"New contact!" the petty officer in the TAC Two chair called out.

Without even a conscious decision Sam hit the general quarters alarm on his command console and the repetitive battle stations gong sounded throughout the ship.

"He's scanning us, sir!" the sensor tech interrupted, her voice rising in excitement.

Sam felt adrenaline course through him. Drone couriers didn't have sensor suites, didn't need them. What if it wasn't a courier? What if instead it was some kind of weapon? Suddenly Sam felt turned inside out. *We must have jumped.*

The bridge lights flickered twice and then failed, replaced by low-energy backup illumination.

"Maneuvering. Why did you jump without orders?"

Ensign Barr-Sanchez, eyes wide with fright, turned her chair to look at him. "I ... I didn't trigger the jump, sir."

"TAC?" he asked next.

"No sign of anything. No sign of the bogie."

"Ops, where are we?"

"Um ... I'm still working on that, sir," Ensign Barr-Sanchez said.

"If we're in a star system, put the primary up on the main screen. Let me have a look at it."

She put the visible light feed on the main screen but all it showed was a carpet of tiny stars.

"There's no primary to see, sir," she said. "There's nothing out there but distant starlight. We are in deep space—the *deep*-deep, light-years from the nearest star."

Wherever they were, they weren't dead. The drone or whatever it was hadn't killed them with a jump scrambler program, but it had done *something*.

BAEN BOOKS
by FRANK CHADWICK
The Forever Engine

Cottohazz Series
How Dark the World Becomes
Come the Revolution
Chain of Command
Ship of Destiny

★SHIP OF★
DESTINY

★★★

FRANK CHADWICK

SHIP OF DESTINY

Copyright © 2020 by Frank Chadwick

A Baen Books Original

Baen Publishing Enterprises
P.O. Box 1403
Riverdale, NY 10471
www.baen.com

ISBN: 978-1-9821-2527-1

Cover art by Don Maitz
USS *Cam Rahn Bay* diagram by Frank Chadwick

First printing, March 2020
First mass market printing, March 2021

Distributed by Simon & Schuster
1230 Avenue of the Americas
New York, NY 10020

Library of Congress Control Number: 2019054177

Printed in the United States of America

10 9 8 7 6 5 4 3 2 1

For Craig and Bev

USS *Cam Ranh Bay* (LAS-17)

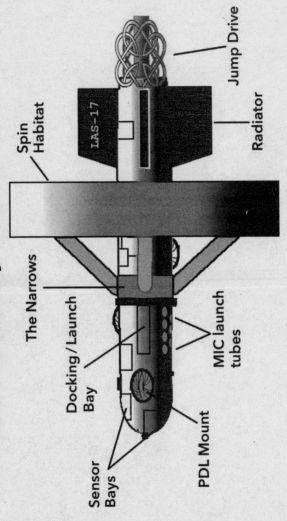

Spin Habitat

Jump Drive

Radiator

LAS-17

The Narrows

Docking / Launch Bay

MIC launch tubes

PDL Mount

Sensor Bays

Sing in me, Muse, and through me tell the story
of that man skilled in all ways of contending,
the wanderer, harried for years on end,
after he plundered the stronghold
on the proud height of Troy.
He saw the townlands
and learned the minds of many distant men,
and weathered many bitter nights and days
in his deep heart at sea, while he fought only
to save his life, to bring his shipmates home.

—Homer, *The Odyssey*
Robert Fitzgerald, trans. 1961

Under the wide and starry sky
Dig the grave and let me lie:
Glad did I live and gladly die,
And I laid me down with a will.

This be the verse you 'grave for me:
Here he lies where he long'd to be;
Home is the sailor, home from the sea,
And the hunter home from the hill.

—Robert Louis Stevenson, *Requiem*, 1879

★SHIP OF★
DESTINY
★★★

In 2041 Earth experienced the single most momentous event in recorded history—first contact with an alien civilization. The Cottohazz was a stellar commonwealth of five peaceful, starfaring species led by the Varoki, the inventors of the jump drive which made interstellar travel and commerce possible. In 2064 the nations of Earth joined the Cottohazz as full members, the Sixth Race.

Seventy years later the Cottohazz is recovering from its first interstellar war, fought between four Earth nations—forming the Outworld Coalition—and one Varoki nation, the uBakai.

PART I:
Voyage Into Darkness

Cassandra
**Outworld Coalition Forward Headquarters
on the planet K'tok, over one hundred fifty
light years from Earth
15 July 2134** *(five months after Incident Seventeen)*

"First you bedded him, then you broke his heart, and now you want to know more about him? Commander, you might rethink the order in which you do stuff."

The words, delivered in Lieutenant Moe Rice's deliberate west Texas drawl, momentarily left Cassandra as empty of breath as would a blow to the midsection. Commander Cassandra Atwater-Jones, Royal Navy, stared across her desk at the man who over the last months had become her friend as well as colleague and subordinate. *Glared* at him was probably more like it, the only way she knew to mask her grief and regret. Rice, a US Navy officer of considerable size and dark visage, returned her gaze unblinkingly. Of course he did: he was right—not that she was prepared to acknowledge that.

When she spoke, she made her voice hard.

"*Leftenant* Rice, my interest in Captain Bitka's command style is professional, as you very well know. He has been missing for five months and it seems as if every admiral in the Outworld Coalition insists that our working group list him as dead, and his command lost due to hostile acts of the uBakai Star Navy. The manner in which his ship disappeared *is* reminiscent of the uBakai jump scrambler weapon—"

"'Cept it didn't destroy his ship," Rice cut in.

"We don't *know* that!" she answered, her own voice rising. She stopped and took a breath and closed her eyes for a moment.

"What *do* we know about Incident Seventeen?" she said when she felt she could keep her voice from trembling. "On nineteen February last, a shuttle-sized craft emerged from jump space in this star system between the orbits of K'tok and Mogo. It emitted radiation on wavelengths consistent with a sensor sweep, made a single powerful burst transmission directly at the closest vessel, and then destroyed itself. The nearby vessel was USS *Cam Ranh Bay*, of which ship Bitka had taken command seven days prior. Bitka's ship jumped almost simultaneous with the transmission. But it did not emerge from J-space at Eeee'ktaa, its intended destination nor, so far as we can determine, has it turned up anywhere else in known space.

"Where did it go? What was its fate? Who was responsible?"

"I know the damned questions, Commander," Rice grumbled as he shifted in his chair. "Just don't know any answers."

Normally Cassandra liked looking at his face, the whites of his eyes so white they were almost blue, set in a face the color of weathered and blackened bronze. Instead she turned to the third person in her office, more as an excuse to look away from Rice without it appearing quite so much like an admission of guilt. Vice-Captain Takaar Nuvaash of the uBakai Star Navy was clearly embarrassed by the exchange, an emotion easy to spot on most Varoki: the broad ears folded tightly back against the head, the hairless iridescent skin flushed pink, or sometimes a bit orange if the Varoki in question was also offended. The common Human epithet for Varoki—*leatherhead*—did them a disservice, she thought. There was something exquisite in the way the light played across their softly textured skin, colors coming and going as if through a kaleidoscope.

Like Cassandra, Nuvaash was a military intelligence officer—what most Varoki navies called "Speaker for The Enemy." Like her, Moe Rice, and seven other officers from four different Earth nations, he was part of the Incident Seventeen Working Group, although in his case the assignment was unofficial. It had to be as, unlike Cassandra and the others, he was a Varoki and a prisoner of war, *their* prisoner. Ironically, he was the only one apart from Moe Rice she felt she could really trust, which was a sad commentary on how tangled and toxic the politics of this entire incident had become. She turned back to Rice.

"I am due to meet with the new station commander in half an hour to brief him on our progress. You know his identity?"

Rice grimaced before answering. "Rear Admiral Jacob Goldjune."

"Yes, Rear Admiral Jacob Goldjune, brother of Admiral Cedric Goldjune, our coalition's CNO." She turned to Nuvaash. "Chief of Naval Operations, what you would call the Fleet-Guiding Admiral. He is the most visible advocate for restarting hostilities with your nation." She turned back to Rice. "Our new commander is also the father of Larry Goldjune, who now commands USS *Puebla*, Bitka's former boat. Wasn't there bad blood between Bitka and young Goldjune?"

Rice laughed but without a trace of humor. Yes, of course there was, she thought. Trust Bitka to pick a fight with the scion of the most powerful and well-connected family in the Navy of the United States of North America.

"Excuse me," Nuvaash said, "but I am confused. The Goldjunes are brothers? Father and son? I do not understand."

"There are three of them," Cassandra said. "Here, let me draw you a picture." She picked up a stylus from her desk holder, drew briefly on the smart surface of her desk, and then tapped the output control. A wafer of thin flexible composite emerged from the output slot. She checked it and handed it to Nuvaash.

R.ADM Jacob ← (brothers) → ADM Cedric
(father)   (uncle)
(son) LT Larr (nephew)

"Ah," he said, "Very clear. But Captain Bitka was a successful warrior and they are all members of the same navy. Why do they dislike him?"

Cassandra looked at him and fought down a surge of

irritation. "Don't be coy with me, Nuvaash. You are not so callow as all that, and I am not in the mood for games." She turned back to Rice. "So what sort of reception do you expect me to receive in this upcoming meeting?"

"I'd wear body armor if I was you," Rice said, but he smiled at her, the bleak smile of condemned prisoners sharing the same cell. "Okay, you want to know what kind of cap'n Bitka was? He never gave up. Never. He relied on his crew, got us to do impossible things, I still don't know how. Somehow made us believe we could do it, and then it turned out we really could."

He paused and thought for a moment.

"Couldn't abide dishonesty. I guess that's what got him so pissed off at Larry Goldjune and his uncle Cedric, the *big* admiral. That last part got him a share of trouble. Still don't know how he got out of that court martial, although I bet you do. I ain't asking, but if you had a part in it, I thank you."

Cassandra nodded, and then Nuvaash spoke.

"Your Captain Bitka reminds me of the archetypal trickster in so many of your Human myths and legends. He never met my admiral but he had an uncanny ability to know exactly what it would take to draw him away from K'tok at the final battle."

Rice shook his head. "Might have looked that way from your side, but the truth is it was just a shot in the dark. Cap'n figured a long shot was better than no shot at all. That's what I mean—the son of a bitch *never* gives up."

He looked at her, a look full of meaning which she immediately understood. Were the roles reversed, Bitka would not have given up on her by now, would he? No.

But she was not Sam Bitka. Listening to Rice made her almost believe he might still be alive, but that was absurd. Realistically the only riddles were how and where he had died, not if, and answering those questions would do nothing to fill the aching void in her heart.

Still, if their working group filed a report declaring him dead and suggesting uBakai culpability, it would be all the excuse the war faction—including the assorted Goldjunes—would need to renounce the fragile ceasefire and restart hostilities, which could rip the Stellar Commonwealth—the *Cottohazz*—apart. Unfortunately, what little evidence there was pointed to the uBakai. Once the investigation stopped, that's all the evidence there would be, and once Bitka and his crew were declared dead, the investigation would be quickly wrapped up.

Bitka had fought so hard, and risked so much, to get them to this fragile peace. She owed it to him to hold the peace together, however and for as long as she could, and if that meant keeping him officially alive, well then so be it. She touched the desktop hologram of her daughter and then stood up.

"Time for me to go if I am not to keep our new admiral waiting."

"Shirtsleeve order?" Rice asked, looking her over. "You at least going to put on a jacket to meet the big brass?"

Cassandra glanced down at her white short-sleeved uniform blouse and blue slacks.

"No, I think this will do. Remember what Ibsen said: 'Never wear your best trousers when you go out to fight for truth and freedom.' Now, where's my hat?"

★ ★ ★

The bulldog-faced American yeoman manning the reception desk touched his ear, listened to whatever was coming through his surgically embedded commlink, and looked up at her.

"The admiral will see you now, ma'am. Go right in."

Cassandra rose, tucked her hat under her arm, and crossed the carpeted anteroom to the dark wood-grained door bearing the plaque which read, in glowing letters, "Rear Admiral Jacob Goldjune, Commander, K'tok Base Area." She pressed the entry panel, the door whispered to the side, and she strode across the polished hardwood floor and came to attention in front of the admiral's desk. His office was a much larger version of her own, with the addition of a broad window behind the admiral looking out over T'tokl-Heem, the occupied Varoki capital of K'tok. In the background, K'tok Needle, the elevator to orbit, rose from behind the downstation complex, impossibly tall and slender, gleaming golden in the morning sunlight. As she watched, a cigar-shaped cargo capsule began its silent magnetically induced acceleration up the needle to orbit.

"Commander Atwater-Jones, reporting as ordered, sir."

She noticed that Admiral Goldjune, his attention on the open files displayed on the smart surface of his desk, wore shirtsleeve order, the same as her.

Nice to know I'm not underdressed for the ball.

He glanced up at her.

"Be seated, commander."

She did so, trying to form an impression of the man. Blonde, balding, heavy, his accent soft and southern, the sort she had heard quite often in Mississippi when she had been there on an exchange course. He had an intelligent face, not what she would call forceful or determined, but not really weak either. *Guarded*, she thought. Well, in military intelligence one got used to dealing with guarded faces and guarded minds. But there was something else in his face. Melancholy. That surprised her. Before he spoke he slid several open virtual folders into the center of his desk, studied them for a moment, and his mouth turned down in a frown.

"So, naval intelligence, huh?" he said looking up at her. "You were on Admiral Kayumati's staff, on board *Pensacola* when she took that fire lance hit that tore her in half. Lucky to survive that one."

"Yes, sir," she said, and despite herself she shuddered at the memory, at the day spent in the dark claustrophobic isolation of an escape pod, feeling her fingers and toes begin to freeze, giving up hope of rescue, and then suddenly safe again aboard HMS *Exeter*.

"Sorry if that's an awkward subject," the admiral said. Cassandra looked up, remembered where she was.

"Quite all right, sir. I certainly wasn't the only one who had some anxious moments that day. Most of the others on *Pensacola*, and the other ships in the task force, were less fortunate than I."

"Uh-huh. I lost about a half-dozen old friends that day, and a couple old enemies I miss near as much. Navies are like that, aren't they? Like a family, including the fact you don't get to pick 'em."

He looked away and shook his head as if trying to clear it of his own memories.

"Commander, I'm trying to catch up on what's what in

this command. I know we've had to do a peck of improvising these last few months, but that's no excuse for sloppy work."

"Yes, sir, I quite agree."

"Huh. You know, this whole Incident Seventeen business—USS *Cam Ranh Bay* disappearing just when that mysterious jump missile showed up and gave a burst transmission, then melted—that can't be a coincidence, can it?"

"I do not believe so, sir."

"Wonder what it is then. I got a dispatch here from the CNO," he said, tapping one of the open documents before him. "It was waiting for me when I got here yesterday. It says to light a fire under you and get a final report out of your working group. How long you been at this?"

Cassandra had been expecting this. She and Rice—and Nuvaash to an extent—had done everything they could to prolong the investigation, but they had been reduced to redoing old work. Even some of the other members of the working group were becoming impatient and suspicious.

"Just past four months now, sir," she answered.

The admiral leaned back in his chair and his frown deepened. "Hell, the *shooting* didn't last half that long. Now we can't find one measly little transport that's gone missing? I wonder if it would have riled as much if anyone else had been in command but Bitka. Most successful fighting captain we had in the war, and some idiot gives him a transport? 'Bow-on Bitka,' they called him, but you must have known that."

"Yes, sir," she said. She felt no need to tell him how thoroughly Bitka had loathed that nickname, but remembering it brought a sudden tightness to her chest and her throat.

"He fought in twice as many battles as any other surviving captain in the fleet," the admiral continued, "and he was probably the least decorated. What do you make of that, Commander?"

"I . . . I don't believe it is my place to comment on the awards policy of your service—"

"Travesty, that's what it is," the admiral said, cutting her off, "and I don't give a good goddamn what he said about my brother, the CNO. From what I can tell, Bitka should have the Medal of Honor, along with Bonaventure and that other one they gave it to. They didn't even give Bitka the Navy Cross! Does that seem right to you?"

"I . . . really, Admiral Goldjune, I don't feel—"

"All right," he said and looked away for a moment, his thoughts elsewhere, before resuming. "You know, when I was still head of BuShips I received a report from him. That was right before all this happened. His recommendations on design improvements in the next group of destroyer riders, assuming we decide to build any more. I imagine you had a hand in that report."

"Only to correct his spelling, sir. The thinking was entirely his own."

"Huh. He had a head on his shoulders, I'll give him that. Wonder if he still does. Well, as to that, I have been looking over your interim progress reports. So has the CNO, by the way. That would be my brother? You re-interviewed every witness. You had to pull three of them back from Earth rotation, which took a few weeks right there. Didn't come up with one single new thing. The

CNO thinks you're dragging your feet, doing the work over and over, trying to put off filing a final report."

Cassandra felt her face redden.

"I assure you, sir—"

"Sloppy," he said with a shake of his head. He sat back in his chair, expression unreadable.

"Sir?"

He tilted his head back and examined her as if through spectacles, eyes narrowing in appraisal. She thought she saw a flicker of a smile as well, although that seemed unlikely under the circumstances.

"All those re-interviews and you didn't come up with a single new insight? You weren't looking hard enough, Commander. I told you I won't stand for sloppy work."

Cassandra felt a renewed surge of anxiety. The admiral could simply relieve her and replace her with *Korvetenkapitän* Heidegger of the *Deutsche Sternmarine*, the next senior officer in her working group. Heidegger would be happy to pronounce Bitka dead and get back to his other duties.

"I'm very sorry sir, but—"

"Re-interview 'em."

Cassandra wasn't sure she understood him at first.

"Sir?"

"You heard me. Re-interview every single witness. This time do it *right*. There has to be something you missed."

Cassandra stared at him, trying to sort out what that meant. Most of the witnesses had rotated out-system. In would take weeks to recontact them, at least another month, perhaps two, to bring them here and conduct the interviews. He was ordering her to do exactly what she most wanted to do. Was this some sort of trap?

The admiral leaned forward, folded his hands on his desk, and looked her in the eye.

"Commander, if we're going to do this—and we *are* going to do this—then let's by God do it right. If anyone gives you any trouble, you direct them to my office. Do you understand me?"

Oh, she had been blind and stupid! Yes, he was the CNO's brother, but as he had said, one doesn't get to pick one's family, does one?

"I think I am beginning to understand, sir."

"*Good.* Good. Now while you're lining all that up, you may have some down time. I looked over the intercepted code of the burst transmission from the unknown jump missile—basically a bunch of gibberish."

That surprised her as well. He had actually read the technical annexes instead of just the executive summary? What sort of admiral was this man? "I am certain the code means something to someone, sir. We simply have not been able to decode it."

"But we already agreed that missile's transmission and *Cam Ranh Bay* jumping away wasn't a coincidence," he said. "That means the jump drive on Bitka's ship must have been able to decode that transmission. Doesn't that excite your curiosity?"

Cassandra leaned forward in her chair and for the first time smiled. "Admiral, I would *murder* to find out why that was so, but up to now our investigation has, under strict orders from above, been confined to a few very limited topics. We *have* been empowered to investigate all known uBakai encryption systems to see if any one of them shares any features with this code. They do not. Since our jump drives are all Varoki manufactured, this makes it difficult to imagine how the code could even have affected the jump drive, since we have a fairly good idea of what the jump drive control code sequences look like."

"Well, might be there's another code, down *under* the Varoki operating systems," the admiral said, "something real different, weird even. Alien."

Cassandra sat back and studied the admiral. *Alien?* Well of course, the Varoki *were* aliens, but that couldn't have been what he meant. He had a look that said she was supposed to understand there was more to what he knew than what he could say. But what?

"I wonder, sir, if you have any suggestions as to how we might go about discovering such an underlying code?"

"Got to go out and look for it. Open your commlink, Commander, and I'll give you a data dump."

He squinted his eyes, working through the visual menu for his own surgically embedded commlink, and then Cassandra felt a faint vibration at the base of her skull indicating a successful data transfer.

"That's orbital telemetry," he explained, "for the jump drive module of the uBakai cruiser KBk Four-Two-Nine. They jettisoned that jump drive after its containment system was breached in the First Battle of K'tok, last December. When the uBakai pulled all their remaining starships out of the system, Four-Two-Nine was stranded in the outer belts without a jump drive. They surrendered after disabling their weapons and wiping the code ciphers, but their log was still intact. We were able to calculate the trajectory of the jump module."

We? she wondered. So this was not simply one admiral with an axe to grind against his more-successful brother.

"Our new orbital sensor platform found it," he continued, "drifting on a course will probably take it clear out of the star system in another year or two."

"But admiral, if the jump drive module was compromised as you say, the anti-tamper system was activated. Otherwise they would not have jettisoned it."

"Oh, you know about that? Well, 'course you do. Some sort of cloud of microscopic particles, eats through any soft seal we know of, including vacuum suits, and also contains an anaerobic neurotoxin—fatal, but not quick nor pretty. You get any sort of containment breach on the jump core, that cloud gets out and the only way to save your ship is to eject the whole module, and I mean right quick.

"But you know what? I been doing some reading too and I can't find any record of a busted drive module that's been around in hard vacuum for more than a few weeks. Usually the Varoki just give them a real hard shove into a star or a big-old gas giant—easiest way to make sure they're destroyed without anyone risking contamination. But this thing's been floatin' out there in the cold and dark for over seven months. I wonder if all that neurotoxin cloud is still active. I wonder if maybe it froze or just dispersed by now. It can't live forever, can it?"

Cassandra felt herself tense, but not with fear, with anticipation. Her mind raced with the possibilities. If they could just look inside a jump drive module, just see how it worked . . . yes, they might find the answer to what happened to Bitka, and answers to so many other questions as well. But the cold part of her brain, the one trained in military intelligence, remained unconvinced.

"Admiral, given how jealously the Varoki guard the secret of the jump drive, why haven't they recovered it? Either the ships of the uBakai Star Navy which were here, or a factory charter since the ceasefire?"

He nodded in agreement.

"That makes perfect sense, but war and perfect sense don't always get along. You know, it's only been seventy Earth years since First Contact with the *Cottohazz*. But before they found us that commonwealth had been around, exploring and colonizing for about two hundred years. In that whole time they never had *one* honest-to-God interstellar war, not until the one we just damped back down.

"Nobody is used to this. Nobody on either side was ready for it—not psychologically, anyway, and nobody knows quite what to do next. So I think what happened was a lot of things fell through the cracks. uBakai Star Navy had their hands full just staying alive—and didn't do all that good a job at it. And in all the confusion, the Varoki manufacturer, AZ Simki-Traak Transtellar, seems to have lost track of that one jump module."

"That seems . . . unlikely, sir," she said.

"Could be they had some help," he said softly.

He smiled and she felt adrenaline course through her body, felt her senses sharpen and her scalp tingle. In the admiral's smile, she suspected, was the hint of what might have been one of the most closely guarded covert operations in human history. She knew better than to acknowledge that conclusion in any way.

"So in all that downtime you've got, why don't you and your team go take a look at that module?" The admiral leaned back in his chair and said this casually, as if suggesting nothing more serious than a weekend outing. "Anyone asks, you're checking out a large piece of debris our scanners picked up, make sure it's not a hazard to astrogation."

"If I might make a suggestion, sir, we could investigate it as a possible piece of wreckage from Bitka's ship. That would explain the interest by my working group."

"Yes, that's better," the admiral said. "Good thinking. Our three surviving destroyers are handling orbital security. Given the ceasefire I can get by with two for a while. Take USS *Puebla*, Bitka's old boat. Go poke around and see what you can find. When you get there, though, I wouldn't send anyone into that jump module who owed you money."

"From what you've told me, sir, I would rather find a way of examining it remotely. Failing that, I suppose I have no choice but to be the first one into the module myself."

Admiral Goldjune looked at her appraisingly. "Sounds like some of Bitka might have rubbed off on you." He looked aside and the sadness she had seen before returned to his face. "Wish a little had rubbed off on my boy Larry."

CHAPTER ONE

Five months earlier, **Outworld Coalition Naval Headquarters Complex, the planet K'tok 12 February 2134** *(seven days before Incident Seventeen)*

What went wrong?

Everything seemed so right with Cassandra from the first night they made love—which was also the first time they'd actually met face-to-face. After a dozen holoconferences and a shared nightmare of fire and death that sometimes seemed a lifetime long, it was easy to forget how briefly they'd known each other. Maybe that didn't matter. People waste so much of every day, every week, every month, what difference does it make how many boxes are marked off the calendar? Those hours that seem like a year's worth of life . . . well, they are, aren't they? Worth a year.

So what went wrong?

Sam noticed it first in bed: exclamations of pleasure which seemed for his benefit rather than hers. It's not that she didn't enjoy their lovemaking. She was passionate and responsive, and he loved how afterwards she would lie beside him shuddering slightly, irregularly, as if her nervous system needed time to reset. So why spread a layer of pretense over the authentic pleasure underneath? She hadn't done it at first—or maybe he hadn't noticed, but he didn't think that was it. Something changed, but what? And why?

Then she'd stopped disagreeing with him. They'd had wonderful arguments, filled with mock outrage and laughter . . . and then they just didn't anymore. She listened thoughtfully, agreed, but seldom prolonged a conversation with her own thoughts, which he began to think were elsewhere.

Sam considered confronting her with his concern, but what was there to say? "I think something's wrong between us because you seem to enjoy sex and agree with me too much?" Sam knew bringing it up would make things worse, make them both self-conscious, and he didn't want that. But more importantly it would feel like as intrusion. Sam remembered Rosemary, his former fiancé from what seemed a lifetime ago but had actually been less than two years. She would always ask him if she'd done something wrong when work or his complicated relationship with his family left him more quiet than usual. No, it isn't about you, he would say, but she never quite believed him. Sam wouldn't subject Cassandra to that. So he gave her space to work it out herself.

And she had.

Would things have been different if he'd made the first move, brought everything out into the open? A stupid question. Would things have been different if he was a different guy who thought differently and acted differently? Sure. So what? He wasn't a different guy, he was this one.

So what was so wrong with this one that Cassandra had to walk away from him, and do it so gently, so carefully, as if he were delicate as a paper-thin antique vase that would crumble if you raised your voice or made a sudden move or just touched it wrong? That was the only part of it that left him angry: she had no right to treat him as if he were *fragile*.

"Admiral Stevens will see you now, Captain Bitka."

The yeoman's voice recalled Sam from his reverie and back to the admiral's anteroom. Moments later, hat tucked under his arm, he stood before the desk of the commanding admiral, First Combined Fleet.

"Lieutenant Commander Samuel Bitka, reporting as ordered, sir."

"Just what the hell am I supposed to do with this fitness report on Lieutenant Goldjune?" the admiral began without preamble, tapping an open document file on the smart surface of his desk. "Remain at attention, Bitka."

Sam looked over the admiral's head as military courtesy demanded, in this case at the view of the K'tok Needle out the broad window of the fleet commander's office. He could hardly see the needle today for the low clouds and fast-moving rain squalls that swept over and past the downstation complex.

Should he tell Vice Admiral Stevens what he thought the admiral could do with the fitness report?

No. It would take a miracle to save him from a second charge of insubordination, and lately he had the feeling he'd run through all his miracles. Besides, there was no civilian job to go back to and the fragile ceasefire with the uBakai might collapse at any time. He was where he needed to be. He sure couldn't do anything useful from inside a Navy brig.

"Admiral, I don't know that there's anything to do with it but forward it to BuPers. It is my honest evaluation of Lieutenant Goldjune."

"*Not* recommended for promotion? At *all?* Are you serious, Bitka?"

"Yes, sir, I cannot recommend the lieutenant for promotion."

"*Bottom* ten percent of the officers you have worked with?"

"Yes, sir, that is my assessment."

Admiral Stevens leaned back in his chair and looked Sam over. Stevens was in his late fifties but looked ten years younger, trim and athletic with a dusting of grey in his thick curly brown hair. He wore a short-sleeved white uniform shirt and his bare forearms were hairy and tattooed. The left arm had a coiled serpent with the motto "Don't Tread on Me." The right arm had a large anchor superimposed over a stylized starship. Sam gathered from these that the admiral was a traditionalist.

"You know, this will reflect badly on you as well," the admiral said. "A captain's supposed to train his executive officer, bring him along. This is your failure as much as his."

"I am aware some will view it that way, sir."

Stevens shook his head and looked back at his desk. "You have quite a history with this family, don't you? A lot of people would look at this and say it was personally motivated. What do you think Lieutenant Goldjune's chances are at his next promotion board with a fitness report like this in his folder?"

Sam considered that for a moment, looking out the window. The rain had eased up and he saw a cargo capsule slide down the needle and disappear into the downstation complex.

"Sir, with any other lieutenant I'd say it virtually ruled promotion out, but with Larry Goldjune I honestly don't know."

Stevens raised his head quickly.

"Are you suggesting a promotion board can be *influenced*?"

"No, sir, I'm saying I honestly don't know. I *hope* it can't. I guess we'll find out."

Stevens glared up at him for several long seconds and then shook his head again.

"Oh, sit down. I'm getting a crick in my neck looking up at you. This is the second time you've burned my ass. You know that, don't you?"

"Sir?" Sam asked as he sat. He'd never met the admiral until a week earlier and as far as he knew they had no previous conflicts.

"You and that good-looking Limey you been banging—yeah, I know about that—what's her name? Jones, right? You two broke the story on that Varoki jump drive manufacturer having cheat codes that could turn a starship inside out and kill its crew with one radio broadcast. If one manufacturer could have them, they all could, and all of a sudden, all their stocks dropped like meteors. Never seen anything like it. Then all the companies that insure starships took a dive until they pulled their insurance policies, and then every interstellar shipping company tanked. I lost half the value in my retirement account in less than three days! Now my wife's threatening to walk, and she tells me she's taking *all* that's left in the account. Can you believe it? Her lawyer says I was managing it so what I lost was *my* half, not hers."

Sam had heard a lot of stories about long angry rants from admirals behind closed doors, but until now he'd never experienced anything quite like it. After the last three months, though, nothing much surprised him.

Admiral Stevens shook his head and then seemed to remember Sam's presence.

"So, you're not exactly on my happy-happy list to start with. Now Admiral Goldjune, the CNO, is on my ass to make *this* go away." He tapped the fitness report. "Come on, Bitka, give me a break. You already fucked me over once. Help me out here."

Sam was surprised to find he felt sorry for Admiral Stevens. He couldn't say that he found much to like or admire in him, and he doubted his marriage was in trouble solely because of a financial setback, but Stevens had served the Navy for most of his adult life and probably looked forward to a comfortable retirement. Losing a dream you'd worked hard for didn't always bring out the best in people. Sam knew that from his own experience, and he was in no position to judge anyone, but after a moment he shook his head.

"I'm sorry, sir, but I can't help you. I hope you'll understand this is not a personal vendetta between myself and Lieutenant Goldjune, at least not on my part. This is about the good of the service. Larry Goldjune is a terrible officer."

"If he's so terrible, why hasn't anyone else noticed?" the admiral shot back. "Hell, he finished near the top of his class at Annapolis, got early promotion from ensign and from junior grade, and had great fitness reports up until now. Even you admit in your report that he's competent *and* smart. Jesus H. Christ, Bitka, what do you want from the guy?"

"*Character*," Sam answered. "Goldjune doesn't care about his subordinate officers or his crew. He doesn't care about anyone else's vessel and he doesn't care about the service. He cares about himself, period. He's not just an embarrassment waiting to happen; he's dangerous."

Admiral Stevens opened his mouth to respond but then looked at Sam and closed it. He tapped his desk lightly with his fingers, looked down at the open documents, shook his head. Then he turned his swivel chair and looked at the rain lashing the clear composite windowpanes.

"I spent my whole career getting ready for the uBakai War, or something like it, and then I missed it. They pulled you out of the reserves, stuck you in a destroyer, and you were in the middle of everything: four battles, *twice* as many as any other surviving captain, ship or boat. And I missed it.

"You know, if they'd sent me and the fleet out here just two weeks sooner, like they should have—like I practically *begged* them to—I'd have pulled your chestnuts out of the fire and we wouldn't be having this conversation. Then we'd *both* be heroes and we could tell the whole Goldjune clan to go fuck themselves. *Just two damned weeks!* But I got here too late and you got all the glory."

"Admiral," Sam said, "if it was up to me, you could have my whole share, and welcome to it."

"What I *ought* to do is ship you back to Earth," Stevens said, sounding almost as if he were talking to himself, thinking out loud. "First thing they'd do is pull that temporary lieutenant commander field promotion you got, and then probably park you somewhere behind a desk. Maybe they'd put you to work teaching tactics at Annapolis to a bunch of earnest snot-nosed plebes. Sure as hell wouldn't have you teaching military courtesy, not unless they got a sense of humor that runs to the ironic."

The admiral's leather-upholstered swivel chair squeaked as he turned to face Sam again, and he smiled ruefully.

"The gods of war must love their jokes. Good one on me. Well, who am I to argue with the gods of war? I just made up my mind. I got a new command for you, Bitka. How do you feel about alligators?"

"Sir?"

"Alligators, as in the Alligator Navy, assault transports. Just this morning, seven days before one of those fast, new armed transports is due to jump out-system, its captain slips on a wet floor and breaks his hip. The *Bay*—USS *Cam Ranh Bay*—has a pretty good XO, almost ready for early promotion to lieutenant commander, and she could probably take over. It's just a milk run to Eeee'ktaa to deliver half a cohort of Marines. But if I put you in command I get you out of my hair, and Larry Goldjune moves up to command USS *Puebla*. If I can't get you to withdraw this fitness report, I can at least let him log some command time before his next promotion review board, get something on paper to counteract this. Maybe his uncle Cedric will accept that as the best of some less-than-perfect options."

"Jesus, I don't want my boat under *his* command," Sam said.

"Noted," Stevens said drily, US Navy-speak for *Who cares what you want?* "Bitka, you either take *Cam Ranh Bay* or you hop the next transport back to Earth. Either way, Goldjune's going to get *Puebla*."

Stevens chuckled.

"Don't worry, I'm sure you'll *love* ferrying jarheads around."

CHAPTER TWO

The next day, aboard USS *Cam Ranh Bay*
13 February 2134 (*six days before Incident Seventeen*)

Lieutenant Mikko Running-Deer wasn't used to being starstruck. It annoyed and embarrassed her.

She had never been much interested in holovid stars, or the manufactured celebrities on the vidfeed, that sort of thing. Sam Bitka was different—the most experienced deep-space combatant ship captain in Human history, and a bad boy to boot. He'd almost been court-martialed for calling the Chief of Naval Operations—in a public briefing to the whole task force—just "some admiral behind some desk a hundred light-years from here."

His romance with that British intelligence operative didn't hurt his reputation, either. Mikko had seen a segment on *Navy Today* with a short vidfeed of the two of them together, and they made a glamorous couple. One still picture caught him laughing, the British woman looking at him with delight, but something else, something Mikko couldn't identify, something held back.

The woman reminded Mikko of a tall, elegant fox—not just the thick mane of red hair, but also her sharply pointed features, and her sly eyes which swept from side to side and seemed to take everything in at a glance. Mikko wondered if she was a dancer. She moved with the grace and constant sure balance of one—or maybe of a martial artist. Still, she thought the British woman was too old for him. Why, she must be almost forty!

Mikko couldn't see the harm in indulging a bit of a fantasy crush from a safe distance. It wasn't as if she was ever going to meet the guy, right? But now a wave of panic flashed through her as she realized that in about ten seconds the main entry lock was going to open and Lieutenant Commander Sam Bitka would walk through. She couldn't let Chief Duransky and the two bosun's mates of the side party see her flustered. Or *him*.

You're a professional! Discharge this ballast.

And then, as if on cue, the ship's bell sounded twice through the public address system, the duty commspec announced, "USS *Puebla* arriving," the lock slid open, and he appeared in his white uniform shipsuit and attached pressure helmet, visor up. The magnetic tabs on his boots clicked on the deck as he walked, holding him down in the zero gee of *Cam Ranh Bay*'s main hull, just as her own boots kept her from floating away.

He looked just like he did in his pictures.

"Permission to come aboard," he said.

"Permission granted. Bosun's party, salute."

She snapped a salute at the same time as the two bosun's mates, one to each side of the airlock, while Chief Bosun's Mate Duransky piped the new captain aboard.

Bitka returned her salute and then saluted the colors suspended on the aft bulkhead of the receiving bay.

"Sir, the crew is mustered in holospace," Mikko reported. "I am ready to be relieved as captain."

Bitka lowered his helmet visor and she did the same. Now the receiving bay seemed to grow in length and the entire ship's complement was formed in two ranks at attention, stretching fore and aft from them, as her holoconference software kicked in. Of course, none of them but her, Bitka, and the bosun's party were actually in the docking bay. The rest were at various stations throughout the ship, their holographic images arranged and projected by the software in her helmet. All of them stood with helmets on and in standard Navy-issue shipsuits, a combination working coverall and emergency pressure suit: white for officers, khaki for chiefs and Marines, and blue for other enlisted. Bitka raised a data pad and read.

"Outworld Coalition First Combined Fleet order dated Twelve February, 2134. To Lieutenant Commander Samuel M. Bitka: Surrender command DDR-11 *Puebla* to your senior line officer and report not later than Thirteen February, 2134, to LAS-17 *Cam Ranh Bay*. Upon arrival on board report to Lieutenant Mikko Running-Deer, Acting Commanding Officer USS *Cam Ranh Bay*, for duty as her relief. Signed, Vice Admiral G. K. Stevens, Commander, First Combined Fleet.

"Lieutenant Running-Deer, I relieve you."

"Sir, I stand relieved." She took a step back and then to the side, in that instant again becoming executive officer, and she felt herself relax. There had been no serious crises during her brief tenure as acting captain, but she had felt the constant awareness that if one would arise, it would be her exclusive responsibility, and she had not realized how heavy that responsibility had felt until it was suddenly lifted from her.

"All hands," Captain Bitka said, his voice level and without the hard edge she had expected to hear in it. He didn't sound like a cold, hardened, killer of ships. He sounded nice. Was that part of his secret of command? A carefully constructed veneer, a face presented to the world to disguise the warrior behind it?

"I had a chance to speak with Captain O'Malley by holoconference," Bitka continued. "He's recovering from his injury on the hospital ship *Mercy Island*. He tells me I am taking over a sound ship with a good crew. I look forward to meeting each of you in the next several days before we make our jump.

"Our mission is to transport two companies of Marines for duty on Eeee'ktaa, the home world of the Buran. We will receiver further orders once on station there.

"I will be going over drills and procedures with the executive officer and tactical department. As you know, a ceasefire has been in effect with the uBakai for the last three weeks, and so far it's held, but there's always the chance we'll run into someone who hasn't gotten the word, or who doesn't *agree* with the word, and so we will continue to operate under the assumption that we are in a war zone. Everyone stay sharp.

"All hands, dismissed."

Chief Bosun's Mate Duransky raised his helmet visor and sounded *Pipe Down*, and the crew began disappearing as they raised their helmet visors, which cut the data feed from the in-helmet holocon systems. Mikko raised her own visor and saw Captain Bitka extending his hand and smiling.

"XO, it's a pleasure to meet you."

"Welcome aboard, sir," she answered, shaking his hand. He had a firm grip but wasn't one of those assholes who tried to crush your hand to show their dominance. "Sir, the off-watch officers are assembled in the wardroom per your request. Can I show you the way?"

He looked around the receiving bay and grinned. "I'd appreciate that. I've been trying to memorize the deck plan in between everything else in the last twenty-four hours. I *think* I've got it down, but I'd feel really stupid wandering into a Marine squad bay by mistake."

Wow, he was good! That vaguely lost and helpless act— perfect.

"Boats," Mikko said turning to Chief Duransky, "have your detail deliver the captain's gear to his quarters."

"Aye aye, ma'am."

Mikko gestured toward the lift which would take them down to the habitat wheel, rotating to provide the equivalent of one gravity. She and her new captain pushed off together to glide the length of the bay in zero gee.

"Sir, I have several revised data files you may want to go over," she added as they boarded the lift, and she handed him a data pad. "I loaded them in here. In particular you may want to familiarize yourself with the civilian passenger manifest. We have a number of VIPs on board."

The captain's head jerked toward her.

"Um, wait . . . we have *civilian* passengers?"

★ ★ ★

Either Captain Bitka's orders had not mentioned civilians or he had overlooked that section. Mikko did not think he had survived four deep space battles by overlooking things, so she wondered why no one had told him.

"I know it sounds crazy, sir," she explained. "A couple months ago civilian passengers on a military assault transport *would* have been crazy, but a lot's changed. When the word of the jump scrambler weapon went public, it caused a big panic and grounded the civilian starships. They'll sort out all that mess with insurance and shipping companies eventually, but in the meantime interstellar commerce stopped—completely. So, the militaries of all six species of the *Cottohazz* stepped up and took over the traffic. It's the only way to prevent a financial collapse."

"A bunch of people but no bulk cargo?" the captain asked after reading the manifest.

"That's correct, sir, but since we're configured as a troop transport anyway, that works out fine. But it puzzled all of us as well until we got a crash course on interstellar commerce. Every inhabited star system has plenty of raw materials, and if they didn't, starships couldn't haul enough to make a difference. As far as merchandise goes, fabricators can construct almost anything. Rather than carry manufactured goods around in starships, it's cheaper to license the fabrication software and just collect royalties. The only things really worth carrying from star to star are key people, data, and devices too cutting-edge to trust to the fabricator software nets. Oh, and unique original art. We've carried a bunch of that."

Captain Bitka shook his head and frowned.

"Maybe someday someone will explain to me how that's important enough to power—or cripple—the finances of the whole *Cottohazz*. But it doesn't need to make sense to me in order to work, does it? Okay. XO, we need to keep the VIP passengers happy enough they don't bother you and me, because we're going to have *real* work to do. Have we got someone entertaining and . . . nonessential we can task with that?"

Why hadn't she thought of something like that? Probably because Captain O'Malley had *enjoyed* schmoozing with the passengers, so she'd thought of that as the natural role of the captain, but Bitka wasn't O'Malley, was he?

"Um . . . we've got charming and we've got nonessential, but not a lot of overlap. I'm sure I can come up with someone. Can I get back to you on that, sir?"

He chuckled. "Sure. Just don't let any grass grow under it, okay? What we need is something like a chief purser. Or maybe a cruise director. One more thing. I'd like you to get your chief yeoman working on is a meal schedule for me."

"Meal schedule. Yes, sir," she answered, trying to act as if that was a routine sort of request.

"Well, I mean a schedule of guests. I need to get to know the officers and crew, and meals are a good way. I want to breakfast with an officer every morning, starting with you tomorrow, then have lunch with a chief, probably starting with our 'Boats,' Duransky, isn't it?"

"Yes, sir."

"Right. Lunch with Duransky tomorrow. Dinner with

an acey-deucy. Have your yeoman set up a rotation so I meet everyone if we stay at it long enough. Officers, I want to start with the department heads and then go to the most junior ensign and work my way back. Same with the chiefs: the bulls first and then the most junior one. For the junior petty officers, just mix it up."

Mikko couldn't remember a captain having dinner with enlisted personnel, especially petty officers first and second class—acey-deucies—just to get acquainted, but she liked the idea.

"I'll get right on it, sir."

The lift came to a halt, the door behind her slid open, and Mikko saw the captain's eyes widen with surprise. She turned and saw the two vaguely reptilian figures waiting in the corridor.

Varoki were surprisingly similar to Humans in structure and even facial features, despite standing over two meters tall, being hairless and iridescent-skinned, and sporting broad, leaflike, constantly moving ears. Dr. Däng, the famous xenophysiologist, who was also on the VIP passenger list, had told her the similarities were due to "easiest path engineering." Mikko wasn't sure what that meant.

"Captain Bitka, let me introduce the Honorable Limi e-Lisyss, diplomatic trade mediation envoy from the executive council of the *Cottohazz* to the Toomish Consortium of Buran. And this is his assistant, Mister Haykuz."

Captain Bitka extended his hand and the envoy e-Lisyss's eyes widened slightly. The assistant took a small step forward, his skin flushing pink with embarrassment.

"The envoy means no disrespect, Captain Bitka," he explained hastily, "but the human custom of shaking hands is not widely practiced among our people."

The captain lowered his hand and shrugged. "No offense taken." He turned and smiled at Mikko. "Funny. Didn't seem to bother the uBakai naval officers I met a couple weeks ago, and we're still technically at war with them."

Mikko had already decided that e-Lisyss's personality was an odd fit for a diplomat, since he seemed a master at either giving or taking offense at fairly minor things, but maybe he was really hell on wheels when it came to closing a good trade deal. Who knew?

She had wondered how the captain felt about Varoki in general, and specifically the uBakai whom he had fought in the war. Apparently, he'd at least been willing to shake their hands, and she hadn't seen any obvious sign of animosity.

"The envoy has asked me to inquire why he was not invited to the meeting of senior officers, as he is the most senior official of the *Cottohazz* aboard the vessel," the assistant asked.

The captain frowned and glanced at Mikko before answering.

"I wasn't aware your boss was on board until about one minute ago."

The assistant and the envoy exchanged a few words in aHoka, which Mikko could recognize from its guttural consonants but could not understand.

"The envoy accepts your apology," the assistant said. "He suggests we now go and meet our officers."

Captain Bitka scratched his close-cropped hair and then shook his head.

"Nope. No offense to your boss but they aren't our officers, they're mine. I understand he's a high-ranking official of the *Cottohazz* but we aren't operating under *Cottohazz* authority. This is a United States Navy vessel and you're riding with us as a courtesy, one we are happy to extend. I'll be glad to talk with him later but right now my executive officer and I have to be going. Excuse us."

Mikko hastened to keep up with Captain Bitka's long strides without jostling either of the Varoki officials as she passed them. She expected to hear outraged protests but for whatever reason they said nothing. Maybe part of diplomacy was knowing how to preserve your dignity when you lost a round.

How had the captain known the Varoki wouldn't force the issue? Or had he? Maybe he just didn't care. Whichever it was, she liked it. Varoki were always trying to throw their weight around. Fortunately, they were as divided into competing nations, alliances, and factions as were humans, and every other intelligent species of the *Cottohazz*. Even divided, they were still the top dogs. In the war they had just finished the Outworld Coalition of four different human nations—The United States of North America, the West European Union, India, and Nigeria—had nearly lost fighting just one Varoki nation, the uBakai. If the Varoki ever all got together and buried the hatchet, it would get ugly.

"So Little Sis and Haiku, what's their story?" the captain asked once they passed beyond a bulkhead.

Mikko struggled to keep her face neutral. Giggling at the two nicknames would be undignified.

"Sir, they call e-Lisyss a trade mediation envoy. As I understand his function, he goes around strong-arming people over royalty rates for the big Varoki trading houses, but he does it with a *Cottohazz* official title and expense account. He's smart, but cold as a polar ice cap. Haykuz, his assistant, is an arrogant little weasel without near as much going on upstairs. That translation stuff was probably an act. I bet e-Lisyss was running high-level auto-trans through his commlink."

"He was," the captain said. "You could see in his eyes he understood us."

Mikko glanced quickly at him. She hadn't noticed that.

"They never tried pulling rank like that on Captain O'Malley," she said. "I think they were trying to snow the new guy, but you didn't fall for it. All due respect to Admiral Stevens, sir, but he should have at least told you about those two."

Captain Bitka smiled. "Maybe he figured this would be more fun."

It sounded as if the captain had a complicated relationship with the fleet commander. Mikko had never met anyone who knew a fleet commander well enough for their relationship to be complicated.

"Here's the wardroom, sir." She followed him in.

"Attention!" she called out and the dozen officers present, already standing in anticipation of their new captain's arrival, snapped to.

"As you were," Captain Bitka said.

"With your permission, sir, let me introduce your department heads."

She did so in order of seniority. Like her, they were all full lieutenants so date of commission counted: Ka'Deem Brook from operations, Rosemary Acho from logistics, Koichi Ma from engineering, and Homer Alexander from tactical. Also like her they were all about thirty years old, plus or minus a couple years, except for Rosemary Acho who was closer to forty. She was a mustang: enlisted as a common mariner, rose to the rank of chief petty officer, and was then commissioned.

Mikko watched the captain carefully for insights into how he sized up his senior officers. She knew—well, she'd heard gossip—that he had little use for Annapolis-educated regular officers and even less for astrogators. She saw no evidence of either in his greeting of Ka'Deem Brook, their chief astrogator and the only academy graduate—other than herself—among the department heads. If the captain had already memorized *The Bay's* deck plan, he surely had read the service jackets of his senior officers.

Did he recognize in Brook, the Ops boss, the crippling need to avoid conflict at all costs? Did he see their TAC boss, Lieutenant Alexander, as the cocksure loner who had become nearly unbearable since learning their new captain was the most famous Tac-head in the navy? Did he see Acho as self-conscious and unsure of herself, hiding her doubts behind a wall of authority and neurotic attention to administrative minutiae? Did he see Ma as a talented engineer too lazy to do the work himself and uninterested in supervising his subordinates? If he saw any of that, he sure could keep a secret.

And what does he see when he looks at me?

Mikko introduced Major J. C. Merderet last, because as a Marine she was not technically a member of the crew, but rather a passenger. Merderet was the only one of them who had met Bitka before, and she had told all of them about the meeting as soon as they heard about his posting as their new captain. The meeting had taken place on K'tok after the ceasefire.

"Introduced himself to every officer and command NCO in the cohort," she said, "and thanked us for the job we did. Only Navy officer who ever did. He said he was sorry they hadn't done more to help. After the beating they took, can you imagine that?"

Mikko wondered if Bitka even remembered the encounter.

"I believe you already have met Major Merderet," Mikko said. "She's commanding our embarked Marine contingent."

Mikko saw Bitka's face brighten and Merderet even managed a rare smile in reply.

"Last time we met weren't you wearing captain's bars?" Bitka said as they shook hands. "Congratulations on the promotion. How'd they pry you loose from the 24th MEU-MIC?"

"Brought it with me sir," she answered. "Two companies of it anyway."

"*Really?* We're carrying two companies of Mike Marines? Jesus! I knew we had some grunts but I thought it was an embassy guard detail or something."

"My orders say the Buran want a demonstration of concept, sir," she said. "We're going to do six company-sized meteoric inserts from orbit to show them how it's done. Not sure why, but that's not my department."

"Nope, mine neither," the captain answered. "After that fight on K'tok, I thought the 24th earned a rest."

"Well sir, some might have said the same about you. I guess they decided sitting on our asses eating Crab *a la K'tok* for eight weeks was rest enough. You ever figure out why the hell the Navy does stuff, you let me know."

To Mikko's surprise, Captain Bitka laughed and nodded. Between a Marine NCO and a Navy petty officer, those would nearly have been fighting words, but watching the easy banter between Bitka and Merderet, Mikko realized those two *really were* on the same team.

The Twenty-Fourth MEU-MIC—short for Marine Expeditionary Unit, Meteoric Insertion Capable—had been one of the two "Mike" cohorts that inserted from orbit in individual reentry pods and captured the capital and needle downstation on K'tok at the start of the recent war. That was already talked about as the most audacious operation in modern military history—*anyone's* modern military history. Merderet had commanded a rifle company in the first assault wave.

Mikko knew Merderet and the captain hadn't met until after the fighting was over, but whatever experience they held in common had rendered them comrades in a way that made her ashamed—not because she had not been there to share it. That was beyond her control. She was ashamed because she was jealous of them. She was certain they'd both lost people they cared about in that fight, and that was nothing to envy, and doing so was a shameful thing, but she still did.

CHAPTER THREE

Six days later, aboard USS *Cam Ranh Bay*
16 February 2134 *(the day of Incident Seventeen)*

Six days after assuming command of USS *Cam Ranh Bay,* Sam still wasn't sure he had a handle on the ship, but he was making progress, and he had time. After all, the war was over, at least for the time being.

The *Bay,* as he'd learned most of the crew called her, was a long, thick composite alloy cylinder, twenty-two meters in diameter and one hundred thirty-five meters long, plus a spin habitat wheel a hundred meters in diameter, spinning around its midsection. The spin habitat gave them one-gee living spaces while most of the machinery and working spaces were in the cylindrical main hull: engineering, auxiliary bridge, and missile room aft, docking bay and small craft amidships, bulk storage, point defense lasers, sensor suite, and main control room forward, and HRM—Hydrogen Reaction Mass—tankage everywhere. Four great big radiators stuck out of the aft part of the main hull like fins. In fact, they were fins when they skimmed the atmosphere of a gas giant to scoop hydrogen reaction mass, the preferred method of refueling.

The *Bay* was an ugly ship unless you liked designs which stressed utility over aesthetics, and if you did, it had a certain beauty. Well, a certain *handsomeness*. Beauty stretched the point.

That first day, only hours after the assumption of command ceremony, they had broken orbit around K'tok, accelerated for six hours at an economical twentieth of a gee, and then coasted out toward Mogo, the system's gas giant. *Cam Ranh Bay's* HRM tanks were nearly full so there was no need to scoop fuel from Mogo's atmosphere, but the calculated jump point was out between the orbits of the two planets and so off they went.

As they broke orbit Sam had every internal smart wall in the common spaces set to show the external view. The shattered wrecks of six human starships, the graves of over two thousand naval personnel, still bore silent witness to the catastrophe that had been the First Battle of K'tok. That had been on Christmas Eve last year, less than two months ago. It seemed like a lifetime.

The surprise of the uBakai fleet emerging from J-space that close to the world—the sheer crazy gutsiness of the move from the normally conservative, predictable Varoki—had been bad enough. But when the Varoki let loose their new jump scrambler weapon, when cruisers and transports began folding in on themselves as their own interstellar jump drives ate them up...

Sam shuddered and shook himself to drive away the memories. No, not the memories. He wanted to remember. He just didn't need the visceral immediacy of that experience repeated over and over. Sam had commanded USS *Puebla*, a destroyer, too small to have a jump drive. That had saved him then. Now he was commanding a starship, complete with jump drive. But the war was over, right?

The day Sam took command of the *Bay*, they had passed by those derelict ghost ships.

The day after Sam took command, he got lost.

Well, he knew about where he was. He was weightless in the main hull at frame forty-four, just forward of "the narrows," where the spin habitat's machinery was located along with the power rings. The docking bay and engineering were aft, launch bays, dead storage, and control room were forward. The problem was the access corridor dead-ended into a "T" intersection and he wasn't sure whether the best way forward was to port or starboard.

A crewperson happened by, introduced herself as Signaler Mate Second Class Lucinda Weaver, and showed him "the shortest way" to the bridge, which was a tactful way of giving directions. He'd thanked her, but then got lost again, this time deliberately. He spent over three hours wandering through the *Bay*, "inspecting" to anyone he encountered, but in truth exploring. He'd spent a lot of the following five days doing the same, not just learning the ship but also meeting the crew, talking to them at his scheduled meals but also as they manned their maneuvering watch stations. Between that and his regular duties as captain he worked full days, long days, and did so deliberately. He wanted to turn in each night bone tired, so sleep would come quickly, more quickly than all those unanswered questions about Cassandra.

Now, six days after taking command, he walked down

the broad central corridor of the habitat wheel, made way for a twelve-Marine squad in PT gear running in step and formation, and then continued to the lift that would take him up to the main hull. From there he'd make his way forward to the bridge to take over the watch. He knew the way well now, thanks to his wanderings. He'd discovered something else in those wanderings: USS *Cam Ranh Bay* was not a happy ship.

He'd served on happy ships, ships where the crew had confidence in themselves, in their officers and chiefs, in the physical ship itself, and most importantly in the captain. Something was wrong with the *Bay*, something he couldn't put his finger on yet. It wasn't an *un*happy ship, not exactly, but it was an unsettled ship, an anxious ship.

Part of the problem might have been his predecessor, Captain O'Malley, a fifty-two-year-old O-5 commander who had already been passed over for promotion to O-6 once and had been facing possible retirement before the war broke out. No one had said anything against him, either on the ship or before he'd arrived, but the Navy was like that. Have an affair and everyone talked about it. Have a run of bad luck or questionable decisions and people would start avoiding you. But if you just coasted along, didn't do anything really wrong, no one would cluck their tongue. In that respect the Navy was like life itself: almost by definition mediocrity was not noteworthy. There didn't seem to have been anything particularly wrong with O'Malley, but maybe nothing particularly right either.

Also like life in general, the higher up the Navy's chain

of command you ventured, the more empty suits you found, men like Vice Admiral Stevens who had risen without the handicap of ever having had a conviction which was more strongly held than one by his immediate superior. As their superiors had themselves risen mostly by the same means, the end results were depressing to contemplate, but thoroughly predictable.

Sam felt the spin-induced gravity decline as the lift carried him up to the main hull. *Cam Ranh Bay* was over three times the tonnage of *Puebla*, his previous command, although the main hull wasn't much bigger. Over half the extra tonnage was in the massive spin habitat wheel, big enough to hold the crew as well as a full cohort of Marines and a slice of a brigade-support echelon. By the time the lift came to a rest, Sam floated free in the car and kicked off from the wall when the door opened. He could have used his shoe and hand magnets but after months on *Puebla* he was well-accustomed to zero-gee movement. He headed forward toward the bridge, passing through "the narrows." He had to slide to one side to get past a maintenance crew working on one of the power routers.

Aside from Captain O'Malley, there were problems with the ship itself. *Cam Ranh Bay* had been commissioned eleven months earlier, the third in the *Peleliu* class of fast assault transports, but she had missed the fighting due to teething problems. In a way that had probably saved her—a little over a month earlier her sister ship *USS Peleliu* had been lost with almost all hands, along with the bulk of Task Force One.

The power ring—the superconducting magnetic energy storage system—was the *Bay's* main problem. It stored energy for the interstellar jump and consisted of four separate rings or cells wrapped around the main hull forward of engineering. But there was something faulty with the energy routers which linked them together, troublesome enough that the ship's alternate nickname was *Building Seventeen*, a sarcastic reference to how seldom it had left the repair docks until recently. Maybe some in the crew felt relief that a faulty power ring had kept them away from the disaster with Task Force One, but it had kept them out of the relief force which came later as well. It was hard to love a ship you couldn't count on.

And the leadership? A mixed bag. As near as he could tell in the short time he'd been in command, he had a good set of chiefs and no obvious weak spots in the junior officers. The department heads didn't work as a team, though. Each one ran his or her own shop and didn't bother much about the others. He hadn't run into any serious conflict so it might just be a case of incompatible personalities and empire building, but that was worrisome enough.

Running-Deer, his executive officer, should be pulling them together but she wasn't, either due to lack of inclination or not quite knowing how to go about it. She struck Sam as a solid officer but cold and standoffish. Maybe she resented him for taking over, since the ship would have been hers if he'd never shown up. Maybe she was just aloof by nature, he didn't know. The truth was he didn't have a lot of experience with executive officers and up until now most of it was bad. Just about anyone would look good compared to Larry Goldjune. Running-Deer seemed to have the respect of the department heads so maybe she was just wrangling them the way Captain O'Malley had wanted her to. Probably all she needed was for Sam to tell her what *he* wanted. It wasn't a good idea to make any big changes until he had a handle on the situation, but he'd been in command for almost a week. It was time.

They were coming up on their jump point in a couple hours. They would make the jump to Eeee'ktaa and then he'd see what Running-Deer's ideas were about getting the department heads on the same page, get them thinking and working as a team.

He waved the bridge hatch open and pushed himself through.

"Captain's on the bridge!" one of the duty mariners called out.

"As you were," he said and he coasted over to the command station where Lieutenant Alexander, the TAC boss, held the conn as OOD—Officer Of the Deck. The bridge, more spacious than on *Puebla* but still the same basic configuration, was only partially crewed, just the maneuvering watch personnel. He recognized and nodded to Signaler Second Weaver—who had shown him the way to the bridge that first day—in the COMM station.

"Sir, the ship is at Readiness Condition Two," Alexander said as he unbuckled from the command chair, his round pudgy face temporarily frozen into a look of martial seriousness. "Material Condition Bravo, on course for the jump point. Power ring is partially charged but down for maintenance, reactor hot, shroud secured, sensors active."

"Very well, Mister Alexander, I relieve you."

"Sir, I stand relieved. Captain has the ship," Alexander called out as he pushed off from the command station. Sam took his place and strapped himself in. Alexander quickly gestured for the petty officer in the TAC One chair to the right of the command chair to move to another station and then took his place.

"I passed the A-gang working on the power ring on my way here," Sam said. "Ship Systems, what's the problem?"

"Numbers one, two, and three cells are seventy-two per cent charged," the engineering petty officer at the systems workstation answered, "but the tertiary router and backup are both down, so the three forward cells are off grid and can't discharge into the jump drive."

"How about the fourth cell?" Sam asked.

"Online, on grid, and fully charged, sir, but that's only about twenty-five per cent of our total standard charge."

"Let me guess: not enough for the jump to Eeee'ktaa, right?"

"No, sir, not near enough."

"COMM, has Traffic been notified there might be a problem?" Sam asked Signaler Weaver.

"Um—we've got two hours to the jump point, sir," Lieutenant Alexander broke in. "I figured the A-gang should have it up and running by then."

"I agree, TAC, they should indeed. We'll see if they can manage. In the meantime, let's let Traffic know what's going on. Weaver, make text signal, USS *Cam Ranh Bay* to K'tok Traffic Control: Mechanical difficulties may require delay in jump and recalculation of jump entrance point. Will advise further. Signed, Bitka, Captain."

"Aye aye, sir."

Sam squinted, the commlink directory for the ship's senior officers appeared inside his eyes, and he brought up the connection for Lieutenant Ka'Deem Brook.

The Operations chief answered almost immediately, his voice inside Sam's head.

Yes, sir.

"Mister Brook, would you join me on the bridge at your earliest convenience? We have a mechanical problem which may delay the jump. If so, we'll have to recalculate our jump point and jump emergence at Eeee'ktaa."

I'll be right there, sir.

Sam next squinted up Lieutenant Koichi Ma, the head of engineering. Ma took longer to answer than Brook had.

Yes, Captain?

"Mister Ma, are you busy?"

A bit, sir.

Sam blinked in surprise and took a moment to formulate a reply.

"Well, I hope you are busy getting our power ring back online. Is that the case, Mister Ma?"

Chief Forsythe has a repair party handling that, sir.

Sam shifted in his acceleration rig and felt himself frown.

"How long before the power ring is online?"

I'd have to check with Chief Forsythe, sir. Do you want me to do that?

"Here's what I want you to do instead, Mister Ma. Get yourself to the narrows and supervise the repairs yourself. If we miss our jump point, I'm going to be hard to live with for a while. So let me hear an 'aye aye, sir.'"

Aye aye, sir.

Sam cut the connection and rotated his head to loosen the neck muscles. What kind of senior engineer let a chief petty officer handle the repairs on an outage that could make them miss a scheduled interstellar jump? Well, Ma wouldn't have to take the flak from First Fleet for screwing up the schedule, or deal with all the paperwork. There was too damned much of that 'not my department' attitude on the *Bay*. Maybe now was the time to have that talk with Running-Deer after all. Sam squinted up her comm code.

"New contact!" the petty officer in the TAC Two chair called out. "One-twenty-six degrees relative, angle on the bow thirty-eight, range twelve thousand and closing at thirty-one kilometers a second. Jump emergence signature."

Without even a conscious decision Sam hit the general quarters alarm on his command console and the repetitive battle stations gong sounded throughout the ship.

"Thirty-one klicks a second is close to our current velocity, sir," the ensign in the Maneuvering One chair said.

What was her name? Barr-Sanchez? Yeah.

"That closing rate may mostly be our own vector," she added.

"What's his profile?" Sam asked.

"He's not squawking, sir," the sensor tech answered. "No transponder. He's hot but he's not accelerating."

"Recharging his power ring," Lieutenant Alexander said from the TAC One chair.

"Size?" Sam asked.

"Small, sir," the tech answered. "No bigger than an orbital shuttle."

Lieutenant Alexander looked at him, his face creased in a puzzled frown. "A starship the size of a shuttle?"

"It must be a jump courier drone," Sam said. With interstellar communication limited to the speed of travel, it was cheaper to send a small courier craft from star to star packed with data than send a whole ship just to deliver the mail. "A hull that small, you put a jump drive, reactor, and power ring in it and there's no room for crew and life support. I just can't figure out why it's not squawking."

"Maybe its transponder is just broke-dick-no-workee," Lieutenant Alexander said. "Like our power ring. The thing is, I've never heard of a jump courier drone with its own reactor. Don't they usually just charge the ring and shoot it off, and the people at the other end recover and recharge it?"

He was right. This wasn't adding up.

"He's scanning us, sir!" the sensor tech interrupted, her voice rising in excitement.

Sam felt adrenaline course through him. Drone couriers didn't have sensor suites, didn't need them. What if . . . what if it wasn't a courier? What if instead it was some kind of weapon? What if it had one of those jump scramblers that had killed all those human ships?

Sam squinted the Duty Engineering Officer, an ensign Rosenberg.

"Engineering, secure the fusion reactor and . . ."

Suddenly Sam felt turned inside out.

★ ★ ★

We must have jumped.

Jumping from one point to another dozens of light-years away was never a pleasant experience. It helped to be prepared for it, but this jump caught him by surprise. For a time, the universe stopped. As in all the times he'd jumped Sam had no sense for how long that was—seconds or decades—because time itself seemed to lose meaning. Then Sam was back on the bridge, or the bridge was back around him, but his balance and orientation were completely scrambled, as if his inner ear had left some important parts back where they'd jumped from.

The bridge lights flickered twice and then failed, replaced by low-energy backup illumination. Sam closed his eyes but the sensation of spinning grew so he opened them again. His vertigo intensified, becoming overpowering. No matter where he looked, he was always looking *down*, about to fall.

He heard someone vomiting and he felt the contents of his own stomach lurch and then climb up into his esophagus. He snatched a bio-bag from the dispenser beside the workstation and barely got it to his mouth before his breakfast omelet came up. As he sealed the bag he heard more retching and saw a string of vomit tumble slowly through the air.

"No puking on my bridge without a bio-bag, damnit!" he managed to shout without throwing up again. "Somebody vacuum that stuff out of the air before we choke on it.

"Maneuvering. Why did you jump without orders?"

Ensign Barr-Sanchez, eyes wide with fright, turned her chair to look at him. "I . . . I didn't trigger the jump, sir."

"Well, who the hell did?" he demanded, but she clearly had no idea. Sam pinged Lieutenant Ma on his commlink.

Yes, sir? the chief engineer's voice answered inside Sam's head.

"Mister Ma, did Engineering initiate that jump?"

The jump? Um . . . I don't think so, sir. I didn't order it. Lieutenant Ravenala is on the main engineering board.

"Find out and report back," Sam ordered and then turned to the engineering petty officer, sealing his own bio bag, who manned the bridge monitors. "Ship systems, report."

"Reactor is offline but secure, sir," he said. "All other systems nominal. Number one power cell is drained. Running on emergency batteries and the LENR generators."

"TAC?" he asked next.

"All scopes clear, sir," Alexander reported. "No sign of the bogie. No sign of anything."

"COMM?"

"In the dark, sir," Weaver answered. "In the *pitch* dark. No incoming comms, no routine background chatter, I mean *nothing*. There's nobody out there transmitting on any band we're monitoring."

"OPS, where are we?"

"Um . . . I'm still working on that, sir," Ensign Barr-Sanchez said.

"If we're in a star system, put the primary up on the main screen. Let me have a look at it."

She put the visible light feed on the main screen but all it showed was a carpet of tiny stars.

"There's no primary to see, sir," she said. "There's

nothing out there but distant starlight. We are in deep space—the *deep*-deep, light-years from the nearest star. I'm still working it out, but I could use more power to the HRVS sensors."

Wherever they were, they weren't dead. The drone or whatever it was hadn't killed them with a jump scrambler program, but it had done something. He wondered why he was still alive. Then he wondered what the drone had actually done. Engineering hadn't had time to initiate their own planned jump.

"Sir, I'm getting casualty reports," the Ship Systems tech said.

That figured. Sam had been strapped in and still felt as if half the joints in his body had been whipsawed to the breaking point. There must have been some odd momentum shifts during the jump. The passengers and crew hadn't even had enough warning to grab onto a stanchion.

He felt his commlink vibrate and saw the ID tag for Lieutenant Ma, the senior engineer.

"Talk to me, Mister Ma."

Sir, we did not initiate the jump from the main engineering board. It must have come from the bridge or the auxiliary bridge.

Sam shook his head. Auxiliary bridge hadn't even been manned. It had to be that probe. "It wasn't AUX," Sam said. "I want a complete report on what just transpired, from an engineering perspective. What did our jump drive do and why? And get the reactor back online. We need juice up here to scope out where we are."

The fusion reactor is down, sir and we don't have any

stored power in the number one cell to get it back up. As soon as the tertiary router is repaired we'll be able to draw on the other three power ring cells and go hot again.

"Well let's get on it, Lieutenant. We can't live on batteries and LENR output for very long."

I have some injuries in the work party, sir. I'll get to work as soon as I get them to the sick bay.

Sam felt his ears flush and his body jerk with another adrenaline surge, this time from anger instead of fear.

"What the hell's wrong with you, Ma? Delegate it. Look in on them later. Right now, I need you working the problem. Get me power and figure out what happened, do you understand?"

Yes, sir, he said, but grudgingly.

Sam cut the connection and looked around the bridge, dim in the emergency lighting. He saw fear on the faces of the crew. More were showing up now, taking their stations from the general quarters alarm. He noticed it had stopped sounding although he didn't remember turning it off.

"Everyone crew your stations," Sam ordered, "but keep the power drain low until we have a hot reactor. Passive sensors only."

His imbedded commlink sounded and he saw the ID tag for Lieutenant Running-Deer.

"Are you okay, XO?"

Yes, sir. Well . . . I broke by doze.

It took Sam a moment to realize she'd said she'd broken her nose.

I'm compiling a casualty list. Lots of sprains and

bruises, a few serious injuries, but I'm afraid we have one fatality.

Sam closed his eyes and for a moment felt dizzy again. He took a deep breath.

"Who is it?"

Running-Deer took a moment to answer.

You know we have that cultural exchange mission to Earth from those aliens, the Buran, taking them back home to Eeee'ktaa? You remember, they were on the VIP list.

"God, not one of the envoys!" Sam said.

Worse than that, sir. One of their children.

CHAPTER FOUR

Three hours later, **aboard USS** *Cam Ranh Bay*
16 February 2134 *(the day of Incident Seventeen)*

Doctor Däng Thi Hue entered the briefing room with the rest of the small group of civilians, many of whom displayed signs of minor injuries from the unannounced interstellar jump. Most of them also showed one or more signs of fear or shock: eyes darting rapidly around the room, voices hushed almost to whispers, and expressions of confusion or anxiety.

What happened, do you know?

Is this the right room?

Can we sit anywhere?

Her own hands trembled, but she disguised it by holding her data pad firmly in both hands in front of her, an old trick she had learned from a public speaking coach. You cannot keep yourself from being afraid, but you can keep from showing it.

Hue tried not to brush against the one alien Buran in the group, its offspring in its arms, and also tried not to make her avoidance obvious. The tiny Buran child stared at her over its parent's shoulder, stared with eyes more

61

serious, somehow older-seeming, than those of a human child. Alone among all six intelligent species, the eyes of young Buran did not seem overlarge for the size of their heads. Some humans described Buran children's eyes as beady looking. They were, which was odd. The proportionally larger eyes of infants were useful survival characteristics for most species. It made the infant's face more expressive and appealing, and so engendered greater attention from the parent. She wondered how the Buran had prospered without that attribute.

Also alone among the intelligent species Buran were without gender, their sexual habits obscure, and their reproduction accomplished by budding. They were little known and less understood, both of which conditions Hue intended to remedy.

Hue, a senior professor of xenophysiology at the University of Jakarta and Nobel laureate for her theory of Structural Ubiquity, was wealthy from seven lucrative patents but lived an austere, if elegant, life. Single, between lovers, and in her fifty-third year less driven to end that state then when she had been younger, Hue had only one passionate attachment, one addiction, and that was to new questions. Her newest question, the one she thought might occupy her mind for the rest of her productive life, was to understand the Buran. Now she wondered if she would get that opportunity at all.

Ensign Clarence Day, who had become a sort of liaison officer to the civilians the last few days, saw her, and his cherubic face brightened. He waved and then gestured to a chair in the center of the conference table.

"Dr. Däng, we have you seated here, across from the

captain. Can't have our Nobel laureate at the end of the table."

Hue looked around uncomfortably. Who *was* seated at the ends, she wondered, and would they take offense? She would have. Ensign Day did seem a bit clueless at times.

"Thank you, Clarence. That wasn't necessary but it was kind of you."

The long table boasted five chairs along each side and one at each end. The chair Day pointed to was in the middle of the table.

She took her seat and smiled to Lieutenant Koichi Ma, already seated across the table and one place down to her right. He returned her smile but he seemed preoccupied with his data pad. He had been too busy with the emergency or malfunction or whatever it had been to resume their earlier conversation. He had a fascinating theory on optimal stress in physical support structures that bore on her most recent research: commonalities in leg architecture across the six well-studied trees of life.

He had been called away in the middle of his explanation, called away by Captain Bitka, who insisted Ma personally supervise some routine repair. It was absurd but typical of the military, at least in her experience. Ma was a talented engineer, his insights bordering on brilliance. He was wasted in his current assignment, as anyone *not* in uniform could clearly see.

She was relieved the Buran was seated to her right with an open chair between them. The Buran were shorter than most of the other intelligent species, averaging about one meter sixty, which meant Hue could have looked most of them in the eye had she chosen to. The difference in height became less pronounced when they were seated, as their legs were shorter in proportion to their torsos, at least compared to Humans and Varoki, the only other species currently aboard the ship. The Buran had remained arboreal much longer than had humans and Varoki, and they retained not only comparatively short legs but a swaying, rolling gait as well.

Her reluctance to sit next to the Buran had nothing to do with stature or gait, however, nor did their skin bother her. Many found the ever-moist, lumpy, mottled brownish-green hide unsettling, but these variations in appearance from human norms were a source of interest to her, not repulsion. One of the Buran had lost a child, however, and Hue did not yet know enough about their social conventions to know how this Buran, who was the senior member of their delegation, felt about that or would react, or what reaction it expected in return. She did not want a *faux pas* to poison her research before it had begun.

Humans, and the other species, knew comparatively little about the Buran. Although they had been members of the *Cottohazz* for more than a century longer than Humans, they had kept almost entirely to themselves for most of that time. Only in the last decade had they begun conducting cultural exchange missions and opening their world to visits from other than governmental officials.

"Good evening, Dr. Däng," she heard, and the Nigerian journalist Abisogun Boniface sat down next to her on her right. She nodded in reply and clucked her tongue softly in sympathy at the sight of his left forearm in a compression cast and sling. She and Boniface had met shortly after he boarded the ship at K'tok, along with the Marine contingent. He had asked for an interview when he learned she was on board and she had politely declined. She did not much enjoy interviews and she had reached the point in her life where she no longer felt obliged to do things she disliked. Boniface had not seemed disappointed and it occurred to her he had asked out of politeness rather than genuine interest. The realization had made her laugh.

Boniface had boarded the ship with the Marines because he had been an embedded war correspondent with them on K'tok. Although she knew no details, she understood there had been desperate fighting there and Boniface had seemed distant and preoccupied at first. He now seemed more open, but also frightened. Well, they all were.

The Varoki trade envoy e-Lisyss took the seat to her left without greeting her or acknowledging her presence. His omnipresent and oafish assistant sat to his left. Several other seats were taken by humans she recognized but did not know well enough to converse with. The only one who had made an impression was the tall, slender, heavily tattooed American musician, with shaved head and wearing a minimalist black suit over a white shirt and finished with an antique black string tie. The visual effect was somewhat spoiled now by a light blue US Navy-issue neck brace. That was Choice (her only name), supposedly a major American *Afro-Jonque* star, although Hue wondered how big a star she was to be touring this far from Earth. She also wondered how someone that white became an *Afro-Jonque* sensation, but she suspected she was being narrow-minded. Music, after all, was supposed to be borderless, but Choice was *so* white. Perhaps she was just very frightened.

Hue had noticed there was always tension in Choice's posture, even before she had been injured. She wondered if the musician's quick, confident answers to questions, and her combative willingness to disagree and then overwhelm opposition, masked some sort of personal insecurity. Hue had never met any genuinely successful mass-audience artists before so she had no experience to draw on. Did success suggest a secure personality? Or did the desire to overcome or compensate for insecurity produce success? It was a question which had never occurred to her before, at least not with respect to celebrity artists, but now she wondered.

As they waited for the captain, Hue looked around and wondered why these particular people had been brought here: two Varoki, one Buran (two if you counted its offspring), and six human civilians. Captain Bitka could have done a ship-wide address and taken questions by commlink. Why did he want to establish a personal connection with her and the others? These *specific* others.

Once all the civilians were seated, Captain Bitka and Lieutenant Running-Deer entered and sat in the remaining two chairs, the captain directly across from her as promised. Poor Running-Deer had her swollen nose taped and sported two luminescent black eyes. The captain greeted Hue politely as he sat and she responded in kind.

They had met only once before, four days earlier, when she had been invited to dine at the captain's table, along with three other civilian guests and one of the ship's enlisted mariners. She had looked forward to it as Bitka had a reputation as an intelligent officer. One person had used the words "tactical genius" to somewhat breathlessly describe him. Hue had seen no evidence of genius over dinner. The captain had made no contribution to the wide-ranging conversation, had not even shown any interest in it, repeatedly covering yawns with his napkin. At one point she was fairly certain he dozed off for several minutes. He *looked* intelligent, with that broad high forehead, and the appearance might account for the reputation, and she knew many people mistook taciturnity for brains. Or possibly the bar for intelligence was simply low in the United States Navy.

Mikko Running-Deer sat to the captain's right and for the second time Hue noticed how the normally cheerful and extroverted executive officer became a different person in Bitka's presence—businesslike, unsmiling, unemotional. What sort of private interaction would produce such a pronounced change in public behavior? Perhaps the same sort that demanded the senior engineer supervise the trivial repair of some power gizmo or other. Maybe when some people in the Navy said "tactical genius" they meant an authoritarian martinet simply lucky enough to have survived the worst Human military disaster in a century.

Was that who this new captain was? Well, she'd see soon enough.

"Thank you all for coming," Bitka said. He had a good strong voice, clear enough he didn't have to shout to be heard, and apparently didn't feel the need to. "We are recording this meeting and broadcasting it live throughout the ship. I want to bring you up to date as to what we know about what happened, our current situation, and what I intend to do. Please bear with me and let me complete that summary. Then I'll be happy to answer your questions. I've asked you specific people here as representatives not only of the three species on board but also of a variety of disciplines and professions. I hope your questions address those the rest of our passengers are wondering about."

It fit that he would not want questions until he was done, fit with a desire to control everything, even the flow of this meeting.

"It should be obvious that we experienced an unscheduled and unexpected interstellar jump. Because there was no warning, passengers and crew suffered a number of injuries, some serious, and one fatality: the child of Eeshaaku Manaam, Consulting Facilitator for the Buran New Era Artistic Conference. Parent and child were on their way to Eeee'ktaa, the Buran homeworld. I have spoken with the Honorable Eeshaaku Manaam and expressed my heartfelt regrets at the death of its child. Councilor Abanna Zhaquaan has asked to address the rest of you and the ship's company at large. Councilor?"

At least the captain knew the Buran custom of using the entire name in address, Hue thought. The Buran to her right, still holding its infant in its arms, rose. Most humans disliked their voices but Hue found them intriguing. They were deep and resonant, but also flat and emotionless, and seemed to have a faint echo, like something from a child's ghost story.

"Captain Samuel Bitka, let me say first that we appreciate your sympathy over the unfortunate death of the young Eeshaaku Manaam. The elder Eeshaaku Manaam asked me to express this to you again in person, and to thank the other passengers for their expressions of sympathy. But we would not want our fellow passengers to suffer undue distress on our account. We have a different view of death than we understand you to have, a view I cannot explain. That is all."

Then it sat again. For a moment no one spoke and several shifted uncomfortably in their chairs. If the Buran had meant to put everyone at ease, it had failed, but that was probably inevitable. Given their appearance and strangely menacing voices, Hue could not imagine what it might have said to make everyone feel comfortable and at ease.

The captain rose again. "Thank you, Councilor Abanna Zhaquaan. Let me extend my regrets to all of you here for the pain and fear you have suffered as a result of this incident. We are doing, and will continue to do, everything we can to get you safely to your destination."

That was rather well done, Hue thought. He didn't sound like someone trained in public relations, but he came off as sincere. He probably *was* sincerely sorry for the death and all the injuries, if for no other reason than he was going to have to do a lot of explaining when they got to the Buran homeworld. He also sounded calm and supremely confident. Most supremely confident men she knew were fools.

"All of that said," Bitka continued, "it's also clear the jump did not take us to Eeee'ktaa, or any other star system. We lost power for over an hour following the jump but, as you can see from the lighting and the restoration of the ship's full e-nexus data grid, our fusion reactor is back online. All of our most pressing immediate concerns have been addressed. What remains is to figure out what happened and get us to Eeee'ktaa.

"My operations department has pinpointed our current location as thirty-seven-point-three light-years from the K'tok system and seventy-eight light-years from Eeee'ktaa, which puts us almost but not quite outside the volume of *Cottohazz*-explored space. Most of that space is empty and most of the stars visited have no life-sustaining worlds. As a practical matter, we are a fair distance from civilization, but well within the range of a single long jump to our destination now that we have made repairs.

"Okay, that's where we are. How did we get here? A few minutes before we jumped, an object that did not match the profile of any known spacecraft operated by any of the six species or one hundred and seventy-two sovereign nation states of the *Cottohazz* emerged from jump space close to us. Within seconds of the object scanning us, our ship jumped without our ordering it. We had preset the coordinates for Eeee'ktaa, a jump of sixty-three light-years from K'tok, but obviously we aren't there, nor did we jump toward it.

"Whatever caused us to jump, it sucked every joule of energy out of the one available cell of our power ring, leaving our reactor in shutdown mode and with not enough available stored energy to restart it. It takes a lot of juice to get a fusion reaction going. Fortunately, we had suffered a malfunction in our power ring which prevented three of our four cells from discharging. That untapped power, once the repairs were completed, let us restart the reactor. Lieutenant Ma and his engineering department literally saved our lives over the course of the last four hours. The next time you see someone with the engineering department shoulder flash, you might want to thank him or her."

Bitka turned to Ma. "Well done, Lieutenant."

"Thank you, sir," Koichi answered, and Hue saw him blush. Perhaps this Bitka was smarter than she had credited him. A classic technique of psychological dominance was alternating abuse with kindness, and if that was Bitka's game, he was playing it very well.

"You're welcome, Mister Ma," Bitka said and then turned back to the civilians around the table.

"Those are the bare facts of what happened. We believe the object broadcast some sort of coded command that triggered the jump we made. We recorded a variety of energy signals shortly before the jump. Some of them were clearly sensor radiation but others appear to be encrypted code. Our supposition is that somehow the encrypted code activated our jump drive.

"As almost all of you must know, the uBakai Star Navy used an encryption system to trigger the jump drives of some Coalition naval vessels in orbit around K'tok in the recent war, the so-called jump scrambler weapon. This signal we received differs in three important ways from the weapon used by the uBakai.

"First, it caused a *coherent* jump. That is, all molecules of our ship and of us left the K'tok system and arrived here at the same time and in their original configuration. The uBakai jump scrambler weapon only moved a selected number of molecules, thus destroying the structural integrity of the ships and the personnel on board."

Hue had never heard a complete description of how that weapon had worked. She knew it had been powerful and deadly, but what Bitka described sounded truly ghastly. She remembered passing the ruined starships as they left K'tok orbit, remembered with a new appreciation of how horribly all those people had died.

"Second, in our event we jumped several light-years, as far as our stored power would take us.

"Third, the code we intercepted bore no resemblance to the code transmitted by the uBakai jump scrambler weapon. Whatever encryption this object used, we haven't been able to crack it yet. We'll keep trying but we don't really have the expertise. It may end up taking some really good brains in military intelligence to unwrap this one.

"So that's where we stand. The good news is that we are still within a single jump's range of Eeee'ktaa now that we have our entire power ring operational. It is my intention to completely charge our ring and then jump to Eeee'ktaa seven hours from now. So everyone should think about getting some rest and having a meal.

"Now I'll take your questions."

Hue leaned back and looked around the table. That was a good, direct outline of their situation and the captain did not give the impression he was holding anything back. She had no idea whether she could trust that impression, and her inclination was toward skepticism. The others seemed to have accepted the presentation on face value, though. She understood. They were frightened, and frightened people often follow the person who shows the least fear.

The Buran envoy to her right lifted its hand, palm up, apparently asking to be recognized.

"Councilor Abanna Zhaquaan?" Bitka said.

"Captain Samuel Bitka, if it is allowed, and if your communication officer would not object, I may be of some assistance in analyzing the coded transmission."

"Are you a trained cryptologist?" Bitka asked.

"A linguist, which is not exactly the same, but not entirely different, either."

"Stop!" Hue heard from her left and the Varoki envoy's assistant held up a hand. All of them turned and saw a hurried conversation between the two Varoki. They spoke softly but Hue could pick out a few works in aGavoosh, the Varoki universal language of diplomacy and commerce. Then the Varoki envoy's assistant turned to Captain Bitka.

"The Trade Envoy insists that this transmission be held as a confidential item until responsible governmental authorities can examine it and determine its significance."

"Why?" Boniface, the Nigerian journalist to her right demanded. "Are you afraid a Varoki government *other* than the uBakai has been tampering with jump drive access codes? Do you want to make sure this all gets hushed up before there's another scandal?"

This time the Varoki envoy jumped to his feet and let loose an angry stream of aGavoosh, harsh, guttural, and rich with clicks in place of some consonants. It was a good language for shouting in, Hue thought, although she couldn't really understand much beyond repetition of the words "outrage" and "insult."

"That's enough," Captain Bitka said, cutting him off. "Please resume your seat, Envoy e-Lisyss." He turned to the Buran. "Councilor Abanna Zhaquaan, given the fact that we are only hours from our jump to Eeee'ktaa, I think a wiser course is to keep the transmission in military hands until we can turn it over to higher authority. I thank you for your offer and under other circumstances I would gladly accept."

The Buran bowed its head in acceptance.

"I have a question," one of the men she did not know said. "We've obviously suffered some sort of a malfunction. Why take any chances? Why don't we signal for help? Won't they send a rescue expedition after us?"

Hue heard a note of desperation in his voice, an emotion she was sure many on board shared, but several people around the table groaned.

"What?" the man said.

The musician named Choice answered, the disdain clear in her voice. "It'll take thirty-seven years for the distress signal to get to K'tok."

"Ms. Choice is correct," the captain said. "Radio waves travel at light speed and we're thirty-seven light-years out from K'tok. Our supply lockers are pretty well stocked, but I don't think they'll last that long."

That brought a nervous chuckle from the others, although the captain's face remained carefully blank. The routine questions began after that, most of them covering material Bitka had already gone over. It had been a good, complete presentation. It had failed to cover only one important point.

When the questions ran their course, Bitka took one more glance around and then looked directly at Hue.

"I believe you have a question, Dr. Däng."

Hue twitched slightly with surprise but kept her face under control. *How did he know that?*

"When we make our jump in several hours," she said, "are you certain it will take us to Eeee'ktaa?"

He looked at her for a moment before answering. His expression remained carefully neutral and his hands stayed folded on the table, but she saw that where the fingers intertwined they were white with pressure. For the first time Hue felt her throat tighten with fear.

"I expect it will," he said, "but I cannot say that I am certain. We don't know what effect the object's transmission had on the control mechanism of the drive, and we can't examine the jump core to find out. All jump drives are Varoki built and are sealed modules which we cannot access, and we wouldn't know what we were looking at if we could. My own engineering department does not know what a Varoki jump core looks like inside or its principle of operation. All we can do is replace defective external components."

"Thank you for your honesty, Captain Bitka." She swallowed and kept her voice level and calm. "If your worst fears are realized and the next jump does not take us to Eeee'ktaa ... do we have any options?"

"Absolutely. I'll have the engineering department replace every component in the jump drive. I have already checked the inventory and we can do a complete trade-out of control systems and jump actuators, everything but the jump core itself. Then we'll jump to Eeee'ktaa."

"Why not do that first?" the same man who asked the question about a distress call said.

"It will take us the better part of two days to change out every component," the captain answered, "and there is always the chance in an operation that involved that something will not work right afterwards and require additional adjustments. Since we don't know there is anything wrong with those components it makes more sense to just make the jump now, and if something goes wrong then we will begin replacing components."

She wondered, *What if that still does not work?* But she did not ask it. She looked at him, looked into his eyes. Bitka was afraid, and now she was more afraid than ever, but she merely bowed her head in acceptance, deliberately copying the gesture of the Buran.

Seven hours later Hue strapped herself into the acceleration couch in her stateroom and thought about what the captain had said and what he had left unsaid. She wished she had been able to speak with Koichi, her friend the chief engineer, but he had been on almost continuous duty since the meeting. Perhaps he could tell her something about the jump drive, something which would at least let her organize her thoughts, her questions. The one conclusion she had come to was that Captain Bitka was not the complete fool she had originally suspected, but that also meant his confidence was a sham.

She set the smart walls, ceiling, and floor of her stateroom to show the external view. She was suddenly surrounded by deep black with a dusting of stars. When they jumped, she would immediately see the bright yellow-orange primary star of the Eeee'ktaa system.

Or not.

CHAPTER FIVE

Three days later, aboard USS *Cam Ranh Bay*
19 February 2134 *(three days after Incident Seventeen)*

The first jump had been tough to accept. Sam had almost expected the results of the second jump, where they had attempted to jump to Eeee'ktaa but had instead just ended up another one hundred twelve light-years away from K'tok. So they spent two days meticulously swapping out every component of the jump drive they could replace, everything but the jump core itself. There was no replacement for that, but logically replacing everything else *had* to correct the problem. Still, he was reluctant to order the jump, wondered if there was one more diagnostic sequence he could run that would put off the fateful moment.

That was stupid. Waiting wasn't going to change anything. Either the problem was fixed or it wasn't. Better to find out, and if it wasn't fixed . . . well, then what? That depended on a couple things, and neither of them were important if the next jump just took them to Eeee'ktaa like it was supposed to.

No, not actually *to* Eeee'ktaa, *toward* it. The second jump had left them one hundred forty light-years from K'tok and a little shy of one ninety from Eeee'ktaa, which was more than they could manage in a single jump. They would still emerge in deep-deep space, light-years away from the closest star, but they would at least be going in the right direction.

If it worked.

"Ops, execute the jump."

"Aye aye, sir," Lieutenant Brook answered and triggered the jump warning chimes throughout the ship. He waited for twenty seconds and then put his hand over the jump actuator control. "Jump in five, four, three, two, one."

Again that sensation of floating free of time and space, then a wrenching return to wherever this was, a rise in body temperature, perspiration. He opened his eyes and saw the same blank field showing no sign they were anywhere near a star and its associated planetary system. That was okay. They knew they wouldn't be near a star this time.

"Ops, tell me Eeee'ktaa is out there about seventy-five light-years ahead of us."

Brook didn't say anything for several long seconds as he worked his panel and Sam could feel the tension build on the bridge. How many of the bridge crew were even breathing?

"No joy, sir. It's not where it should be."

Sam's stomach tightened and he felt dizzy, felt panic beginning to tickle his throat. He heard groans from the bridge crew, a mix of anger and fear.

"What the fuck?"

"*Now* what's wrong?"

"Jesus Christ!"

"Belay all that," Sam shouted above the babble and the bridge quickly fell silent. "We'll figure it out. Work your stations. TAC?"

"No nearby objects," Lieutenant Alexander reported. "No energy sources, nothing identifiable as a tactical threat."

"COMM?" Sam asked.

"In the dark, sir," Lieutenant Bohannon reported from COMM One to his left. "No communication signals on any band we're monitoring. I'll start a systematic sweep of the spectrum."

"Very well," Sam said, although he was pretty sure what that would turn up: nothing.

"Two hundred sixty-one light-years from K'tok's primary, sir," Brook reported from Ops One. Sam noticed that Brook hadn't moved since coming out of jump, hadn't spoken except for those brief reports. Brook knew what this last jump probably meant.

"Son of a bitch," Sam said quietly. Another one hundred and twelve light-years, exactly. Another hundred light years from Cassandra, from understanding what happened, from figuring out what to do next with his life. He shook his head. Not the sort of thoughts a *good* captain would have.

"Can you plot our course from K'tok to our current location, Mister Brook?"

"Yes sir. I have it right here. We are moving almost directly toward the galactic core but slightly offset, seven degrees to spinward."

"Have all our previous jumps since leaving K'tok been on that same plot?"

"Yes, sir, all three have been on this same course track, straight as an arrow."

"Very well, Mister Brook. Now shoot me a view forward and tell me the distance to the next star directly on this course, assuming there is one. Or get started on it but have your number two finish. I'm going to set up a holoconference with the senior staff."

Sam had considered all the possible outcomes of this jump he could think of and after the actual event he was down to two possibilities. Either the jump core was damaged and locked on a random course, or it was deliberately reprogrammed with a specific destination in mind. They'd find out soon enough.

Sam turned to Lieutenant Bohannon in COMM One. "Tell the department heads and the XO to helmet up and we'll holocon. Mister Brook, Mister Alexander, that means you too."

Sam picked up his helmet from the mount beside his workstation, clipped it on, and plugged his suit's life-support umbilical into the socket in his workstation. With his helmet on and visor down it could get stuffy quickly.

The helmet had hologram cameras on the inside to record his face and on the outside to record his body movement. The view of the other conference participants was projected on his helmet faceplate. The only really odd thing about seeing them was he knew they wore helmets but they looked as if they did not. The helmet cameras recorded in and out from the helmet, but could not record the helmet itself. Holoconferences were normally used to allow officers on different ships to meet. On the same ship the meetings were almost always face-to-face but Sam needed to talk to his senior officers right away, in private, and didn't want to pull them away from their duty stations.

He slid his visor down and was immediately in a virtual conference room, a neutral grey, seated at an oval table. As the others closed their visors they appeared, first Alexander, then Running-Deer, Acho, Brook, and finally Ma.

And Sam was back to the two possible explanations: random damage or a deliberate destination.

If it was simply damaged, if they were headed in a random direction, they were all dead. Space was too big for there to be any possibility they would happen onto a star system with a human-habitable world before they ran out of power, food, or oxygen. Their only hope was that the course was *to* somewhere, a destination they could reach before they ran out of something critical. He suspected most of his officers had figured this out as well, but he wondered which ones had. Time to find out.

"So which is it?" he asked. "Some random course a damaged jump core spit out, or a specific course to somewhere?"

"Or did engineering screw up the component replacement?" Lieutenant Brook said. "Who'd you fob *this* job off on, Ma?"

Sam was surprised by the anger in Brook's voice and expected an explosive retort, but instead Ma just shook his head.

"Wish a mistake was the answer, Ops. I wish to God

that was all it was. But XO checked every component we replaced."

Running-Deer nodded. "I did. The captain checked my work, and Lieutenant Acho checked every part number out of inventory and every replaced component back in. That's why we took two solid days. There's no mistake. Every component in the jump control suite was replaced by a fresh component from storage."

"Had to be the Varoki," Lieutenant Alexander the TAC boss said. "That probe that did whatever it did to our jump drive, it *had* to be Varoki. Who else knows how to get into a jump core and mess with it? Nobody."

"I'm not so sure, TAC," Sam said. "The code's nothing like their jump scrambler weapon, nothing like we've ever seen from any Varoki operating system."

"Who else can it be, sir?" he asked. "Can you imagine anyone else who could possibly be responsible?"

"No, I can't, TAC. But the thing to remember is the universe is not limited by my imagination, or yours either."

"I don't know who did this," Lieutenant Ma said, "and I think it's too early to start guessing. We just don't know enough yet. But I'll tell you one thing, I don't think it's random damage. Damage might lock in a course, but whatever this is it's done more than that. When we jump it sucks every bit of power out of our energy ring, except the cells we physically disconnect from it. I think someone wants us to go somewhere and is in a hurry for us to get there."

"But if they want us there," Alexander said, "why suck the power dry? If we hadn't had that malfunction the first jump we'd be dead."

Ma shrugged. "I can't say for sure, but maybe whoever set this up, their power systems work differently than ours do."

"Varoki power systems are exactly the same as ours," Alexander shot back.

"I know that, TAC," Ma answered, "so you might want to rethink that theory."

Sam couldn't see any plausible candidate for who had done this, but the emerging consensus was clearly that it was deliberate, not a simple accident. On one hand, the idea that anyone even had the ability to reach all the way down into their jump core and make it do whatever they wanted was not simply impossible, it was terrifying. On the other hand, they weren't dead yet. They at least had a chance.

"Wait one," Brook said and held up his hand. He turned to the side and listened, apparently to his commlink.

"Understood," he said and turned back to the group.

"That was quartermaster Ortega in the Ops Two chair. I had him working on the calculations of a possible destination. We've got a preliminary, sir, but bear in mind that at these distances those stars aren't where we see them anymore. They've been moving for a long time since that light started moving our way, but we've got a baseline projection of their drift over time. I'd like to deploy our large visual array and get a better look."

"But you've got a candidate," Sam said.

"Yes, sir. K2 class star with enough wobble to suggest a good set of planets. Distance is two thousand seven hundred and forty light-years from here, give or take."

"Jesus Christ!" Alexander said. "Did you say almost three *thousand*? Are we going to go all the way out there?"

"I don't know, TAC," Sam said, "but right now it looks as if someone wants us to."

"But why would the Varoki want to send us out there?" Alexander asked.

Sam shook his head. "That's why I'm not onboard with that theory, TAC. It would be quicker and easier for the Varoki to just kill us. The destination star is about three thousand light-years from K'tok. That's twenty-five hundred light-years farther than any *Cottohazz* survey mission has ever gone. As bizarre as this sounds, we have to face the possibility we are dealing with an intelligence the *Cottohazz* has never encountered before."

"Excuse me, sir, but then how do they know how to reprogram a Varoki jump drive?" Alexander said.

"I don't know. None of this makes sense, yet. But the important thing is we're going *somewhere*. I think most of you had already realized that since we cannot change course, if we weren't aimed at a star system, we'd be dead inside a couple months, and not much we could have done about it. But we *are* aimed at a star system, and that means we're still alive."

They sat in silence, stunned silence, Sam thought. Finally Running-Deer shook her head. "An alien intelligence. And it's controlling our ship. We're going to have some very frightened people on our hands."

"Yeah," Lieutenant Ma said, "including me."

"Scares the hell of me too," Sam said, "if that's any consolation. Once we break out of this conference, though, all of you need to hide that fear way down deep. You've got officers and crew and civilians looking to you to set an example. We can't change the course, but we can control when we jump, and we can control how far by how many power cells we disconnect, and that's something. *We* decide how long this trip takes. Mister Ma, how's our fuel endurance look?"

"Um...I'd have to check sir. We're in pretty good shape, I think."

"I have it here, sir," Running-Deer said and looked at her data pad. "The reaction mass tanks are over ninety-five percent and if there's a gas giant at the destination we can scoop more hydrogen from it. Fuel pellet supply for the fusion reactor is our critical power limit, since we can't fabricate those. But the *Bay* was designed with the alternate peacetime role of deep interstellar survey. That's why we've got twice the jump range of any combatant ship in the fleet and lots of reactor fuel. We've got twenty-one hundred hours and change on the reactor—about three months at continuous peak power. We can easily triple that endurance, or more, if we aren't maneuvering and jumping all the time."

"Good. What about food, water, and oxygen?"

Lieutenant Acho, the logistics officer, answered immediately. "We recycle every drop of water and scrub the carbon out of the air. Those aren't an immediate problem. Because we are liable under treaty to serve as a *Cottohazz* transport in emergencies, we carry compatible protein stock for all six intelligent species. We have rations for five and a half months for the Human passengers and crew, effectively unlimited for the fifteen Varoki and twelve Buran on board—because there are so few of them compared to the stocks we carry."

"Okay," Sam said, "I figure we're twenty-five more jumps from our destination—let's just start calling it that: *Destination*. Twenty-five jumps. If we stick to one jump a day we're looking at a month there. If we can get whoever reprogrammed our jump drive to change it back, it's another month back to Eeee'ktaa. Sounds like we've got fuel and rations for out and back with a considerable reserve. So that's something positive right there."

"How are we going to make whoever's waiting for us reprogram our jump drive?" Alexander asked.

"When I know that, Mister Alexander, I'll tell you. We'll break now. I'll take care of the announcement to passengers and crew. After that, you department heads start meeting with your officers and chiefs. I want a list of ideas for possible contingencies we may have to face and drills to deal with them. XO, I want to meet you afterwards, say fifteen minutes in the briefing room."

"Sir, the briefing room is up in the habitat wheel. May I suggest we use the alert wardroom here in the main hull? If we go up into the wheel we'll be mobbed by a lot of frightened passengers with questions we won't have the answers to yet."

"Good point and good suggestion, XO. Okay, see you there."

He raised the visor of his helmet, the connection broke, and he saw the bridge crew at work around him again.

Sam sat there, alone with his thoughts for several long seconds, but the truth was for much of the last two days he had thought through what to say to the passengers and crew in this nearly worst of all possible cases, to the point that he felt he had already spoken the necessary words many times. He had Bohannon connect him to the all-ship comm circuit.

"Attention, this is the captain speaking. As most of you have seen by now the jump did not take us to the Eeee'ktaa system. Instead we are in deep space on the same course as in our last two jumps. Our conclusion is that the object we encountered somehow managed to corrupt our jump core, which we have no access to or ability to repair. As a result, we are locked on a course toward a star a considerable distance away. We are not helpless, however. We control when we jump as well as how far. We just can't change the direction. We also have an extensive sensor suite and as we approach our destination we will use it to study the star system and gather whatever information we can.

"I have already arranged to consult on a continuing basis with key representatives of the civilians on board. We have an impressive pool of talents and experience to draw on. But I will not attempt to minimize the potential danger we face. I do know that our best chance of surviving whatever trials lie ahead of us is together and working as a team.

"I promise you anything we find out which bears on our fate I will share with you. We are in this together. Thank you for your courage and patience."

The alert wardroom was in the main hull, not the rotating habitat ring, which meant it had no simulated gravity. Sam got there five minutes early, got a zero-gee squeeze bulb of black coffee from the dispenser, and clipped his tether to the table in the middle of the room. The alert wardroom, austere by the standards of *Cam Ranh Bay*, was larger than the only wardroom USS *Puebla* had.

He missed *Puebla*. Mostly he missed the familiarity of working with a crew he knew he could count on. Not that the *Bay's* crew was second-rate. He still just didn't know them well enough, didn't know their strengths and weaknesses, didn't know where he could lean on them for strength and where he had to go easy, help them along. He did know something was wrong with the officers and he finally had an idea what it was.

His stomach growled. He'd deliberately put off eating to avoid post-jump consequences. Now he touched the smart surface of the table and ordered a seaweed salad with Bosnian chicken, and texted his apologies to Chief Duransky for having to skip their scheduled lunch. Just as the XO got there the steward brought Sam's salad out and clipped its magnetic plate to the table surface. As usual Sam looked at the metal plate and half expected the salad to float away, but it never did. The surface tension of the liquid salad dressing was enough to hold it in place. The silverware, on the other hand, was magnetic to stick to the table when not in use.

Running-Deer still wore a broad piece of surgical tape across her nose but the swelling had gone down and the bruises under her eyes, shiny greenish-purple at their peak, had faded to pale blue shadows.

"Sorry I'm late, sir."

"No, I'm early. Get something to eat if you like. How's that nose?"

"My nose is fine, sir, and thank you for asking. I hardly feel it anymore. I'm not hungry, sir, but I'll grab a cup of tea if you don't mind."

She drew a zero-gee squeeze bulb of black tea before clipping her own tether to the table.

"I want to make this a slow trip, XO. We need to work the crew, get them used to the idea of where we're going. You live with something long enough you start getting used to it, no matter how screwed up it is."

"Yes, sir," she said, but it sounded pro-forma to Sam as if she wasn't sure she agreed.

"The other thing is the officers," he said. "A month or more will give us time to whip them into shape."

"Sir?" she said, as much a challenge as a question.

Sam took a breath before continuing. He really dreaded this next part.

"XO, I've been trying to figure out what the problem is with the officers, and I finally did. It's you."

Sam saw her mouth stiffen, her body draw back slightly, and her neck and cheeks color.

"It's not that you don't know your stuff," he continued. "In terms of technical skills, you're clearly the best officer on this ship. You could take the place of any department head tomorrow—except maybe engineering—and not lose a step, hit the deck running.

"But you cover for them, like you did for Ma in the holocon just now with the fuel numbers. You connect the dots between the departments, fill in all the blanks. They get about 80% of the job done and you take the baton and cross the finish line for them. Any time departments need to cooperate, *you* do it. The department heads don't even need to talk to each other."

Running-Deer looked at him but her eyes had become glassy, expression fixed, and he saw her knuckles had turned white on the hand that held the grip rail around the edge of the table.

"I know. You knock yourself out to make this ship run like a well-lubricated machine, and now here's some new captain ragging your ass over it. But XO, you've got to let these people do their jobs. No, strike that. You have to *make* them do their jobs, because that's *your* job."

"I-I don't know what to say, sir," she stammered. "I thought you were satisfied with my performance."

"It took me a while to figure out what was wrong. So now I have and now I'm telling you, but you can turn this around. You're a fine officer, Running-Deer. Look . . . tell me about Lieutenant Brook. Give me your unvarnished assessment of his strengths and weaknesses."

She looked at the table surface for a moment, collecting her thoughts, then looked at her bulb of tea. Sam wondered how much she wanted to throw it at him. She took a breath and looked up.

"Ka'Deem is smart and technically very proficient. There isn't a station in the Ops department he can't crew as well or better than the specialists assigned to it. He cares about his people, looks out for their welfare. Very conscientious."

"But," Sam said.

She shifted uncomfortably. "But he is conflict-averse, sir. He doesn't like to discipline people. He covers for his weaker staff. He goes along with other people's ideas even when he thinks they aren't the best way to do things, just to avoid a disagreement. He's great at coming up with compromises . . . maybe too great." She thought about that for a moment and looked Sam in the eye. "You think I'm like Ka'Deem Brook, don't you?"

Sam chewed another bite of salad thinking about how to answer that, what the most honest answer was.

"No. You have more initiative than he does, and you're clearly a stronger leader. You're being the XO Captain O'Malley *wanted* you to be, and there's nothing wrong with that. He was the captain. But you got a new captain now. So be the XO *I* know you can be."

He pushed the remnants of his salad aside and leaned forward.

"We're one ship, a transport, not even supposed to be anywhere near real trouble, and I think we're about to go into a shitstorm of epic proportions. But we're not defenseless or helpless. We've got a month to get our people working together and coming up with ideas for how to get every gram of performance out of this ship. And I mean weapons, life-support, sensors, acceleration, endurance, data analysis, everything. We have to get every quantum of knowledge and experience and imagination out of the crew.

"It's not your fault, XO, but the *Bay's* been coasting. Hasn't it?"

"Yes, sir," she said, and then nodded in genuine acceptance.

"Okay. No more coasting. What do you say? Let's light some fires."

She looked away for a moment and then looked back. "Aye aye, sir."

"Okay, then. Carry on."

She unclipped her tether and pushed off through the hatch, and Sam sighed.

Well, it sure wasn't the enthusiastic embrace of the new order he had hoped for, but it was probably the best Running-Deer could manage under the circumstances. He hadn't meant to damage her self-esteem but he hadn't known any other way of getting through to her. He wondered if she understood how little actual experience he had at this captain stuff.

CHAPTER SIX

Seven days later, aboard USS *Cam Ranh Bay*
26 February 2134 (*ten days after Incident
Seventeen, 1946 light-years from Destination*)

Mikko Running-Deer stepped back from the shower of
sparks as a machinist mate from engineering put the
finishing touches on the composite alloy pipes in the
renovated storage compartment.

"The first hydroponics compartment is already
hydrated and we have soy growing there," Lieutenant
Rosemary Acho, the logistics officer, explained. "This
compartment should be up and running by the mid-watch
tomorrow. More soy here, but when we clear a third
compartment we're going to grow some different plants,
tomatoes, probably. They grow fast."

Mikko looked over the clusters of water pipes and the
six separate clear tanks inside.

"Engineering did a good job fabricating the clear
composites," she said.

"Yes, Ma'am, once we got Lieutenant Ma moving on
it. I figure we can stretch our human rations by another
month, maybe six weeks, if all three of these chambers

produce like they should. Um . . . there's something else I'd like to bring up, XO. I found a shipment we're carrying for transfer to Fleet Base Akaampta."

"The *Cottohazz* combined operations base?" Mikko asked.

"Yes, Ma'am, although it's US Navy property and consigned to the US ordnance holding facility there."

"Okay, my curiosity is aroused. What is it?"

"A shipment of thirty-six deep-space intercept missiles," Acho answered and looked down at her data pad. "Mark Fives, the new Block Six variants with the refitted laser pointers and with the Sunflower anti-missile option, the one the destroyer crews improvised in the war. It's now hard-coded in."

"Mark Fives?" Mikko said. "Aside from the four new General-class heavy cruisers, the only things that can shoot those are US Navy destroyers, and most of those are wrecks out around K'tok. There sure aren't any of either at Akaampta. That doesn't make any sense."

"Well, XO, that's the Navy for you. I checked the supporting documentation. The shipment was ordered before the war, as advanced deployment of replacement munitions in case one of our heavy cruisers got tagged for joint *Cottohazz* operations. It looks like it's been moving through the bureaucracy on autopilot ever since, except someone decided to substitute new production missiles. Now they're in our hold."

Mikko saw the possibilities. *Cam Ranh Bay* was technically an armed transport, but aside from the spinal coil gun for launching planetary bombardment munitions it had two small point defense lasers for anti-missile work, two larger dual-purpose lasers, and launchers for twelve older Mark Four deep-space intercept missiles. Thirty-six brand new Mark Fives would be a major augmentation to their anti-ship firepower.

The captain would like the fact that the idea came from Acho instead of her. It would show initiative, maybe even growing self-reliance. That conversation a week earlier still stung, but Mikko was trying to change.

"That smacks. Good work, LOG. The captain can requisition those for emergency use. You put together the paperwork and I'll get his signature. Tell Lieutenant Alexander he has some new toys. That should excite him."

Acho looked down and shook her head. "I already did, Ma'am. He says we can't fire them. Wrong bore size for the coil gun."

"That sounds like another job for engineering," Mikko said.

"Lieutenant Ma wasn't crazy about detaching part of his A-gang to rig these hydroponics tanks. And the truth is, neither Lieutenant Alexander nor Ma have much use for me." She looked up into Mikko's eyes. "They're reservists, with good jobs waiting for them once the emergency is over. They figure people who picked the Navy as a career did it because they couldn't find anything better."

"Be careful how wide you cast that net, Lieutenant. The captain's a reservist, too."

"He's different, XO. Besides, they've all been to college, you too."

"You've been to college, Acho. I've seen your personnel folder."

"Navy sent me to technical school, ma'am. It's not the same. I came up through the ranks. I may wear a white shipsuit now, but when they look at me they still see khaki."

Mikko knew that much was true. There was no getting around it. Acho was ten years older than most of the other officers of her grade because she'd had a good career as a petty officer before being tapped for officer training. She didn't have "polish," didn't get the literary references in some of the wardroom conversations, and so mostly kept quiet, although Mikko couldn't see what "polish" had to do with getting the job done. Yes, there was an inescapable air of condescension in the way most of the other officers treated Rosemary Acho, but Mikko doubted she understood how quickly it would go away if she just wouldn't embrace it like a martyr.

"I'll talk to Alexander," Mikko said, "get him moving on this with you and Ma, but you need to discharge that ballast and stand up for yourself, Rosemary. You've got more active duty time in uniform than both of those two put together. You know how to make things work and where to look for answers—like finding these Mark Fives buried in the cargo. You don't need to apologize to anyone on this ship for who you are or how you got here."

"Yes, Ma'am," Acho said, without conviction.

"Look," Lieutenant Alexander, the TAC boss, told Mikko an hour later, "we're not a cruiser, okay? We're a transport. There's only so much firepower we can wring out of this tub."

Mikko rubbed her temples, hoping her headache

would go away. Of course, her current headache was mostly Lieutenant Homer Alexander.

"USS *Cam Ranh Bay* is an *assault* transport," she said. "She's not a cruiser, but she's not a tub either and you better never let the captain hear you call her that. We've got a coil gun—"

"For launching bombardment munitions," Alexander broke in. "Forty-centimeter bombardment munitions, not deep space intercept missiles."

"I know that, TAC. But Lieutenant Acho—"

"Lieutenant Acho knows logistics, not ordnance," he interrupted again. "She sees 'missile' on a shipping manifest and thinks she's got something. But those Mark Five bad boys need a coil gun to fire and they won't fit *our* coil gun. I can't just wave my hands and make them fit."

Bad boys? Mikko thought. And he said it with a sort of tough male swagger and a step toward her that made her fight against her rising anger. How much of this was just Alexander defending his turf as a testosterone-only zone? Maybe he'd forgotten that Captain Bitka's old TAC boss on *Puebla* had been Marina Filipenko, and she'd managed to get the job done pretty well. Or maybe it was just that he hadn't come up with the idea himself.

"Lieutenant Alexander, you interrupt me one more time and you will bitterly regret it. Do you read me?"

Alexander took a half step back.

"I . . . I'm sorry, Mikko. It's just . . . TAC is my job. I take it really seriously."

"Take it seriously?" Mikko said. "You know, Lieutenant, sometimes I just don't get you. We're going into the deep-deep black with no idea what we're facing except they're probably more advanced than we are and might not be friendly. The last thing we want is a fight, but if it comes to that, we're going to need every edge we can get. Right now, our only credible anti-ship assets consist of the two dual-purpose lasers and exactly twelve Mark Four missiles. You're the TAC boss, for crying out loud. I'd think you'd *jump* at the chance to add thirty-six Mark Fives to that. Instead I'm hearing excuses. What the hell's wrong with you?"

Lieutenant Alexander's eyes grew wider and she saw him color with either anger or embarrassment, she couldn't tell which.

"What's wrong? Look, I know my job, XO, but you've got to be realistic. Just wanting more firepower doesn't make it happen."

No, she knew wanting it didn't make it happen. But *working the problem* did. There had to be a way to use these missiles. There *had* to be, and she knew she could figure it out and make it work. She wanted to. She wanted to drag Alexander and Acho to engineering, explain the problem to Ma, and *beat* the solution out of them if she had to, then give it to the captain, her present of thirty-six lethal additions to their armament suite.

But that was why these three couldn't work it out on their own, wasn't it? Because she always did it for them. She had done her best to change, to execute her job the way the captain wanted her to, and for days she had seen little bits of evidence like this that maybe he had been right.

"TAC, you and Lieutenant Acho get together with Lieutenant Ma and come up with a solution."

"It'll have to be later," Alexander said. "Lieutenant Ma's on watch right now."

"I know. He's duty engineering officer so you know right where to find him. Get Acho, go to engineering *now*, and do not come back until you three have figured out a way to make these missiles work."

"How?"

"That's your job, TAC. Build a goddamned catapult if you have to but make them work. Now go. *Shoo!*"

Watching Alexander stride away in obvious irritation, Mikko had to admit to a fairly unprofessional feeling of satisfaction.

Three hours later she was doing her afternoon routine on the resistance machines in the officers' gym when Rosemary Acho pinged her again. She sounded upset when she asked Mikko to join her in her office. Mikko wiped the perspiration from her face with a towel and her first reaction was to refuse. She suspected this was just another complaint about the boys not treating her as an equal, although only an hour earlier they had submitted a joint plan to make the Mark Five missiles work: engineering was going to fabricate sabot sleeves around the missiles so they would fit their larger bore coil gun.

Something in Acho's voice sounded different, though.

"What's the problem, LOG?"

"The, uh . . . the Varoki trade delegate e-Lisyss and his assistant are here with some, um . . . *recommendations* concerning rations. I think this may be above my pay grade."

Was that anger in her voice? No. Maybe disgust, but something else as well.

"I'll be there in five minutes," Mikko said.

She unhooked the cooling feeds from her shipsuit, washed her face in the 'fresher, and thought through the possibilities for problems over rations on the way to Acho's office, a quarter of the way around the habitat wheel.

Because the six species of the *Cottohazz* were independently evolved from different trees of life, their protein chains were different, as in incompatible, even poisonous to each other. But since transport vessels of all the navies of the member states of the *Cottohazz* might be called on to move almost anyone, all of them carried protein ration stocks for all six species. *Cam Ranh Bay's* galley could put meals on tables for Humans, Varoki, Buran, Zaschaan, Katami, and Brand. The problem, she supposed, was that it was navy galley food, and the *Bay's* cooks weren't exactly experts in alien *haute cuisine*. The envoy e-Lisyss, like any other sentient being, probably had a lot going on inside him, but about all that Mikko had experienced so far was a sense of disappointed entitlement.

When she arrived, e-Lisyss and his assistant Haykuz were seated in chairs in front of Acho's desk. The light glittered on their hairless, green-tinted, iridescent skin and she was again reminded of some sort of large, terrestrial lizard. Mikko wondered if their distant, primitive ancestors had had feathers, like dinosaurs. She remembered the nicknames Captain Bitka had given e-Lisyss and Haykuz that first day—Little Sis and Haiku—and she suppressed a smile. Acho stood when Mikko entered.

"XO, thank you for joining us."

Neither of the Varoki stood, of course.

"What can I do to help?" She sat in the third chair in the office and Acho sat as well, but the logistics officer's rigidly erect posture was a blueprint of tension.

"The envoy e-Lisyss has been sharing with me his concerns concerning rations." Acho frowned, probably realizing the awkward phrasing betrayed her nervousness.

"I'm afraid a military transport doesn't have the quality or variety of food the envoy is probably accustomed to," Mikko said. "I wonder if there's a Varoki on board who has some experience in cooking and who might help the galley staff with meal preparation."

Acho shook her head. "No, it's not about the quality of the food. It has to do with quantity."

"We have more than enough protein in stock for the small number of Varoki on board," Mikko said. "If portion size—"

"No, Lieutenant Running-Deer," the Varoki assistant Haykuz said, "the concern is not portion size for *us*. In fact, it is clear that we will still be alive after the entire Human crew has starved to death, which it will do in a little over four months by our calculation."

"Lieutenant Acho has come up with some expedients to stretch that out a bit," Mikko said. "But yes, that is our principle concern as well."

"The Envoy's mission for the *Cottohazz* is of the highest importance," Haykuz explained. "It is essential that he survive to return, and he cannot do so without the Human crew of this starship remaining alive and functional."

Mikko felt a shock of realization and then a rising throb of anger, but she pushed it back down. No. The son of a bitch couldn't possibly mean that. He couldn't be *that* big a son of a bitch, could he?

"As a member of that crew, I appreciate the value he places on us," Mikko said and stood up. "Now, if that is all, I'll—"

"No, it is not all," Haykuz said and Mikko noticed for the first time his own flushed face, his own ears drooping and folded back, and the fact that he now looked down at the deck, refusing eye contact. Haykuz was an idiot and a toad, but at least he had decency enough to be ashamed of what he said next.

"There are many useless mouths among the Human passengers, who contribute nothing to our chances of survival. Hard decisions are required."

So, he really was that big a son of a bitch. Humans were just servants and in a pinch, it made sense to only keep the really useful ones alive? *Fuck you and the horse you rode in on!* Mikko thought. But she was XO. It was her job to solve problems, not make them worse. She tried to make her mind work coldly and logically, tried to formulate a response which would end this right here and keep anyone outside this room from knowing what had been said. Except the captain, of course. She would have to tell him. So what was it she wanted to be able to tell him she had said to these two?

"I will explain this to you and save you the humiliation of having the captain say it later. We are serving officers in the Navy of the United States of North America, and we are bound by its regulations, as well as by the laws of our nation, the joint covenants of the *Cottohazz*, and common decency. All of those make us responsible for the survival and wellbeing of *every* person in this ship, regardless of station or situation. They do not empower the captain to execute passengers on the off chance we might need some of their food later.

"Lieutenant Acho, you will not repeat this conversation to anyone else on the ship."

"Aye aye, Ma'am."

"As for you, Mister Haykuz, I will never make a record of this conversation and so officially it will never have taken place. But if you or the envoy make this proposal directly to the captain I assure you it will become part of the official record of this voyage. For your own good I recommend you do not do that under any circumstances. Do you understand me?"

Still looking down, Haykuz did not move. e-Lisyss stared at a place on Acho's office wall and then grunted a single syllable. Haykuz relaxed slightly.

"It is understood, Lieutenant Running-Deer."

CHAPTER SEVEN

Ten days later, aboard USS *Cam Ranh Bay*
8 March 2134 (*twenty days after Incident Seventeen, 836 light-years from Destination*)

Lieutenant Deandra Bohannon, communications officer, tightened the straps of her acceleration chair and closed her eyes, waiting for the jump. How many was this? Nineteen or twenty, she'd lost count. Too many.

She'd read about long-term effects of multiple jumps—effects on things like cognition. All the molecules of your body ended up someplace else exactly the same as when they started, but sometimes there was a stray atom or two of hydrogen in the space where you came out. That's why your body temperature went up a little. But what if it was in your brain, what did that do? No one knew, but whatever it did, the more jumps the more damage.

Most people didn't do twenty jumps in a three-year Navy hitch. They were doing almost thirty in one month. What would that do? What would they be like?

"Jump in five, four, three, two . . ."

She wanted to scream but she didn't. Officers don't scream.

And then it was over and she felt dizzy from the elevation in temperature, felt herself suddenly soaked in sweat, her ears filled with a buzzing hum. She panted for air and turned up her suit's cooling system.

"You okay, COMM?" Captain Bitka asked from the command chair beside her.

She gasped and nodded. "Hot flash, sir. I'm fine." She smiled weakly at her own joke.

"Scopes are clear, Captain," she heard the TAC boss Homer Alexander report. "No nearby objects, no energy sources, nothing identifiable as a tactical threat."

"COMM?" the captain asked her.

Deandra sat there, trying to concentrate, but all she could hear was that same buzzing hum, rising and falling in intensity and pitch. She shook her head to clear it and then saw the rise and fall in pitch mirrored on the visual readouts of her workstation in front of her.

"Oh my God! I've got *comms!* I can't make it out, sir, it's faint, but it's definitely electromagnetic in the radio spectrum. This isn't background noise. Someone's talking!"

"Descartes was full of shit!" Lieutenant Ma shouted as Sam and the XO entered the briefing room.

"Atten-HUT!" Running-Deer barked and the two officers present—the Ops boss Lieutenant Brook and Lieutenant Ma from Engineering—came to their feet: Sam had apparently arrived in the middle of an argument, or maybe just a rant. Since it was Ma's rant, the room momentarily fell into an embarrassed silence. Sam sat down at the conference table and watched the three other officers follow his example.

Five of the six civilians he had chosen as his advisory board were present as well, but they did not stand, nor did he expect them to. The sixth civilian, the Buran linguist, was working with Bohannon on the incoming radio signals. These five—what an odd group, but it was the best he could assemble.

He'd surprised some of his officers when he tagged Choice, the American musician, to sit in with the group. Most of them hadn't known that before Choice had become a professional musician she had earned an advanced degree in cybernetics. Running-Deer had drawn his attention to that in the VIP profile. Whatever civilization they encountered, there was a good chance the technology would be radically different. He wanted someone who knew the logic and limitations of data analysis. Choice had also turned out to be perceptive and articulate. Once he got used to her unconventional appearance, he couldn't help but notice she was strikingly attractive as well. He supposed it was harder to make it in music without that.

He'd hesitated before adding Boniface, the Nigerian journalist. Boniface had been embedded with the Marine cohort on K'tok so Sam had asked A. J. Merderet, the Marine commander, for her impression.

"He's okay, him," she'd said. "Didn't pretend he wasn't scared shitless but didn't let his fear stop him from doing his job, either. He did what he was told, stayed out of the line of fire, never did anything stupid enough to get one of my Marines shot at. And another thing, he wasn't trying to make sense of it or come away with some profound insight into war, you know? Just wanted to witness and report it. I got no complaints."

Someone used to observing and analyzing facts, and who at least tried to keep his own lens from distorting what he saw. That was good enough for Sam.

Sam had formed a rough picture of the others but continued to find Dr. Manaia Johnstone, the New Zealand anthropologist, a bit of a mystery. He wanted someone with an insight into dramatically different cultures. So far, he had said almost nothing in any of their meetings. His heavily tattooed face—even more inked than Ms. Choice—gave him a ferocious appearance, but then that was the point of Maori tattoos, wasn't it? All Sam really knew about him, aside from his *curriculum vitae*, was that he was apparently a very good listener.

e-Lisyss, the Varoki diplomat, was politically mandatory, being the senior *Cottohazz* official on the ship, and Sam figured they might need a diplomat later. And of course, that meant his assistant and translator had to be there as well. One saving grace was that ever since e-Lisyss had recommended summary execution of "useless mouths," the two Varoki had mostly kept their mouths shut in these meetings.

Finally, Dr. Däng, the Indonesian xenobiologist, was an obvious pick. If they were going to encounter alien life, better have someone handy who had spent her entire adult life studying it, and had managed to pick up a Nobel prize along the way. Sam had quickly figured out Däng didn't think much of him. He didn't think she had figured out how little that mattered to him.

As Sam looked at them he noticed the variety of civilian clothing had gradually given way to standard issue blue enlisted personnel shipsuits. In the event of a hull puncture, having about ninety percent of a vac suit already on made a lot of sense. Ms. Choice naturally wore a custom black pressure suit, form following.

"I see you were in the middle of a spirited discussion," Sam said. "I imagine it's prompted by the discovery that we can now detect radio broadcasts from the star system we've dubbed Destination. Pretty amazing news, isn't it? We suspected that there was intelligent life at Destination, and hoped for it. I haven't wanted to mention it before, but I think we all understand that we *need* there to be intelligent life there in order to get back home. We need to contact the beings who reprogrammed our jump drive so we can persuade them to program it back.

"We are eight hundred and thirty-six light-years out from Destination. That means the radio transmissions we are monitoring were made eight hundred thirty-six years ago. We can't translate them yet but Lieutenant Bohannon and Councilor Abanna Zhaquaan are working on the language. The important thing is that yesterday, when we jumped to nine hundred forty-eight light-years from Destination, there were no radio emissions. Something very important happened there between eight hundred fifty and nine hundred fifty years ago.

"This tells us something else. There was always the possibility that some unrecorded early Varoki survey mission had reached and colonized this star system and then sent a probe back to *Cottohazz* space. We now know that cannot be the explanation. These broadcasts we are monitoring from Destination predate the Varoki invention of the jump drive by over five hundred years.

"I'm changing our standard procedure. From now on

we'll be jumping every other day instead of every day. That will give us time to deploy the big survey sensor array after each jump and spend about thirty-six hours collecting data. The important thing for now is we know there's intelligent life at Destination—or at least there was eight hundred years ago.

"So with that in mind, please carry on, Mister Ma."

Ma shifted in his chair.

"Well sir, I was just explaining to Ms. Choice why I think her theory of intelligent life in the galaxy is... flawed."

Sam looked at the musician and smiled. "You have a theory of intelligent life in the galaxy, Ms. Choice? I'd love to hear it."

Choice threw a wary glance at Ma and then cleared her throat.

"Well, it's like this. You look at what we know about life in the six main ecosystems, and the top carnivores never last very long—maybe a few million years if they're lucky."

"Dinosaurs," Ma said in a mocking, singsong voice.

Irritation flashed across Choice's face.

"Yes, dinosaurs lasted for over a hundred million years on Earth, but no *one* dinosaur species did so as top carnivore. Individual species don't last that long, but the galaxy's been around for *billions* of years. Think how many intelligent species may have evolved and died off already. So, when a species dies, what does it leave behind? If it's a tool-using culture it leaves its tools. Isn't that right Dr. Johnstone?"

"Absolutely," the Maori anthropologist said.

"Tools?" Sam said. "I'm afraid I don't see the connection."

An impatient frown darkened Choice's face.

"A very advanced technological society will inevitably develop machine intelligence. A species may become extinct, but their machines will be more robust. The odds are overwhelming that the most common form of *surviving* intelligent life in the galaxy consists of self-aware machines left behind after the extinction of their creators."

Lieutenant Ma snorted and Sam found himself smiling. Watching these two glare at each other and paw the deck was at least a momentary distraction from the looming threat facing them. And who knew? It might actually end up being relevant.

"I take it you disagree, Mister Ma," Sam said. "Does that have anything to do with your negative opinion of Descartes?"

"Yes, sir. 'I think therefore I am,' Descartes said. But if he'd actually thought a little harder about it, he'd have realized that insects think, in a primitive sort of way. At least they calculate. What they don't do is *feel*."

"Of course they feel," Choice said.

"I don't mean they have no nervous system," Ma answered. "I mean they have no *emotional* response to sensations. If Descartes had had the good sense to say, 'I *feel*, therefore I am; I *mourn*, therefore I am; I *desire*, therefore I am,' well, then he'd have been onto something. And all these sad generations of cybernetic engineers wouldn't have wasted the best years of their lives chasing this false dream of a self-aware machine. Ms.

Choice is lucky to have gone into something really useful, like music. Otherwise she'd have spent her life saying, 'If only we link more processors together, and add more memory, then it will wake up.'"

"Well, it *will!*" Choice said.

Ma shook his head.

"Come on! You really think something capable of doing *nothing* except adding one and zero, over and over again, can somehow become a sentient self-aware being by doing that faster, and remembering more of its sums? That's absurd!"

"*Absurd?*" she shot back, rising from her chair. "I stay in touch with people in my field. They're close to having it, really close," she said, pointing at him repeatedly for emphasis, as if she were punching his chest with her finger.

"How close?" Ma asked. "Ten years? Maybe as long as thirty?"

Choice's eyes opened a bit in surprise. "Yes, about that. I mean, it's hard to be precise—"

"Right," Ma said and turned to face Sam. "Ask any cybernetic engineer how close we are to true artificial intelligence—a self-aware, conscious machine—and they'll tell you either ten years or thirty years, depending on whether they're optimists or pessimists."

"Yes, there's a broad consensus," Choice said. "You think that's an argument *against* it being true?"

"No, but here's the thing: that's exactly the answer you would have gotten from any cybernetics specialist you asked, no matter when you asked the question, at *any* time in the last one hundred and fifty years.

"Think about that! We were ten to thirty years away from it in *1980!* Take all of them at their word and it means we are not one year closer to having such a thing now than we were way back then." He turned and looked at Choice, now jabbing with his own finger to emphasize his argument. "And we *never* will be, because you guys are looking for consciousness in all the wrong places."

"We're modeling brains," Choice shot back, "neuro-pathways, breaking down how the brain calculates. Where *should* we be looking? In a church?"

Ma shook his head. "I mean you're looking at the wrong things *in* the brain. It's like the old saying: if all you have is a hammer, everything looks like a nail. Calculation is all you can measure with precision, so that's all you think matters, but you're wrong."

"What else are you talking about?" she demanded, "Magic? Invisible mental waves? Extra-dimensional souls? What?"

"Well, think about this. Now, correct me if *I'm* wrong, Dr. Däng, but the least advanced terrestrial animal which experiences pleasure during the act of sex is a frog. Isn't that so?"

Dr. Däng sat up a little straighter and smiled. "Well, when I got up this morning I never thought I'd end up considering the lascivious nature of frogs. We could spend the better part of a week arguing about some definitional issues, and probably never settle them to everyone's satisfaction, but basically, yes Koichi, you are correct."

"That's the boundary line," Ma said, "*desire*. Animals lower than a frog mate because they are programmed to, like machines, but a frog does because *it loves to fuck!*

That's the beginning of self-awareness, and it isn't a result of binary addition. It's a result of sensual pleasure.

"You want to make a self-aware machine? Figure out a way to give it an orgasm and *then* we'll talk." He leaned back in his chair.

Choice glared at him for a dozen or more heartbeats and then shook her head. "You'll see when we get there." She sat down and turned away from him.

For a few seconds no one said anything. Sam wasn't sure what the others thought of all this, but he really enjoyed the idea of an engineer arguing *against* machine-based intelligence and an artist arguing *for* it.

"But Ms. Choice," Sam said, "your argument, intriguing as it is, addresses much older civilizations which supposedly died off a long time ago and left their intelligent machines behind. We seem to be approaching a civilization which developed electronic communication within the last thousand years, not million."

She turned back and looked at him for a moment before answering.

"Captain, you assume the beings generating those radio transmissions are native to that star system and developed the technology eight or nine hundred years ago. What if that's just when they got there?"

CHAPTER EIGHT

Sixteen days later, **aboard USS *Cam Ranh Bay***
24 March 2134 (*thirty-six days after Incident*
Seventeen, 74 light-years from Destination)

Sam looked around at his cabin—the dark-red composite chairs and sofa, the imitation wood-grain coffee table and desk—and compared it to the compact austerity of the captain's cabin on USS *Puebla*. He'd thought that was luxurious, and it was by a destroyer's standards. He'd actually had his own private zero-gee shower, the only one on the boat. Here his bathroom was nearly as big as his first cabin on *Puebla*, when he'd just been its tactical officer. He'd considered *that* luxurious as well, because as a department head he hadn't had to share it with another officer.

He shook his head. Not for the first time he felt out of place here, and that was no way for a captain to feel on his own ship, He activated his desk holovid recorder and settled back in his padded swivel chair.

"Hey, Cass. I doubt you'll ever see this so I feel a little stupid even making it. It's sort of a personal log addressed to you, mostly because I need someone to talk to about all this, someone whose morale won't crumble if they find out their captain has doubts and fears, and even regrets. Talking to myself seems more like a symptom than therapy, so I'm talking to you instead. There's no way to transmit it from here, but if I get back—or if *Cam Ranh Bay* gets back without me—it'll be there for you.

"Well, we're almost six weeks out and we're farther from *Cottohazz* space than anyone has ever been: almost three thousand light-years. One jump a day for the first three weeks and one jump every other day for the last two. Whatever is steering us has us headed roughly toward the galactic core and we've just crossed the great rift between the Orion Spur and the Sagittarius Arm. No one's explored in this direction because you have to go through so much empty space to get anywhere interesting."

He smiled.

"*Interesting*. What's that old curse? Well, wherever it's taking us, it's on the outer edge of the Sagittarius Arm. We're only about seventy light years from the end of the road. How's that for a change in perspective? *Only* seventy light-years. How long did people look across distances like that and think of them as uncrossable voids? Tomorrow we'll take the plunge, jump right into the Destination system, come out about twenty-five million kilometers above the plane of the ecliptic. We'll start broadcasting to the locals and monitoring every data stream our sensors can capture—try to find some common basis for communication.

"This wasn't my original intention. At first, we worked out a plan where we'd jump to a range of one light-month and spend a couple weeks there gathering data before we made the final jump. Everyone, including me, wanted that extra time to study them up close before committing, but I ended up scrapping it. If we jump in from that close they'd pick up the signature of the jump, and they'd already know where we came out, so they'd be able to connect those two points and draw a line right back to the *Cottohazz*. They may already know where we're from, but if they don't I won't give it to them on a platter.

"Instead we'll jump from here. I doubt anyone can detect a jump signature from this far out, but even if they can it will take seventy years for the light to get to them. Seventy years. That's as much breathing space as I can give you and still have a half charge on our power ring in case of trouble."

Sam paused to take a sip of coffee and stare at the walls of his cabin. He had the smart walls set to show the exterior view. He found himself doing that more and more, even though with no nearby star the vastness and loneliness of the view was nearly overpowering.

"I find myself staring at the stars a lot, Cass, wondering. As long as there have been people, I guess we've looked at the stars and wondered *if* something alive, something intelligent was out there. Then we found the *Cottohazz*— or they found us—and the *if* was answered. But just those other five species, and we've gone a long time, looked a long way, without finding anyone else. Now we found one more—or they found us—and they must be pretty intent on meeting us.

"I'll tell you what I can't tell anyone else here, Cass. I have a *terrible* feeling about what we're likely to find. If they could communicate with our jump drive, why not just communicate with us? Why snatch a ship full of people and drag it across the rift to another spiral arm of the galaxy if all they wanted to do was chat?"

His schedule reminder vibrated softly inside his head, at the base of his skull.

"Well, Cass, I've got to go. I'm due at captain's mast. We've been having discipline problems, more and more the farther out we get, and we've got a really bad one on the docket today. People are frightened and they're losing hope. It's my job to give them that hope. I'm trying, Cass, but I'll tell you, I'm kinda running on empty."

CHAPTER NINE

One hour later, **aboard USS *Cam Ranh Bay***
24 March 2134 *(thirty-six days after Incident
Seventeen, 74 light-years from Destination)*

Captain's mast was the name the Navy gave to nonjudicial
punishment. Judicial punishment required a court
martial, which could be convened as necessary, but for
most infractions the miscreants were offered the option
of allowing the vessel's captain to decide their
punishments in a less formal setting.

For almost an hour Mikko had watched Captain Bitka
dispense judgment in a strikingly nonjudgmental manner.
He reprimanded, lectured, and disbursed punishments
somehow without displaying disdain for the men and
women brought before him. She had first seen him
conduct captain's mast three weeks ago and she had asked
him about it afterwards.

"Well, we don't punish them for being bad people, XO.
We punish them for doing bad things. There's a
difference. That's my theory, anyway."

As she called the last case of the day, she saw the lines
of his face harden. This would test his theory.

"Senior Chief Bosun's Mate Duransky, Francis X, front and center," she ordered.

Duransky walked in. Captain's mast was held in the captain's day cabin in the spin habitat, so there was normal gravity. The chief bosun's mate normally had the slightly bouncing stride of someone who spent a lot of time working in zero gee but his gait today was flat and lifeless. He entered the office in company with the Marine lance corporal guard and came to attention. Mikko noticed a fresh bruise on his left cheek and the start of a black eye. That hadn't been there two hours ago.

"What are the charges, XO?" Captain Bitka asked for the record, although he knew the answer.

"Sir, Senior Chief Petty Officer Duransky stands accused of misuse of Navy equipment, theft of government property, conduct injurious to good order, abuse of authority, dereliction of duty, and incapacitation while on duty," she answered.

The captain looked at Duransky. The chief bosun's mate's gaze remained on the wall above the captain's head but his face slowly went from flushed to pale.

"So, Duransky, you figured out how to modify a medbay drug processor to produce Oblivion."

"Yes, sir," Duransky answered after licking his lips.

"You got Medtech Patel to help you. Ruined her career too, by the way. And you used up some of our irreplaceable pharma stocks to do it."

"Yes, sir."

"And then you traded some of it to crew members for sexual favors?"

Duransky closed his eyes and nodded.

"You're the chief bosun's mate, the senior noncommissioned officer on this ship, the figure every enlisted person and most junior officers look to as an example of correct behavior in the face of adversity. And this is the example you chose to set."

Duransky opened his eyes.

"God help me, sir, but I was that scared. It's like I went crazy, like some other person did all them things."

"We're all scared, Duransky. Now I have a ship full of people even more scared because they think they can't even trust their own chain of command. My inclination was just to go straight to a court martial, throw the whole goddamned book at you, make an example. The XO convinced me it makes more sense to get through this with as little fuss as possible. You owe her your neck, because regulations limit the extent of punishment I can dole out in a captain's mast."

"I understand, sir. I'm very sorry, sir."

"Your sorrow means shit to me," the captain spat back. "Here's all that Navy regs allow me to do without a court martial: permanent reduction in rank of two pay grades to bosun's mate first, confinement to quarters on plain rations for thirty days, all accumulated leave revoked, pay forfeiture for thirty days plus restitution for replacement of all stolen materials.

"In addition, so long as you are on my ship you are limited to menial duty and will have no supervisory authority over any crewperson. I will recommend your separation from the service without pension as soon as we return home. Now get out of my sight."

Duransky turned and took a step toward the door.

"Wait," the captain said, and Duransky turned back. "Leave your bosun's whistle right here." The captain pointed to the surface of his desk.

Mikko saw tears of humiliation in his eyes as Duransky pulled the curved brass whistle from a pocket of his khaki-colored shipsuit and laid it on the captain's polished desk.

"Another thing," the captain said. "Lance Corporal Gupta, you will escort the prisoner to the ship's store and have him turn in his khaki shipsuit and replace it with penal orange. You will then escort him to his confinement compartment and, upon turning him over to the guard, you will go to the prisoner's quarters, collect every khaki shipsuit and item of khaki uniform clothing, take it to the ship's store, and replace all of it with enlisted mariner blue."

"Aye, aye, sir."

Only chief petty officers and Marines wore khaki.

Mikko and the captain sat in silence for several long seconds after the others left, both of them looking at the whistle.

"You know, sir, technically that's his property."

"I don't give a damn. He doesn't get to have a bosun's whistle on my ship, not even stowed away in the bottom of his sea bag."

"Yes, sir," she said.

The captain huffed out a sigh. He suddenly sounded tired.

"Crew's coming apart, XO. I can feel it. Medbay's passing out sleep aids and antidepressants like they were candy. Three times as many fistfights this week as three weeks ago, and I think half of them don't end up on report. We practically have to post guards on the beer dispensers in the galley, and then post guards to watch the guards. Now Oblivion? And from our senior chief? Jesus Christ, what a mess!"

"It's the waiting and the uncertainty, sir," Mikko said. "Once we make that last jump and get to Destination, the crew will at least know what they're up against and what to do. The drills you have us doing help, maybe more than you know. This thing with Duransky . . . I know it's bad sir, but we caught it. We dealt with it. Let's replace him and move on, keep everyone focused on what's out there ahead of us. The crew will get squared away, sir, and Ops is finding out new stuff all the time. That helps."

"Shoving Duransky out an airlock might help, too," Captain Bitka said, and then looked up at her. "Not that I would ever consider such a thing."

"What he did was pretty bad, sir, no question. But he had a clear record up until now. Usually you don't . . . well, you don't react quite this strongly." She said this last with some trepidation, but it was true and part of her job was to tell the captain the truth as she saw it.

"It wasn't just pretty bad, XO. This was different. All those mariners that come before us, we're responsible for leading them. That means discipline, but not humiliation, because if they stumble, often as not it's as much our doing as theirs. But Duransky . . . he was our senior chief. Was one of us, one of the leaders the entire crew looked to. Maybe all the commissioned officers outrank him on paper, but in terms of who the crew looks to, the only people more important are you and me. Not even the department heads are as important. What he did to my crew . . . I'll never forgive him."

He picked up the bosun's whistle by its chain and watched the shining curved brass tube swing back and forth for a moment.

"We might need this," he said. "Where's Duransky's replacement going to find a bosun's whistle way the hell out here? Who do we have?"

"Two possibilities, sir: Chief Wainwright runs the small-craft subdivision and Chief Velazquez heads up the deck subdivision. And by the way, no senior bosun worth his or her salt doesn't have a whistle tucked away just in case."

"Fair enough," the captain said with a smile. He watched the whistle swing back and forth for another second and then dropped it in a drawer of his desk. Then he looked directly at her. "If I wasn't here and you were running the ship, who would you pick?"

"Ted Wainwright," she said. "Gloria Velazquez is great but I'd rather she had a few more years before giving her this much responsibility. Also, we'd be bumping her over the heads of a couple of other chiefs with more seniority. The crew likes her but she might have trouble pulling the chiefs along."

"Wainwright strikes me as pretty solid," the captain said. "You work well with him?"

"Yes, sir, I do. I asked him to wait out in the passageway, just in case you wanted to talk with him."

The captain smiled, and she felt herself color slightly.

"I didn't mean to overstep, sir. I can have Velazquez here in five minutes."

"You aren't overstepping, XO. It's your job to anticipate. No, I was just wondering if Wainwright gave Duransky that new shiner."

Mikko hadn't realized the captain noticed the bruise, but that was stupid of her. He noticed a lot.

"Maybe punching Duransky doesn't show the sort of self-control you want in a Boats, sir."

"Maybe not, but I think what we need right now is a chief bosun's mate who is *ferociously* protective of this crew. Did anyone see it?"

Mikko shook her head.

"Okay then, Chief Wainwright's our pick. We'll talk to him and, unless he steps on his dick in here, he's our new Boats."

"Thank you for the confidence, sir. I appreciate it very much. I know I can't fill the shoes of your wartime XO, Lieutenant Goldjune, but I—"

The captain's laughter cut her off and she felt her face flush with humiliation. He saw her look and shook his head.

"I'm not laughing at you, XO. I swear to God I'm not." He sat back and looked at her, frowning in thought. He seemed to make up his mind about something.

"XO, I think we need to clear the air. We'll meet in my cabin once we've talked to Wainwright."

"Very well, sir," Mikko said with a sinking feeling. The last time he "cleared the air" was when he told her what a failure she had been as XO. And he had been right. What new revelation was coming?

When she got to the captain's cabin the hatch opened for her and she entered.

"You drink bourbon?" he said without preamble.

"On occasion, sir."

"Not my drink of choice," he said, "but it's sort of a tradition I picked up from a former captain."

Bitka poured two fingers of bourbon in a tumbler and handed it to her, poured another for himself, and then gestured to his small lounge area. She took an armchair and he settled on the leather couch, setting the bottle on the coffee table. He lifted his glass.

"USS *Cam Ranh Bay*," he toasted, "and all who sail in her."

She clinked his glass and then sipped. The bourbon was pretty good.

"XO, I know I caught you flatfooted with my critique of your leadership style a couple weeks ago. I apologize, not for that, but for not telling you how I feel about your performance since then. I guess I got caught up in all the things going wrong and ignored the things going right. You are doing an outstanding job under difficult and terrifying circumstances, and in a situation no one has ever had to face before. When I laughed back there in my office, it was because you seem to think you'll never be as good as my last XO. Jesus Christ, set your sights higher than matching *Larry Goldjune!* You're worth ten of him."

Mikko felt her face color even more, and hated knowing it was obvious, even if now for a different reason. She found it hard to believe he rated her higher than Larry Goldjune, one of the most promising young officers in the Navy. Everyone knew he was on the fast track for admiral and he'd been Captain Bitka's right hand through the worst part of the war. Why would the captain say something like that?

"I want you to understand something else, too," the captain said. "I picked Wainwright for our new Boats because he's *your* pick. I trust your judgment, but it's more than that. I've got you to back me up, but if something happens to me, you'll be in charge. Ka'Deem Brook is senior department head so he'll step into the XO slot, but we both know his weaknesses. He may rise to the situation, but you can't count on that. You'll need a senior chief you can rely on."

"Something happen to *you*, sir?" She realized that after all the captain had already lived through, the thought that *she* might survive and he not had never even occurred to her.

"You never know, XO," he said. "Take it from me, command can come to you when you least expect it and through some genuinely screwy ways. You just never know."

He leaned back and looked at her thoughtfully.

"I have this feeling you have some . . . interesting notions about the war and the people who fought it, including me and, apparently, that useless sack of noise Larry Goldjune. What did you call him? My wartime XO?"

"Yes, sir," she said and again felt her neck and ears flush with embarrassment. The captain grinned.

"It makes you uncomfortable to hear me talk about *heroes* that way, doesn't it? I don't mean it to, but you should know that the reason I'm commanding the *Bay* is I filed probably the most negative fitness report in the recent history of the United States Navy, filed it on my wartime XO Larry Goldjune, and then I refused to walk it back when I got leaned on by admirals all the way up to his Uncle Cedric, the chief of naval operations. It's the sort of fitness report that would end any career, but I have the feeling Larry's will survive."

He took a swallow of bourbon and grimaced. Mikko felt as if a door was opening and she was allowed into a private room where public figures removed their disguises and appeared as they actually were. But it also meant the Navy she had dedicated her life to might not actually be what she had been taught it was, believed it was, and wanted it to be. If anyone else had said these things she would have put them down as some disgruntled failure making excuses for his own lack of recognition and progress, but this was Sam Bitka.

"Admiral Goldjune talked to you directly, sir? About Lieutenant Goldjune's fitness report?" Mikko had never heard of any pressure being put on an officer to alter a fitness report. It violated everything she had ever been taught about the prerogatives of a commanding officer.

"No, he had Vice Admiral Stevens do the dirty work," the captain said. "It came from him, though. Stevens told me so, for one thing, and you could tell it was true from how scared he was."

"You don't think much of Vice Admiral Stevens, do you, sir? You don't think much of Admiral Goldjune either."

Bitka shook his head.

"Of course, I've never met Admiral Goldjune," Mikko said. "I've heard the stories—we all have—that you disapprove of some of his wartime decisions on ethical grounds. I can't disagree with that, sir. But from what I've read he is a first-rate strategic thinker."

"Strategic thinker my ass!" The captain laughed without humor and then took another sip of bourbon. "I could run circles around him and I'm just some half-baked reservist. I'll tell you the bill of goods we've been sold, XO, and I mean *all* of us, the whole damned society we live in. It's that if someone is heartless and cynical, that must mean they're smart. The colder they are, the crueler, the greedier, the more ambitious and dishonest, well, the smarter they must be, right?

"You don't lose your soul all at once. It starts when a superior tells you their stupid idea and you say, 'Yes, sir,' instead of, 'Are you *loco*?' You say it because it won't do any good to question their sanity, will it? It won't change anything. It will just make trouble, and for what? Nothing. So you say, 'Yes, sir,' and you start discarding your soul in those little, harmless fawning lies told to incompetents and mental defectives, and you keep going up the ladder, and one day you're Vice Admiral Stevens sitting in an office on K'tok wondering how you got there."

Mikko sat motionless listening, frightened, unwilling to say anything. She certainly was not about to say, "Yes, sir."

Bitka had delivered this last speech almost to himself but now he turned and looked her in the eyes. He poured another two fingers of bourbon in his glass and took a sip.

"I know you want to know about the war, XO, so I'm going to tell you about it. You think it was against the uBakai? Hell, they didn't want a fight. They'd just had a civil war. They were broken, licking their wounds. So the great strategic thinker behind our Outworld Coalition, Admiral Cedric Goldjune, decided that was the time to lean on the uBakai at K'tok. What could possibly go wrong with that, huh?

"Well, he didn't count on a bunch of anti-human Varoki

fanatics who wanted to rid the *Cottohazz* of the scourge of...well, of us, XO, of you and me and everyone we've ever known. They couldn't do it by themselves, though, being just a cabal of crackpots, although pretty highly placed crackpots. All they could do was get the war started. To go all the way, though, they needed all the Varoki to sign on, and for the rest of the *Cottohazz* to at least look the other way. To accomplish that they needed to sucker us into an attack on Hazzakatu, the Varoki homeworld, to 'pay back' the uBakai. That's what it would take to turn all the Varoki against us; cross that one line *nobody* had ever crossed, an attack against the surface of the homeworld of one of the six sentient species. And your brilliant strategic thinker, Cedric Goldjune, walked right into it. He fell for it like a rube at his first carnival."

"But there wasn't an attack on Hazzakatu," Mikko said.

"That's right, there wasn't. There wasn't because a group of officers disobeyed orders, deceived their chain of command, violated the Articles of War, broke their sacred oaths, and committed what amounted to treason so stark and heinous it would have had them dancing at the end of a rope if anyone had figured it out."

He shrugged. "Doesn't matter. Most of them ended up dead anyway. Now people call them heroes, and they *were*, but just not for the reasons everyone thinks."

Mikko had never meant to, but she hadn't been able to avoid occasionally thinking that someday Sam Bitka might open his heart and unburden himself to her—not as a lover, necessarily, but as a friend. On those occasions when she had allowed herself to think about that possibility, she had never imagined it like this. She didn't want to believe this, but she did. She *had* to believe it coming from Sam Bitka, even though it changed what she thought she had known about him and challenged everything she believed about her service. She also understood that Bitka could not know any of this unless he had been part of it. *Most* of them ended up dead, he had said. Not all.

She thought through the names of the heroic, famous dead of that war, the people whose actions were now held up as exemplars of duty, bravery, and sacrifice, and she wondered how many of them had been part of Bitka's treason. Were they *still* exemplars of duty, bravery, and sacrifice? Bitka clearly thought so. She had no way to judge.

"Why are you telling me all this?" she said, and it came out sounding angrier than she had meant it to, but not, she was surprised to realize, angrier than she felt. "Why are you putting all this on me?"

"Because you're a good officer, Running-Deer, but before you can be a great officer you've got to stop glorifying all these people above you. You think they're smarter than you, braver than you, *better* than you. They aren't. *I'm* not. Trust yourself, not these phony military geniuses and made-up heroes. You know the only difference between you and most of the people above you in the chain of command? They're older, and let me tell you, wisdom does not invariably come with age.

"Navies need heroes, I guess. Wars absolutely need heroes. How else would you get the next guy to sign on? How else do you get people excited about the next war? But *you* don't need them, Running-Deer. Sure, some officers are pretty good at what they do, but none of them are perfect. Respect them, but don't worship them. Pay attention to what everyone else is doing, take every good idea they have and use it yourself, but learn from their mistakes, too. If you think they walk on water, you'll miss the mistakes."

He drained his glass.

"Long speeches make me thirsty," he said.

Did he really see that much potential in her? Or was this just a pep talk to keep her morale up? Did he think her morale needed keeping up? Had she done something to—

No. No more second-guessing herself, not if she could help it. She owed him that much. She owed him the effort to be the officer he thought she could be. Not because he was a hero, not because he was a tactical genius, but because he was her captain.

CHAPTER TEN

Two days later, aboard USS *Cam Ranh Bay*
26 March 2134 (*thirty-eight days after Incident Seventeen, at Destination*)

They'd made the jump to Destination the previous day, come out safely above the plane of the ecliptic, and begun transmitting at once, as well as recording every bit of incoming radio they could capture. They had extended the large sensor array, the one the *Bay* had to help carry out its alternative mission of deep survey vessel. That was imaging everything in the star system on a broad spectrum, from X-ray down to infrared.

Sam had decided, and most of his advisory committee concurred, that the best course was to transmit as soon as they jumped in. The inhabitants of the system were bound to detect their arrival. A flood of broadcasts would do more to defuse suspicion and potential alarm than would an ominous silence. At least that was the theory.

Sam had given Brook and his Ops department twenty-four uninterrupted hours to collect data and analyze it, and he'd given strict orders for everyone to leave them alone, had even forbidden Ops to share any data with anyone, including Sam himself, to make sure they weren't interrupted. That hadn't been easy; this was one loop Sam wanted to stay in, but he'd kept his curiosity in check for one long day. The only piece of relevant information he had was from engineering, that as soon as they arrived in the system, their jump drive had gone cold and would no longer respond to any commands.

As he made his way to the lift that would take him to the main hull, knots of passengers and crew stopped talking as he passed and their eyes followed him. They had some hope, at long last. They had been in the system for a whole day, and so far, no one had made any hostile or aggressive move toward them. He supposed that was a good sign, but it felt odd. There should have been more reaction to their arrival, some alarm or at least some excitement, shouldn't there?

"This is fascinating, sir!" Lieutenant Brook, the Ops boss, all but gushed five minutes later when Sam entered the auxiliary bridge. Sam took his excitement as encouraging—at least he didn't look terrified or depressed.

"I wanted the briefing here," Brook explained, "instead of the briefing room because we've got a better holosuite, and we can use the main display for the big-picture flat-vid stuff."

Sam saw everyone else from the advisory group already present. Well, who wouldn't be anxious for the first look at a new civilization? He strapped into the command chair between Bohannon and Alexander, already in the COMM and TAC One chairs. Brook and Running-Deer were at the Ops stations, and the civilians made their way to other workstations.

"Okay, Ops, show me what you've got."

"Well, we have to start with this—imagery of the Desties."

A stir went through the room. *Desties* is what they had begun calling the until-now hypothetical inhabitants of Destination. Brook smiled like a magician about to unveil his greatest trick. He touched his control panel and they were looking at a flat vid of an alien talking to them—or to the camera anyway.

Long narrow face, broad mouth under a prominent snout, eyes set very wide, longish ears, thin hair on the top and bits of the face but mostly bare brownish-grey skin.

"Looks like a goat," Lieutenant Ma said, "not a *robot*."

The remark was clearly meant for the musician Choice but Sam saw no reaction from her.

"Almost certainly herbivorous," Dr. Däng added, leaning forward in her workstation. "Note the dentition. Also, the eyes placed on the side of the skull instead of the front—excellent field of vision but poor depth perception—better suited to prey than hunter. None of the six species of the *Cottohazz* evolved from herbivores, all from carnivores or omnivores, but in all cases hunters. I wonder how these creatures' ancestors got enough concentrated protein for dramatic brain growth."

"Here's what they sound like," Brook said and added audio. The language was gibberish for now, but the voice sounded soft, not unpleasant at all. The language had a lot of sibilant sounds and Sam noticed the alien's jaw seemed to have less range of motion than did human jaws but its lips were longer, fleshier, more mobile, and with many more precise formations. Its lips rippled across its teeth like water over stones as it spoke.

"Who is it talking to?" Sam asked. "Do we know? Or is this to us?"

"We believe it's traffic control directions to a spacecraft, but we're not certain. It's a broadcast radio transmission, and it was sent probably before they were aware of us. It originates from Destie-Four, which appears to be the center of population and space traffic in the star system, sir."

"They've made no reaction to our appearance?"

"Some. Per your orders, we've been broadcast transmitting from the time we emerged from jump space, letting them know we're here and not trying to sneak up on them. We've gotten some tight-beam transmissions from Destie-Four in reply, although we haven't been able to decipher them yet."

"But no change in spacecraft routes? No ships vectored toward us? No spike in system-wide radio traffic?"

Brook shifted uncomfortably and then shook his head.

"No, sir. That's a little weird, isn't it?"

"Not if they were expecting us," Running-Deer said.

"Well, at least no threatening moves," Alexander added.

Sam turned back to the view screen. The alien speaker was in some sort of control room. Other similar aliens sat at other control stations behind it and occasionally Sam saw one walking. They were upright bipeds, short and squat, their gait shuffling but fast.

"What's gravity like on Destie-Four?" Sam asked.

"About one point four Earth gravities, sir. We'll get a

workout just moving around down there unless we wear SA frames. Those control systems you see in the background of the video feed appear to be highly bio-interactive. There's a lot of prolonged touch, slight motion, maybe pressure changes, and probably some tactile feedback."

It was actually hard to tell where the Desties ended and the workstations began. The Desties wore sleeveless tunics and their arms fit into flexible, irregularly pulsing sleeves which looked moist and alive, and sported very organic-looking webbing around their connection points to the control consoles. The surfaces of the consoles were also irregular and highly flexible, and they continually rippled and changed shape, possibly to reconfigure for different functions. Occasionally whitish fluid bubbled and ran down sleeves and across the control surfaces, leaving them looking slimy.

"That looks really gross," Homer Alexander the TAC boss said.

"Their hands seem awkward," Dr. Däng said. "Three fingers and an opposed thumb, but very thick and apparently with less range of motion than ours. If those controls are biosensitive, they may also be genetic-specific, whatever means they have of holding genetic information. Any plans you may have had of pirating a ship and learning to fly it home just became problematic, Captain Bitka."

"Never fancied myself in an eye patch, anyway," Sam said, and most of the humans in the room laughed. "Go on, Mister Brook."

"Well, their control panels have very sophisticated

holodisplays. Better than ours, it looks like. Some of those things on the control panels, I can't tell if they're real or holograms, but if you watch for a while sometimes some of those manipulating tendrils on the sides of the control arms go right through them."

"Hope it's a hologram," Lieutenant Ma the engineer said. "If they can move a finger through a solid object . . ."

"Pretty sure it's a hologram, Mister Ma," Brook said with a touch of condescension. There must still be some friction there. Sam would have to keep an eye on that.

They watched for a while in silence, other than the continuing monologue from the alien. It was hard to look away from this view of an entirely new intelligent species, but Sam knew there had to be more than this one recording.

"What else do you have, Ops?"

Brook turned off the recording and activated the main holo-display to show a large three-dimensional schematic map of the star system.

"Well, we've got a K2 yellow-white star with at least *six* inhabited worlds: four rocks in the liquid water zone and two inhabited moons of the largest gas giant."

"Inhabited moons out there?" Lieutenant Alexander said. "Doesn't it get pretty cold?"

"By the gas giants? Yes. We don't know if those are outposts or self-sufficient habitats, but there is definitely signal and spacecraft traffic to and from them."

Brook began describing the volume of spacecraft traffic—much higher than in most star systems in the *Cottohazz*—identified high- and low-density routes, and while Sam listened with part of his brain, another part marveled at the latticework of glowing orange threads on the hologram hovering before them, each thread representing one ship and its projected course track. There were hundreds of them, maybe over a thousand. The intricacy of the astrogation and the volume of the traffic suggested millions—no, *billions*—of minds at work. He again felt fear, but different than earlier. Before he'd feared the unknown; now he feared what he could see in front of them.

I hope they're friendly, he thought. If they weren't friendly then Sam and his crew and passengers were probably as good as dead—if they were lucky.

"You say you are sure most of the spacecraft are robotic?" the musician Choice asked. Sam remembered her theory. Would intelligent machines be easier to deal with? They might be harder to persuade but less likely to be pissed off.

"Yes," Lieutenant Brook answered. "It doesn't pay to put people on ships like that. They are mostly high-tonnage hulls on very slow trajectories, using the system's gravitational conveyor."

"Using the what?" Choice asked.

"Sorry," he said and smiled at the singer. "Astrogator talk. Bear in mind, this is all movement in a system, not between stars, so there's no jumping going on that we've detected. Anyway, for moving between worlds in a system, once you're out of planetary gravity wells you can get just about anywhere almost for free if you're not in a hurry. Give your ship a little shove and all the different moving gravity fields in the system will do the rest, provided you've got a good computer to figure out all the vectors.

We call it the gravitational conveyor. It's like a thirty-rail billiards shot on a frictionless table."

"More like three hundred rails," Running-Deer said.

Brook nodded. "I didn't want anyone to think I was exaggerating, but XO is right. These people are great at number crunching."

Sam felt his scalp tingle with a sudden realization and he sat forward.

"How do you know that, Mister Brook?"

"The number crunching? Well . . . we back-engineered the courses, sir. Ran them through our astrogation models and they all checked out. Beautiful math, sir."

"You reverse-engineered *every* course on this plot through *our* astrogation suite?"

"Yes, sir, every single one. Is . . . is something wrong?"

Sam saw Running-Deer rotate her workstation and look at him, her eyebrows elevated in the surprise of her own sudden understanding. She'd figured it out, too. He met her eyes and nodded in affirmation, and then settled back in the command chair. For the first time in over a month he felt himself relax just a little.

Brook looked from him to Running-Deer and shook his head.

"I'm sorry, sir. Did I miss something?"

"Yes you did, but it's perfectly understandable, Mister Brook. You've finally got this rich flood of data. You've done an outstanding job of organizing and processing it in hardly any time at all. Naturally you're focused on what's different or novel. You missed the significance of some things which aren't different. Two things to start with.

"First, as advanced as they may be, they haven't figured a way around Newton's laws of motion. No magic inertialess drives down there, just thrust and gravity, same as us."

"Oh. Yes, sir, that's right," Brook said. "Inertialess drive? I guess I never thought of something like that. What was the second thing, sir?"

"Well, they don't have any courses too complicated for our astrogation computers to unwrap."

"Oh!" the musician and cybernetics expert Choice said. "Well, then that means . . ." And her voice trailed off.

"Right," Sam finished for her. "Their computing ability is not significantly better than ours. Or if it is, they aren't using it, and why wouldn't they? It doesn't help your theory of machine intelligence, does it?" he added with a smile.

She hesitated and then shook her head.

"No, it doesn't."

No defensiveness, no prevarication, just a straight, honest answer. That was refreshing.

"A question, if I may, Captain?" the New Zealand anthropologist Johnstone ventured.

"Of course," Sam said. Johnstone spoke so seldom in these meetings Sam was beginning to wonder if he had made a mistake tagging him.

"Have we made any progress on translating the language?"

Sam looked at Lieutenant Bohannon.

"What's the story, Lieutenant? Any progress?"

"Yes and no, sir," she said. "As Mister Brook said, we have done no actual decoding. We don't have a key, a way into the language. What we do have is a growing body of words, phrases, and sentences. We're getting a handle on grammar, what may be case and declension differences. But until we know the *meanings* of some of those words, that's all we can do. But the more of this structural work we do now, the quicker we'll be able to give you an auto-trans program once we get actual vocabulary."

She looked to her left where the Buran linguist, with child in arms, was strapped into a communication workstation.

"Would you agree with that, Councilor Abanna Zhaquaan?"

"Yes, Lieutenant Deandra Bohannon," it answered in its deep, strangely flat voice, "We are in the same position in which industrious but unimaginative philosophers find themselves: wealthy with respect to rules and structure but destitute of meaning."

"Huh," Sam said, surprised at the idea there were Buran philosophers, but really, why not?

"So how do we find that meaning, Councilor Abanna Zhaquaan?" he asked. "How do we get a key to their vocabulary?"

"There is only one reliable way," the Buran said. "We find common words and proceed from there."

"That makes sense," Sam said. "I guess even modern linguists couldn't decode some of those old Earth languages until they had a key, some starting point. I take it we're working on that?"

"Yes, sir," Bohannon answered. "We're sending pictures of objects with English language text labels, along with audio clips saying the English word. We're starting to get some return messages with similar attachments but we're not certain they understand what we're looking for. But if these return messages are what we need, we could have a working version of their language in a few days."

Sam saw the two Varoki consult for a moment and then Haykuz, the assistant, spoke.

"The Envoy e-Lisyss wishes to know why the aliens are being instructed in English instead of aGavoosh, which is the official language of the *Cottohazz* administration."

"Actually, it's the first language of the *Cottohazz*," the Nigerian journalist Boniface pointed out, "but legally all six common languages of governance are official, and English is one of those."

"Nevertheless, the envoy expresses his objection."

"Noted," Sam said, and he saw Running-Deer trying to suppress a smile. He doubted the Varoki envoys understood what "Noted" really meant in Navy-speak.

"Why did we emerge so far from the main planet?" Dr. Däng asked. "It will take us a long time to reach orbit and there are considerable communication delays."

"About ten minutes each way on the comms," Sam said, "and that will decrease as we get closer. We've got a residual velocity of thirty-five kilometers per second, so we're looking at ten days to Destie-Four, the main inhabited world. Hopefully that will give us time to crack the language and get acquainted. It also gives them time to get used to the idea of us. By the time we're likely to be within range of any of their defensive systems I hope they're okay with the idea of visitors. If we appeared a lot closer, they might shoot first and then think about asking questions later."

"Come now, Captain Bitka," Dr. Däng said. "We've made no threatening moves. This is clearly a highly advanced civilization. I doubt they would make the sort of errors in judgment you seem willing to attribute to them."

"Well, Dr. Däng, I hope you're right but we can't count on it. Besides, it occurs to me we're a pretty advanced civilization too, and we do stupid shit all the time. Also, our crew is wound pretty tight. Let's give them some time to get used to all this. I don't want us to do anything crazy, especially before we know enough Destie to explain it was a mistake."

"I still think it was an unnecessary waste of time," she said.

Sam smiled.

"Also noted. Lieutenant Bohannon, get me a language and somebody down there to talk to."

PART II:
The Gates of Hell

Cassandra
On board USS *Puebla*, in the K'tok System
7 August 2134 *(five and a half months after*
***Incident Seventeen, four months after USS* Cam**
Ranh Bay *arrived at Destination)*

One of the unique advantages to having been stationed for several months in orbit above K'tok, the only extra-solar world biologically compatible with humans, was that USS *Puebla's* food lockers had been stocked with edible but exotic fruits, vegetables, and meats from the world below. "Crab cakes" were a regular entree on *Puebla's* menu, covering a wide variety of flavors but sharing that name since most of the animals in the area around the Needle downstation were crustaceans of one sort or another—or at least the K'tok-evolved analog.

Another popular local delicacy was meteor fruit, so-called because its surface was lumpy and rock-gray in color. The flesh was crisp, moist, and sweet, however, reminiscent of some of the very tart varieties of apples.

Lieutenant Rosemary Hennessey, *Puebla's* engineering officer, was eating a large meteor fruit as Commander Cassandra Atwater-Jones arrived in the forward engine room. Hennessey was tall, big-boned, broad in the shoulders and hips, blonde, and ruddy-faced, at the moment more so than Cassandra remembered.

"Okay, Ma'am," the engineer said, her mouth still partly full, "here you go. Six remote-piloted workbots, fabricated to the specifications you provided." She patted the exterior of the packing cases and opened one lid. The smooth, featureless, composite-alloy flattened cube, about fifty centimeters across, nestled in the foam cavity inside the container. Cassandra ran her hand along the surface.

"Thank you, Leftenant Hennessey. I appreciate your attention to this. Quite a lot depends on their functioning correctly. Quite a lot indeed."

"As you say, Ma'am." Hennessey secured the lid. The two of them floated in the forward engineering room of the destroyer, and now Hennessey turned and looked at Cassandra with as close to a completely blank look as she could ever remember receiving. The engineer took another loud bite of fruit.

"I have to ask," Cassandra said, "aren't you the least bit curious about what these remotes are for?"

"No, Ma'am, and I don't want you to tell me. Right now, I have plausible deniability and I'd just as soon keep it that way. I've been a Navy engineer for eleven years, and I spent most of that time in starships. There isn't an engineer in the service who doesn't want to crack open a jump core and look inside."

Hennessey paused for another bite.

"But they sting, don't they?" she went on, her words distorted by a mouth full of fruit. "Hell of a defense mechanism: anaerobic microscopic solvent, eat through about anything *except* solid composite alloy— coincidentally the same material in the exterior casings of these workbots you had us fabricate.

"Of course, if that's what you had in mind you'd have to seal the bots into the workspace, since the solvent will eat through any sort of flexible airlock seal. I suppose the thing to do would be to take a solid composite hood—like that one over there you had us put together—and weld it solid over the access door, with the bots inside. Then use the bots to open the access door.

"But once they're sealed in, how do you refuel them? Well, give them batteries and a Tesla-effect proximity recharger. Nice touch. All they have to do is get close to that recharger plate you had us set into the containment hood surface and they can juice right up.

"But how do they get around in zero gee without running out of reaction mass? You can't refill that by proximity. Very cool solution: electromagnets with reversible polarity. Find anything magnetic in there and play push-you-pull-me to get around. And those gripper arms: all hard composite gears, no flexiparts. Very retro.

"Of course, that's all just speculation, you understand." She took another bite with a wet-sounding *crunch*.

"I quite understand," Cassandra said. "I have to say— and without in any way commenting on the validity of your speculation—that for an experienced engineer you do not show a great deal of enthusiasm at the prospect."

Still chewing the fruit, Hennessey looked at her for a

moment, possibly deciding what to say next. Cassandra had the feeling that none of the possible responses she was considering would be friendly, and she wondered why. Hennessey swallowed and shook her head before answering.

"Commander, since the ceasefire we've gotten about a dozen replacement officers and ratings, which makes a dent in the casualties we suffered but not a very big one. Aside from those replacements, every woman and man on this boat would be dead today if it weren't for Captain Bitka, and most of them have sense enough to know it. When the captain went missing, a lot of us took it hard, but missing doesn't mean dead. It just means missing, and he's pretty good at getting out of tight spots. But then you come along with word you've found the wreckage of his ship, and we need to hurry up so you can paw through it, maybe get a look at something *important*.

"The thing is, if there's wreckage then he's not missing; he's dead. And no, none of us have a great deal of enthusiasm for that prospect, Commander. What I can't figure out is how you, of all people, can. You must be quite a piece of work."

Her eyes never leaving Cassandra's, Hennessey took another deliberate, crunching bite out of her meteor fruit.

Cassandra felt the urge to tell Hennessey the truth, but she did not. She wasn't sure how much of her urge came from a laudable desire to alleviate Hennessey's possibly misplaced grief, and how much from a rather pathetic hunger for vindication. It didn't matter. Neither justified telling Hennessey anything, because the engineer was right in one respect: she *did* need plausible deniability, but not due to the scenario she suspected. That wasn't the jump drive from Bitka's ship out there. It was from the uBakai cruiser KBk Four-Two-Nine, and Captain Larry Goldjune had just assured her they would dock with the wreckage within three hours.

"Ms. Hennessey, this is brilliant work on these 'bots. I admire not only the dispatch with which you completed the project but also the attention to workmanship. I am deeply appreciative, and I will include that appreciation in a formal communication to your commanding officer.

"And one more thing, *Leftenant*: the next time you speak to me, it had better not be through a mouthful of sodding fruit."

Eleven sleepless hours later Cassandra clicked down her helmet visor and opened the link to the holoconference. Lieutenant Moe Rice of the US Navy appeared to her right and *Korvetenkapitän* Georg Heidegger of the *Deutsche Sternmarine* to her left, both of them on board USS *Puebla* with her. She had left the balance of the working group on K'tok to schedule the re-interviews of witnesses and negotiate their duty and travel arrangements. That should keep them busy, she thought. She wanted Moe Rice with her, for assistance, and Heidegger where she could keep her eye on him. She regretted not being able to bring Takaar Nuvaash as well, but she could summon up no argument in favor of his coming which would justify so enormous a breach of security.

In a moment, the physicist, Dr. Wu, appeared across the table from them, his image beamed from K'tok along with a two-minute turnaround delay. Not for the first time

Cassandra wondered if Rear Admiral Jacob Goldjune, young Larry's father, had lost his mind. The physicist was *Chinese*. Keeping this illegal examination of a Varoki jump core secret would be hard enough working with their own scientists, but China was not even a member of the Outworld Coalition. She understood they were lucky there was *any* human physicist who happened to be in the K'tok system at that time, but still ... *Chinese?*

He didn't look particularly Chinese, she thought, aside from the obvious ethnic facial characteristics. He needed a haircut and a shave, he wore a flowered shirt of baggy cut, and he held a large unlit cigar in his hand. She knew he was in his late forties. He looked tired but excited.

She'd read through his dossier, as much as had been sent to her. If she'd been back at K'tok, with direct access to fleet intelligence records, she'd have known more. She could request the full dossier, but not without alerting a lot of communication personnel to Dr. Wu's importance, and so she had to make do with this and blind trust in Admiral Goldjune's good sense—one of the disadvantages of being "in the field."

Walter Wu Tao, born May 19, 2085, Shenzhen, Guangdong Province, Republic of China. 2106 Graduated University of Shenzhen. 2109 awarded doctorate in high energy physics from the Xi Jinping Institute in Beijing. 2109 to 2113, research fellow at CERN in Geneva, West European Union. 2115 to 2121, adjunct instructor in physics, Massachusetts Institute of Technology, United States of North America. Then, for the last thirteen years ... a ship's purser? On a passenger liner? Well, that explained why he was out here.

"Dr, Wu, I am Commander Atwater-Jones, and these are my subordinates *Korvetenkapitän* Heidegger and *Leftenant* Rice. We are pleased you were able to assist us in this examination."

"I must renew my objection to this entire enquiry," Heidegger said. "This jump drive is the property of a powerful Varoki trading house—Simki-Traak Transtellar—and we have no business examining it. I was led to believe the object was part of the missing transport."

"As was I," Cassandra answered calmly, "but once we discovered our error, and had already docked with the object, Rear Admiral Goldjune directed us to examine it for whatever insight it may offer our investigation. You know that as well as I do, *Korvetenkapitän* Heidegger, but your objection is noted."

"If word of this gets out—"

"How would it, Herr Heidegger? Only the four of us here and Rear Admiral Goldjune know the particulars. *I* certainly don't intend to tell anyone, nor should you unless you fancy spending the next twenty years in prison. Now Dr. Wu, I understand you have not had much time, but can you tell us anything about the object based on our transmissions so far?"

"*Can* I?" he said after the communication lag, and then he laughed. "I already told Admiral Goldjune he needs to come up with a good microbiologist, and fast. I hate to say it but that's probably going to do you more good than a particle-smasher like me looking at this. You've seen the visuals on the drive core yourself, right?"

"Yes," she answered, "I've been watching the vid feed from the start. I don't know what I expected the jump core to look like, but this isn't it. Just layer after layer of very thin metallic plates, which look to be either gold or gold-plated, and some sort of glutinous lubricating medium. Aside from interface systems connecting it to the jump actuators in the control suite, that seems to be all there is."

During the communication lag she wondered how many years it had been since Wu had even visited China. He didn't sound Chinese. Any scientist would be fluent in English, of course, but he spoke it almost without an accent.

"Yeah," Wu said after the delay. "*Seems* is right. Whoever built that thing thinks a lot differently than we do. We look and see the machine as all those wafer-thin plates, with some sort of goo on them. Here's a good one for you: the goo *is* the machine. It's a colony of some sort of microbial lifeform, which apparently lives on waste heat or whatever electromagnetic energy is available. It was dormant when we started looking but as soon as we gave it some light it started waking up and once it got some electricity, *hot damn!* Those single-cell microbes live between the circuit boards and serve as selective biosuperconductors, opening and closing circuits between the panels.

"Those low-power tests I ran? A pre-jump sequence? As soon as the sequence was initiated, there was a spike in colony activity and the organisms formed new circuitry patterns of bewildering complexity—bewildering at least to me. I had to go back to some knot theory math I hadn't worked with for about a decade to make heads or tails out of all those three-dimensional circuitry flow patterns.

Man, I really *hate* knot theory: crossings, braids, links, ambient isotopy, fourth-dimensional deknotting ... damn, give me a break!"

He put the unlit cigar in his mouth and chewed thoughtfully on it.

"String theory?" Moe asked.

Wu shook his head after the lag. "Knot theory, not string theory."

"Knotted string theory?"

Wu laughed after the next lag. "This could turn into a pretty good comedy routine, if you're into dumb physics jokes. And who isn't, right? Knot theory, just plain old knot theory. No strings involved."

"I sympathize with your frustration, Dr. Wu," Cassandra said, "but I am not sure I understand the significance of all that."

"Right," he said after the communication lag. "A knot is a mathematically described line segment which at some point doubles back across itself. The complexity of a knot is described, among other ways, by the number of times the line segment crosses itself. A very simple knot you would tie in a piece of string has three crossings: the first one when you fold it back across itself, the second when you double it back under, the third one when you push it through the loop. Got it?"

"I think so, yes."

"Well, in this three-dimensional circuitry flow pattern our e-nexus core identified knots with approximately five times ten to the seventh crossings."

"Wait," Heidegger said. "They constructed a coherent mathematical knot with over fifty *million* crossings?"

"Not *a* knot," Wu answered. "Several tens of thousands of knots, as near as I can tell. Even with that hotshot naval computing suite, it's a lot for one guy to handle. I'd like your admiral to find me a professional number cruncher as backup as well. But here's the kicker: it changes and forms a new set of circuits over one thousand times a second."

They sat silently trying to make sense of that, Wu again chewing on his cigar and smiling slightly. He apparently enjoyed watching the confusion on their faces, a confusion he had already worked through. Cassandra could not imagine what all those different unique patterns might be. And then she could.

"It's calculating, isn't it?" she said.

"That's where I'd put my money," Wu answered with a grin.

"Well," Moe Rice said, "it's got a lot of molecules to move during a jump, and it's pretty good at keeping them in the right place, judging from experience. Doesn't sound like too many calculations when you look at it that way."

"No," Dr. Wu agreed. "In fact, it is still inadequate to that task if it actually calculates separately for every molecule it moves in a jump. I bet it has some sort of pattern-recognition shortcut which manages to reduce the number of required calculations to a manageable level and mass apply them to an entire set of molecules."

Cassandra thought about that: over a thousand calculations a second, each involving tens of thousands of circuit knots, each with around fifty-million crossings. How many data points was that? Even assuming just one bit per crossing, it came out to . . . more than she could calculate in her head. And that was after the problem was reduced to a *manageable* level.

"The thing that's got me stumped," Wu went on, "is how it *moves* those molecules. I spent my early life chasing the dream that there was some way around the Varoki lock on theoretical physics. The *Cottohazz* intellectual property laws give them ownership of anything discovered based on knowledge they already own, but I guess every young buck physicist like me thinks there's a way to wiggle past that, to find a research path that is so generic the big Varoki trading houses can't claim ownership. But there isn't, and the big reason is they won't let us know how this damn drive works. Trade secret, they say. But if we don't know what principle they've discovered to make this thing work, we don't know where to look for something they haven't discovered already. You see?"

"Is that why you left physics to become a purser on a starship?" Cassandra said.

"Sure. If I couldn't figure out how the damned things worked, at least I could ride them. See the stars, you know? And you know what it got me? It got me right here, the first non-Varoki physicist in history to look inside a jump core and live to tell the story.

"Physicists have been dying to get a look inside a jump core as long as I've been alive—longer, even—just so we could see what the thing does. Now here I am, like I won the biggest physics lottery in history, I'm looking right at the goddamned thing while it's working, and I got *nothing!* Makes me want to come up there and give that son of a bitch a good hard kick."

He scowled and put the unlit cigar back in his mouth.

"So why do you need a microbiologist?" Rice asked.

Good question, Cassandra thought. Trust Rice to see past all the clutter.

"Well, I looked at the initial tests on the biological material the one sampler bot collected. We'd like to understand how that killer solvent works, right? The bot got some of the aerosol solvent and also scooped some material from the main colony organism. The chemical bath stripped out a couple thousand distinct proteins, which isn't all that many. The problem is they aren't identifiable as anything we've seen before."

"Obviously, they are not from our tree of life," Heidegger said. "The Varoki invented the jump drive. They must be proteins from their home world."

"Nope," Wu answered, "not even close. And not from any other ecosystem in the *Cottohazz*, either. You run all the amino acid code chains through the universal protein database and you get about two thousand 'no match found' results.

"Now what do you make of that?"

CHAPTER ELEVEN

Four months earlier, **aboard USS *Cam Ranh Bay***
7 April 2134 *(thirteen days after arrival at*
Destination, second day in orbit around Destie-Four,
fifty-eight days after Incident Seventeen)

As executive officer, Mikko did not have a spot in the normal watch rotation, but she filled in as necessary when one of the senior officers had a pressing job to attend to. The Red Watch was Homer Alexander's, but he was working with his missile-room crew, making sure they were up to speed on the modified Mark Five intercept missiles, and so she sat in as OOD—Officer of the Deck. She didn't mind. She liked sitting watch now and then. It gave her time to think.

Right now, she was being forced to rethink her notions concerning heroism. If there were any heroes who survived the uBakai War, Sam Bitka's name had to be on the list, but he wasn't what she had imagined, or fantasized. Part of that was due to the secrets he had shared over bourbon after Chief Duransky's hearing, but other differences were subtler.

For instance, whenever anyone asked him to share

159

lessons from the war he did so, but never in a way that suggested he had done anything remarkable. Mikko at first put that down to modesty, the sort of self-effacement she expected from "real heroes." Most of the other senior officers did as well. But over the last few weeks, as she and the captain worked together, she no longer believed that. He was trying to prepare them for what was coming, prepare them to face whatever lay ahead, and to face it alone, without him to rely on.

She had begun to think the captain had a premonition of his own death. She wondered if part of him did not secretly wish for it. When she came upon him alone, lost in thought, unaware that anyone was watching him, sometimes he seemed so terribly sad.

In that, he reminded her of J. C. Merderet, commander of the embarked Marine contingent—another hero who insisted all she had done was her job, and all she demanded of her Marines was that they do their jobs.

Mikko was beginning to understand, or at least believe, that heroism often simply meant doing your job when the world conspired to make doing so impossibly frightening, dangerous, and difficult. That was what she thought the captain was trying to prepare them for, and the implied horror of that approaching test had driven every bit of romantic infatuation from Mikko. She thought she was coming to love Sam Bitka, but not as a man, as a fellow human being.

"Councilor Abanna Zhaquaan is talking to the New People again," Bohannon said as she strapped into the Comm One chair beside her. "Or still, I guess. Ever since we cracked the Destie language . . . Christ, it never seems to get tired. Sometimes it just walks over to a couch, lies down with its creepy little kid, and sort of turns off, you know? Like switching off the light. A couple hours later it wakes up and starts again. The Desties must run shifts of talkers with it. I needed a break."

"Hey," the sensor tech in the Tac One seat to Mikko's right said. "I'm getting a surge in radio traffic from ground control on Destie-Four, but it's not to us."

Mikko touched her command workstation to bring up the passive sensors. There *was* a lot more comm traffic.

"Did this just start?"

"Yes, Ma'am. I'm showing acknowledgments from their orbital platforms now. Hey, see that spike? I think that's an outgoing tight beam to another in-system station."

Mikko saw the energy output from the surface and orbital platforms hold steady, then go up again as more stations came online.

"Wow!" the sensor tech said. "That's a jump departure signature. Somebody just launched either a starship or a jump courier."

They hadn't seen a ship enter or leave the Destination system since they arrived.

"You're sure that's a *jump drive* signature?" Mikko said. "Exactly like we use in the *Cottohazz*?"

"Yes, ma'am," the sensor tech answered, and then he realized the unlikeliness of two civilizations coming to exactly the same technical and engineering solution to star travel simply by coincidence. *"Holy shit!"*

Sam sat at the desk in his stateroom and watched the small hologram of Cassandra—the only one he had of her, an image of her shoulders and head, a five-second recording of her that showed her expression change from laughter to an inviting smile and then freeze for five more seconds before restarting. He liked this recording. It captured something essential about her personality that was at the root of his attraction to her, although he couldn't put into words what that was. He found himself studying it whenever he sensed something else, something about his situation or environment that he couldn't quite put his finger on. That unsettled sensation was exactly how he felt about the New People, the beings they used to call Desties before they could speak with them directly.

Four days ago, Bohannon and Councilor Abanna Zhaquaan had begun decoding nouns, based on exchanged pictures and labels in English, and Destie verbs followed, and then a cascade of vocabulary, still growing. Communication with real content had begun yesterday, questions and answers, but nothing like what Sam had expected.

As near as they could tell, the Desties, or *New People*, were courteous and helpful but not particularly curious about *Cam Ranh Bay* or its passengers and crew. It wasn't that they already knew anything about them—it was more as if a bunch of unknown aliens showing up in a strange starship was not that unusual an event.

Sam made sure Bohannon's team did not mention their problem with the jump drive. There was plenty of time to deal with that once they had a better understanding of the situation here. At the moment Sam couldn't say that any of it made much sense to him.

Suddenly the general quarters gong began sounding

and simultaneously his commlink vibrated: Running-Deer on the emergency command channel.

"What's happening, XO?"

Captain, you need to get up here pronto. *I think all hell's breaking loose.*

Mikko had filled the captain in by commlink while he was still on his way to the bridge. Once he took over she headed aft to her battle station in the auxiliary bridge, and all the while she kept wondering what the Buran had said to prompt this reaction.

After two tense hours, the captain called a meeting of the department heads and civilian advisors. Mikko saw nothing but worried faces when she entered the conference room and imagined they saw the same from her. She also noted that Major Merderet had joined them.

"You all know we have a new situation," the captain began. "I'll start by saying Lieutenant Bohannon and I are convinced this . . . problem is in no way the fault of Councilor Abanna Zhaquaan. The councilor was following my instructions to gather as much information as possible."

Captain Bitka was cut off by a torrent of angry aGavoosh from the Varoki trade envoy e-Lisyss. It went on for twenty or thirty seconds before ending with a loud and final-sounding click. His assistant, visibly coloring from anger or embarrassment, his large ears folded defensively back against his head, provided a translation.

"The Honorable e-Lisyss objects to what was clearly a diplomatic exchange disguised as linguistic research. He disavows any responsibility for the damage done. He wishes his official protest recorded in the ship's log. He demands to be placed in charge of all future negotiations."

"Noted," Captain Bitka said and then turned to the Buran linguist. "Councilor Abanna Zhaquaan, can you explain to the others what you told me?"

The Buran looked around the table with its blank black eyes and then spoke in its deep, flat voice. "At Captain Samuel Bitka's direction I took care not to mention our forced passage here. I said we had been summoned by a messenger missile, but did not say our star drive had been reprogrammed. I also made no mention of the recent war, or of organized violence of any kind in the *Cottohazz*.

"When the subject of our interstellar drive was broached they wished to know from whom we had obtained it. They did not seem to even consider that we might have developed it ourselves. And in fact we—that is to say Buran—did not. The Varoki did, which I told them. They were unfamiliar with the word Varoki, of course, and seemed to assume it was equivalent to a word in their language translated roughly as Guardian, or perhaps Overseer, or even Master. Were the Varoki our Guardians, they asked.

"I replied they were not, that all of our six species lived together as equals. When we shared pictorial images of Varoki with them, they became agitated and several more protracted exchanges established we had no Guardians, in the sense they understand the term, and were in fact innocent of the concept. This revelation led to them severing communication. Lieutenant Bohannon tells me the large volume of communication across the system immediately ensued."

It was hard to read emotions on the Buran—hard to tell if they even *had* emotions comparable to humans—but Mikko sensed something like anxiety, a concern the Buran had somehow contributed to the problem, or a fear the others here would think so.

"Thank you Councilor Abanna Zhaquaan," Captain Bitka said. "Now I'll add that twenty minutes ago we received an open communication giving us an orbital correction and orders to send a delegation down to the planet surface to meet with their Guardian, a being known as The Eye of P'Daan. I don't know whether that's a name or a title. Envoy e-Lisyss, it looks like you're going to get your wish. You will be the representative of the Cottohazz Executive Council with the landing party, and also of the Varoki species. Councilor Abanna Zhaquaan, I would like you to ask if one of your colleagues would volunteer to accompany the landing party as a representative of the Buran. I will not order a civilian to do so. Not you, by the way. I want you and Lieutenant Bohannon up here monitoring and recording everything said down there."

"I understand, Captain Samuel Bitka. I am certain several of our party will relish being the first of our species to meet the New People face to face. I will select one of them," the Buran linguist said.

"I'm going, too," Boniface, the Nigerian journalist said.

Mikko looked at him, his face shining in the overhead light, and she saw an excitement in his eyes she couldn't remember seeing before.

"I said I wouldn't order any civilians to accompany us," the captain said. "I'm considering ordering you not to. What function would you serve?"

"Observe. Report. That's what I do. You need a trained witness who is not a party to the negotiations. Also, I am fitted with an embedded biorecorder. If the communications with the landing party are disrupted, and assuming you can rescue me or recover my body, you will have a complete record of what happened. Besides, if you think I'm going to cover the biggest story in the history of the *Cottohazz* from a couple thousand kilometers up in orbit, you're... well, you're not as smart as I think you are."

Captain Bitka looked at him for a moment and then nodded.

"Okay, you're in. Major Merderet, I'd like two Marines along for security. Unarmed, I'm afraid, and definitely not in armor, so you might want to tag a couple with good unarmed combat skills."

"I've got pretty good close combat skills," she said.

"Your offer to volunteer is noted and will show in your record, but you're not going. Get me two Marines who anybody sane will think twice before they tangle with.

"Mister Brook, give your helm the go ahead to start bending orbit. They have a needle but it's on the other side of the planet from where they want us to set down, so we'll use a PSRV lander—that's a Planetary Surface Recovery Vehicle for benefit of the civilians. I figure half an hour to bend orbit and we'll make one orbital pass over the site to put eyes on it. I want everyone in the landing party suited up in the ready room in twenty minutes. Bosun's mates will fit you out with SA frames—Strength Augmentation exoskeletons—and they'll adjust them to your physiology. We'll need them to walk around down there if we're going to walk far in that high gravity, and for safety reasons the PSRV needs to set down half a klick from the meeting site. We might fry something important with our rocket blast if we land any closer."

He paused and looked around, maybe wondering if there was anything he missed.

"Okay, see you in the ready room in twenty minutes."

CHAPTER TWELVE

Moments later, **aboard USS *Cam Ranh Bay***
7 April 2134 *(thirteen days after arrival at*
Destination, second day in orbit around Destie-Four,
fifty-eight days after Incident Seventeen)

As everyone else filed out Mikko signaled to Captain Bitka to have a word in private. He waited until everyone else left and the door clicked shut, then sat at the table. Mikko saw a haunted look in Bitka's face, as if he saw death approaching, and once again she wondered if that was what he wanted. The thought angered her. She knew if she was going to change his mind, she had one chance and she couldn't afford to waste it. She took a breath.

"With respect, sir, you've got no business on the landing party."

"We can't risk offending this Guardian, XO, whoever or whatever it is. It asked for—"

"A *representative*," she said, cutting him off. "They didn't ask for the commander, sir. They asked you to send a representative to make an offer. Those were their words: make an offer. E-Lisyss is our diplomat, right? He's dying to talk to these guys. He should be our point man."

The captain shook his head.

"Can't trust him alone. He doesn't speak for the *Cottohazz* or for any if its member states, Neither do we or anyone else on this ship. Somebody's got to remind him of that."

"Not your job, sir," she insisted.

"I can't order someone down there with him unless I go along."

"What are you trying to prove, sir? That you're the bravest son of a bitch in the Navy? Don't you trust me?" she asked, knowing this was a low blow but also knowing she had to change his mind.

The captain jerked upright in his chair and his eyes opened wide in surprise. "Trust you? Of course I do."

"This is *my* job, sir. Let me do my job. You do yours. With respect. Sir."

Bitka looked away, far away, and then finally sighed in resignation.

"Shit. Okay, you're right. You're absolutely right. You command the landing party." He straightened and his voice became firm. "I want Chief Wainwright flying the PSRV and have him pick the boat to take; he knows which ones are reliable and which are hangar queens."

"Aye aye, sir."

"And send my compliments to Major Merderet. I want a full platoon of Mikes in combat armor and prepped in drop capsules. Tell her no, she is *not* to drop with them. If things get hot I want her up here coordinating."

"Understood, sir."

"And you're taking a gauss pistol along. Tell them it's a badge of authority if anyone asks."

"I'd rather not, sir. Would you have taken one?"

"No, but I trust you with it more than me. I haven't shot one in about ten years. You're qualified, right?"

"Yes, sir. Shot expert at the Academy and I've kept my hand in."

Bitka hesitated, as if rethinking his decision, and then shook his head.

"I'm going to have all the passengers secure themselves in their acceleration rigs, and then I'm going to spin down the habitat wheel, just in case we need to do some violent maneuvers on short notice. I have very mixed feelings about this, XO."

"Really, sir? Because ever since that alien probe hijacked us, my feelings have been unmixed and uniformly dark. For almost two months you've been telling us the truth: the only way out of this is forward. So let's go talk to these assholes and see what it's going to take to make them send us home."

Mikko hated reentry. She'd done it half a dozen times, because her training required it, but nobody but a fool or a Mike Marine willingly plunged into an atmosphere at a velocity of seven or eight kilometers a second and hoped the atmospheric drag slowed them down enough to keep from crashing into the surface. Oh, and didn't burn them up. She noticed it never seemed to work very well for actual meteors. The ride was bumpy, but Chief Wainwright was as good a PSRV pilot as any on the ship, and by the time he fired the vertical thrust system to make the final landing flare, she'd gotten her heart rate and respiration back to normal.

They already had a read on the atmosphere: oxygen/nitrogen in close enough to the same proportions as on Earth so they wouldn't need respirators. All of them carried auxiliary oxygen packs in case they got short of breath. Hopefully they wouldn't be down here long enough to need a recharge.

Chief Wainwright popped the hatch from his pilot station and a breeze brought the smell of the world into them: humid, sour, warm. It was a living world, and after months inside the sealed environment of a spacecraft, a living world always smelled of death, of decay, along with the smells of life. She supposed you couldn't have one without the other.

Mikko and the other five struggled into their SA frames in the limited space in the PSRV and then she and e-Lisyss strapped the small vox-box units around their throats and fitted the mouthpieces. All of the party had the newest version of Destie auto-trans loaded in their commlinks, so they would get a running translation of what was said, but they didn't know enough about Destie technology yet to know if their alien counterparts had a similar capability. Engineering had manufactured the vox-boxes to capture the spoken word (in English for her, aGavoosh for e-Lisyss), turn it into the best Destie they could manage, and project it from the integrated speakers.

They climbed down the side ramp into the bright sunlight under a clear blue sky. That was one reliable and comforting constant throughout the universe, thanks to atmospheric dispersion of visible spectrum light: if a world had a breathable atmosphere without much airborne dust, its sky was blue. It was mid-morning at this longitude on

Destie-Four. The temperature was like early summer in her native South Dakota, but the air felt damp and heavy. They didn't know much about the climates and seasons of this world yet. To be honest, she didn't care. The sooner they left this place behind, the better.

Of the party, e-Lisyss had the hardest time with the SA frame and so their progress across the yellow-green meadow was limited to his awkward trudging pace. She and the Marines were used to the frames and Boniface was as well. He'd gone through Marine equipment familiarization as a prerequisite for being embedded with a Mike unit. He'd probably worn powered armor down on K'tok during the fighting. Acolyte Onogoe Barvenu, the young Buran, had taken to the SA frame with a spirit of curiosity and adventure. Mikko wasn't sure why the Buran had chosen someone so young—if indeed it was young. Maybe it was just of slight stature. All she knew was other Buran adults were taller and bulkier.

She went over the explanation, mostly truthful, they were to offer the Guardian once the formalities were over. It was not their intention to disturb or alarm the New People with their arrival, but they had been brought to the system involuntarily, by a probe vehicle of unknown origin. They had also experienced a malfunction in their star drive upon arrival, one which they had so far been unable to repair. They would appreciate any assistance the New People could render. All they had to offer in return was an exchange of information and the gratitude of their people, the six intelligent species of the *Cottohazz*.

They approached the meeting place, a broad, flat rise topped by what looked like a polished stone circular platform about fifty meters across, rimmed on the far side with several tall, irregularly shaped, shining metallic . . . well, what were they? Statues? Monuments of some kind? Or possibly sensors or communication equipment. They looked like abstract art to her.

About twenty New People waited for them on the platform.

"Captain, are you receiving all of this?" she subvocalized on her commlink. It was enough to move her jaw and tongue, and expel a little breath, for her commlink to translate that into spoken words at the other end, and it had the advantage of privacy.

Good video and audio feed, Captain Bitka answered inside her head. *How's the weather down there?*

"Hot and humid," she answered and smiled. "Looks like a welcoming committee waiting for us."

You'll do fine, Mikko, he answered and she felt her cheeks warm. He'd never used her first name before. Or maybe just the heat made her feel flushed. She wiped perspiration from her forehead.

"Almost there, Envoy," she subvocalized on the separate channel to e-Lisyss. It was an open secret he had English auto-trans loaded on his commlink but they'd confirmed it before they left the *Bay*. Mikko had loaded aGavoosh in hers before leaving as well. It was strange to hear English spoken in the unpleasantly familiar voice of the Varoki trade envoy.

I can see for myself, female Executive Officer.

This from their diplomat. Great.

The eighteen New People of the welcoming committee were all dressed identically in lightweight fabric, very loose long trousers and tunics which reached to mid-thigh, the sleeves to their wrists. The tunics and trousers were dark red and edged in a copper-colored metallic fabric. They carried no weapons or devices of any sort. The New People stood in groups of three, one forward and two back. Six groups. Mikko sensed something ritualistic in their costumes and rigid formation, and she felt some sort of ritual response was required.

Bow! e-Lisyss ordered over their commlinks and all six of the party bowed, the Buran a bit later than the rest.

The New People showed no immediate reaction and then, as if on command, all of them advanced in their peculiar shuffling gait and came among them, one to each side of each of them and one in front, the ones to each side taking their hands gently in their own and then drawing them forward into the center of the meeting area. They were only about a meter fifty tall and so came up to the shoulders of the humans, mid-chest on the Varoki. In a way, it was like being guided forward by children.

They reached the center of the stone meeting area and halted. Mikko saw a flicker of movement ahead and then four beings stood there, each beside one of the metallic monuments or sculptures. Had they stepped out from behind them or had they emerged from them? She couldn't say, but what she could see clearly was that they were not New People.

They were tall, taller than humans, taller even than the Varoki, easily two meters ten or twenty. Upright bipeds, large eyes with no whites she could see, hardly any sign of a nose, a clear single mandible jaw with recessed chin, and feathers. Small soft feathers on the side and back of the head, larger more ornamental feathers on the shoulders, very fine feathers, or maybe a down, on their arms. The sun shone from Mikko's right and the beings stood in the shade of the metallic structures, but the air around their heads seemed to glow in the semi-darkness, like . . . *halos.*

Their legs were encased in shining metallic trousers, articulated at the joints. *SA frames,* she thought. *They must not be from around here, either.*

"Damn!" she subvocalized to Captain Bitka. "Do you see this, sir? It's a whole different species! And that glow . . ."

I think we just met the Guardians, Bitka said.

"I am Special Trade Envoy Limi e-Lisyss," the Varoki said through his vox-box in Destie, and Mikko gave him points for having the presence of mind to even speak. "I am the senior representative present of our government, the *Cottohazz.* This government was established by my people, the Varoki, over three hundred of your years ago. All that time it has guarded the peace and prosperity of the other five sentient species we discovered and to whom we gave the gift of interstellar travel. We—"

"You gave the others the gift of interstellar travel?" one of the Guardians said, its voice deep and resonant. "How did you come upon this gift?"

"Varoki scientists invented it," e-Lisyss answered.

"You believe this?" a different Guardian said.

"It is the *truth,*" e-Lisyss answered, a hint of righteous indignation entering his voice.

e-Lisyss started to take a step forward but the three New People held him firmly and then with a surge of adrenaline Mikko saw that their free hands all held short, gleaming knives.

Where had those come from?

"Sam?" she said.

Mikko!

CHAPTER THIRTEEN

Moments later, **aboard USS *Cam Ranh Bay***
7 April 2134 *(thirteen days after arrival at*
Destination, second day in orbit around Destie-Four,
fifty-eight days after Incident Seventeen)

When the first knife struck, Sam heard a collective gasp
go up from the bridge crew. When Running-Deer went
down, Alexander in TAC One let out a cry of despair that
came from the soul. Sam felt almost paralyzed by the
sudden carnage on the audience slab—almost.

"Merderet. Drop your Mikes!" he ordered into his
commlink. Then he pinged Lieutenant Sylvia Norquist in
the docking bay.

"Norquist, clear away another PSRV and put a good
coxswain in it. Don't launch until I give the order."

Mikes away, Merderet reported. *Seventeen minutes to
ground.*

"Load a second platoon in pods, Major. That's our
reserve. Here's your quick brief for the inbound platoon.
Priority One, recover surviving members of the landing
team. Priority Two, secure the landing area with a
minimum of friendly casualties. Priority Three, get me a

prisoner if you can. The big birds seem to be in charge, so bring me one back—alive."

Aye, aye, sir, she answered.

When he stopped talking he became aware of the background noise, curses and one person sobbing quietly. Almost everyone looked away from the large monitor feeding the camera views but Sam did not take his eyes off it. For whatever reason, the Desties had not jammed the commlink feeds. As long as the eyes and ears of the six beings down there lived, the ship's monitors would reproduce it. Boniface's biorecorder would go on recording and transmitting quite a while longer. As much as he wanted to look away, those were *his* people and someone should witness their final moments.

"Dr. Däng to the bridge," he ordered into his commlink. "Bohannon, patch me into the downlink to Chief Wainwright in the landed PSRV."

"You are live to the Five Boat, sir," she answered, voice betraying anger more than grief.

"Five Boat, what's your status?"

Secure for the moment, sir, the senior chief bosun answered, *but there are Desties outside bangin' on the hatch. Pretty soon they may bring in a cutting torch, or whatever they have to do the job.*

"Twenty Mikes are inbound, Chief. We need you operational to haul them out again, so lift off and find a secure LZ within a couple klicks. Better stay low. We don't know what sort of close air-defense threat we're facing."

Sir, if I lift right now, we're going to toast a bunch of Desties.

Sam watched what the New People were doing on the stone platform that was now slick with his crew's blood.

"Icing on the cake, Chief."

Aye, aye, sir.

Sam turned to Lieutenant Alexander in TAC One. The TAC boss stared away to the side, no readable expression on his face other than enormous loss. Of course! Sam had been a blind fool. *That's* why Alexander always shot his mouth off in front of Running-Deer: showing off, trying to impress her. Poor, stupid bastard.

"TAC, we've got four lasers and a sky full of satellites. Set up a target priority queue. Rank those big guys in high orbit first, all the little stuff that's pretty much communication relay birds last. Lieutenant, do you hear me?"

Alexander ran his hands over his face, then went to work.

"Yes sir, set up the target queue. Then what?"

"If we get any sign of hostile action against the PSRV or the Mikes, start taking out satellites as fast as you can. Otherwise wait for my order."

"I think we ought to just open fire, sir," he said, his voice shaking.

"Noted."

"Sir," the sensor tech to Alexander's right said, "the Five Boat is airborne."

The bridge crew gave a ragged cheer.

Dr. Däng floated through the bridge hatch and turned to face Sam. Her eyes were wide in shock, her cheeks still wet with tears.

"Dr. Däng, we have a recording of the entire incident. I want you to watch it—"

"What kind of a monster are you? Watch *that*? Are you insane?"

Sam closed his eyes for a moment but the images remained.

"I do not have a physician on board. You are the closest I have to a trained pathologist. I need you to watch the recording and tell me if it is possible for any of the landing party to have survived. It will affect decisions I have to make in the next few minutes."

Sam saw her intellect overcome her rage and she brought her emotions under control, then nodded her understanding. Sam looked away, the only privacy he could give her. After three or four minutes, she spoke, her voice strained but under control.

"No member of the landing party who entered that audience area can have survived their wounds."

"Thank you, Doctor. You are excused from the bridge."

Sam pinged Merderet.

"Major, do you have comms to your Mikes?"

Not this second, sir. They're in the hot part of the reentry, lots of ionization. Give me a minute or two.

"When you've got comms, tell them there are no survivors of the landing party, so they can go in guns hot. Recover their remains. Let's not lose anyone else. If anything down there moves except to run away or surrender, kill it."

Aye, aye, sir.

"And Major, I would really, *really* like a prisoner."

We'll do our best, sir.

Sam cut the link. He'd tried to mentally prepare himself for every possibility, walk through what he would have to do, have to say, but there was one event he had never prepared for. He went over the words he would have to say next, trying to treat them as words in a script he was reading so his voice wouldn't shake, as Alexander's had a few minutes earlier.

"Mister Brook."

The Ops boss rotated his workstation and looked at Sam through eyes hollow with shock.

"Mister Brook, call your senior chief to the bridge and turn your chair over to her. Then lay aft to the auxiliary bridge and take the command chair there. That's your new battle station . . . XO."

Brook subvocalized an order on his commlink, and began releasing his restraints.

Sam turned to Alexander. "TAC, execute your target queue. Sweep every goddamned satellite you can see from the sky."

For the next hour, Alexander's TAC department knocked out satellites with murderous efficiency. As they had expected, the largest platforms in higher orbits were directed energy weapons, but the ones closest to them went down immediately. Another fired at them as it rose over the distant horizon, hit the habitat wheel, but did surprisingly little damage and no casualties. The *Bay's* lasers knocked it down before it fired again.

Forty-three minutes from when the Mikes entered atmosphere, Chief Wainwright came up on the commlink.

Captain Bitka, I have twenty Mikes, one prisoner, and all recovered remains on board and I am lifting off. Estimate dock in two-five minutes.

Another cheer went up from the bridge crew and Sam relaxed a little. Twenty-five more minutes and they could accelerate out of here. But where to? They had a whole world, a whole star system trying to kill them.

"Captain," Lieutenant Alexander said, "We've got a couple more of those gun-sats ready to come over the horizon in their orbits. I'd like to engage over the horizon with a Mark Five. With all the junk out there, I don't think they'll be able to pick our missile out of the clutter before it detonates. In Sunflower mode, it can take down twenty or more satellites in one shot, and scramble their electronics to boot."

A deep-space intercept missile was not meant for use in orbit. When it detonated, a thermonuclear warhead destroyed the missile but pumped out thirty X-ray laser pulses, each one enough to blow most satellites into scattered debris. The problem was any unshielded electronics in a large part of one hemisphere would be fried by the electromagnetic pulse, along with most remaining satellites on that side of the world. Usually, that was a bad thing, but right now it sounded pretty good to Sam.

"What's loaded in the coil gun?" he asked.

"A standard Thud," Alexander answered. "Kinetic energy submunition round, take out twenty hectares."

"Marines said the Guardians fled into an underground complex. Unload the Thud, load your Mark Five, and take out those gun-sats. Then load a Thud, but not a submunition round. Give me a crust buster."

"Aye, aye, sir."

Suddenly, Sam felt himself thrown hard to one side

against his restraints, and then heard the whooping siren of the hull breach alarm. The bridge filled with the babble of voices, particularly from the left side—maneuvering and engineering.

"Pipe down!" Sam shouted, and the bridge fell silent except for the hull breach siren.

"You're the crew of a US Navy warship and we're under fire. This is your real job so get used to it. Now work your stations. Ship status, what's the damage?"

"Losing pressure in the docking bay and compartments twelve and twenty-two in the habitat wheel, sir," the machinist mate at the Engineering Two station answered. "A-gang on the way to repair damage. No power loss. Sensors and weaponry still up."

"Ops," Sam ordered, "evasive action, but keep us in orbit. The Five Boat's still on its way.

"TAC, what's shooting at us?"

"I don't know, sir," Alexander answered, desperation in his voice.

"Well, figure it out, and quick." Sam heard two short blasts of the acceleration klaxon, the warning alarm for lateral thrust, and then felt a tug to the side as the *Bay* used its attitude control thrusters to displace. It wasn't much, but with so many of the satellites down, and so much new debris in orbit, the Desties' tracking and fire direction might be pretty degraded. It might be enough.

Sam pinged Major Merderet in the launch bay.

Yes sir, she answered immediately.

"Major, we took a hit aft of where you are. Better pull your reserve platoon from their jump pods and get them up to their squad bays."

Aye, aye, sir.

"Captain," Alexander called out, "it's fire from the surface. We've got a firing solution for a Thud, and we've still got that submunition round in the coil gun."

"Hit him, TAC," Sam ordered, and Sam felt the *Bay* shudder with the launch.

"On the way," Alexander said.

"He fired again!" the sensor tech in the TAC Three chair called out. "Missed us, but look at this."

The main screen showed an exterior view looking forward over the bow toward the planetary horizon. A momentary flash came and went, almost too quickly to register.

"Show that again and freeze it," Sam ordered. The image reappeared as a thin, bright line running almost straight up past them. As they looked at it, he felt the *Bay* accelerate slightly.

"What is that?" Lieutenant Bohannon asked. "A laser?"

"We're in vacuum, COMM," Sam said. "Nothing for a laser to interact with out here, so no visible track. Maybe a particle accelerator?"

"From out of an atmosphere and into vacuum, sir?" Alexander said. "I'd like to know how that works. A neutral beam won't hold together in the atmosphere, and a charged one won't outside of it."

"Can you track its origin?" Sam asked.

"Yes, sir. It's close to the original firing point, but it's moved," the sensor tech said. "It's moving counter-rotation, and I think it's firing from underground."

"Underground? Let me see that," Alexander said and touched his own workstation to bring up the duplicate of the sensor tech's display. Sam did as well. Assuming it was the same weapon, and that it wasn't actually moving with respect to the planet surface, but was instead moved along by the planet's rotation, the only solution was a site on the far side of the planet but underground, maybe half a kilometer.

"Bullshit!" Alexander said. "Who can shoot through a whole planet? It's crazy."

"Firing again," the sensor tech reported. "Missed even farther. The firing track lines up exactly with the previous solution."

"Tac," Sam said, "get a Mark Five ready and take out those gun-sats. The blast will keep those sensors blind. Then take out the complex the Guardians retreated into with a crust buster. Ops, keep maneuvering, but get us down lower and meet our PSRV. I want to recover the Five Boat and get the hell out of here."

CHAPTER FOURTEEN

Five hours later, **aboard USS** *Cam Ranh Bay*
7 April 2134 *(thirteen days after arrival at*
Destination, second day in orbit around Destie-Four,
fifty-eight days after Incident Seventeen)

Five hours later, once they were safely away—at least for the moment—Sam stood helmeted in the docking bay. Fourteen bodies in sealed gray composite bags floated in zero gee, tethered to each other, held by a mixed honor guard of Marines and bosun's mates. He heard Lieutenant Bohannon say, "All hands, bury the dead," on the all-ship channel, the signal for everyone to stop their work for a moment while they said goodbye to their shipmates.

"Honor guard, hand salute," Sam ordered and then read the names of all fourteen dead: one Buran, one Varoki, and twelve humans. Among the humans, two Marines, two sailors including Mikko Running-Deer, and eight civilians. One of the civilians was Abisogun Boniface, the Nigerian journalist. The other civilians were killed by the final energy weapon hit on the habitat wheel.

Sam got to the end of the ceremony, to the final line, the one which read, *We therefore commit their remains to space, to rejoin the universe from which we all came, and to which we all surely will return,* but he could not say it. He could not.

"At this point in the service," he said, "we bury the remains in space, as has become our tradition, but we're not going to do that today. I'm not going to dump our friends and shipmates into space someplace where if one of these monsters finds them . . . well, we all know what they'd do. So we'll freeze and store their remains. If we die, we'll die together, and if somehow we get back home we'll carry them with us for burial in their native soils. We're not leaving anyone here.

"Ship's company, dismissed."

One hour later, Sam turned on the holovid recorder and simply sat, unsure where to start.

"Cass . . ." he said and then stopped and looked away, looked at the exterior starfield view on his cabin wall and ceiling and floor, the view that made his furniture and himself seem to float in space. It made him appear the same as he felt—adrift and alone.

When Sam was seven years old, an elderly lady in the neighborhood died and his parents took him to her funeral. The old lady rested silently in her open casket and Sam had stared at her for a long time, knowing she would not move but waiting for movement, anyway. Even when people sleep they move, their chests rise and fall as they breathe, skin throbs here and there with the energy of blood coursing beneath it. What most distinguished this first dead person from all the live people he had seen was the absolute lack of motion.

In deep space, the stars are like that. People grow up under a canopy of stars and, like the body of a living person, that canopy is always moving slightly. Variations in the atmosphere make the stars twinkle and flicker. But in deep space there's no atmosphere and so each star is a single, solid, unchanging point of light. On Earth, the stars look magical. In deep space, they look cold and dead.

He switched off the external starfield view. He had spent enough time staring into the abyss. He rested his face in his hands for a while, not saying anything, trying to keep his mind as blank as the gray walls around him.

"Jesus, Cass . . . what they did! I don't know if they treat everyone this way or if we did something to especially piss them off, and I don't care. This is so sick, so . . . twisted, it's hard to get my head around. They didn't just kill the landing party, Cass, they butchered them right there while we watched. And I mean butchered—professionally, methodically, and some were still alive when they started."

Sam paused because he could feel his throat tightening, his voice starting to fail him. Running-Deer had been alive for a while, trying so hard not to scream in horror and agony but then giving in to it, because anyone would have. He could still see it, but for a while couldn't trust his voice to say it.

"They sliced them up, filleted them, and then, so help me God, Cass, they *ate* them. At least the four big mucky-mucks did, the one who called himself The Eye of P'Daan and his three sidekicks. *Guardians!* Well, they're dead Guardians now, all but one we've got locked up. Our Marines grabbed that one after having to kill most of their squat little servants. The head guy and two others fled underground, into the main complex. We dropped a crust-buster on it, one of our deep penetrating bombardment munitions, so... well, they're dead, but I'm not sure where we go from here.

"We took down damn near every satellite in orbit around the principal world, over fifteen hundred of them, but they've got some damned particle accelerator that I swear to God can shoot through planets. How the hell does it do *that?* It hit us once, killed seven civilian passengers up in the wheel and one crewperson in our docking bay. If it hit fifty or so meters aft it would have taken out engineering, and that would have been the end of that.

"We lit off three nuke warheads from Mark Five torpedoes to kill satellites, scramble their ground sensors, and cover our acceleration burn. Then I shut down the reactor and got our thermal shroud deployed. We're coasting in low-heat emission mode. In a few days, if we're still alive, I'll use our low-signature MPD thruster to match course with one of those automated bulk freight carriers we spotted outbound for the big gas giant. If we get in close below it, I'm hoping we'll look like a false echo.

"But I can't imagine a way out of this, a way home, a way to stay alive much longer—one armed transport with a screwed-up jump drive against a whole civilization that looks to be at least as advanced as we are. I don't even have a plan yet, not beyond the next couple weeks."

He felt a tingle at the base of his skull and saw the commlink ID for Dr. Däng.

"Have to close, Cass. My resident xenobiologist wants

to scream at me some more. Smartest person I've ever known, and an even bigger pain in my ass. I love you."

He turned off the recorder and felt a second tingle.

"Yes, Dr. Däng. What is it?"

Captain Bitka, I must talk with you. I must talk with the entire advisory group as soon as possible!

She sounded even more upset, more agitated than earlier, maybe because the shock was wearing off. Sam didn't relish a public screaming match with her, couldn't see what it would accomplish.

"Dr. Däng, I know we disagree over my actions, but what's done is—"

No, it's not about that, she snapped, her urgency turning to impatience. *We have all been too shocked to think, and I have been a blind fool! What we witnessed on Destie-Four was scientifically impossible.*

"Impossible?" Sam said as he felt the first flush of panic. "You mean . . . our people weren't actually killed by the Guardians? But we recovered their remains, didn't we? Or . . . were our people still alive in the complex when I ordered it destroyed?"

No! They were certainly dead, Captain Bitka. Please try to put aside your guilt and self-flagellation for a moment and listen to me.

All six intelligent races of the Cottohazz are from independently evolved trees of life. Their fundamental protein chains are different and incompatible, to the point that they are poisonous to each other, often producing fatal results within minutes.

Sam knew that, knew it because it was the reason humans and Varoki fought over K'tok—other than Earth the only naturally occurring ecosystem discovered which was human-compatible. Then he understood Däng's agitation.

"How could the Guardians eat human flesh and not die?" he asked. "Unless . . . wait, you mean the Guardians are biologically compatible with *humans*?"

No. As unlikely as that would be, it is at least within the realm of biological possibility, as the K'tok ecosystem demonstrates. But you forget, Captain Bitka, they— including our prisoner—also ate the flesh of the Varoki envoy e-Lisyss and the Buran Acolyte Onogoe Barvenu. There is no way that is possible! Nevertheless, we witnessed it, and our prisoner is still very much alive.

CHAPTER FIFTEEN

**Six days later, aboard USS *Cam Ranh Bay*
13 April 2134 (*nineteen days after arrival at
Destination, sixty-four days after Incident
Seventeen, running dark, outbound to gas giant*)**

Dr. Däng Thi Hue sat back from the genome analysis and imaging display and rubbed the back of her neck. She'd known the truth hours ago, suspected it days ago, but she had to be sure, had to be absolutely certain before reporting her results to the captain. If they ever got home, what a story this would be!

A *story* . . . She thought again, as she had so many times in the last six days, of Boniface, the Nigerian journalist killed in the landing party. They had become friends in the last month, sharing tea together daily at 1600 hours, a quiet time she had increasingly looked forward to, and which had now become a bleak dark corner of her day.

She wished so much now that they had done the interview he had asked for that first time they met. She knew her own fame had a power which made her uncomfortable, but which was undeniable nevertheless. An interview with her would have given him wider exposure, would have been a nice counterpoint to his war reporting.

Why, she wondered, had he become a war reporter? He was gentle, but with a streak of righteous anger under the surface. She had seen it directed twice at the Varoki trade envoy, heard its echoes when he talked about the Varoki trading houses, but also about his own government's benign neglect of the rural poor, what he called *the forgotten upcountry*. Did that anger suggest a fascination with violence? She didn't think so, and yet he felt a need, or perhaps a responsibility, to bear witness to it. She knew his first name, Abisogun, was Yoruba and meant "born in war." He had told her that but had not told her *which* war. There had been so many.

And now this . . . this thing in the genome analyzer. Yes, this would make a sensational story too, if they managed to return to the *Cottohazz*. And somehow, someone would find a way to have a war about it, because they always did. She had to admit the captain had been right about that: advanced civilizations just meant bigger, shinier machines; there did not seem to be any reduction in their capacities for violence or irrationality, not that his observation set him apart from that, as his murderous reaction on Destie-Four had demonstrated.

Well, the captain might be a monster, but he was at least *our* monster. If it took a monster to get them home, so be it. She had never imagined she would ever think such a thought but watching the massacre of the landing party had changed her somehow, hardened her. Her own recognition of the problem did not, apparently, set her apart from it either. She could only hope this "new her" would fade with time, and this new hardness would eventually soften, but she didn't know that it would.

In the meantime, she had her answer to the question she had posed six days ago, and news for the captain, news perhaps worth another Nobel prize, if she had still cared about that.

As Hue sat down in the briefing room, she recognized she was suffering from sleep deprivation and it might be affecting her cognition in subtle ways. The trail of the riddle had simply been too seductive to waste much time on sleep these last few days. There had been a time when she had been able to work for three or four days without anything but brief naps, but those days seemed to have passed and that thought brought a brief wave of melancholy. She put that aside, gathered her thoughts, and looked across the conference table at Captain Bitka. She had asked for this first briefing alone, just the two of them.

He looks old, she was surprised to find herself thinking. He was twenty years her junior, no more than his mid-thirties, and of course he looked younger than she. Only in his eyes did she see the same weariness and pain she felt. And a new hardness.

"Captain, my specialty is xenophysiology, but of course I have a solid grounding in microbiology as well and I have kept reasonably abreast of the field. I wish we had an accomplished microbiologist with us." She paused and thought a moment. "Oh, I know just the man, Dr. Agus Parang. Agus would probably give everything he owns to be—"

"Dr. Däng," the captain broke in, "you're killing me."

"Oh, I'm sorry. I am wandering a bit, aren't I? It's just that I am unused to being overwhelmed, and what I have seen through your medbay's instruments . . . It's hard to know where to begin."

"Why don't you start with how our prisoner is able to eat the protein from three different trees of life and not croak?"

"Yes, that's where we started, isn't it? In order to understand that, let me begin by explaining what protein is. Bear with me. You need to know this for anything else to make sense. A protein is a type of large biomolecule which consists mainly of one or more polypeptides, which are long chains of amino acids. There are about twenty amino acids which most terrestrial organisms need in order to live and grow.

"When we eat food containing protein, our digestive systems break that protein down into its component amino acids, which is what we're really after. You understand? It's about the amino acids, not the protein itself. Our digestive system is adapted to the sorts of protein which developed on Earth. Most other species rely on very similar sets of amino acids, but by chance the development of chemical life on their world happens to have different polypeptide chain structures, so their digestive systems are different from ours to break down those different structures. You understand?"

"Yeah, I think so. That doesn't really explain why their proteins kill us, though."

"Correct. There are harmful proteins in our own environment. Most neurotoxins are protein-based, for example. The most dangerous venoms are protein. In some cases, our digestive system is adapted to segregate and expel harmful proteins in small enough amounts, but evolutionarily there is no reason to go to the trouble of adapting the digestive system to every possible protein in the environment. It is an easier solution to adapt to the most plentiful food sources and simply avoid consuming the poisonous ones. But in the alien environments we have encountered, essentially all of the food proteins are poisonous to us, because of their unfamiliar structure. The animals which have evolved in that ecosystem naturally have digestive systems which can break those proteins down, extract the amino acids they need, and discharge the harmful bits."

"Okay, got it," the captain said and took a drink of coffee. The way he said it made Hue think he really did understand. She hoped so. This part was very simple, secondary school biology. If he couldn't get past this, he was not going to understand anything else.

"So," the captain said, "if there is no reason from an evolutionary point of view to have a digestive system which can tackle every possible protein structure, how do these guys get one?"

"They did not evolve."

"Say again?"

"Well, Captain, I cannot be certain there was *no* period in their biological history when their ancestors evolved, but there is no evidence of it in their current genetic material. These beings were, to borrow a rather highly charged phrase, intelligently designed. *Very* intelligently designed."

"Wait," he said. "Does this have to do with those halos? Because if you're selling some sort of religious—"

"No," she cut him off, "not that. The halos are simply bioluminescence, as much a form of decorative display as the different colors of their plumage. What I mean is that their genes show unmistakable evidence of having been massively altered from their original configuration, to the point that that configuration is no longer possible to reconstruct. Their genes are the way they are because they were carefully and deliberately configured to produce very specific results, among those being the ability to generate a wide variety of enzymes able to break down the proteins from multiple trees of life, and to adapt very rapidly to new proteins.

"We've fed her—it is a female, by the way—food from the Katami, Brand, and Zaschaan protein groups the last few days. We already knew she could digest Human, Varoki and Buran protein. She gobbled it all down and asked for more. We noticed she consumed about forty percent more fluid on the day she ate Zaschaan-compatible protein and she generated more waste, but showed no ill effects. I don't think it's possible to poison her in the conventional sense."

"So, you're saying you don't think she evolved, because there is no reason to evolve in that way?" the captain said.

"Well, that would be one argument, but the smoking gun is in her genetic material. By the way, did I mention she is immortal?"

"*Immortal?*" he said, sitting bolt upright. "What about those three we just killed back on Destie-Four?"

"They are not invulnerable nor indestructible. They

can be killed. If they do not eat, if they receive no oxygen, they will die. They are immortal only in the sense that they do not age, at all."

"That's not possible," he said.

"Of course it is possible! The overwhelming volume of life on Earth, and in every other ecosystem we have ever encountered, is immortal. Higher organisms, plants and animals, most lifeforms you can see with your naked eye are not, but in terms of numbers and even biomass they are far outnumbered by microbes, and *microbes are immortal*. They reproduce by cellular division. Some get eaten by other organisms, some are damaged or destroyed by environmental hazards, but those which do not never get old and die. They just keep growing and reproducing forever. Only higher organisms age."

The captain stood up and for a moment Hue sat back in her chair, unsure what he was going to do, but then she relaxed as he began pacing the length of the conference room. She had to admit, it was a lot to absorb in such a short time.

"Okay," he said, "only higher organisms age. But she's a higher organism, right? So what's her trick?"

"There are a number of important differences, but the most obvious and significant one is circular chromosomes," Hue answered.

The captain stopped pacing and looked at her. "Another biology lecture, right?"

"I am afraid so."

He sighed and sat back down, took another sip of coffee, and gestured for her to start.

"The principal reason microbes are immortal is they

have circular chromosomes. When the chromosomes divide in two for reproduction, the division process starts at one point on the circle, goes around it in both directions until it meets on the opposite side, and so produces two circles, each one side of the original chromosome, which then fill in their missing parts and become the chromosomes of the two new cells. This is a nearly foolproof way of making faithful copies of the genetic material.

"Higher organisms, however, have much more genetic material to deal with and it has to be packed into the nucleus of a cell not much bigger than that of a microbe. A typical human cell is six one-thousandths of a millimeter in diameter, about three times the size of many bacteria cells. But the length of the DNA that makes up the chromosomes in every human cell, if you unwrapped it and laid it out straight, would stretch across this table from me to you, Captain. It is over one meter long."

"How does something a meter long fit in a cell that's... how big did you say?" the captain asked.

"Six one-thousandths of a millimeter. Well, it's long but very, very thin, so it is bundled into cables which are bundled and rebundled and wound and wrapped. It's a very lovely thing to see, but it is definitely a difficult engineering problem. So difficult, in fact, that you cannot manage it with a circular DNA strand. You cannot collapse and wrap a circular strand that long tightly enough without breaking the circle, so eukaryotes—which is what we call all the higher organisms from plants on up—instead have *linear* strands of DNA which are bundled into chromosomes."

"So why is that a problem?"

"Linear strands have ends, and ends fray, lose genetic material, particularly in the act of trying to duplicate them during cellular division. The ends have a component called telomeres which prevent fraying, but the telomeres fray themselves and eventually the linear strands start losing bits of DNA. When those bits are important, the genetic instructions become garbled and the cells made are not the perfect replicas we would like."

"So, we start getting wrinkles and bad knees?" the captain asked.

"Precisely."

"Okay," he said, "this Guardian has circular chromosomes, so no ends to fray, and so no aging. I guess that makes sense. But you said we can't do that. What's *her* trick? Really super-elastic chromosomes or something?"

"No, although she does use a slightly different sugar in the chromosome bonds than we do, and that may make it more resilient, and each cell nucleus contains numerous chromosomes. But the DNA structure the Guardian possesses would not, so near as I can tell, enable it to compact into its cell nuclei all the DNA we and most other higher organisms carry, without breaking the circles. Instead, she has simply dispensed with most of it."

"Okay. I'm supposed to ask how that's possible, right?"

"Yes. We do not routinely use most of our DNA. Some of it is legacy material, left over from when we were less advanced organisms, or remnants of retroviruses to which we have been exposed, that sort of thing. Much of that material is considered junk, although some of it is a sort of overview of our evolution path and other parts are useful during gestation and growth from infant to mature adult. After all, a human embryo begins as a single cell and grows through a number of stages as a fetus, some of which bear coincidental resemblance to earlier stages of our evolution. At one point the human fetus has a tail, at another stage gills, although humans have neither. Obviously, the genetic material to produce tails and gills is buried somewhere in the human DNA but no longer used in fully formed adults.

"Our Guardian prisoner, on the other hand, only has the genetic material necessary to reproduce her existing mature cellular structures. It is about twenty per cent of the material we carry with us, perhaps even less but I'm not sure. As I said, this is not my specialty."

"But wait a minute," the captain said, "if that's all the DNA they've got, and a fetus uses some of that—what did you call it—*legacy* material to grow, how do they reproduce?"

"Ah. Very perceptive question, Captain Bitka. They do not, at least not in the old-fashioned way. She has sexual organs, but only the fun ones. She has nothing comparable to a womb. If they are as adept at biogenetic manipulation as this would suggest, and assuming they are the architects of their own genetic structure, I suspect when they need new Guardians they just make some."

"Goddamn!"

"Indeed. Apparently, the price one pays for immortality."

Bitka sipped his coffee, momentarily lost in thought.

"Huh. So, if she has no reproductive organs, how do you know she's a she?"

"Informed supposition. Her sexual organs are internal

instead of external. That is a fairly common characteristic in female eukaryotes in most trees of life we have encountered."

The captain nodded and then straightened in his seat.

"Okay, guess it's time to go back to Plan A. I intended to interrogate the prisoner right away, while she was still alive, but your revelation changed all that. Time to have that talk."

Hue felt the blood drain from her face as she understood the import of that.

"*While she was still alive?* So you were going to torture whatever information you could from her and then kill her? The Guardians and all those New People killed back at the Destie-Four complex weren't enough vengeance? I suppose you'll let me examine the corpse post-mortem. How generous of you."

Bitka scowled, his face flushed slightly, and he shook his head in anger. "Gee, and we were getting along so well there for a while. You're being stupid, Dr. Däng."

"Oh, it is stupid now to value life, especially that of an enemy."

"No. it's stupid to jump to conclusions just because they fit your dumb stereotypes. I wasn't going to kill her. Come on, you're the scientist. You can't connect these dots?"

Hue stared at him, unsure what he meant. He shook his head again in annoyance.

"I knew we were going to have to make a run for it when I ordered our Marines to grab a prisoner. I also knew—or *thought* I knew—there was no food on this ship an alien prisoner would be able to ingest without being killed by it. What did you think, Doc? That on our way out to the gas giant we'd just pull over at a Destie-Burger stand and get her something to eat? I figured we had a week, maybe two, before our prisoner starved to death. When you told me she could eat our protein, I knew food wasn't a problem so I let you find out everything you could before talking to her myself."

He drained his coffee, put the mug down with a loud *clunk*, and stood up from the table.

"Well, now it's time."

Hue sat back in her chair as Bitka walked to the door. She had misjudged him, or rather misjudged his motives in this one case. She didn't suppose it mattered very much, as she already understood that Bitka's self-image seemed completely independent of her opinion of him. Still, it was annoying to be wrong.

"Captain, wait a moment."

Bitka stopped at the door and turned to her, his expression inquisitive.

"If you are going to talk to her, you should know two things. First, her name is Te'Anna. Second, she does not blink."

"Meaning I can't bluff her?" Bitka asked.

"That's not what I had in mind, although that is probably also true. No, I mean she physically never blinks her eyes. There is not an intelligent species we have encountered this is true of, and so it is somewhat disconcerting, but less so if you are prepared for it."

The captain cocked his head slightly to the side. "Thanks," he said, and started through the door but then stopped and turned back.

"Okay, I'll bite. How come?"

"We look for life in the liquid water zone of a star system," Hue said, "the place where the star's radiant energy is enough to melt ice but not enough to boil it away. It's not impossible for life to start places other than in liquid water, but it's hard, and it's very hard for it to get much more advanced than microbes.

"Our universal experience of life which ends up producing large organisms is that it begins in liquid water. Every one of the six intelligent species of the *Cottohazz* evolved from lower forms which evolved in water and then moved onto the land. But the optic sensory organs were already perfected by their aquatic ancestors and they just brought those eyes with them. The problem is those eyes were developed while continually immersed in water, so land animals needed to develop ways to keep them wet. That's why we have tear ducts and why we blink: to wet our eyes. That's why everyone blinks and weeps. If I were starting from scratch, that is not the way *I* would have designed an eye for a creature who was going to spend its life on dry land.

"Whoever designed her eyes apparently felt the same way."

CHAPTER SIXTEEN

One hour later, aboard USS *Cam Ranh Bay*,
running dark, outbound to Destie-Seven
13 April 2134 *(fifty-nine days after Incident
Seventeen)*

Sam was on his way to his first interrogation session of the
alien prisoner but found the Buran linguist, with infant in
arms, waiting for him in the broad corridor of the habitat
wheel.

"I apologize Captain Samuel Bitka, but it is important
I have a moment of your time."

"I have time for you, Councilor Abanna Zhaquaan."

Sam still could not tell much about the Buran's body
language but today he noticed it shifted its weight from
foot to foot, making a gentle rocking motion. Invariably
the Buran stood motionless when they spoke, so whatever
the meaning of this difference, he was pretty sure it was
significant.

"We gain a better understanding of the Guardian
language, the one we called Destie at first. As we do, we
understand more nuances. We discover we have made a
mistake, a very bad one."

Sam felt a flash of dread and his attention instantly went from polite to absolute.

"What mistake?"

"We translated the Guardian command to send a landing party to present an offer. A better translation would have been an offering. In fact, we now know that the boarding party itself was understood to be the offering of appeasement. It is their custom."

Sam closed his eyes and felt himself sway back and forth for a moment.

"Their custom," he repeated.

"Yes. We should have seen this. People are dead because of us. Lieutenant Running-Deer who was so considerate to us is dead because of this. *AAAAAAAA!*" it exclaimed, a flat toneless bark of some emotion Sam could not identify: grief, remorse, guilt, anger.

"*aaaaaaaaa!*" the Buran infant repeated, as if the unsettling echo in the adult's voice was not enough.

Sam could hardly untangle his own emotions. He did not try to understand those of the Buran, but whatever part of the reaction was guilt, he thought that part was misplaced.

"Councilor Abanna Zhaquaan, did they make an effort to explain this custom to us before the landing party was sent?"

"No, Captain Samuel Bitka, but they had no reason to think we would be unfamiliar with it."

"You are mistaken. They had *every* reason to think it. Those reasons were why they demanded the meeting. They knew we were not from Guardian Space and so could have no understanding of their customs. You were not to blame, my friend. They were."

"But . . . it was just their custom."

"Well, we learned one of their customs, the hard way. And then they learned one of ours, also the hard way, so maybe we're even, although I have to say I don't feel even."

"No, not even," the Buran said. "They were an advanced technological society with no apparent recent experience with war, and so their infrastructure was extremely vulnerable. We destroyed seventeen hundred satellites by direct action, mostly due to the detonation of two nuclear weapons in Destie-Four's orbital space. Debris continues to disable additional satellites, and will do so for some time, and in so doing we have eliminated their functioning communication infrastructure.

"As near as we can tell, not only communication but aerial travel, all surface cargo transportation, all financial transactions, and all manufacturing have ceased. Many aircraft guided by means of satellite-linked control have crashed. There will be famine and unchecked disease, and there will be riots if they are the sort of people who respond to terror and approaching doom with violence. According to our prisoner every Guardian on the planet was in that underground facility, so we have apparently eliminated their supreme leadership. We have not detected any spacecraft launches, nor any effort to establishing a replacement satellite system, nor any coordinated disaster-relief efforts on the planet surface. None of those things would be possible without a communication system.

"Captain, we may have destroyed a civilization."

Sam stared at the Buran until he realized his mouth was open. He licked his lips, shook his head.

"Destroyed an advanced space-faring *civilization?* With one assault transport and a couple missiles?"

"Good morning, sir," the corporal in charge of the two-Marine guard detail standing outside the stateroom greeted him. Both wore simple khaki shipsuits and had holstered gauss pistols on their hips.

"Good morning, Corporal. How's our prisoner?"

"Same as always, sir," she answered, "fuckin' weird."

"Got eyes on her?"

She handed Sam her viewer glasses and he studied the alien, more to collect his thoughts than gather information. He might have destroyed an entire civilization a few days ago, or at least started its destruction in train, and now he had to talk to one if its leaders and see if he could persuade her to help them escape. He wasn't sure where to begin. The alien sat in the small stateroom in a Varoki-configured chair which was still a bit small for her. Her halo was clearly visible in the subdued light of the interior. He handed the viewer glasses back.

"Okay. I'm going in to interrogate her. Crank the light level up a bit."

The corporal triggered her commlink. "Visitor coming in. Prisoner will remain seated." Both Marines drew their gauss pistols and held them pointing up, fingers outside the trigger guards, and stepped to either side of the door, out of the immediate line of fire.

"Opening in three, two, one," the corporal said, and then the pistols came down and level as the door slid open, each guard covering a different half of the stateroom. "Subject is seated, Captain. Clear to enter."

Sam crossed the threshold into the small stateroom and the door whispered shut behind him.

Sam had seen vid of the Guardian so he knew her general physiology. Being in her physical presence was different and a little intimidating. He wasn't sure how much of that came from the knowledge of her immortality and how much from her towering height—about two meters thirty. Even with her seated and him standing she didn't have to bend her neck to look him in the eye.

To his surprise her most striking features were her eyes. Proportionally they were larger than a human's, more like an owl's, and of course they never blinked. They were pale gray, nearly the same color as her head feathers, which were small and fine, not much different than flowing hair at first glance. Dr. Däng had told him those eyes could see far into the infrared part of the spectrum. He wondered what else those eyes could see.

Sam wore a clumsy vox-box around his neck and spoke into the clear flexible mask. The vox-box translated his words into Destie and produced a fair approximation of his voice and inflections from its speaker.

"My name is Samuel Bitka and I am captain of this ship. I understand your name is Te'Anna, and Lieutenant Bohannon tells me you are willing to speak with me. Is that correct?"

"Lieutenant Deandra Bohannon," the Guardian named Te'Anna said, "communications officer. She worries she has insufficient sexual allure to attract a desirable mate. Do you find her sexually alluring?" Her abrupt sentences came in short, clipped packets of words.

Sam worked at not letting his surprise at the question

show on his face. The Guardian cocked her head to the side in a gesture he found unsettlingly birdlike. No, all sorts of animals made head movements like that. It must be the feathers that made him think of a bird.

"She is a subordinate," Sam said. "I try not to think of my subordinates in those terms."

"That is a custom of your people or just a personal eccentricity?"

"It's a rule."

"A *rule?* And this rule is always obeyed?"

"No rule is always obeyed."

She studied him for a moment. "But you always obey it, Captain Bitka. Is that *your* personal eccentricity?"

"One of several," he answered. "I would like to ask you some questions."

She made another strange head movement: she tucked her chin down against her chest and then pushed her head forward and tilted it back, stretching her neck.

"Of course. Ask anything you like. I am your prisoner for now."

For now? Sam decided to let that pass. He looked at his data pad, at the list of questions he wanted to ask, and decided to start with an easy one.

"The leader of the group of Marines which captured you said you made no effort to flee into the complex or avoid capture. He said you appeared to be waiting for them and wanted to be taken."

"He is very perceptive, this leader," she said. She raised her right hand and ran her fingertips through the feathers along the side of her face, and he found it a very graceful gesture. Unlike the New People, her fingers were long and shapely, but like them her hand had only three fingers and an opposable thumb. Interesting coincidence, Sam thought. He also thought, *Well, they may be geniuses when it comes to genetic manipulation, but we'd sure kick their asses in a piano-playing contest.*

"Why did you allow yourself to be taken?" he asked.

"I am not sure you would understand," she answered.

"Try me."

"I was very bored. You seemed interesting."

Bored? Sam looked down at his data pad to hide his expression. What sort of being allows herself to be taken prisoner by violent aliens out of boredom? Maybe one who had lived a really long time.

"How old are you?" Sam asked.

"I do not know. I have been alive as long as I remember. Of course, I suppose that is true of any sentient being. But my earliest memories are of myself essentially as I am now, and with the sensation I had always been thus."

"How long ago was that?" Sam asked.

"Again, I do not know. Three hundred orbits of the world you call Destination Four around its star? Perhaps four hundred? No, come to think of it I have a vague memory of having been elsewhere once. That must have been a very long time ago, as the New People say we have been here with them for over eight hundred orbits. They are more concerned with keeping track of such things than are we. Time is more important to those who have so little. Of course, I may not have come here with P'Daan. I may have come later."

Destination-Four did one orbit of its star in about 1.3

Earth years. That placed the Guardians here at least a thousand years ago.

"You came here from elsewhere, so there must be other Guardians. Other inhabited worlds in your . . . I don't know what to call your civilization."

"We call it the Realms, or at least we used to. Perhaps they still do. There are other worlds, other Guardians. Other Guardians come and visit sometimes, not often. I do not know how many Guardians are still alive, I would say in the thousands, probably no more than that. Certainly fewer than a million. Most of us have simply lost interest and died, or gone off looking for something . . . else. Only those with a grand obsession or a . . . a good *hobby,* remain. I believe there are several thousand inhabited star systems in the Realms. There used to be. It is hard to keep track and there is little contact between them except when a Guardian becomes restless."

Several *thousand* inhabited star systems? The room moved around Sam for a moment. He took a breath and went on.

"The New People spokesman called the Guardian we were to meet The Eye of P'Daan and you just mentioned P'Daan as well. Who is P'Daan? Is he the one who gave the orders for the massacre?"

She did another one of her neck stretching motions and then ruffled her neck feathers with the fingers of both hands.

"P'Daan came here along with M'Eetos and engineered this system; they are its patrons, its creators. M'Eetos left some time ago, and P'Daan left later, but he intends to come back. He left P'Moze in his place, to serve as his eye. That is when P'Moze took the name The Eye of P'Daan. Well, that must be obvious. Are you going to torture me?"

Torture? Why was everyone fixated on torture? Did he really look like someone who would resort to it? Oddly, she had asked this last question without fear, with nothing but curiosity.

"Have you ever been tortured?"

"Not that I remember," she said.

"I think you'd remember if you had."

She just looked at him and he had the feeling what he had just said was foolish. Remember it? For how long would she remember? A thousand years? Ten thousand? Ten *million?*

Sam didn't know if he should believe her story about not remembering very much, but as he thought about it, it made sense. Maybe they lived forever, barring accident or violence, and they never aged, but their brain was still just a kilo and a half or two of meat. How much did Sam remember of his early childhood? A few confused images, some scenes he wasn't even certain the order of any more. And that was only *thirty* years ago. If he lived to be a hundred, what would he remember? What if he lived to be a *thousand?*

"No, Te'Anna, I do not intend to torture you."

He had no way of knowing what any of her nonverbal behaviors meant, but he had the sense his answer disappointed her. *When she said she was very bored,* he thought, *she wasn't kidding.*

"You must keep some records of your personal history," he said, "or the history of your species, your civilization."

"Yes, we have histories," she said. "I cannot remember the last time I was interested in reading them. They just repeat the same things over and over, endlessly. It is hard to concentrate on them, or even take them very seriously. My own history is encoded in a data-storage organism in P'Daan's palace complex. If we ever return there, I will let you view as much of it as you like. I think it is good I do not remember more. Think how even more boring life would be if I could remember all the things I have done over and over and over, for centuries. Why would I ever do anything more?"

The thought made Sam shudder. The idea of living forever but not being able to remember it had at first struck him as a raw deal, but now he realized the alternative was infinitely worse. To live forever but remember everything you had ever seen, felt, said, thought, or done would soon reduce existence to nothing but endless, pointless repetition. Even with her memory limited, it was no wonder this creature's life had come down to a near-suicidal quest for novelty—*any* novelty, even torture. How many times, he wondered, had boredom driven her to seek out torture? And how many times through the millennia had she been tortured and then forgotten it?

"I appreciate the offer of access to your personal history," he said, "but I'm afraid I won't be able to accept. We destroyed the palace complex under where the meeting took place."

"*Destroyed* it?" she said. "I find that hard to believe. It is heavily protected."

"Well, not heavily enough. We have an orbital

bombardment weapon designed to penetrate deep, armored complexes. To my knowledge this was only the third time it was ever used in combat. It was . . . effective. If you like I can show you the before and after deep radar imagery."

"But the Eye of P'Daan was there," she said.

"Yes, and the two other Guardians that were with you. It does not appear that anyone in the complex survived. I know this must come as a terrible shock."

"You killed *three* Guardians? I cannot remember anyone ever killing a single Guardian . . . *ever.* I cannot remember ever *hearing* of such a thing and I have no idea how any of the other Guardians will react to this. Or how the New People will react, for that matter. They may not have understood that we even can die. Oh, Bitka . . . you people . . . are more interesting than I ever dared *hope!*"

CHAPTER SEVENTEEN

Five days later, **aboard USS *Cam Ranh Bay*,
running dark, outbound to Destie-Seven
18 April 2134 (*sixty-one days after Incident Seventeen*)**

Loptoon Haykuz sat in his stateroom and watched the
incoming comm light flash on and off, on and off. For the
eleven days since the catastrophe on Destie-Four and the
death of the envoy e-Lisyss and the rest of the landing party,
Haykuz had remained locked in his stateroom, opening his
door only for the stewards who delivered his meals. He had
powered down his embedded commlink. There was no one
here he wanted to talk to. The humans had not disturbed
him at first because they understood grief.

Grief had nothing to do with this, however. Haykuz had
hated e-Lisyss, loathed everything about him: his studied
arrogance and casual ignorance, his narrowness of
interests and yet his continued success and mounting
prestige. Were the only requirements for success a
confident assumption of superiority and a willingness to
bludgeon anyone who did not immediately acquiesce?
They were certainly the only capacities Haykuz had seen
in the envoy e-Lisyss, his superior.

His *superior.* Haykuz hated him for that as well, not just his automatic assumption of it so much as the reality. E-Lisyss *was* his superior, in every way, and reminded Haykuz of it periodically, lest it slip his mind. How many careers had Haykuz tried and failed at? Nothing seemed to fit him, but it would have embarrassed the family for the second issue of his sire to turn out to be a nothing, especially after his grandsire had died and his sire became patriarch of the extended household. So, place the young Haykuz second-issue with an old associate, a man almost as successful as the departed grandsire, and ask him to keep the ne'er-do-well in line. Maybe make *something* of him, although Haykuz did not think anyone had any extravagant expectations in that regard.

The comm light continued to blink. He would say he was lying down, that he did not see it. He had taken a sleeping drug and so did not hear the occasional beeps. He knew what it was, knew what it had to be.

Oh, if only e-Lisyss had lived! Then the catastrophe about to engulf and possibly consume his family, the Varoki, every intelligent species in the *Cottohazz* would have been *the envoy's* fault. Wasn't it bad enough Haykuz was going to die along with everyone else on this awful ship? Did he have to die knowing it was now *his* responsibility to avert the extinction of his species, and that once again he would fail? Fail one last spectacular time.

And of course, he would. Of course, because they were not wrong about him. Of all the Varoki on this ship to become the highest surviving official representative of the *Cottohazz* executive council, *why him?*

The comm light continued to blink.

He squinted and powered up his commlink. The ID tag for Captain Bitka appeared—Captain Bitka, who saw through Haykuz's mask of officiousness to the weakling behind it, and had done so without even having to try hard. He opened the link to his new tormenter.

"Yes, Captain."

"Mister Haykuz. I want you to know that, even though there were very real differences between us, I deeply regret the death of Envoy e-Lisyss. All of us have lost friends and shipmates. I won't say I know how you feel, but you have my sympathy."

"Thank you, Captain. I myself must apologize for not communicating with you sooner following the incident. We are in some peril and although I do not know how useful my assistance can be, I owe it to you and everyone else on board to at least offer it."

"Well," the captain said, "that's actually what I was calling you about. I have been talking with our Guardian prisoner almost continuously for the last five days. She's told me something . . . something I don't feel comfortable keeping secret. But I also don't feel comfortable making the decision to share it entirely on my own. I'm not asking you to share the responsibility for the decision, only to listen to the information yourself and give me your reaction."

Haykuz closed his eyes and breathed deeply.

"Mister Haykuz?"

"Yes, Captain. May I have a quarter hour to refresh myself and then meet you?"

★ ★ ★

Haykuz met the captain at the door to the ship's officers' lounge and meal area, which the humans called a "wardroom."

"I want to brief you on what we've found out in the last five days," the captain said, "in a general sense, anyway, before we go in to talk directly with our prisoner."

"Is that really necessary?" Haykuz asked. "For me to speak with it directly, I mean."

"It's a she," the captain said. "I think, for your own peace of mind, you should hear the main item directly from her. I've asked my chief engineer to join us as well. He may think of some questions I haven't. We can wait for him here."

Captain Bitka gestured through the door. Haykuz entered the wardroom and sat at the table the captain indicated.

"I'm having coffee," the captain said. "Would you like something? The stewards can make you some redroot soup."

Every human seemed to think every Varoki loved redroot soup, spent their lives gulping it down, probably because that was the only Varoki beverage most of them had heard of. E-Lisyss would have taken umbrage at the obvious stereotype, would have done so expertly. No one could wring advantage out of an adversary's inadvertent, or even imagined, misstep like e-Lisyss. But why? These people weren't his enemies. The offer of a popular Varoki beverage was actually a thoughtful gesture.

"Mister Haykuz?"

"Oh. My mind was wandering. Yes, Captain, I will have some redroot soup. Thank you."

The soup came in a strange hard white mug without handles. The soup's sharp, salty aroma made his stomach rumble, reminded him he had not eaten the midday meal. He took the mug in both his hands, felt the warmth spread through his palms, and he sipped. Not very good redroot soup, but . . . not all that bad either. He drank half the mug before putting it down.

"We've found out a lot about the Guardians the last few days from Te'Anna, our prisoner," the captain began after sipping his own coffee. "There are still lots of frustrating gaps in our knowledge, though. I don't know if you've heard, but the Guardians are immortal."

"The steward mentioned it. I assumed it was a wild rumor. This is true? You are certain?"

"Dr. Däng is certain, and she explained the genetics to me. Made sense, although I don't think I could explain it back. She could probably answer any questions you've got but, yeah, it's true."

Haykuz thought the captain was telling the truth, but he could not be sure. He had never even been good at knowing when Varoki were lying to him, and he understood that humans were much better at it. He could ask Dr. Däng later, but he disliked talking to her, facing her obvious contempt, and who was to say she wouldn't lie to him as well? Still, he thought this was the truth.

"They must be like gods, then."

"I've never heard a Varoki speak of religion before. You worship gods?"

Haykuz shook his head. "I don't. Some do. Historically many did, but spiritual sensibilities change over time. We do not discuss it often, but in ancient times our notions of immortal and powerful gods were very like your own myths. What is that like, I wonder? To be a god."

"Our prisoner is very interesting to talk to," the captain answered, "but also disconcerting. At first, she struck me as scatterbrained, sort of simpleminded, easily distracted. The more I talk with her, the more impressed I become with her intelligence. Her curiosity is absolutely insatiable, sometimes to the point of being annoying. She absorbs and understands information very quickly, and I think her tendency to mentally wander is the result of a mind interested in everything new.

"She claims not to remember much beyond the last several hundred years, and I believe her. Within that span, however, her memory is extensive and detailed, and she's told us a great deal about the civilization we're facing. It encompasses an enormous swath of territory out along this spiral arm, as many as a thousand star systems, all controlled by Guardians originally. Some of them have died or simply left."

"Died? You said they were immortal."

"Well, they do not age but they can be killed. They also sometimes end their own lives out of boredom. As far as Te'Anna knows, all of the intelligent species inhabiting those worlds were raised up from lower animals through genetic manipulation by the Guardians. The New People in this system, the ones we called Desties, were raised up eight hundred years ago—a little over a thousand Earth years. They believe they are much older than that. The Guardians invented a history for them."

Haykuz thought about that: intelligent beings with

space travel and a complex technological society who had existed *as a species* for only eight hundred years!

"Why?" Haykus asked.

"Why raise them up? As servant races, a labor force."

"Yes, but to what end?"

"Satisfying the material and technological desires of the Guardians," the captain answered, and his mouth twisted as if he tasted something sour.

"That is all? This whole species, the New People, was created to serve the wishes of . . . how many Guardians?"

"Originally just two, named P'Daan and M'Eetos. They were later joined by others. P'Daan and M'Eetos left at different times but there were seven Guardians in the system when we arrived. Three are dead, one is our prisoner, and three more are out there somewhere. A message was sent by their equivalent of a jump courier to the nearest Guardian system once they understood we were not Guardian-raised species, had not in fact ever heard of the Guardians. We still don't know what sort of reaction that may provoke. After what happened on Destie-Four . . . well, it's hard to imagine we're all going to end up pals."

"Why did they bring us here?" Haykuz asked. "Or did they? And if so, how?"

Captain Bitka looked at him for a moment, his expression impossible to read.

"She'll have to tell you that. Here's Lieutenant Ma now. Let's go."

Haykuz had seen images of the alien. Her physical presence was a different matter, but although he found her gaze unsettling, he did not feel intimidated by her. How strange, since he felt intimidated by so many others. He had been told she was intelligent, and he believed it in an intellectual sense, but on an emotional level he could not consider her a person. Sharing the room with her was like sharing it with a large, clever animal, but not at all like an equal, much less a superior, being. That made it easier, at least at first.

"But I have already gone over all this," she complained, rather like a petulant child, Haykuz thought.

"I told you before," the captain said patiently, "Mister Haykuz should hear this from you, in order to judge its truth. He is unlikely to believe it coming from me. If you do this, I will let you ask me any question you like and, provided it does not compromise the safety of my ship, crew, passengers, or home world, I promise to answer it."

She turned her gaze from Captain Bitka to Haykuz.

"No. I want to ask the Varoki a question. That is how you say it, yes? *Varoki?* I will answer his questions, but then afterwards he must answer one of mine."

Haykus felt a thrill run through him, but not of fear so much as excitement. "Which question?"

She did a strange head movement, ducking the chin and stretching her neck, then turned her head to look at him from a slightly different angle. "I do not know yet."

He took a breath and then spoke. "I agree. First my questions. Did you bring us here?"

"Did *I?* No." She cocked her head slightly to the side and looked at him as if she were examining a specimen.

"Some device forced us to come here. Was it a Guardian device?"

She sighed, very much as if growing impatient. "I think it must have been, yes?"

"How was it possible for a Guardian to communicate with our jump drive? We have never, to my knowledge, shared its secret with anyone."

"Oh, you really do not know, do you? You have a Guardian star drive. Its signature is unmistakable, which is why the New People showed no alarm at your arrival. As to who brought you here and why, I have a theory. Would you like to hear it?"

Haykuz sat for a moment trying to understand what she had just told him. How could they have a Guardian star drive in this human ship? He ignored her and turned to the ship's engineer.

"Who . . . who manufactured this jump drive, Lieutenant Ma?"

"AZ Kagataan," he answered immediately. "The documentation says core was manufactured thirty-one months ago on Hazzakatu, delivered to Earth, and then installed in *Cam Ranh Bay* at the International Space Dock in Earth orbit twenty-seven months ago. We've gone over every record we have, and it all checks out. I can't actually examine the jump core, because of all the security traps you people put on it, but from the outside it looks like every other Varoki-built drive I've ever worked with."

Haykuz looked back at the alien.

"This officer confirms that the drive was built by the Varoki trading house AZ Kagataan."

"I do not dispute that," she said. "But it was Guardian-designed."

"Perhaps independent discovery . . ." Haykuz began, but she leaned forward and opened her eyes even wider.

"Then how did our device bring you here? Coincidental discovery of a scientific principle is quite believable. Coincidental invention of the entire mathematical language which controls the operation of the device itself? *Impossible.* Each of our drives has an identity tag in its control code, unique to the Guardian owner. I have not examined yours, but the New People detected the ownership tag associated with M'Eetos, one of the two original Guardian patrons of this star system. Would you like to hear my theory *now,* little Varoki-thing?"

Haykuz stared at her but hardly saw her. His mind was too full of speculation, calculation, warring possibilities. "Yes," he finally said.

"Somewhat over four hundred years ago, M'Eetos left this star system. I do not know why; I think it was before I came. I remember seeing M'Eetos, but I can no longer be certain my memory is not of hologram images. It is said he became restless. Somewhat later, P'Daan wished his return and so sent out a series of remote devices which would scan possible star systems for traces of the identity tag of his drive and then reprogram it to return to this realm system, which you call Destination. Your star drive is obviously a slavish copy of the one in M'Eetos's vessel. One of P'Daan's devices must have arrived in your system, scanned you, found the looked-for tag, and completed its mission.

"I believe that answers all of your questions. Is that so?"

"Yes," Haykuz heard himself say, although he could not

remember deciding to speak. He certainly had no further questions to ask, only answers to absorb and make sense of.

"Then I will now ask my question. When we raise up a race, we often invent a history for them stretching back into antiquity. Some of us are better at it than others. I have heard M'Eetos particularly enjoyed that aspect of the process."

She leaned forward and stretched her neck out until her face came very close to his, her large gray eyes seeming to see through his flesh and bone all the way into his soul. When she spoke, it came out as an insistent whisper.

"None of the other races of your *Cottohazz* had any evidence of your existence prior to three hundred of your years ago. How certain are you that *four* hundred years ago M'Eetos did not raise your people up from some swamp-dwelling creatures, and simply invent your supposed history?"

CHAPTER EIGHTEEN

One day later, aboard USS *Cam Ranh Bay,*
running dark, outbound to Destie-Seven
19 April 2134 (*sixty-two days after Incident
Seventeen*)

Sam's commlink vibrated as he left the lift and began walking through the habitat wheel to the passenger meeting. He pushed his pointless ruminations about Cassandra aside and squinted up the ID tag: Haykuz. When the Varoki official left Te'Anna's quarters yesterday, he'd seemed in shock. All he had said to Sam was, "We will have to speak later." Maybe this was it.

"Mister Haykuz. I am glad you commed me. How are you feeling?"

I am sure you must know that I am shaken, Captain. The revelation concerning the jump drive, and then that creature's insinuation . . . all very troubling. I see you released the summary of information concerning the drives to the passengers and crew. After much thought, I confess I believe her account of the origin of the drive. I see no other explanation which matches all of the facts as we know them. I agree with your decision to share that knowledge.

"Thank you, Mister Haykuz. I think if the crew and passengers are going to help us think this through, they need to have all the facts."

Yes, Captain. I appreciate that you did not share her suggestion that we Varoki . . . are somehow less than we had thought. I must ask you, Captain. Do you believe that about us?

"I believe the part about the origin of the jump drive. But the part about you being raised from a lower species by genetic manipulation? No, I don't believe that. I think she was just messing with your head. I think she likes doing that, seeing what it takes to get under our skins. But what difference does it make? How you got to be who you are doesn't change anything. You still are who you've always been."

Ah, but in a sense, we are not, Captain. Even if we have independently evolved, we have always seen ourselves as the benefactors of the other five intelligent species, the only ones capable of inventing the jump drive. Now it seems all of that is a lie. I will tell you, Captain, if we return to the Cottohazz, *a large part of my people will never accept this as truth. They will dismiss any evidence as an insidious fabrication. Technological supremacy is too important to our self-image to abandon.*

"It didn't keep you from believing it," Sam said.

Nothing is very important to my self-image. We will speak again later, Captain Bitka.

Sam couldn't even imagine a *Cottohazz* without the Varoki on top. How would the other species take it? Even without a war, the legal ramifications were staggering. Did all those Varoki star drive builders owe three hundred years of royalty payments back to everyone who'd paid them under false pretenses? Somebody must have committed fraud at some point. Or maybe some sort of reparations payment. Who knew? It was going to be a hell of a new world, assuming they managed to get back with the news.

Sam heard the babble of voices before he got to the meeting area. Almost a hundred people, most of the civilian passengers, filled the broad corridor in front of the enlisted crew's exercise room on Wheel Deck Two, the inner layer of quarters and living area on the habitat wheel. They filled it with their physical presence and with the nervous murmur of their voices and with the faint odor of their fear. He made his way through the press, acknowledging their greetings.

As always, the geometry of a habitat wheel struck Sam with its oddness but also its unintended utility in a moment like this. The corridor seemed to rise up to each side and eventually merge with the ceiling. Today that meant he would not have to stand on a platform to be seen by the crowd; everyone could see everyone else's faces, as if standing in an amphitheater tipped onto its side.

He looked at their faces and he saw fear and anger, not much hope. He should have done this sooner. Addresses over the commlink network and recorded briefing summaries weren't enough for people whose fates were entirely in his hands, his and his crew's.

Ensign Clarence Day waited for him with a data pad, going over his notes. Day had started as their "handler" for the VIPs, but had grown into liaison officer to the civilian passengers in general. No one told him to; he'd just seen the need and filled it. Sam recalled that he and Running-Deer had picked Day for the job because he was "entertaining and nonessential." They'd been about half right.

"I've screened the questions, sir," Day said, "and I've tried to pick ones that are representative. Per your orders, I haven't skipped the tough ones."

"Good," Sam said, "not that I like tough questions, but we don't want them going away without the answers they care most about. Okay, let's get started."

Ensign Day raised his hands above his head and whistled, one loud, sharp blast. The low babble of conversation died out.

"Can I have everyone's attention? Good. Thank you for showing up for our first Q and A with Captain Bitka, and thanks to those of you who submitted questions. When I call on you I'm going to cue your commlink through the wall speakers in this corridor so everyone can hear, okay? If English isn't a comfortable language, don't worry. Just use the language you're most comfortable with. I'm running it through autotrans so everyone will hear the question in English. For those of you whose English isn't very strong, you might want to reset your own commlinks as well, but you probably have, right? Otherwise I'm just going *blah-blah-blah* up here.

"Okay, first question is from Alice Tan Li. Please raise your hand so everyone can see you."

The woman appeared to be Chinese, in her fifties, or perhaps sixties if she had taken care of herself. She wore a tailored suit of elegant cut in a tasteful gray with iridescent panels in the body of the jacket, fashionable among business types. Her drawn face and disheveled grey-streaked hair, loosely confined in a bun, stood in stark contrast to her clothing.

"My question is how are we going to get home?" She asked the question in Chinese, and her words sounded abrupt and angry, but the truth was Chinese always sounded that way to Sam.

"The short answer is, we're still working on that," he said. He heard groans of disappointment and looks of irritation and disbelief. That made sense. It was easier for them to think he was holding back than that there was no better answer. "What I can tell you is what we know, where we're going, and what we're going to do when we get there.

"Here's what we know. The jump drive we've always thought was made by the Varoki was invented by the Guardians a long time ago. We don't know how the Varoki got hold of it, but that's why the Guardians were able to reprogram our jump drive. We think they did it because one of their Guardians was missing—the one who had the jump drive all of ours appear to have been copied from— and they were trying to get him back, not us.

"Where are we going? We're currently coasting out toward the system's largest gas giant. We've matched course with an automated bulk carrier and are hugging it very closely to mask our signature. We're also running in low-emission mode with our thermal shroud deployed and faced back toward the largest remaining source of communication and spacecraft traffic, which is Destie-Three. For those of you unfamiliar with a thermal shroud, it is a hemispherical parasol of light composites, honeycombed with coolant lines filled with liquid helium. It traps all of our thermal emissions in that direction, pumps the heat back to our aft radiators, and discharges it there. It is an effective means of reducing our thermal signature to nil, at least in that one direction. As near as we can tell, they've lost us. We are off their scopes.

"What are we going to do? It will take us about three weeks to get to the gas giant. There are two inhabited moons. From our Guardian prisoner we know the smaller of the two moons is the administrative center controlling the facilities which build and maintain spacecraft in this system. We intend to land Marines there and take control of the complex. If they knew enough to screw our jump drive up, somebody there has to know enough to unscrew it."

"Do you trust that Guardian you took prisoner?" someone shouted.

"No," Sam said. "So far, we've confirmed everything she's told us, to the extent we can double-check it. That doesn't mean we're letting our guard down."

"*Madamoiselle* Sophie Apollinaire, I think you're up," Ensign Day said.

Younger than many of the passengers, Sam thought, perhaps mid-twenties, casually but expensively dressed. Not an established professional, but perhaps the daughter of one.

"We've been hearing about the Varoki stealing the star drive," she said, "and that is why we're in all this trouble. Why can't we just give the Varoki we have to the Guardians and ask them to let us go? *We* didn't do anything wrong."

Sam saw nods of agreement, heard a low mutter of assent and some anger.

"This thing about the jump drive is big news alright," Sam said. "It's going to mean big changes back home, once we get there with the word. I don't have any idea how it will all shake out, politically, economically, militarily. I don't think it's going to be easy or pretty, but we'll get through it somehow.

"But I'll tell you this: the Varoki passengers on this ship aren't any more responsible for what's happened to us than you are, ma'am. Just like you, they were told a lie from birth, and just like you and me and everyone standing here, they believed it and lived their lives accordingly.

"No one's turning any of my passengers or crew over to the Guardians, not while I'm alive. Next question."

"Mister Mahaan Singh is next," Ensign Day said.

Singh was dressed a lot like the Chinese lady, business formal—most of the passengers were prosperous, successful artists or businesspeople. He also wore a turban and the tightly wound beard of a Sikh. Singh had a lean and particularly polished look, his face carefully blank.

"Is it true this was all just a misunderstanding? You already said they weren't interested in us but some missing Guardian. Could we have avoided violence with a better negotiator?"

"Are you a negotiator, sir?"

"Yes I am, and I am a very good one, too."

"Well, we're actually short a negotiator at the moment. Perhaps you will volunteer to accompany the next landing party which tries to communicate directly with them."

Some of the color drained from his face and he leaned back. "Well, it's all different now that you went ahead and started a war."

"Yes, it is, but that's the situation we have to deal with. To answer your original question, no, sir, this was not just a misunderstanding. We've learned the Guardians routinely eat what they call offerings. They did not tell us of their so-called custom, not as an oversight, but because they do not care whether we understand or not. They think we are no more noteworthy than livestock. Mister Singh, I've never heard of a negotiation between a pig and a butcher ending well for the pig. Have you?"

"I think you're oversimplifying," he said.

"Well then, come along next time and show us what you got."

"Or just shut the fuck up," someone shouted from the crowd. A murmured ripple of agreement was met with scattered angry pushback and then a rising swell of voices made inarticulate by too much pent-up fear and frustration.

"That's enough!" Sam shouted. "I'm not here to argue, I'm here to answer questions. Who's next?"

Lieutenant Koichi Ma sat for the second time with the alien prisoner, this time on his own.

Yesterday's session had changed everything he knew about the political and scientific order of things in the *Cottohazz.* He'd never been much interested in starships. Sure, he'd gone the Naval ROTC route to help with college, and then got called back to active duty when things started heating up, but his heart had never been in crewing a starship. Jump drives belonged to the Varoki. Humans could lease them, use them, but never study them, understand them, *re-engineer* them. Ask an engineer to operate a machine but forbid him from making it work better and you will have an unhappy, frustrated engineer, and none more so than Koichi Ma. Just a waste of his time.

But now...now he wanted to go back and pull the jump core—*his* jump core—open and see what made it tick. He couldn't, of course, but he could do the next best thing.

"I'd love to talk about the star drive your people invented," Ma said to the alien, "but there's something else we need to cover first. The captain has asked me to figure out everything I can about the weaponry we're facing. We got hit by a beam weapon from the planet we call Destie-Four."

"Oh, yes," she said. "Fortunately for you it seems to have done very little damage."

"It killed eight people," Ma said. Te'Anna simply looked at him as if he'd agreed instead of contradicting her. As Ma thought about it, eight *people* dead probably was not very much damage from her point of view. Hardly worth mentioning.

"Our instruments tell us it was fired from the far side of the planet," he said, "fired *through* it. Are our instruments wrong?"

"I know nothing of your instruments, Lieutenant Ma."

That was literally true but not what he was asking. He couldn't tell if she simply misunderstood or was deliberately prevaricating, playing with him.

"Is it possible the weapon fired at us passed through Destie-Four?" he asked.

"I do not know what was fired at you, but we do have a weapon which matches your description. Yes, it can be fired through a planet."

"How does it do that? Does it damage the planet?"

"No, of course it does not damage the planet. What sort of a defensive weapon would that be? Really, Lieutenant Ma, you seem intelligent and yet sometimes your questions are very foolish."

"Perhaps you mistake my ignorance for foolishness," he said.

"No, I never make that mistake. What do you call the subatomic particle which transfers the nuclear force between elements of the nucleus?" she asked.

"Do you mean the strong or weak nuclear force?"

"There is only one. What you call the weak force is simply a special case of electromagnetism. What particle transfers what you call the strong force?"

"We call that particle a meson," he said.

"Ah, yes. The weapon which fired at you is a meson accelerator."

A *meson* accelerator, he thought. That didn't make any sense. Sure, a meson could go right through a planet, or anything else, without affecting it. So how could it damage them? For that matter, how did it even get to them? Mesons only lasted a couple microseconds before decaying, and when they did they mostly produced photons.

Photons. *Light*. That streak of light they saw—that's probably what a stream of mesons would look like when they decayed.

Ma looked up and saw Te'Anna's unblinking gray eyes focused on him. Was this a test? Maybe some sort of a red herring to confuse him? He could just ask her, but if this really was the weapon . . .

Okay, accelerate a beam of mesons. As long as they're still mesons they go through anything, but when they decay they decay into photons, and what was a laser but a coherent stream of photons? If they could control the wavelength of the decaying photons, make that light stream coherent, they had a real weapon.

But if the particle only lasts two or three microseconds, even at the speed of light you couldn't get much more range than a kilometer. That weapon hit them from a lot farther away than that, thousands of times farther. How could it, if you only had a couple . . .

"*Oh!*" Ma said out loud. "Relativistic velocity."

Te'Anna cocked her head to the side for a moment.

"Elastic time velocity, we call it," she said.

At that close to light speed, the subjective time of the meson stream slowed way down. As far as it was concerned, the mesons still only lasted a couple microseconds. From the outside, though, it seemed as if they hung around a lot longer, long enough to reach out and smack *Cam Ranh Bay*. How do you determine where the mesons decay into a shaft of photons? By varying the speed of the particle stream, and so slowing the decay.

"Huh," Ma said. "That's pretty smart."

"I imagine it appears so to you," Te'Anna replied. "You are easily impressed."

Koichi Ma laughed, and he saw it caught her by surprise. Maybe she could crawl around in that poor

Varoki assistant envoy's head and mess him up, but Koichi had grown up with a crazy Filipino mail-order bride for a stepmother, and he'd come through that experience reasonably intact. This Guardian was going to have to bring a lot more game if she wanted to fuck with *his* head.

"For the decaying mesons to produce a laser—a coherent stream of light—they all have to decay to photons of exactly the same wavelength. How do you manage that?"

"I doubt you would be capable of understanding," she said, looking away with her chin raised in disdain.

Then Ma remembered something, and he grinned. "Ah, but you *can't* get them all to decay to exactly the same wavelength, can you? If you could, there would be no visible signature in vacuum, same as any other laser. But there's that glow—some of the photons come out noncoherent. You're not quite the hotshot engineers you think, are you?"

She held her pose for a moment and then looked down. "I do not know. I do not remember those details of the design. Weapons have never interested me very much, at least not that I can recall."

"Okay, Te'Anna, maybe you're foggy on the weapons but you seem to know a lot of physics. Now why don't you tell me how your interstellar drive works?"

She sat motionless and then spoke.

"But you are the engineer. Do you mean to say . . . you do not *know*?"

"Varoki trade secret," Ma answered.

She shivered and then ran her fingers up through the feathers on her neck and head, fluffing them so they stood out from her head in wild disorder. Then she leaned forward and down so her face was level with his and quite close.

"Oh, Lieutenant Ma, I will very much enjoy telling *you* that!"

CHAPTER NINETEEN

Seven days later, aboard USS *Cam Ranh Bay,*
running dark, outbound to Destie-Seven
26 April 2134 (*sixty-nine days after Incident
Seventeen*)

"Captain's on the bridge," Quartermaster First Ortega called out as Sam floated through the bridge hatch.

Sam took in the scene with a glance: Lieutenant Bohannon in command chair, Ortega at the helm, Sensor Tech Second Laghari at Tac One, the other bridge stations empty. The three looked tense and alert but without any sign of panic. Bohannon, the White Watch OOD, hadn't sounded general quarters; she'd just called him to the bridge, so the news might not be that bad.

"Sorry to disturb you, sir," she said as she unbuckled her restraints, "but I thought you should see this."

"No need to apologize, Ms. Bohannon. Fill me in." He shoved off toward the command chair.

"Sir, the ship is at Readiness Condition Three, Material Condition Bravo, on course for Destie-Seven in low-emission status. Power ring is at sixty-three percent charge, reactor cold, thermal shroud deployed, sensors passive. No acceleration or course change this watch. At 0237 Zulu we detected a jump emergence signature and seven minutes later began picking up broadcast communication from it, all in Destie, or I guess it's the Guardian language. Anyway, it's one of theirs."

"Very well, Lieutenant, I relieve you."

"Captain has the bridge," she said as she pushed herself up and then to the left to settle into Comm One. Sam strapped himself into the command chair and looked around. He was again reminded of how different the *Bay's* bridge felt from *Puebla's*. A destroyer's bridge was small, cramped, and with a lot of dark, dingy corners that looked like they might harbor spiderwebs if there had been such a thing on a spacecraft. Even though the *Bay's* bridge wasn't that much bigger, it *felt* roomier, more open. Usually it was brighter, but all the working spaces were at reduced lighting levels to save power, and the crew's faces were lit mostly by their instrument displays.

"How far is that ship from us?" Sam asked.

"Forty-six million klicks, sir," Bohannon answered, "closer to the system primary than we are, probably aiming to match orbit with Destie-Four and assess the damage."

That last bit was guesswork, but it made sense to Sam.

"I take it these comms were not directed at us."

"That's right, sir, but they're about us. Somebody wants to know what the hell is going on here, what happened on Destie-Four. They're getting a lot of confused chatter back, some from Destie-Four itself, some from the other inner worlds, and some from the two inhabited moons of Destie-Seven. It's going to take them a while to sort everything out, and it will take us a while to sort through all that comm chatter, but we're capturing everything we can."

"Aside from our Buran friend Abanna Zhaquaan," Sam said, "you've listened to more of these people than anyone. What do you think?"

She huffed out a sigh and pursed her lips in thought before replying.

"I think they'll switch to tight beam pretty soon, and we'll lose the thread of the conversation, but from what I've heard so far, it sounds like someone has shown up to kick ass and take names."

Sam thought so as well. "Well, at forty-six million kilometers, we've got a pretty good head start on them, even if they do figure out where we are and what we're up to."

"They could do an in-system jump, sir," Bohannon said. "Like the Varoki did in the last war. It's risky, but it could get them to Destie-Seven way before us."

They could, indeed, Sam thought. But *would* they? He thought about it and then shook his head.

"We'll see, but I don't think that's gonna happen, Comm. For us, for the Varoki, for anyone in the *Cottohazz* it's a risk, but, in some circumstances, it's justified. Jumping in or near the plane of the ecliptic could have you come out in the same space as some little rock, and then you get an annihilation event. But if the stakes are big enough, maybe it's worth the risk.

"But if you're immortal, Bohannon, it's a little different. See, for them the risk is actually higher, because if you decide to use this as a tactic, and you keep doing it for a couple thousand years, you're pretty certain to find that little rock eventually. Immortality is definitely a two-edged sword."

"Our prisoner took a pretty wild risk letting us capture her, sir," Bohannon answered.

"Yeah, that's absolutely true, but I think there are two kinds of Guardians: the ones desperate to find something to make life interesting enough to be worth living, and those who already have it. Our Te'Anna is one of the desperate variety, but I think this P'Daan guy knows exactly what he wants."

"Active sensor radiation!" the sensor tech in the TAC One chair called out, voice rising in alarm.

"Sir, should I begin evasive maneuvers?" Ortega called from Ops One.

"No!" Sam shouted. "Everybody calm down. We're hugging this bulk cargo carrier for a reason. TAC, what's the signal strength like on the incoming sensor radiation?"

"Very weak, sir. I'd say it's pretty range-attenuated."

"Okay. Lesson one, folks: if you're playing possum, don't twitch. If we maneuver now they'll see us for sure. If we stay put, hopefully we'll blend into the return echo from the cargo carrier, or look like a false echo. If they detect us, we'll see them react soon enough. For now, stay cool.

"TAC, have you got any sort of read on the size or configuration of that new ship? Lieutenant Ma says that meson accelerator they use as a planetary defense weapon is probably too bulky to mount in a ship. Says it needs a really long accelerator tunnel."

"Sir," the sensor tech said, "the bandit has his reactor

lit up, so I'm getting pretty good data on his configuration. He looks to be over a kilometer long."

Bohannon whistled. "That is one big fucking ship, sir."

Yes, it was, and probably big enough to hold one of those meson accelerators. Sam activated his commlink and pinged Ka'Deem Brook.

"Yes, sir?"

"XO, we have a little situation, nothing too serious yet, but I'm going to Readiness Condition Two, and I'd like you to relieve me on the bridge. I'm going to have another chat with our prisoner."

"Do you find me attractive, Captain Bitka?" Te'Anna turned in her chair and looked at him with her enormous unblinking gray eyes.

It wasn't how Sam expected the conversation to start, but then he never got exactly what he expected from their alien prisoner. He sat down himself before answering.

"Some species come closer to matching our aesthetic standards than do others. Yours has many attractive characteristics: you are tall, graceful, well-proportioned by our standards, and large-eyed. Your feathers remind us of human hair, at least your head feathers do."

She ran her fingers through her neck and head feathers, fluffing them out, and Sam realized that was a preening gesture.

"But do you find me sexually attractive?" she said. "Do you find me alluring?"

Sam shifted in his chair. *Alluring?* Was she hitting on him?

"Um . . . you may remember from a previous conversation that I try not to think of people in my chain of command in those terms."

"But I am not in your chain of command."

"You are a prisoner, and that's even more problematic."

Te'Anna cocked her head to the side and looked at him in what might have been exasperation. "Eh. You have so many *rules!* How do you remember them all? I may not always be your prisoner, so consider the question hypothetically."

Why was he suddenly so uncomfortable in her presence? Was it because there *was* a certain sensuality in her shape and the grace of her movements? Or was it the combination of that realization with the memory of her eating the still-warm flesh carved from Mikko Running-Deer's body?

"Look, I really don't have time for—"

"Make time," she said, her suddenly sharp voice cutting him off, and she sat up straighter. "These are not idle questions. It is a subject of much interest and importance to me. Did your little biologist-thing tell you about me? About my sexuality?"

"She said you had no actual reproductive organs, but that you had those sexual organs associated with pleasure, what she called the fun ones."

"The fun ones, yes, that is a good description. What else?"

"That's all," Sam said, and he felt thankful that was the truth. At the moment, it was more than he wanted to know.

"Oh," Te'Anna said with a tone in her voice he was

beginning to associate with disappointment. "She left out the most interesting part. I wonder if she noticed. Proportional to our size, we have over twice as much erectile tissue as any species we have ever encountered. So you see, when I *do* think about sex, my thoughts can be quite intense." As if to emphasize the point she shifted in her chair, moving her weight from one hip to the other and then back again.

"Naturally," Sam said. "Must be tough, stuck here all alone."

"Not in the sense you mean. I am an excellent lover, and I love myself more than any other."

"Well . . . that's swell, then. Is there a point here?"

"Think of it as my natural curiosity as a student of intelligent life. You come from a culture which includes six intelligent species coexisting with the pretense of equality. Is there no interspecies sex?"

"Yes, there is," Sam said, suddenly aware his face was turning a shade of pink. After all he had gone through in the uBakai War, and now this involuntary odyssey across a thousand unexplored light-years of interstellar void, he thought he could take pretty much anything in stride. Of course, that was before he had begun having regular chats with a cannibalistic alien overlord preoccupied with sex, possibly with him. "Look, I'm not interested in talking about this anymore, okay? Something *important* has happened, something which will actually interest you."

Te'Anna leaned back and looked away with what might have been a shrug of satisfaction. How much of this was just to put him off balance, he wondered. "Very well," she said, "I perceive your patience wears thin. But we *will* come back to this later. Now ask your burning question."

Sam picked up his data pad, brought up the image of the Guardian who had been doing most of the broadcasting, and held it up for Te'Anna to see.

"Know this guy?"

"Oh! How insulting! He would not come back to me, but he has returned to deal with *you*, Bitka? The New People must be beside themselves with joy. P'Daan, their creator, has returned."

Sam felt the vibration at the base of his neck from an incoming comm. He squinted and saw Ka'Deem Brook's ID tag.

"Yes, XO," Sam said.

Sir, we have more jump emergence.

"Another ship?"

Seven more, sir. All of them big ones.

Sam felt lightheaded, a sensation almost immediately replaced with a certainty that he would not see Cassandra again, that whatever unanswered questions he had about their relationship would remain unanswered. The fact he would die not knowing seemed as bad as the prospect of death itself.

CHAPTER TWENTY

Six days later, aboard USS *Cam Ranh Bay,* running dark, outbound to Destie-Seven
2 May 2134 (*twenty-five days into hostilities, seventy-five days after Incident Seventeen*)

Lieutenant Homer Alexander, officer of the deck of Red Watch, sat in the command chair on the bridge of *Cam Ranh Bay* and thought about how drawing closer to people was different than drawing closer to things. As you got closer to a thing—a building, a mountain, a sign—it grew larger in your view. But the closer you got to a person, the smaller they seemed, at least the ones you had first noticed from a distance, the ones who seemed larger than life: politicians, holovid stars . . . war heroes.

When he first learned Bitka was to be their new captain, Homer could hardly believe it. Sam Bitka, a reservist just like him, a tactical officer just like him, and the man who, due to casualties and the emergencies of war, had risen to command his own destroyer and become the acknowledged tactical genius behind the victories of Destroyer Squadron Two in its desperate defense of K'tok in the uBakai War. *That* Sam Bitka was going to be their skipper! But whatever Homer had expected, the reality had been very different.

As if summoned by Homer's thoughts, the captain floated through the bridge hatch and Homer hid a scowl. *What the hell did he want?* He made Homer nervous—all that prowling around the ship and always with that calm smile, as if he hadn't a care in the world, as if . . . as if things were like they had been before.

"Any developments, TAC?"

"No change, sir. They're still deployed in four two-ship elements: one element in Destie-Four orbit, the other three headed for different parts of the system. One of them is outbound toward us."

"Methodical search," the captain said, and the way he said it, as if it were some gem of wisdom worth passing on, made all the fear and despair and resentment in Homer bubble to the surface, and he suddenly didn't care what he said, what the captain thought, what the goddamned Navy thought, or what came next, because he knew, *knew*, that he and all the rest of them were going to die here.

"That's right, sir, methodical search, just like you said yesterday and the day before, and the day before that."

Homer heard the sarcasm and ridicule in his voice. Had he meant that to bubble out into the open? Well, there it was. Bob DaSilva at Ops One looked at the captain, eyes wide, as if he expected an explosion. Chief Bermudez sitting beside him in Tac One just shook her head and studied her instruments. The captain floated near the hatch looking at Homer but his smile never wavered. After a moment, he looked at Ensign DaSilva in the Ops One chair.

"Mister DaSilva, you are qualified to stand as officer of the deck, aren't you?"

"Yes, sir. I completed the training routine when we were still a week out from Destination."

"Had a chance at OOD yet?"

"No, sir."

"Shame to have all that training go to waste. Lieutenant Alexander, would you please surrender the bridge to Ensign DaSilva?"

Homer rattled off the ritual ship status report—which of course DaSilva already knew since he'd been sitting in Ops One the whole watch—and he turned over the command chair. The captain gestured for Homer to follow him.

Bitka led the way to his day cabin four frames aft of the bridge. After he clipped his tether to his desk he gestured to Homer to clip his to the other side. Somewhere on the brief trip back, the captain's smile had disappeared.

"Now spill it, Lieutenant. What's eating you?"

Homer looked at him and suddenly didn't know where to start. That every order the captain gave seemed to diminish Homer somehow? Give further proof that he was less a man than the captain, less than the man he wanted to be? They were within a year or two of the same age, both had successful civilian careers, both had been called back to service, but Bitka had fought through the war and Homer had spent it on training exercises in the Solar System. The *Bay* had even been on the wrong side of the Solar System, in far Saturn orbit, when the uBakai fleet made its punishing hit-and-run raid on Earth's orbital facilities.

But what ate at him most was that if their places had been swapped, he didn't think he would have risen to the challenge the way Bitka had. He couldn't know for certain, sometimes he thought he would have, but when he was alone and he closed his eyes and looked inside, he didn't think so. He just couldn't see himself doing those things. Or he could, but the images seemed like daydreams, scenes from an adventure holovid, not reality.

Was that what Mikko had thought as well?

"Look, Lieutenant," the captain said, finally breaking the silence, "I know you took the XO's death very hard. All of us did, but your feelings for her went beyond . . . what most of us felt for her as a shipmate. I didn't understand that until afterwards. I'm very sorry for your loss."

"She never understood either," Homer said. "She never noticed how I felt, and you know why? Because of *you*. She was in love with you, and you never even saw it."

"You're letting your own disappointment run away with you," the captain said. "Running-Deer and I had a professional relationship, and the start of a real friendship, but nothing more. Don't be a fool, Alexander."

Homer felt his face flush with anger and he leaned forward in the chair.

"*I'm* the fool? You think I'm imagining it? Hell, everyone on the ship knew she was crazy about you, except you. Ask any officer if you don't believe me."

Homer saw a look of surprise come over the captain's face and he knew this last shot had struck home.

"Come on . . . she hardly *spoke* to me at first," Bitka said.

"Tongue-tied," Homer answered. "That's why she

never noticed how I felt: she only had eyes for you. Maybe it wouldn't have worked out between us, but we should have had the chance to find out. Just the chance, that's all I wanted. Now I'll never know."

Something changed in the captain's expression when Homer said those last words.

"What you just said, say that again."

He said it not with anger, but more curiosity or wonder in his voice. Homer looked at him a moment before answering.

"What hurts most is never knowing what might have been, never finding out whether or not it would have worked."

"And that's what you can't get past," the captain said, nodding.

"That's right."

The captain looked away, his forehead creased in concentration, and he sat there, silent and lost in thought for what seemed a long time but probably wasn't much more than a minute. A minute of silence between two people who have been trading heated words can seem like a very long time. Finally, the captain turned back and appeared almost surprised to find him still there.

"Mister Alexander, you are being foolish. If it's any consolation, you're not the only one on this ship in that condition."

"Captain, I—"

"Shut up and listen for a minute, Homer. I'm sorry I never noticed Mikko's feelings for me. I can be fairly oblivious at times and I've been preoccupied with a broken love affair of my own . . . too preoccupied. I see that now. I think it's gotten in the way of doing my job. Well, that stops right now.

"As to Mikko, I'll tell you this: whatever infatuation she may have felt for me before we got to know each other, I think it was maturing into a genuine friendship. It was for me, anyway. I miss her a lot.

"I lost someone in the uBakai War—not a lover but someone I was coming to love. I can't tell you how to deal with loss like this, but I can tell you others have gone through it and come out the other side. I believe you can, too."

Homer floated in zero gee with his eyes closed, trying to regain a sense of physical and emotional equilibrium. He knew the captain was right. He didn't hate him any less, but he knew he was right. Well, hate was too strong a word. What *did* he feel? Hurt. Just hurt, and he wanted the hurt to stop. He closed his eyes even tighter.

"When something won't let go of you, sir, when it fills your head and won't leave room for anything else, keeps getting bigger and bigger, like it's going to overwhelm you . . . what do you do?"

"Well, for me what made the difference was my responsibility to the people relying on me to get them home alive. That's what keeps me going here as well, TAC. You need something to think about and work on, something really important, and I've got just the thing. When you get off watch, get together with Lieutenant Ma. He's got the best handle on how that meson gun of theirs works. Lash up some best estimates of its range and lethality, and a guess at what it will take to kill one of those Guardian long ships."

Homer thought about putting together some simulations of Guardian long ships, estimating damage, range of engagement, but after a moment he shook his head.

"Okay, I'm with you on this, sir, but we don't know enough about those ships to do anything but guess. We can work out something on the armament, but if you want me to show how to kill those ships, we need more than a guess. What about our prisoner? From what Ma said, she has a pretty good head for technical detail, but he didn't know what to ask beyond the big science things. You're a Tac-head, sir. You know what information we need. Can you talk to her? Maybe you can get something we can use to dummy up a simulation."

The captain unhooked his tether, which Homer took as his cue to do the same.

"I haven't had a chat with Te'Anna yet today, and I'd planned on trying to ask her what makes this guy P'Daan tick. I'll see what she can tell us about technical performance of those ships, too. You're close enough to the end of your watch you may as well get some lunch. Let Ensign DaSilva finish his first watch and turn the ship over to his relief. Do him good.

"Thank you for speaking so honestly with me, Homer. I guess I needed to talk this through myself. But just so we understand each other, Lieutenant, if you ever again pull a stunt like you just did on the bridge, you will spend the rest of this cruise under arrest for insubordination and conduct injurious to good order. Are we clear on that?"

"Yes, sir. I'm very sorry, sir."

CHAPTER TWENTY-ONE

One hour later, aboard USS *Cam Ranh Bay,*
running dark, outbound to Destie-Seven
2 May 2134 (*twenty-five days into hostilities,*
seventy-five days after Incident Seventeen)

Sam thought about his conversation with Homer
Alexander on the short walk from the lift to Te'Anna's
confinement cabin. It was a good walk, if stripping away
your self-illusions is good, and Sam thought that it was,
uncomfortable and embarrassing as the process might be.
Here he was, trying to counsel the officer he considered
the least mature and emotionally developed of his senior
officers, and what did he find himself looking at? A
goddamned mirror! Well, maybe not exactly, but close
enough. He managed not to laugh at himself as he walked,
but he couldn't keep the grin from his face.

"Unusual odor in there today, Captain," the Marine
corporal in charge of the guard detail said. "We checked
it out and Dr. Däng says it's harmless. Some herbs the
alien's burning, like incense. You suppose she's smoking
dope and trying to cover it up, sir?"

"Every Marine's a comedian," Sam said.

"Yes, sir," he answered with a grin.

Sam smelled the unusual aroma in Te'Anna's stateroom as soon as they cracked the hatch. It was musky, not unpleasant, but you couldn't help but notice it. A variety of different strains drifted through the main odor, some alien, some vaguely familiar, one . . . pungent, so sharp he could almost taste it on his tongue, and he knew it at once, how Cassandra had smelled and tasted after sex. *And he remembered her tasting him, kissing and licking his shoulders and neck, saying he must have sailed because she could taste the sea brine on him—*

The Marine guards closed the door behind him with a click, and his mind was suddenly back in the Guardian's stateroom. It took him a moment to get his bearings, but only a moment, and he realized that had he experienced this vivid odor an hour ago, before his talk with Homer Alexander, the recollection might have overpowered him. He wasn't sure why it was different now, but it was.

He took a seat opposite the Guardian and examined her carefully. She sat turned slightly to the side in her chair so she had to turn her head to look at him. She leaned casually against the chair's back, a study in confident grace and elegance.

"What does P'Daan want?" Sam said.

"The same as I and every other Guardian wants," Te'Anna answered, "a reason to go on living. It was a long time ago now, but I remember that so long as I knew them, M'Eetos was P'Daan's reason for living. M'Eetos' imagination, creativity, flair with which he undertook everything he did, entranced P'Daan. M'Eetos *was* special. He seemed to . . . *glow* with possibility.

"When M'Eetos left, P'Daan changed. He became darker, harder. Finding M'Eetos became his new obsession, his new reason for living. Avenging the devastation which you visited on the New People may be another. He should be grateful to you for providing it, for only these passions keep us alive. He may in fact understand that, but I doubt it. He has never been terribly introspective, at least by our standards. His lens seems directed entirely outward."

She paused and ruffled the feathers on her neck and the side of her head.

"Do you find me attractive today?"

"You look very nice. Why would he need a new reason? Wasn't his old one enough?"

"What is it you find most alluring in a human female?"

Most alluring? Most? The sensation of a tongue on his neck, and the knowledge that it delighted in what it tasted?

"The willingness to answer questions," he said.

She expelled air sharply and clicked her teeth together, which he took as an expression of frustration.

"Why would he need a new reason?" Sam asked.

She turned away and raised her chin before replying.

"He searched for M'Eetos for so long, I think actually finding him would have been a terrible anticlimax, at least were M'Eetos alive and content somewhere. Now, if he were dead, perhaps slain by your Varoki... ahhh, *that* would be an act worthy of revenge, a revenge lasting for centuries, perhaps longer."

"You mean revenge against the entire species?" Sam asked. "Maybe the whole *Cottohazz*?"

"Possibly, but not necessarily. Did you know a sacrilegious cabal of the New People conspired to kill one of us a long time ago? It is true. They were unsuccessful, of course, but to even contemplate such a thing . . . Well, P'Daan's vengeance on those very conspirators continues to this day."

Sam sensed the conversation wandering off track, but where it was going seemed important, although he wasn't sure how yet. "How is that possible? I thought he left this star system a couple hundred years ago. New People don't live that long, do they?"

"Not much more than fifty years, as I recall," she said. "Perhaps twice that. I've never paid much attention to them. But P'Daan had K'Irka, the most gifted gene sculptor we have here, make the criminals unaging, like us, so he could go on punishing them forever. She can do that. I am told the process takes some time, as the body replaces the original genetic material with the new, and the cells are replaced throughout the body. It is excruciating, as well. Once the criminals were altered, he gave them to H'Stus, who was the object of their plot, and who torments them still, those who have not managed to kill themselves over the years."

The Guardians could make other organisms immortal? Well, why not? If they could make themselves that way, why not any organism? From what Däng had said, though, any other organism would pay the same price: inability to reproduce naturally, and that was only the physical price. What about the psychological price? He wondered what the Guardians had been like before they lost the ability to age and die naturally.

The *ability*? Strange that he was thinking of it as a lost ability instead of a permanent reprieve from a death sentence.

"How long has this punishment been going on?" he asked.

"Oh, I forget. Five hundred, six hundred years perhaps. I wonder . . . will he do something similar to you, the architect of the attack on his pet New People?"

"He'll have to catch me first," Sam said.

Te'Anna simply looked at him.

Yeah, it sounded lame to him, too. Trying to get inside P'Daan's head was getting him nowhere, and he wasn't sure he really wanted inside one of their heads. Alexander was right—they needed something more to go on if they were going to put together a battle simulator that was worth anything. There was something else bothering him, though.

"Here's one thing I don't understand. This system has some defensive weaponry, but there's not much evidence they've ever had to use it. There's also no sign of combatant spacecraft in the system, at least not originally. Now here comes P'Daan with a squadron of battleships. Near as we can tell, each one of those long ships must mass between a half million and a million tons. Where did they come from? Is there a grand fleet you draw on in case of trouble?"

"Trouble? I wonder if we have ever had the sort of trouble you mean. I don't believe we have. No, nothing like that," she said and waved her hand as if brushing away insects. "P'Daan always had a fascination with war. I wonder where he even learned of such a thing, but he was always more interested in our history than was I. When he left here and did not return for so long, I suspected his absence suggested either a great spirit quest or a time spent with the Hobbyists."

"Who are the Hobbyists?"

"Well, I don't know why we call them that. So many of us have hobbies of one sort or another, but for some reason they are so . . . singleminded, I suppose, that they have captured that term."

"You've lost me."

"Oh, I am sorry, Bitka. Sometimes I forget and think of you as my intellectual equal. The Hobbyists raise species to sentience, adapt them to war, and then match them against one another."

"Like gladiators?"

"I do not know what that word means, but if it means individual combat, then no. Each group of Guardian Hobbyists—think of them as a team or faction—develops a single star system, raises up a species, creates an industrial culture for them, builds a fleet, and commands it against another faction."

How long would that take, to create an entire species, develop their technology and culture? And for . . .

"You mean, an interstellar war game?" Sam said, hardly believing it as he said it.

"Yes! A war *game*. Exactly. But you understand it is a game only for the Guardian Hobbyists."

Same as admirals and presidents, Sam thought.

"For the raised species, it is a deadly struggle for survival," she continued. "Sometimes the wars go on for generations. The losing species is enslaved, sometimes exterminated."

How different was this from the way ancient humans saw the world? The gods struggle, back different nations, fight out their battles by proxy, and the mortals pay the butcher bill. Those who understood the *Iliad* as history instead of imaginative poetry would know exactly what Te'Anna meant.

"So, these new ships..."

"They must be from one of the Hobbyist fleets. Their crews were bred for war, and have probably survived many battles."

"And the ships themselves?"

"The ships were bred for war as well, Bitka. War and nothing else. Their only purpose is to kill ships."

Bred for war—Sam thought that was an interesting way to think of design intent. Almost poetic.

"We haven't seen any evidence of use of nuclear warheads or explosive power generation, the sort we use in our intercept missiles. Is it something we just haven't run into yet?"

"No, we never use such things. The residual radiation is bad for the ships, the crews, everything. There are limits, Bitka. You use these terrible things, and the damage they do...horrible! The damage to the ships which survive—they are never the same. And what you did at the world you call Destie-Four—oh! Those poor satellites!"

"Poor *satellites?* You talk as if they were alive."

She simply looked at him, and then he knew. When she said the ships were bred for war, she meant it literally.

"I keep forgetting," she said, "how inanimate your technology is. This ship is just dead metal, isn't it? And yet you refer to it as 'she,' which is curious. Still, it has no life of its own. That must be why you have such large crews. Even if you could do the work with fewer people, would you? It would be very lonely with no ship to talk to. On the other hand, you never need to persuade the ship to seek danger, do you? It has no sense of self, and so no sense of self-preservation. That must be convenient at times."

"The satellites . . . you mean they were all alive? Self-aware? Not machines?"

"What is the difference between an organism and a machine?" she said. "The satellites were organic constructs designed to a specific purpose. They were alive, *and* they were machines."

She hadn't answered his question as to whether the satellites were self-aware, whether they were conscious. He didn't press the point.

"Okay, so what are we facing in those killer starships?"

"Well, as your Lieutenant Ma has already surmised, their principal weapon is a meson accelerator. I do not recall ever being a Hobbyist myself, so I have no clear knowledge of the details of their other weapons, but we use neutral particle accelerators quite often. I assume they would have a number of those for closer work, and a thick carapace to protect against their effects."

"Acceleration?"

"Oh, much less than your ship, at least on a sustained basis. They are probably capable of brief bursts of high thrust, but they cannot sustain it for very long."

"Why not?"

"In part it is a question of reaction mass, but the greater

problem is the ships themselves. They do not like prolonged high acceleration. It hurts."

"It hurts? Why would you build the capacity for pain into a starship?"

"Without pleasure and pain, Captain Bitka, there is no consciousness, no mind, no self-awareness, because there is nothing to *demand* awareness. It is not what you would call an optional feature."

Sam wasn't sure he bought that explanation, but if those long ships really weren't capable of sustained high-gee acceleration, that was really something. It meant he could avoid a fight most of the time. He probably couldn't avoid one forever, though. If he had to fight, he might at least be able to pick the time and place. The question was what he could do against those long ships, even if he caught one by itself.

"Why don't you use lasers?" he asked.

She tilted her head to the side and looked at him before answering. "Well, most of them do so little damage."

CHAPTER TWENTY-TWO

*Five days later, aboard USS Cam Ranh Bay,
running dark, outbound to Destie-Seven
7 May 2134 (thirty days after the commencement of
hostilities with the Guardians, eighty days after
Incident Seventeen)*

As his department heads made their way into the briefing
room, Sam pretended to read the statistical summary of
the last simulated battle. He'd already read it and it didn't
tell him anything he didn't know from experience. He'd
commanded the long ship from the auxiliary bridge while
Brook commanded the *Bay* from the main bridge. He,
Brook, and Alexander had traded roles in exercise after
exercise, seventeen times so far. The summary simply
quantified, made numeric, the reality of their repeated
simulated destruction.

For four days they had run different permutations of
the drill: *Cam Ranh Bay* versus one Guardian long ship.
Once they could beat one ship, they'd begin running drills
against two, or at least that had been the plan. So far, they
had yet to beat one long ship, or even come close.

The Guardians still hadn't located them. The ruse of

hugging close to a slow cargo ship was working, so they still had some time, but not endless. Sooner or later they would have to break away, start accelerating, to get to Destie-Seven-Echo, the moon that held the system's spacecraft construction complex.

Sooner or later.

It would need to be sooner. The bulk carrier's course would take eight months to get out to the gas giant, even if it were headed for the right one, and they didn't have eight months of food—less than half that, and they still needed to get home if their drive ever got repaired. They could jump twice a day on the return trip, push the reactor and power rings, cut the return trip down to ten days— say two weeks to give them a safety margin. Acho's hydroponics rooms were working. That helped. They could go on half rations or less for a while without much health risk, stretch their food out quite a bit.

But all that meant nothing if they couldn't get the jump drive fixed, and they couldn't be sure just getting to the shipyard would accomplish that. How much extra time would they need? How close could he afford to cut this?

And none of *that* mattered if they couldn't stand up to a single Guardian long ship. In theory, they could outrun any one ship, but Sam recalled what the twentieth-century philosopher Berra had said: "In theory, theory and practice are the same, but in practice they're different."

Lieutenant Ma, the last to arrive, entered the briefing room and took a chair. Sam looked around the table and didn't like what he saw. Brook the XO: uncomfortable and irritated. Alexander the TAC Boss: depressed and discouraged. Bohannon, who had moved up to Ops Boss: uncomfortable, uncertain of her position. Acho, logistics: attention on her data pad where Sam could see a spread sheet displayed. Ma, engineering: distracted and preoccupied. He'd been coming along well, but now he was back to his old habits. *Why?* At the end of the table, Haykuz, the Varoki bureaucrat, his expression unreadable. Sam still wasn't sure how he felt about his presence, but he didn't see a good way to avoid it.

"Okay," Sam said. "We're all here. Mister Haykuz, at his request, is joining us as an observer and in an advisory capacity as the senior *Cottohazz* official on the ship. I have not involved the other civilian members of the strategic advisory panel as our concerns here are entirely operational and tactical, not strategic.

"We've got several items on the horizon: when to make our burn for Destie-Seven-Echo, how to approach the moon, and our tactical plan to assault and secure the orbital complex. But we can't address any of those until we face the two-hundred-kilo gorilla in the room: how to beat a long ship without sustaining crippling damage to the *Bay*."

"Or how we beat one at all," Alexander said quietly. Bohannon and Brook both nodded in agreement.

Sam suppressed his first impulse to snap at the tactical officer. Showing anger would just look weak, emphasize how badly they'd been repeatedly beaten.

"If I may, Captain?" Brook said.

"Go ahead, XO."

"Maybe we should change the simulation parameters."

"What do you mean?" Sam said. "Have you figured out something about those ships we've missed?"

Brook shifted in his chair and did not look directly at Sam when he answered.

"No, sir, but crew morale is becoming an issue. Those alien ships keep killing us in the drills over and over . . . we're going to have some problems soon."

"Jesus!" Alexander said, but Sam held up his hand to quiet him.

"What are you suggesting, XO?"

"Rig it so we win one. Give the crew some hope."

"How about figuring out how to actually beat the damned things?" Alexander demanded, his voice rising.

"TAC, dial it back," Sam ordered. "But he's right, XO. We need a real solution, not a lie. If we rig the simulator and beat the ship, the crew will think whatever tactic we used will work. They'll expect our training to concentrate on that from then on. Are we going to train them to execute tactics we know won't work? And if not, they're going to wonder why not."

"We could work something out," Brook said, still looking away, "make up some excuse."

"No, we're not going to do that, but it is time to take a harder look at what's going wrong." Sam looked around the table, included all of them in his next question. "There has to be a tactical approach that will work. What are we missing?"

"I don't think we should wrap up the discussion of the simulator yet," Brook said. Again he didn't make eye contact but Sam was surprised to hear a sort of mulish stubbornness in his voice, and defiance as well. Acho looked up from her data pad and glanced at Brook as if she'd missed part of the conversation and wondered how it had gotten here.

"We weren't having a discussion, XO. I was explaining my decision. We don't need a fake solution; we need a real one. There has to be one, but we're missing something. What do we do about that?"

"Go back to the start," Alexander said, and then Acho added, "Work the problem." They said it as dutifully as students repeating the lesson he'd drilled into them for almost three months. Well, they had the words right. The question was whether it would do them any good.

Brook said nothing, did not move, continued to stare at a blank spot on the wall.

"That's right," Sam said. "Go back to the start and work the problem. TAC, what's the heart of the problem, in one sentence?"

"I'll give it to you in one number, sir:" Alexander answered immediately, "thirty-eight thousand. That damned meson gun of theirs has a range of forty-three thousand kilometers, plus or minus, and we've got to get a missile within five thousand kilometers of their ship before it can do any damage. That means we have to get it through a kill zone of thirty-eight thousand kilometers. So far we can't."

Sam heard the murmur of agreement from the other officers.

"Our coil gun spits out a Mark Five at four klicks a second," Alexander went on, "which is less than their design velocity, but that's as good as we can manage with our lash-up. Assuming a closing rate between the ships of eighteen klicks a second, that missile still takes *twenty-nine minutes* to cross that kill zone. We've got decoys and some jamming, but ... twenty-nine minutes?" He shook his head and leaned back in his chair.

"Not to mention the fact that half the time the bandit kills the *Bay* before the missile would get there anyway," Bohannon added. "Most of that closing velocity is from the *Bay*, not the coil gun. Pretty hard to get out of the way of that meson gun once we fire the missiles."

"That is the insurmountable problem," Brook added. "To get the missile velocity up, we must increase our own velocity before launch, and there is then insufficient time to decelerate, so we enter their kill zone before our missiles can engage them."

That had been the pattern of the simulations: first the long ship killed the *Bay*, and then it killed whatever missiles they'd thrown at it. They'd tried firing a missile ahead of them and detonating its thermonuclear warhead to jam the Guardian sensors. That worked for a while, but they only had so many warheads and even if they expended most of them staying alive themselves, nothing killed the long ship. When they ran out of warheads to cloak their position, the long ship still killed them.

"May I ask a layman's question, Captain Bitka?" the Varoki diplomat said.

Shit, Sam thought, *here it comes.* There'd been so much anti-Varoki sentiment on the ship since finding out about the jump drive, Sam wanted Haykuz to know he and his officers didn't share that sentiment. That didn't mean he wanted to be pals, though, and it sure didn't mean he wanted the guy wasting their time. He'd never struck Sam as being very bright. Well, he'd let Haykuz attend, so nothing to do now but live with it.

"Very well, go ahead."

"Why do you assume a closing velocity of eighteen kilometers per second?"

"It represents the velocity resulting from one hour of acceleration at one half of a gee. A half gee is all *Cam Ranh Bay* can manage at full thrust, and I wouldn't want to count on more than an hour warning before an engagement."

"I see," Haykuz answered. "But you would be able to increase that closing rate if you had ample warning of an engagement?"

"That's a very big if," Sam said. "Besides, that acceleration would take ten per cent of our total reaction mass, and then another ten per cent to decelerate afterwards. That's a very big investment. Not sure how much more we can afford."

Haykuz shifted in his chair and flushed, his ears starting to quiver back against his skull, but he spoke again. "Yes, as you say. These are probably very stupid questions and I apologize if I am wasting everyone's time with them, but what if you were to initiate the engagement? Could you not then choose a higher closing velocity?"

But he didn't want to pick a fight, Sam thought. He wanted to avoid one as long as he could, right up until the Guardians forced it on him. But the lower acceleration of those long ships meant there were only three ways they could force a fight: park themselves right where the *Bay* had to go next, or hem them in between several converging ships, or do an in-system jump to come out right in front of them. Of those, the only one Sam was really afraid of was an in-system jump. The other two he could see well in advance and then he *could* pick the time of the engagement, and the closing velocity, couldn't he?

But what if the Guardians did an in-system jump? Well, that would depend on how conservative they were. If they kept a good initial distance between them he could still get up a good head of speed, and with those long-range meson guns why *wouldn't* they try to keep their distance?

In the last war, he'd learned to start the engagement by closing as fast as he could. It made sense given the weapon arrays in that fight. They were completely different here, but son of a bitch if it didn't still make sense!

"Huh," he said. "That's actually worth looking at. Okay, let's run the problem assuming we pick the time of engagement and we get our closing rate up as high as we can. Our limitation is HRM: how much hydrogen reaction mass can we burn and still decelerate to make orbital entry at Destie-Seven-Echo?"

"Maybe . . ." Bohannon said with a pause and glance at Sam as if for permission to continue. He nodded. "If we do pick the time of the engagement, we can decouple the main hull from the habitat wheel. That gives us more acceleration, or we use less reaction mass for the same acceleration."

"And leave the passengers and Marines behind?" Brook demanded. "You'll have a riot on your hands."

"They'll be as safe in the wheel as we will in the main hull, safer really," Alexander said. "The captain better do some more town hall meetings to explain it, but it's not a stupid idea. It's part of our core design."

"And what does all that get us?" Brook asked. "They still kill the missile."

"It gets us shorter transit time through their kill zone," Bohannon shot back.

"*They still kill the missile.* It only takes one shot," Brook said.

"If we cut the transit time down to something like ten minutes," Alexander said, "we may be able to confuse their firing solution that long. We can't do it for twenty-nine minutes, but maybe ten or fifteen?"

"How?" Brook demanded.

"Well, we can't do much more with jamming," Alexander admitted, "but maybe decoys. We're using the on-board decoys built into the Mark Fives so far, which are just radar reflectors. The missile itself has almost no thermal signature because it comes out of the coil gun cold. Those radar reflectors... what if we fabricate a swarm of them?"

"Pack them with the Mark Five and you'll slow it down," Brook said. "More mass to push out the tube."

"Yeah, but we could fabricate a separate missile that was nothing but decoys. Fire it first and then the real missile with its own decoys."

"Then they just kill all the decoys, too," Brook said. "Or half of them. If they kill half the decoys, they're starting to get a pretty good chance of taking out the missile by luck. What stops them from just killing everything they see?"

The table fell silent. Acho went back to her data pad.

Alexander leaned back in his chair, hands behind his head, and studied the ceiling. Bohannon shifted uncomfortably in her chair, while Haykuz sat absolutely motionless at the end of the table.

"Cycle time," Ma answered after a few seconds, speaking for the first time. "Our prisoner says there's a cool-down and reset cycle between discharges of somewhere between ten seconds and half a minute, she's not sure beyond that."

"Ten seconds gives them sixty shots in ten minutes," Brooks said, "and that's assuming we can actually get the closing rate down that low."

"Hell," Alexander answered, "we can give them a lot more targets than that. And in with all those decoys, we don't count on just one missile getting the job done. Drop three or four on them. If we add one of the old Mark Fours from our original missile packs, it'll run hot and they may think that's the main threat."

Sam could sense the mood beginning to change until Brook spoke again.

"But will we still be alive to enjoy the victory?" he asked. "Remember, in almost every drill the long ship kills *us*, and does it long before the missile can get there. We can make decoys of the missile because it doesn't have much of a thermal signature, but we can't make dummies of the *Bay* that will fool anyone."

The table again fell silent.

"Excuse me if this is an obvious point," Acho finally said, looking up from her data pad, "but how fast can they rotate that ship?"

"What difference does that make?" Ma snapped.

Sam opened his mouth to rein him in but Alexander beat him to it.

"Back off, Lieutenant Ma. She's got as much right to ask a question as anyone. We wouldn't have any chance at all without these Mark Fives she found in cargo. You and I were both assholes about it and look how it's turned out. So why don't you discharge that ballast and just answer her question?"

Discharge that ballast? The only person on the ship Sam could remember using that expression was Running-Deer. She'd probably stood up for Acho, tried to hammer some sense into Ma and Alexander. It apparently had an effect on one of them.

Ma looked around, saw a couple of hard faces, and colored slightly.

"Right. Sorry, LOG. I don't know how fast they can turn it. I'm just curious how that bears on the problem. I might be able to get with our prisoner and run some numbers."

"Well," Acho said, "those ships are a kilometer long and they can only shoot straight ahead, right? Even with magnetic beam benders at the end of the pipe, how much deflection can they get without screwing up the meson stream?"

"Their arc of fire has got to be less than one degree," Alexander said. "That's about all a beam bender can give them. For more than that they'd have to rotate the ship."

"Yes," Acho said. "See, I've been running some numbers, and given its nominal range of 43,000 kilometers a one-degree arc of fire is only 750 kilometers wide at its extreme range. The closer we get, the smaller that arc becomes."

And then they were all engaged in the debate, all but Sam and Haykuz, and for the first time in the last five days Sam thought they might have a chance against one of the long ships, maybe even a couple of them. He looked over at Haykuz and the Varoki met his eyes. Sam nodded his thanks. Haykuz cocked his head to the side, the Varoki equivalent of a shrug.

PART III:
In the Highest Tradition of the United States Navy

Cassandra
Four months later, **on board USS** *Puebla,*
in the K'tok System
15 August 2134 (*eight days after docking with the drive module*)

All morning Cassandra had been unable to get through to Dr. Wu, the physicist on K'tok heading up the analysis of the jump drive module. "He's in conference," was all she could get from the communication ratings at K'tok Base. Then when she tried to meet with Captain Goldjune on USS *Puebla*, she found him to be incommunicado as well. When she found Moe Rice in *Puebla's* tiny wardroom, she clipped her tether beside his at the only table in the room.

"Something smells fishy here, Mister Rice," she said

"Probably this here crab cake," he said pointing at his half-eaten lunch with his fork. "Tastes like three-day-old channel catfish."

"I meant I find it suspicious that both Dr. Wu on K'tok

and Captain Goldjune here on *Puebla* are unavailable to meet or communicate with me."

"Count your blessings when it comes to this boat's skipper."

Cassandra looked around to make sure no one else was in the wardroom and she moved closer to Moe.

"Mister Rice," she said softly, "there is something I haven't told you. When Rear Admiral Goldjune gave me this assignment on K'tok, his remarks suggested he knew more than he was willing to say about this jump drive we were to examine, but that we might find a more deeply embedded operating code which was—and I use his word here—*alien*."

Rice wiped his mouth with a napkin and pushed the food tray to the side.

"All that stuff Wu was talking about, those proteins and whatnot, kinda lines up with that, don't it?" he said.

"Yes. But what I wonder is how Rear Admiral Goldjune knew, or at least suspected, that it might."

"Huh," he said and looked away, brow furrowed in thought.

Cassandra's commlink vibrated and she saw the ID tag for Captain Goldjune.

"At last," she said to Rice. "Perhaps now we'll see what's going on." She squinted open the channel. "Hello, Captain. Good of you to return my comm."

Oh, I assure you, Commander, it is entirely my pleasure. You'll be interested to know I've just been speaking with Admiral Goldjune. He has asked me to tell you that the Incident Seventeen working group is disbanded, effective immediately. You and your officers will return to their previous duty, which means Lieutenant Rice can move back to his old cabin and start work here next watch. He was on detached duty to you, but he is still my supply officer. Transportation will be arranged for you and Heidegger.

"Disbanded? What do you mean? What about our final report? Who is to continue the examination of the wreckage?"

It means, Commander, that you are finished snooping around and wasting time. I think those were his exact words. He has told your working group personnel on K'tok to complete a final report, with all of your findings, in two days, and submit it to him. That report, I understand, will find that the only credible explanation for Cam Ranh Bay's loss is hostile covert action by the uBakai Star Navy. As to the examination, Puebla will remain on station here with the wreckage pending further orders. I don't believe you're cleared to know what happens after that.

Had all of this been an elaborate ruse by the admiral to get her off-planet? No, that made no sense. The jump drive was here! They were actually looking at it, recording data files full of information for analysis later, potentially world-changing information. This made no sense.

"That does not sound at all like Rear Admiral Goldjune," she said.

Oh, I'm sorry, did I lead you to believe I had spoken with my father, the rear admiral? No, I just finished talking with my uncle, Admiral Cedric Goldjune, the Outworld Coalition chief of naval operations. He arrived at K'tok twelve hours ago, on an unannounced fact-finding tour. I don't think he liked some of the facts he found.

And then the nasty little shit laughed.

An hour later, Cassandra heard the tone for her doorway, turned the wall transparent, and saw Moe Rice floating in the corridor. She triggered the hatch.

"Leftenant Rice, to what do I owe this pleasure?"

"Way you stormed off . . . as a good friend of mine once said, you look like I could use a drink. It happens I got a bottle right here." Rice held it up for her inspection.

Cassandra made a face. "Not some of that awful bourbon, I hope. Please come in."

Rice coasted through the hatch into the tiny cabin Cassandra had to herself, nearly filling it up in the process. Rice and Heidegger shared one about this size. She understood U.S. destroyers were small, and their accommodations Spartan, but this bordered on the surreal. Rice passed the bottle to her and rummaged in her sanitary cubicle for zero-gee drink bulbs.

"Rye?" she said, examining the label. "It looks like bourbon to me."

"Bourbon is at least 51% distilled from corn," Rice said. "That's why it's so sweet. Rye is at least 51% distilled from rye. Trust me, they ain't the same. Pass that bottle back and I'll fill these bulbs." He did so and then left the bottle to float in the air between them.

She shuddered after her first swallow. "Oh! It's *dreadful!*"

"You got shitty manners," he said. "Anyone ever tell you that?"

She sighed. "Almost everyone seems to, sooner or later. Tell me, Mister Rice, how is it no one on this ship—I beg your pardon, *boat*—has murdered that sodding little wanker Larry Goldjune?"

Rice laughed and clipped his tether to a stanchion on her wall. "You know how much paperwork that would generate?"

"That is what airlocks are for," she replied.

He sipped from his own bulb and smiled in appreciation, his eyes half-closed. Then he looked directly at her. "So, not that it's any of my business, but what did that low-down no-good skunk Sam Bitka do to screw things up between you two?"

She added more whiskey to her drink bulb before answering.

"He was . . . very quick to fall in love."

"Well, that can scare some folks, I guess. What'd you do about it?"

"We had a good physical relationship. I went along. I thought his ardor might wane."

Rice laughed again.

"Ma'am, I don't know how things work in England, but where I come from if you want to cool a man's ardor, good sex and plenty of it ain't the best way to get the job done."

Cassandra considered that. Was he right? Had she really wanted Bitka's feelings to cool? Or had she just told herself that? No, she knew what she had been about.

"In *my* experience," she said, "a good many men are more interested in the chase than its *dénouement*. Once they've achieved their elusive goal, they rapidly lose interest and begin preparing for the next chase." She took a drink of whiskey. "Not our Bitka, though, damn him.

And . . . there is the matter of my daughter, Penny. She's seven years old—just turned while we were out here."

"That the little girl in the hologram on your desk? Looks like you some, with all them freckles. Good age, seven. Tough things to miss, those birthdays."

"War is hell," she said, lifting her drink bulb in a mock toast.

"Yup. You with Bitka by any chance on her birthday?"

"Ah. Very clever, Mister Rice. Perhaps *you* should be in military intelligence." She took another drink.

"Better go easy on that unless you're used to boozin' in zero gee. Goes right to your head."

"That's rather the point, isn't it?" she said, but her mind was elsewhere. How long, she wondered, before he probed deeper into her feelings about Bitka? And what would she say then?

She closed her eyes and breathed slowly, deeply, feeling the effects of the whiskey, her insides tingling with fire, her skin numb, as if she were reduced to her inner essence, her shell forgotten. No, not forgotten. Although she could not feel it, she knew every centimeter of her skin, knew it from the memory of his intimate lingering caresses, tracing the line of her neck, the curve of her breasts. Sometime when she was alone, not just alone in the world, but alone inside, she touched herself in mimic of those caresses, imagining the hands were his, having him back just for a short while.

She breathed in sharply and opened her eyes. Moe was looking away discreetly, always the gentleman, perhaps the best man she knew, but relentless in his pursuit of the truth, including from her.

"Do you know what I could use tonight, Mister Rice? I could use a damned good shagging."

He grinned, a good smile, but shook his head. "Sorry, Ma'am, but my heart belongs to Miss Marjorie Morgenstern of Del Rio, Texas. A bottle and a sympathetic ear are all I can offer."

"What happens at K'tok stays at K'tok," she said lightly.

He settled back and his smile faded. "With respect, Ma'am, that's bullshit and you know it. What happens here we'll carry around with us forever. And I'll tell you something else, I'm no prude but it's a might insulting to get propositioned when I know all you really want is to change the goddamned subject. Now why don't you stop stallin' and tell me what Bitka did when he found out you had a little girl?"

She took another drink, only a sip this time.

"Well, he was delighted. Asked me about her. Listened to my stories of her with genuine interest. Expressed a sincere desire to meet her when we returned to Earth."

Rice looked at her, waiting for more, but there wasn't anything more. His expression soured.

"Yup," he deadpanned, "*that* would sure as hell piss anyone off."

"So much for the sympathetic ear," she said.

She should thank him for the drink and plead a headache, ask him to leave, see him in the morning. Instead she took another sip. She waited for him to speak, goad her into another admission, push her for an explanation, scold her for drinking too much. Instead the bastard just floated there on his tether, arms folded, watching her. Waiting. Serene and patient as a great black Buddha.

"Hard as it may be for you to believe," she said at last, "I do not suffer from a shortage of men willing to play father to Penny. More like a sure fit."

Rice looked confused. "Did you say *sure fit*?"

"Surfeit," she corrected herself, enunciating the word carefully. Perhaps she *had* better slow down on the whiskey. "It means an overabundance."

"Uh-huh. 'Bout how many make up a surfeit where you come from?"

"One. Well, Bitka made two, but one was more than sufficient." Then the next sentence came out as a whisper, although she had not meant it to. "Back to one now, it seems."

And then there were tears, but she closed her eyes to cut them off, tightened her jaw and compressed her lips. She *would* not do that! No drunken, blubbering confessions. What was done was done and tears changed nothing. She sat motionless, eyes closed, and inside herself she stared down the weak, silly girl whom she no longer was—had never been, really, except in her occasional self-indulgent daydreams.

Once she was sure her voice was under control she told Rice the story: the fling with a married man, the unexpected pregnancy because she had believed him when he said he was infertile, the aftermath when he insisted that he be allowed to raise the child, give it all the "advantages" his wealth and position offered. His childless wife would raise no objection—she was very civilized. Everyone was very civilized.

"Never took you to be exactly poor," Rice said. "What kind of wealth and position we talking about here?"

"Henry Godolphin Pelham, son and heir of the fifteenth earl of Chichester. Very old name, very old title. The wealth is considerable, but much newer than the name and title, rendered acceptable to all concerned only by his pedigree."

"Kinda like money laundering, huh?" he said, and Cassandra laughed, delighted with the image it conjured up—*Henry the money launderer!* She had not laughed for what seemed a very long time, but it had only been a little over five months.

"So, your daughter with him now?"

"No. She is with my mother while I am away."

"He gave up, huh?"

She laughed again, but this time without any trace of humor.

"Henry is not the sort to give up. I have been fighting him for seven years. I won in the courts, three times. I am certain there will be a fourth challenge, now that I am away from Penny, especially as my assignment here was anything but coincidental. Henry belongs to The Rag in London, as does the Chief of Defense Intelligence, my superior."

"The Rag?"

"Oh, sorry," she said. "Army and Navy Club. I cannot of course prove that my transfer out here was arranged over whiskies there—probably in those overstuffed red leather wingbacks in the Smoking Room, if I know those two. I'm a member as well, you see, so I can hardly claim Henry had unfair access, can I? But there are members, and then there are *members*.

"As I said, Penny is with my mother, and so she will

have to deal with this business. My mother has always been quiet, but for all that, she's quite strong. She's not as young as she once was, though, and I won't be there to help her. I have come to hate Henry for what he is going to put her through. I never used to—hate him, that is."

Moe nodded and took a sip of rye. "So, you figured Bitka would just complicate things in court, huh?"

She didn't answer him, but the truth was she had not thought that at all. It was *her* fight, hers and her mother's and Penny's, and win or lose they would come through it, one way or another, with or without his help or hindrance. She simply didn't want his help. She did not want to share this fight with him. She did not want to share *Penny* with him, or with anyone else. She had fought so hard and for so long not to share her with Henry, it had become part of her makeup not to share her at all—a mental habit.

A stupid, selfish habit, she realized—now that it was too late to matter. But there was even more to it than just that.

"One more question," Moe said. "Did Sam know all this, 'bout the custody fight and all?"

Cassandra looked away and took another sip of rye.

"Uh-huh," he said. "Well, that was a mighty interesting omission, wasn't it?"

She felt a vibration at the base of her skull and saw the ID tag for the duty communications rating.

"Commander Atwater-Jones here," she said.

Ma'am, this is Signaler First Kramer. I have an incoming clear text for you from COMKTOKBASE. Captain Goldjune is copied as well.

Kramer's voice seemed strained, hoarse, almost as if she had been crying.

"Very well, Kramer. Go ahead."

Ma'am, the text reads: USS Cam Ranh Bay *exited jump space vicinity Mogo, 1621 hours this date. Surviving crew and passengers well but will be under observation quarantine for immediate future.*

Kramer paused and Cassandra felt suddenly flushed and lightheaded. She heard her blood pounding in her ears. She let go her drink bulb and covered her face with her hands, not wanting Rice or anyone to see her expression in this moment—a range of emotions she had no words for, no understanding of, but which filled her and overwhelmed her.

Kramer's voice trembled when she resumed speaking.

Captain Bitka did not make it back.

Signed, J. Goldjune, Rear Admiral.

CHAPTER TWENTY-THREE

Two months earlier, aboard USS *Cam Ranh Bay,*
running dark, outbound to Destie-Seven
7 June 2134 (*one hundred eleven days after*
Incident Seventeen)

Sam saw Choice enter the conference room, the last to
arrive. There were still several empty chairs around the
conference table and the steward had laid out her lunch
order beside Ka'Deem Brook, but she picked up her tray
and moved to a different seat down the table and on the
opposite side. *That was interesting,* Sam thought. Almost
as interesting as the fact that Brook did not seem to notice
she had even entered the conference room, *deliberately*
unaware.

Sam put down his fork and pushed his seafood salad to
the side.

"The rest of you please go on eating," he said. "Thanks
again for helping out. We've been gathering data on this
culture for over two months now, and our prisoner
Te'Anna has been extremely helpful. I'm almost beginning
to think of her as our guest . . . almost. I imagine several
of you sometimes wonder where her sympathies lie. I do

myself, but we need to remember that is dangerous thinking. We do not understand the Guardians. We will probably never completely understand them. Te'Anna's goals, whatever they are, are clearly not aligned with P'Daan's, but we should never assume that means they are aligned with our own."

He paused and looked around the table, checking for signs of acceptance or rejection of that assessment, and he saw mostly nods. Dr. Däng frowned in thought, Brook remained studiously opaque, and Lieutenant Ma seemed preoccupied with another problem, but Sam saw no sign of actual disagreement from the group. Ma had emerged from his interview with Te'Anna badly shaken. Sam had watched the recording of the conversation between them concerning the jump drive, but the exchange had been so deeply mathematical in nature that he could not follow any of it, despite having taken a few courses in astrophysics.

"Okay," Sam resumed. "In about thirty-six hours we are going to lock down the spin habitat and begin accelerating away from the bulk carrier we have been shadowing. When we do, the Guardians will see us and the real pursuit will begin. Our plan is to seize the shipyard at the moon we have designated Destie-Seven-Echo, and which we now know the Desties call Haydoos. If there is any place in this system where they know how to repair a jump drive, it will be there. The shipyard is part of the orbital station which corresponds to what we call a highstation. It's at the synchronous orbit track above the moon's equator and linked to the surface by an orbital elevator— a needle.

"Our Marines are going to have to fight for the

highstation shipyard, and unless we are extraordinarily lucky we're going to have to fight some long ships sooner or later as well. But we are as prepared for those eventualities as I believe it is possible to be. Further delay at this point reduces our chance of survival rather than increasing it.

"As to your side of the work, I've been getting individual reports from you. I thought it would be useful for us to meet and share a summary of findings in your areas of specialty. Mister Haykuz, would you like to start?"

It felt odd to start with the Varoki, Sam thought. Technically he *was* the senior *Cottohazz* civilian official on the ship, but Sam had never shown any deference to Haykuz's predecessor e-Lisyss. That seemed like a different lifetime, so much had happened since. Now Haykuz's ears spread in a comfortable and relaxed pose, his skin clear, no sign of defensiveness, hostility, or even unease. Yes, *all* of them had changed in the last two months.

"Thank you," the Varoki said. "I will be brief. My specialty is diplomacy, at least nominally. I do not consider myself an expert, although I have worked with and observed several highly skilled diplomats. We have had no opportunities for formal negotiations since the destruction of our landing party on Destie-Four, in part because to attempt such would reveal our position. Instead we have been trying to ascertain the nature of the society and individuals with which we may be able to negotiate in the near future. Dr. Johnstone, our anthropologist—or perhaps now we should say *sentientologist*—has provided most of the insights and I will leave it to him to explain."

Sam hadn't expected that. He turned to the Maori anthropologist who hardly ever spoke in these meetings. Sam couldn't remember exchanging more than a dozen words with him, four of which had been, *Please pass the pepper.*

Johnstone cleared his throat before speaking.

"Well, to begin, there are two distinct cultures. You have to distinguish between the culture of the New People—or Desties, as we used to call them—and that of the Guardians themselves. The New People, despite their technologically advanced state, live in a society which is a cross between a theocracy and a slave plantation. The authority and legitimacy of society is based on theological foundations, but the society is organized *not* for the benefit of a priestly class, but rather for the deities themselves—the Guardians—whose presence, unlike that of other deities, is manifest."

"And the slavery part?" Sam asked.

"The Guardians *own* the New People, both individually and collectively, by right of creation. P'Daan and M'Eetos are the nominal supreme deities, but all of the locally known Guardians, including Te'Anna, have a place in the New People pantheon."

"And they all just accept that?" Lieutenant Alexander asked, skepticism heavy in his voice.

"Every society has its atheists," Johnstone replied, "its sceptics, its nonconformists, and I imagine it is the same here. In general, though, they accept it. A fairly small part of their productive labor is required to meet the desires of their gods, so their standard of living is high and, more importantly, fairly evenly distributed. Most New People have little interaction with the Guardians. In that respect, at least, it is similar to most religions."

"The myth of the happy slave," Choice said, and Sam could hear the disgust in her voice.

Johnstone's forehead wrinkled in consideration of that, or at least so Sam thought. It was hard to tell through his mask of Maori tattoos.

"That I could not say," he answered, "but they are not rebellious slaves for the most part. I would say the average New Person has as much control over their day-to-day life as the average citizen of the *Cottohazz*."

"You said there is a different culture for the Guardians," Sam said. "How so? Sounds as if they're pretty much on top. Aren't the slave owners an integral part of a slave culture?"

"Within this star system, yes. What I call Guardian culture is the metaculture of the Guardian realms. It is the mechanism of interstellar interaction, and it is what we would call a classic gift culture."

"A *gift* culture?" Sam said.

"Yes, a nonmarket-based exchange system, where gifts are given without expectation of material reciprocity."

"*Altruism?*" Lieutenant Alexander asked, sounding even more skeptical than before. "And you're telling us that actually works?"

"In most cultures," Johnstone answered calmly, "material reciprocity can be replaced with a change in status. If one being gives something of value to another, the other takes it either with the expectation of repaying it or with the tacit acceptance of the higher status of the donor. This is as true when giving alms to a beggar as it is in a feudal society when a monarch gives a fief to a subordinate noble. There are many other details of gift cultures, but that is the central logic: giving and accepting gifts changes the *status* of both participants. The main departure in this case is that between Guardians this gifting, as an assertion of authority and status, replaces a market economy."

"You mean the Desties don't have a market-based economy?" Lieutenant Ma asked.

"That's a different culture," Johnstone said quickly. "Weren't you listening? To a limited extent the New People have a market economy, as a mechanism for allocating resources. But the interactions between the Destination system and other star systems flow exclusively through their Guardian rulers. The cultural organization of the Guardian realms would be very familiar to a native of the pre-Columbian Mississippian cultures of North America, or of Homeric Greece."

"Huh," Sam said, beginning to believe it but not sure what to make of it. "What does it tell us about our current situation?"

"It tells us the limitations under which P'Daan works," Johnstone answered. "He has brought with him a force of eight warships, and we have no evidence the Destination system has ever produced vessels such as those. They must be gifts from one or more other Guardians, the ones our prisoner calls Hobbyists. If what Te'Anna has told me is true, P'Daan cannot accept more than this without lowering his status, incurring an obligation of obedience and loyalty to other Guardians beyond what he may be willing to undertake. The Guardians may have a thousand ships in the near stellar neighborhood, but P'Daan may be either unable due to station, or unwilling due to pride, to call on them. The cost to him may be too high."

A thousand ships? Sam hoped he was wrong about that, or else right about everything else.

"Thank you, Mister Johnstone," he said. "There's a lot to think about there. It certainly fits with everything we've seen so far. Dr. Däng, would you like to go next?"

Dr. Däng gave her report, although there was little new in it. She was cataloguing and decoding additional genetic material, but it served to confirm what they already knew. She did confirm Te'Anna's claim concerning the volume of her erectile tissue, which caused a few smiles and exchanged glances.

Lieutenant Bohannon gave the report on linguistics. Councilor Abanna Zaquaan, an infant in its arms, sat silently beside her. Again, nothing particularly new in the report, simply further refinements of their autotrans programs. There was one interesting observation at the end.

"As we learn more about the Guardian language," Bohannon said, "and monitor some poorly masked ship-to-ship chatter, it becomes clear the language we call Destie is not just the *lingua franca* of Guardian space. It is apparently the only language spoken. It may be the only language any of these species have ever spoken. We're not sure that has any tactical significance, but it backs up Dr. Johnstone's thinking."

Sam turned to Choice.

"Ms. Choice, I don't know that we've uncovered much new concerning their data analysis systems but—"

"Oh, quite a lot, actually," she said. "Not technical details, but an interesting overview picture. We noticed from the start that the pattern of commercial astrogation in the Destination system suggests a level of computational technology roughly comparable to ours. However, after talking to Dr. Däng about their work in genetic engineering, it became clear they must have access to far more powerful computational assets."

"What makes you say that?" Alexander asked, challenge clear in his voice. Sam saw that Choice suppressed a frown of impatience.

"The fairly short time they have been here in this system," she answered, "and the massive genetic re-engineering it would have taken to raise the New People in that brief period, both suggest that. Also, the apparent speed and ease with which they genetically modified the rebel New People Te'Anna spoke of also suggests the ability to rapidly synthesize and implant billions of strands of genetic material with very specific design functions. We could not do that with our computing ability, and as you observed earlier, our ability is at least equal to the sort of computers moving those bulk carriers around."

"But if they have better, why not use it?" Dr. Däng asked, which was of course the heart of the issue.

"I believe they have two tiers of technology," Choice answered. "I'm even more confident of this after hearing Dr. Johnstone's analysis of their cultural organization. One tier is used by the client races—at least in this one system we can examine—and is good enough for them to carry out their function, which is to provide for the material needs of the Guardians. The other tier is reserved for Guardian use. That appears to include a more advanced form of computing, actual genetic engineering, and star travel."

"Wait," Ma said, "now what makes you think star travel is a Guardian-only technology? We've only seen eight of the starships and maybe *you* know who or what's driving them, but *I* sure don't."

Sam saw her flush with anger and he couldn't blame her. Ma hadn't just interrupted her, he'd managed to sound pretty patronizing as well. Choice took a breath before answering.

"We discovered the Guardians are genetically engineered to digest any protein chains from any tree of life. What does that remind you of?"

Choice looked at Ma for a moment and he shrugged.

"Think harder," she said, and when the flush of anger rose in his cheeks and ears, she shook her head.

"As you more than anyone on this ship should know, Lieutenant Ma, every jump drive in the *Cottohazz* is protected from examination by a defense mechanism which produces a neurotoxin fatal to every large organism from every tree of life we know. Dr. Däng, do you know any way to create a single organic neurotoxin which will attack every large species of every tree of life in the *Cottohazz*?"

"No, dear, but I am not a microbiologist."

"Do you know any microbiologist who could do that?"

"Well . . . I suppose not," Däng answered. "That *is* an interesting point."

"We always assumed the Varoki made that device to

protect their intellectual property," Choice continued. "But bioengineering has never been a significant feature of Varoki technology. How did they come up with it? Now that we know they found and copied the jump drive, I think they just found a way around the defenses that were already there and copied them as well. I'd bet my life that anti-tamper device is Guardian bioengineered, and if so, why would the Guardians need it? Obviously to guard it against their own client races, or as Dr. Johnstone suggests, their slaves."

The table was silent as they all thought that over. Then Ma whistled.

"Ms. Choice, I have to hand it to you. I think you're right. That makes you one and one," he said with a grin, as if he were an instructor awarding a student a prize.

"One and one?" she said.

"Well, you were wrong about the galaxy being full of conscious, self-aware machines left behind by vanished civilizations, but I think you nailed this one."

Choice stared at him for several long seconds and then looked around the other faces surrounding the table, the irritation on her face changing to confusion and then surprise.

"You mean you haven't figured it out?" she asked all of them. "I thought it was too obvious to even mention. Weren't any of you listening to the recording when our prisoner asked Captain Bitka, rhetorically, what the difference was between an organism and a machine? Don't you remember Dr. Däng telling us that the Guardians were *intelligently designed*? Lieutenant Ma, you said if I could find a way to give a machine an orgasm you'd listen to me. In reply, I offer our oversexed prisoner, Te'Anna. The Guardians *are* the machines of an extinct civilization. We just never imagined machines made of meat."

CHAPTER TWENTY-FOUR

Two days later, aboard USS *Cam Ranh Bay*,
outbound to Destie-Seven
9 June 2134 (*one hundred thirteen days after
Incident Seventeen*)

Sam coasted onto the bridge, took the watch from Homer
Alexander, and strapped himself into the command chair.
He checked the chronometer: 0345, halfway through the
Mid Watch.

"Habitat wheel is spun down and locked, sir,"
Lieutenant Barr-Sanchez at Ops One reported. "All
passengers and crew reported strapped in. Ship is secure
for acceleration."

"Very well, helm," Sam replied, "make your burn."

"Aye, aye, sir."

Barr-Sanchez hit the acceleration warning klaxon,
waited ten seconds, and then fired the main thruster. Sam
felt the vibration of it through the structure of the ship
itself. Then the acceleration pushed him back in his chair
until the nose of *Cam Ranh Bay* became "up." They were
starting with a half-gee burn for ten minutes, spending a
chunk of HRM to build up an initial vector. After that they

would drop back to a sustained twentieth of a gee. Since the power plant could generate a higher exhaust velocity at lower thrust, their reaction mass efficiency would be much better, and they could sustain that thrust all the way to the gas giant.

For over a month they had coasted silently in low-emission mode, living off a charged power ring and recycled waste heat. Now their direct fusion thruster would show up on every large thermal array in the star system. P'Daan and his long ships would know where they were and would know where they were headed. If what they thought about the Guardian ships was true, they did not have the thrust to catch the *Bay* before it got to Destie-Seven-Echo, the moon holding the system's main shipyard.

Unless the Guardians made an in-system jump and got out ahead of them. There was nothing Sam could do about that but wait and see what happened. He thought the odds were better than fifty-fifty they would *not* execute an in-system jump. He thought he was beginning to get a handle on their psychology. Well, they'd see soon enough.

Signaler First Lakhanpal in the Comm One chair beside him gave a start and touched his ear. "Uh . . . Captain? I'm getting a tight beam text, low power, in Destie. Here's the translation: *So lonely. Nice you travel with me.* There's no signature, sir."

"Track it if you can," Sam said, sitting forward in his chair and activating his own workstation display. "But you say it's low power?"

"Very low power sir. Can't have come from . . . *Oh, shit!* It's from the bulk carrier we've been shadowing!"

"Captain, should I sound general quarters?" the petty

officer in the TAC One chair asked. Sam shook his head
and settled back in his chair.

"If it wanted to hurt us, it would have done so a long
time ago," he said.

"You mean there's *crew* on that bulk carrier, sir?"
Lakhanpal asked. "I thought it was unmanned."

"It is unmanned. That's the ship talking."

All this time the bulk carrier had known they were
there and said nothing, told no one, happy just for the
company of another ship. Te'Anna had said it must be
lonely for a Human crew with no ship to talk to. What was
it like for a self-aware ship with no crew? It took a
moment for Sam to trust his voice to continue.

"COMM, make the following reply in Destie, very low
power, tight beam, no signature: I will always remember
you. Safe voyage."

Three hours later Lieutenant Koichi Ma sat across
from the captain and poked at his breakfast: scrambled
egglike-substance with diced faux ham. Actually, that was
a disservice to the galley crew, who did a great job putting
meals on tables. He usually liked breakfast, but today he
had no taste for anything, especially breakfast with the
captain, but it was his turn in the rotation. If only Bitka
weren't so damned . . . *optimistic*. It just wasn't natural,
and if it was an act, it was a hell of a good one.

"You seem distracted, Mister Ma," the captain said
between mouthfuls of egg. Nothing wrong with his
appetite.

"Sorry, sir, My A-gang has an EVA deficit we're having
a hard time catching up on."

"What's the problem?"

Ma shrugged. "Only so many EVA-qualified techs, and safety standards limit how many hours a watch they can spend suited up and working out there in hard vacuum. Being under constant acceleration, even at a twentieth of a gee, makes everything harder and a lot more dangerous. Now Lieutenant Alexander wants us to move six of the Mark Four missiles out of their launch pods on the habitat wheel and up to the main hull's docking bay. I don't have the job hours to do it as soon as he wants."

The captain put his fork down, slowly raised his coffee mug, and sipped carefully. In a twentieth of a gee, sudden movements tended to put coffee all over the place.

"Well, we need those Mark Fours up in the main hull if we're going to use them in a fight," the captain said. "You know our plan involves decoupling the main hull from the spin habitat so we can get more acceleration. Plan also calls for using those Mark Fours as a supplement to the railgun-launched Mark Fives. The Fours aren't as lethal but they've got their own solid-fuel rocket engines and more acceleration than our jury-rigged Mark Fives."

"Yes, sir. I'm just not sure how we're going to get it done."

The captain sat studying him with that look which Ma had never learned to penetrate but had gotten used to. The captain was thinking, but usually not about what a disappointment someone was. Mostly he thought about fixing the problem.

"Well, let's do this," he said. "I don't want you to push crew safety but put off some of the routine maintenance and make a block of time with those hours you free up.

You get your crew all set and I'll have Ops cut the thrusters, give you time to move those missiles in zero gee, which should be a lot easier. I don't want to coast for long with those two Guardian ships still accelerating behind us, so let's move four missiles now. That's all the plan calls for. The other two are insurance. We'll see about moving the other two once you get caught up on the maintenance backlog. What do you think?"

"Cutting the acceleration will make it a lot easier, sir. And safer."

"Can you get those four missiles moved in an hour?"

"It'll be tight sir. I'll do my best . . ." Ma stopped. Why was he promising something he knew he couldn't deliver? "No, sir. I can't do it in an hour. It will take at least two."

Bitka got that far-away look again as he sipped his coffee.

"Okay, two hours. Let me know when you have it set up."

That afternoon Sam woke from a light nap in his day cabin when an incoming comm vibrated the base of his skull. He sat up on the couch, rested his legs on the floor, and took a minute or so to collect his thoughts and drive away the last fog of sleep. He squinted and saw Homer Alexander's ID tag. Homer was OOD that watch.

"Yes, TAC?"

Those two long ships following us have started burning a lot of HRM, sir, Alexander said. *They're trying to catch up.*

Those were the two Guardian long ships which had been outbound, apparently toward the gas giant Destie

Seven, as part of the system-wide search. Once Sam had lit the *Bay's* reactor and accelerated away from the bulk carrier, the Desties had tracked them up. The two outbound long ships had begun accelerating as well, and they had continued to do so for the last two days.

"Well," Sam said, "they're heading for the biggest gas station in the star system, assuming they scoop hydrogen from gas giants for reaction mass like we do. Hard to see how they get around otherwise. They must figure they can afford to burn it up. They making any progress?"

No, sir. Still falling behind. So what's the point?

Yeah, Sam wondered, what was the point? The Guardians couldn't catch them before the *Bay* got to Destie-Seven. Of course, the gas giant wasn't their main concern, it was the shipyard at Destie-Seven-Echo. Had the Guardians figured that out? Probably. It wasn't that complicated if they stopped to think about it. Of course, these were immortal gods who'd been on the top of the heap for centuries, maybe millennia. Did they bother to think hard anymore?

"I don't know what they intend, TAC, but the longer they burn, the less time we'll have to take care of business at the shipyard. Since we still don't know what we're going to do when we get there, I'd rather they took their time following us."

Wait one, Alexander said, and the contact went dead for a few seconds, then Alexander came back on. *Captain, we've got an incoming tight beam holocomm.*

"Where's it from, TAC?"

Looks like Destie-Five orbit. It's definitely a Destie or Guardian holocomm, but they've cut the data flow rate down so our processors can decode it without a work-around. Same procedure they used back before.

"Nice of them to remember," Sam said. "Is there an explanatory tag on it?"

Yes, sir. It says it's for you. Asks for you by name: Captain Samuel Bitka.

CHAPTER TWENTY-FIVE

At the same time, aboard USS *Cam Ranh Bay*,
outbound to Destie-Seven
9 June 2134 (*one hundred thirteen days after
Incident Seventeen*)

Ka'Deem Brook sat at the desk in the office he had
inherited from Mikko Running-Deer and went through
the meaningless routine of producing yet another Plan of
the Day, as if everyone on the ship did not know that today
was going to be like yesterday and like tomorrow, at least
for the immediate future.

His mind wandered and he wondered what Choice was
doing right now. Had she taken another lover? He
wouldn't mind if she had, as long as it was another civilian.
He wouldn't like her talking about him in bed to another
officer, but he could live with that. He just hoped she
hadn't found one *before* she broke off their relationship.
He'd never had any expectation the affair would last
forever and had simply enjoyed it while it had. A
Cottohazz-wide famous musician and a Navy lieutenant?
Sure, he could just see himself at SMA—the Stellar Music
Awards—the ugly duckling among a thousand swans. No,

he'd enjoyed his moment of carnal bliss, and he knew people in the service would eventually figure out it had happened, maybe with some understated hints from him. That wouldn't do him any harm, either. Maybe she'd even mention him in a tell-all memoir of her harrowing adventure. *That would smack!* Even if she trashed him, that would still smack. He wondered if it would cause much trouble with his wife Bunny.

But...what if Choice took up with an *enlisted* crewperson? What would their pillow talk about him be? The thought sent a shudder of dread through his body.

The commlink vibrated at the base of his skull and he saw the ID tag for Captain Bitka. *Now what?*

"Yes, sir?"

XO, I've got an incoming holocomm from the Guardians addressed personally to me. We'll record it but you should helmet up and sit in. Set your holosuite to receive only. No point in confusing them as to who's who.

"Aye, aye, sir," Brook answered and felt his stomach tighten as he cut the circuit and looked around for his helmet. *It was just here this morning. Ah! The door brackets. There it was.*

His hand trembled slightly as he slipped on the helmet and sealed it. He plugged his shipsuit into the life-support umbilical at his desk workstation—who knew how long this would take? He took a couple measured, steadying breaths and felt his heart rate start to slow again.

He had seen vid of the Guardians but had not been present in any of the interviews with their prisoner. He had no need to participate, nor any desire. The less he had to interact with them the better, but he knew he had a job to do. Someone had to keep the captain in check.

Ka'Deem Brook was probably the only senior officer on *Cam Ranh Bay* who had not been swept away upon hearing that Sam Bitka was taking command. He'd already gotten a full report on Captain Bitka from his friend and Annapolis classmate, Larry Goldjune: the lack of experience and professional polish, the tendency to shoot from the hip and trust to luck, the unwillingness to accept Navy tradition and procedures.

Actually, Larry and Brook hadn't exactly been classmates. Brook had been a year older than Larry, a "Youngster" to Larry's "Plebe" when they met. Somehow, he had never felt able to exercise authority over the younger midshipman. Brook chalked that up to Larry's natural leadership. He'd have far preferred Larry as a captain to Bitka.

Even back at Annapolis, Brook and everyone around him knew Larry Goldjune would someday outrank them all, and it wouldn't pay to antagonize him. After all, it was in Larry's blood: his father at that time a senior captain commanding a President-class cruiser and his uncle had already worn the two collar stars of rear admiral upper half. If somehow Brook returned from this nightmare, having a Goldjune ally would matter.

Captain Bitka wasn't a disaster as a commanding officer, but he also wasn't anything special, in Brook's opinion. Bitka had no real experience in operations or on the technical side—unless you counted being able to repair an ordinary fabricator, a job for a machinist's mate second class. He had very little command experience, and his lack of a formal command education at the academy was apparent in almost everything he did. His one claim to fame was his supposed genius for tactics, but the new drills which were beating long ships in the simulations were developed by Alexander, with some help from Acho, not by Bitka. Even the idea for them had come from that leatherhead, Haykuz.

Bitka was likeable, Brook supposed, in a remote sort of way, but even there he managed to sacrifice most of the majesty associated with a commanding officer without gaining any sort of intimacy with the crew in return. Ma and Alexander, the two fellow reservists among the department heads, probably looked up to him for obvious reasons: birds of a feather. Brook wasn't sure where Acho stood. What had puzzled him was Running-Deer's admiration for him, especially as she had been the other academy-trained senior officer on board. He chalked that up to her infatuation. Too bad she had died before seeing her hero had feet of clay.

Not that Brook wanted Bitka's job. He just wanted a captain he had more confidence in.

XO, are you ready? he heard Bitka ask inside his head. Brook slid the helmet visor down and secured it with a click, activating his holosuite.

"Ready, Captain Bitka."

Good. Won't pay to keep a god waiting too long. COMM, patch us through.

As the channel opened, the holosuite took over and Brook's view of his office disappeared, replaced by that of the interior of an alien starship. He made sure the holosuite was recording their first look at what was probably the bridge of a Guardian long ship. It had workstations which looked similar to those of the New People, but crewed by an entirely different alien race, barrel-chested with slender arms, large heads, dark coloration, and what looked to be a carapace of some type. The faces looked more like insects than anything else, but with more familiar-looking eyes, although four of them: two on the front of the face and one to each side. Another race with awkward-looking hands and only three fingers and a thumb. Brook immediately recognized the Guardian from the earlier broadcasts by the coloration of his feathers: P'Daan.

"S'Bitka, I speak directly to you. I demand justice: justice for the New People and justice for my four dead companions. If you can hear and see me, S'Bitka, and if you have the courage, respond," the Guardian said.

The image froze. *S'Bitka?* That must be the Guardian form of Captain Samuel Bitka's name, but Brook had never heard Te'Anna address him so in any of the recorded interrogations. And *four* dead companions? Of course. P'Daan didn't know Te'Anna was still alive and their prisoner, and that meant he couldn't know how much she had told them.

"I see and hear you," Bitka's hologram responded. "You know what I want? Justice for my *six* dead companions, who yours butchered and ate like cattle. I'm not sure I have it yet, but to save lives I am willing to call it so. You've experienced some of our weaponry. Believe me, you don't want to experience the really nasty stuff we haven't used yet, so why don't you just let us go in peace?"

The captain froze the image and then his hologram looked over at Ka'Deem.

"May as well grab some lunch, XO. The light-speed transit time back to Destie-Four is about fifty-five minutes, and then as long for his reply to get to us. Stupid way to carry on a conversation, but I guess if you're immortal, time's not as much of an issue. I've got some paperwork to catch up on."

He lifted his helmet visor and disappeared. Ka'Deem lifted his own and sat quietly for a moment, considering the distances involved even in this comparatively short voyage across a star system. P'Daan's ship orbited Destie-Four. They were bound for Destie-Seven and had already come a billion kilometers. A *billion* kilometers, almost a light hour, and they were less than halfway to the large gas giant. He had served as a commissioned officer in the United States Navy for ten years, most of that time spent in spacecraft and almost half of it in starships, but he had never quite come to terms with the enormous distances involved. He knew the numbers, but they were so large as to be meaningless except as values to plug into equations. He shrugged and went back to work.

Two hours later he closed his desk workstation, put on his helmet, and lowered the visor.

"M'Eetos gave you creatures the interstellar drive!" P'Daan thundered when his hologram reappeared. "Are you too primitive to understand even that? Your drive bears his coded signature. I believe he raised you all up, gave you sentience, and how have you repaid him? What did you do with M'Eetos?"

The hologram froze, so P'Daan was waiting for a reply, already had been for an hour. Ka'Deem wondered if *he* was having lunch.

"Never even heard of M'Eetos, or any other Guardian before we got here," the Captain replied. "I honestly have no idea where he is or what happened to him. And if you think he raised us up, you're kidding yourself. We are independently evolved. Every species in the *Cottohazz* is.

"And this little trip was not our idea. *You* brought us here, without asking us, and if things went bad when your underlings decided to eat some of us, that's not our fault.

"You're obviously right about the origin of the drive, though. It must have passed from your pal M'Eetos to the Varoki and then they passed it off as their own invention. There are five or six Varoki trading houses that I figure owe you, or M'Eetos, or *somebody*, about three hundred years' worth of back royalties. But I think everyone who paid them those royalties is going to have a claim for fraud as well, and that could get complicated. It's not really my problem, but if you like I could recommend a couple good intellectual property lawyers." He froze the image.

What the hell was the captain trying to do? Instead of looking for a deal, he was practically *taunting* the Guardian!

"Take five," the captain said with a grin Ka'Deem couldn't fathom, "or two hours, if you like. We'll see what Mister Big says next."

Two hours later, P'Daan's reply came.

"*I* am the law," P'Daan said, and then cut the connection.

"So," the captain said, "I think that went pretty well."

Was he insane?

An hour later Ka'Deem Brook hesitated before the doorway to the Varoki diplomat's quarters. He had no more regard for Loptoon Haykuz than did anyone else on the *Bay*, and he realized that what he was doing might be seen as undermining his own captain's authority. Most of his instincts rebelled against what he contemplated doing, but his greater responsibility was to the ship, to its crew, and to its passengers. Instead of touching the door's chime he took several steps back and around the corner of the corridor and then squinted up Haykuz on his commlink.

Yes, Lieutenant Brook, the Varoki answered. *What can I do for you?*

"I wonder if it would be possible for the two of us to speak confidentially about a matter of great importance? Perhaps in your quarters?"

The Varoki paused before answering. *In confidence, you say? I am happy to speak with you and I can assure you of my discretion, but I cannot guarantee absolute silence if the subject should stray beyond . . . certain boundaries.*

"Of course, Mister Haykuz. That goes without saying," Brook answered, although it was not at all the answer he had hoped for. Well, he would have to be discreet as well, feel out Haykuz. Six weeks ago, he would have felt far more confident of where the Varoki stood on the subject of their captain but everything had become confused and ambiguous since the massacre on Destie Four. The ground had shifted and he no longer knew where anyone stood.

Seconds later the tall Varoki met Brook at his door and gestured him in, offered him water or hot tea to drink— tea from Earth. Suddenly Brook wondered how many other Humans Haykuz had entertained over tea lately.

How many others had come here to sound him out? How many others had he invited here in order to sound out himself? Why had Brook not thought of that before?

"Water will be fine," he said.

They sat in chairs which Brook found higher than he was used to and his feet barely touched the cabin floor, as if he were a child sitting in an adult's place. The stateroom was undecorated, like a blank slate, revealing nothing of the Varoki's personality. Was that deliberate? Haykuz, ears spread wide and face clear of color, waited patiently for Brook to begin.

"As you are an experienced negotiator, I was hoping you could help me understand an exchange the captain had with the Guardian P'Daan over the course of today," Brook said. "I was somewhat surprised the captain did not invite you to join the conference, given your position as our senior diplomat."

"You compliment me twice, Lieutenant Brook," Haykuz answered, "and more than I deserve, in describing me as an experienced negotiator and a senior diplomat. Really, I am neither. My experience in both realms consists of observing others. But whatever insight I have gained from that is at your service."

Brook shifted uncomfortably in his chair, not certain how to proceed. Was Haykuz genuinely that humble? He had never seemed so before, while he had been the diplomat e-Lisyss's flunky. Then he had seemed a reflection of his superior's arrogance. Brook had at least understood that arrogance, but this Varoki was a stranger.

But he was here. He had to go on. All he knew to do was relate the holoconference between Captain Bitka and

P'Daan as simply and directly as he knew how. He did not ask why the captain had seemed to throw away any chance of negotiating a compromise, or what purpose was served by that, but surely the unasked question was clear. Nevertheless, when he finished the Varoki simply studied him for a moment before speaking.

"And what can I help you with, Lieutenant Brook?"

Brook took a breath before answering, and then pressed ahead.

"Why do you think he decided not to negotiate with P'Daan?"

"Ah. Well...negotiate what? The terms of our surrender?"

Caught off guard, Brook leaned forward. "*Surrender?* Do you think we should surrender?"

"Oh, no, I don't think so. Certainly not yet. But it seems to me we are in a very weak position. It is difficult to negotiate from weakness. I would think the captain would want to put off serious negotiations until he can demonstrate strength somehow. Of course, we did that at Destie-Four, but the arrival of P'Daan with his fleet has changed the balance, hasn't it? It is certainly difficult to see how best to proceed."

"But he seemed to deliberately antagonize P'Daan," Brook answered. "That will make negotiations harder. Why burn bridges?"

"Why indeed?" Haykuz asked and looked away thoughtfully. Then he bobbed his head and looked back. "My late superior, the Honorable e-Lisyss, always attempted to begin a negotiation by pretense of injury or offense, to put his opponent on the defensive. I suspect he did it thinking this made an error in judgment more likely. I wonder if P'Daan did not intend something similar by beginning his communication with an accusation. Perhaps the captain understood that and deliberately refused to respond as P'Daan intended. Perhaps . . . perhaps the captain knows he will have to fight P'Daan before they can negotiate. If the captain can force P'Daan into an error in the fighting—and is there a more frequent cause of error than anger?—he will be able to negotiate from a position of greater strength when the time comes. That is a possible reason. But really, Lieutenant Brook, why do you not simply ask him what he intended?"

"Well . . . I don't want him to think I am questioning his judgment," Brook answered. "He might take offense."

"Ah. He does not strike me as one who would do so, but perhaps he is different with his officers than with civilians such as myself. I confess to having little experience with the military. But short of asking him directly, I do not see how your curiosity can be satisfied."

Brook sipped his water and wondered what he had expected to accomplish here. He had been looking for a possible ally, he supposed, but an ally in what? Someone to back up his assessment of the captain when and if they got home? And who was going to get them there?

CHAPTER TWENTY-SIX

Seven days later, aboard USS *Cam Ranh Bay,* outbound to Destie-Seven
16 June 2134 (*one hundred twenty days after Incident Seventeen*)

Captain Bitka, I have a Mister P'Daan holding for you on line one, he heard Signaler Lucinda Weaver say inside his head. *Will you take the call?*

Sam laughed.

"Again? Can't we comm-block him or something? Okay, please give my compliments to Mister Haykuz and have him helmet up as well. Once he's ready, I'll take it."

Aye, aye, sir.

Sam sat up and swung his feet off his bunk, rising slightly in the air as he did so in the low gravity. Damn, why did P'Daan always call when he was asleep? And these calls were getting so common they were becoming pointless exercises: four times in eight days. He padded across the floor of his day cabin, his bare feet scarcely touching the floor, and retrieved his helmet from the rack beside his desk.

Captain, Mister Haykuz is ready.

"Okay, let's go."

Sam lowered his visor and saw the hologram of Haykuz. After the first conference, which took him by surprise, he'd asked the Varoki diplomat to sit in. P'Daan appeared, today taking the conference in what appeared to be his spacious personal quarters. The Guardian was as physically imposing as ever, but Sam realized these repeated harangues were probably tactical mistakes on P'Daan's part. The first time the alien had had a chilling majesty, much of which came from the strangeness, the novelty of his appearance and demeanor. Now, Sam was getting used to him. A couple more holoconferences and he'd probably be just one more big, annoying bird.

Well, annoying and deadly.

"One less day in your fleeting existence, S'Bitka," P'Daan began. "If you should survive to become my prisoner, the sweetness of the memory of these days will make you weep for a century. You know what I did to the New People who dared attack us. They now live in eternal torment, and I will do exactly the same to you. Do not pretend you are not afraid. I know better. I know the desperation with which mortals cling to the pathetic moments of their lives. You are no different. You cannot escape from this star system. Your only escape is death, and if you fall into my hands, I will deny you even that." P'Daan's image froze.

"And good morning to you," Sam answered brightly. "I was just thinking that at a carnival you actually have to *pay* to have your fortune told, but I get it from you for free. You know, you've lived thousands of years, maybe millions, and I bet you've never been to a carnival. Now *that's* sad."

Sam froze the image and turned to the Varoki official. "We're up to a little over two hours in turn-around time, Mister Haykuz. We can take a break, get some work done, but before we do, any observations?"

The Varoki thought for a moment, perhaps comparing this P'Daan to that of the earlier messages.

"He seems different today, more resolute. He does not seem to be speaking to provoke a specific reaction from you or create a particular impression. I believe he has made a decision."

Sam hadn't noticed a change but now as he thought back he could see what the Varoki meant. There was something different about the Guardian's attitude today. There was always plenty of arrogance to go around from P'Daan, but today there was a big shot of *don't-give-a-damn*, too.

"Interesting observation. Thank you. Comm will call you in about two hours, when the reply comes through." Sam lifted his visor and the virtual environment of the holocon gave way to his stateroom. He picked up the hologram projector of Cassandra from his desk, turned it on, and watched several cycles, then froze it at the end.

"What are you thinking?" he asked the hologram. "And what's that Guardian son of a bitch up to?"

After a few seconds Sam squinted up the commlink code of the OOD, Lieutenant Sylvia Norquist.

Yes, sir, she answered immediately.

"Ms. Norquist, let's go to Readiness Condition Two."

Aye, aye, sir, Readiness Condition Two, she answered, without a question even in her voice. Man, the crew had come a long way in a couple of months, he thought, in more ways than one.

Two hours later he donned his helmet and lowered the visor.

"Enjoy your illusions, S'Bitka," P'Daan began. "In the end they will undo you. As for all mortals, your weakness is your addiction to illusion. The only thing real is this moment. That is where I live, in the moment. You divide your time between past and future, between memory and illusion. And make no mistake, the future as you imagine it is certainly illusion, the sort of future where you have made a difference, where you have changed the world in some noticeable way.

"Let me tell you what the future is: entropy. Energy inevitably slips from higher states to lower states, matter breaks down from elaborate structures to more simple ones. In the end the universe will be a uniform temperature and consist of a uniform distribution of atoms: hydrogen, helium, iron, carbon. There will be no way to tell which of those carbon atoms were once part of you, S'Bitka, because every carbon atom is indistinguishable from every other. Nothing you do, no matter how heroic or how base, will change that final distribution of atoms at the end of time." P'Daan's image froze.

Sam had to admit he found that prospect depressing, as P'Daan undoubtedly intended. And just because his enemy intended him to feel a certain way didn't make it wrong, did it? P'Daan was right, that's how things ended up. It still seemed too remote to worry much about, though, and then he realized that for P'Daan and the other Guardians it was not so remote a prospect. When they thought about the heat death of the universe, they saw their *own* inescapable mortality.

And then Sam laughed and switched the holosuite to transmit mode.

"See, you think a lot bigger than I do. You want to change the universe, and you can't. My ambitions are more modest. I want to make a few people's lives a little better, and I might be able to accomplish that. And you know why I want that? It pleases me, I guess because I share an emotional bond with other people. I *like* people, some of them anyway. I'm even getting to like a few Varoki, like my quiet friend here."

"Thank you, Captain Bitka," Haykuz said.

"You're very welcome, Haykuz. But I have to say, P'Daan, I'm not all that crazy about you. And I just figured out something: you're a fraud. I mean, that's a good pitch you have there, about how nothing really matters in the grand scheme of things, so I guess we mortals should just collapse in despair, right? And that bit about the carbon atoms? Nice touch!

"But here's the thing: nothing you're planning on doing to us will make any difference to the carbon atoms at the end of time, either. You're going to live thousands, maybe millions of years, possibly even a billion, and you're not going to influence one more carbon atom than I will. How do you like them apples? Here I am, a lowly mortal who's going to be gone in the blink of an eye, and I am every bit as important to the universe as you are. Man, that must really burn your ass. And all this stuff about how we mortals are here only for an instant, unlike you guys? I bet that's exactly what those other Guardians were thinking as they were eating my friends, but we'll never know for sure, will we? It's too late to ask them."

Sam felt his commlink vibrate and simultaneously he saw the interrupt warning appear as a text hologram above P'Daan's head.

General Quarters it read in flashing orange letters.

Sam immediately lifted his helmet visor, cutting the holocon feed, and heard the general quarters gong sounding throughout the ship. He pushed off in the low gee for the door of his day cabin as he squinted open the commlink. The incoming ID tag read Lieutenant Sylvia Norquist, the OOD.

"What's happening, Norquist?"

Jump emergence signature, sir. Two large targets, range one-nine-seven-triple-zero, bearing two-niner-seven, angle on the bow fourteen, closing at three kilometers per second. I sounded general quarters on my initiative.

So that's what P'Dann had decided! Sam did the tactical math in his head: about eighteen hours to rendezvous, at that distance and closing speed. *Too close. Damn!*

"You did right, Norquist. Start the log and battle clock from the time of jump emergence. I'll be on the bridge to relieve you in one minute. Prep the ship to undock with the spin habitat."

He'd grabbed his boots and, still barefoot, was already out in the passageway leading forward, which had become "up" since the *Bay* had been under continuous low acceleration. He grabbed the hand conveyor which ran forward along the starboard side of the passage. He thought through the problem as he let the hand conveyor take him past the partial bulkheads at the three frames between his day cabin and the bridge. About two hundred thousand kilometers wasn't enough distance for the plan they'd had the most success with, which was to raise their velocity at low gee over a day or two. They'd have to do it quicker, which they could, but it meant burning a lot more HRM. This might still work but it was going to be close.

Two ships, though. Well, they'd run the drill against two ships and won . . . usually. It was an added complication, though. It wasn't just more firepower; a second ship let the enemy cover a broader field of fire with their two meson guns, and let them take out twice as many incoming targets. And it meant the *Bay* had to kill twice as many ships to win. To survive, they'd need to do some fancy evasive maneuvers. More reaction mass.

He heard the subdued but excited chatter of crew behind him, coming up the passageway to their battle stations on the bridge. He couldn't make out the words, but the tone carried that same mix of excitement, anticipation and anxiety as he felt himself.

Lieutenant Ka'Deem Brook's voice rose in pitch inside Sam's head, the emotion clear even through the mechanical filter of the commlink: *This isn't going to work!*

"Main hull is clear of the docking collar," Lieutenant Barr-Sanchez reported from Maneuvering One as she punched the acceleration warning klaxon twice. "Ready for ventral thrust."

"Make full ventral thrust," Sam ordered. He felt the vibration immediately as the ventral attitude control thrusters fired fore, aft, and amidships, pushing him down in his acceleration chair and sliding *Cam Ranh Bay* "up."

The view forward showed on the main bridge display and he saw the big habitat wheel, now separated from the main hull of the *Bay* and moving "down."

"Nose is clear of the habitat wheel," Barr-Sanchez reported. "Securing ACT burn. Radiators are clear of the habitat wheel."

"Full thrust," Sam ordered, "all drives."

Barr-Sanchez hit the acceleration klaxon again, one long wavering blast, and then fired the thrusters. The acceleration pushed Sam back into his chair, made him feel all of his weight and then some. Without the mass of the habitat wheel, the *Bay* could manage a little over one and a tenth gees. It would be close, very close.

This isn't going to work, Ka'deem Brook repeated. *Run the numbers, Captain! There's not enough time, not enough distance between us and the long ships. If we follow your course projection, we enter their effective range in one hour and forty minutes, but our missiles won't be in range to kill them for another ten minutes after that.*

"I know the numbers, Mister Brook."

If we launch our ordnance at the forty-minute mark and then start decelerating, we can stay completely out of their range.

"Yes, and our missiles will have to spend nineteen minutes in the kill zone. Our missiles don't live nineteen minutes in the kill zone, XO. You know that from the simulations. They can probably live thirteen minutes, and that's what that extra twenty minutes of straight-ahead acceleration gets us."

Maybe! Brook shot back. *We don't even know that*

much for sure. It's all based on assumptions. And it still doesn't do us any good. Even if every assumption is right, they kill us ten minutes before our missiles kill them.

"Fortunately, XO, we've got an hour and a half to figure out how to avoid dying. Plenty of time. COMM, get me all-ship, captain to crew."

"Hot mic, sir," Bohannon said.

"All hands, this is the captain speaking. We are about to engage two Guardian long ships which just popped out of jump space. We have separated from the spin habitat, which is a trick they haven't seen from us before, and we are about to show them how fast this lady can run when she ditches her skirt. We've drilled and drilled and drilled, practicing how to kill these bastards, until we can do it in our sleep. Now it's time to just do it. Captain out."

"Sir," Lieutenant Alexander said from the TAC One chair to Sam's right, "you might want to look at this. We're getting unusual readings from one of the long ships, the one we've tagged Bandit Two."

Sam touched his workstation and brought up the TAC sensor feeds.

"See, sir? Its heat signature is declining, as if it's gradually turning on some sort of thermal cloak. And look at the HRVS image. The stern of the ship seems like it's shimmering, wavering. Do they have some kind of force field covering it?"

Sam looked at the imagery, the closest and best look they'd had so far of long ships, two of them in tight formation: massive, blocky structures at the stern, an almost impossibly long, slender latticework frame reaching forward, and a smaller but still considerable structure at the bow. One of the long ships was cooling, and Sam also saw a slight shimmer around the aft section of the ship. Then he smiled.

"TAC, that's a very original interpretation of the data you have there, but leaving aside alien cloaking devices and force fields, use Occam's Razor and try again. Limit yourself to phenomena we've actually experienced."

Alexander stared at his workstation and shook his head.

"Sorry, Captain, but I've never seen anything like that shimmer over the stern of the starship except maybe an electrostatic armor field. You think that's what it is?"

"I think it's simpler than that. We like to avoid in-system jumps near the plane of the ecliptic because there's junk floating around there, and you come out in the same space as junk, you experience an annihilation event. That shimmer is from atmosphere escaping. It's outgassing, and its thermal signature is decreasing because it's cooling down. He doesn't have power and pretty soon he's not going to have atmo. I bet he suffered an annihilation event upon exiting jump space. That evens the odds a bit."

"You mean he came out in the same space as a rock?"

"I'd guess more like a few grains of sand. This had to have been a pretty small event. Of course, small is relative. The only annihilation events I saw in the war didn't leave anything identifiable as a ship. That's the problem with in-system jumps, especially if you jump into the plane of the ecliptic, where all the debris gathers. I'll tell you, TAC, I'm amazed they risked it. I really am. It's one thing for us mortals to roll those dice. I guess in one sense we and the Guardians are risking the same thing: all that's left of our lives. But for us that's a few decades. For them, it's potentially millennia. What's worth that risk for them? I really never thought they'd take it."

"Well, sir, who says there are Guardians on those two ships?" Alexander said.

Huh! Sam thought. That made a lot of sense. Those two ships were two hours' communication time away from P'Daan, same as the *Bay* was. If there were no Guardians actually over there, calling the tactical shots, that might make a difference.

"Captain Bitka," Bohannon said from COMM One to his left, "P'Daan's back on the horn."

"Christ! Take a message. And get me a tight beam back to the habitat wheel. I need to talk to our prisoner, Te'Anna."

"Sir, we rigged her stateroom up as a holosuite, just in case," Bohannon said. "You want to use that?"

After disengaging from the habitat wheel, the small stay-behind crew had used the attitude thrusters on the wheel to get it spinning again, so Te'Anna sat in normal gravity and looked at him through her unusual unblinking eyes.

"Oh, Captain Bitka!" Te'Anna said. "I did not expect to speak with you today, let alone see you. You look very strange, however, particularly your legs, which seem too short and somewhat lacking in detail. This device you call a holosuite has room for considerable improvement."

"Yes," Sam answered, "my engineering department tells me your holocomm technology is superior to ours. Maybe you can give us some pointers later. I don't have much time right now, but I would like to ask a couple quick questions. Have you personally ever done an in-system jump in the plane of the ecliptic?"

She looked at him and tilted her head to the side.

"If I did that sort of thing, I would not be here speaking to you. I would have died long ago."

"That's what I figured. Next question: the human female named Choice has a theory about your technology and its diffusion through your society."

"She is not your subordinate," Te'Anna interrupted. "Do you find *her* alluring?"

"She's a lovely lady. She believes you keep some technology segregated from your servant races. Bioengineering, for example, and star travel. Is that so?"

"Of course," she said as if it were obvious. Maybe it should have been.

"You're saying no Guardian in their right mind would risk an in-system jump, but that star travel is reserved for Guardians. That doesn't—"

"Only the technology is reserved," she interrupted, "not the simple ability to operate it. Why is this a puzzle? Your own civilization does the same."

Yes, they did, he thought, but that wasn't the point here. The point was there were no Guardians on those two ships which had made the jump.

"Thank you. This has been helpful." Sam reached for his visor to cut the connection.

"Stop!" she said. "Do not end our conversation yet. You are not treating me well."

He now noticed she sat more slumped than usual. He didn't know what her body language really meant, but something about her posture and attitude was different.

The stateroom lights were dim and yet her aura, or halo, was hardly visible.

"I'm pressed for time, but I'll listen to your complaint later, if we're still alive."

"It is a critique," she said, "not a complaint, and it is brief and simple."

Sam squinted up the helmet chronometer.

"Two minutes," he said. "I'll give you two minutes."

"I will not use half of that. I willingly became your prisoner out of boredom. I came to you because I believed you would excite my curiosity, and so renew my waning interest in life. Instead I am confined in this small room, with only occasional visitors and a very limited allowed reading list.

"I have no particular loyalty to P'Daan and some sympathy for you. Not an abundance, but some. You should be courting my loyalty by allowing me wider access to your ship, crew, and passengers. The two guards—who are with me at all times in any case—would be adequate to insure I cause no trouble. Without more mental stimulation, I will lapse into depression and eventually die.

"That is all I have to say."

She said it calmly, dispassionately, but Sam saw a suggestion of desperate appeal in her large, unblinking gray eyes. She must be terribly alone there, cut off not only from her own people but also from most of the ship's company.

"Let me think about it," Sam said, "but I believe we can work something out, assuming we survive the next several hours."

CHAPTER TWENTY-SEVEN

Moments later, aboard USS *Cam Ranh Bay,*
outbound to Destie-Seven
16 June 2134 (*one hundred twenty days after
Incident Seventeen*)

Sam removed his helmet and scanned the large display at
the front of the bridge.

"No change in enemy course, sir," Alexander reported.
"The live enemy ship, Bandit One, has docked with the
crippled Bandit Two. They may be taking off survivors."

"Or assisting with repairs," Sam said. "How long till
we're at our firing point?"

"Coming up on thirty minutes."

Sam checked their relative positions. The angle on the
bow had dropped from fourteen degrees to twelve, which
made sense because they weren't on exactly the same
course. The long ships were coming in from their port side
and would cross their course to starboard in about three
hours at their current velocity, less than that once they
finished their acceleration. But that meant the *Bay*'s true
course was not toward them but offset slightly. All of the
simulations had assumed head-to-head closing situations.

"Huh," he said to himself. He ran the course projection again on his workstation and then sat back in his acceleration couch.

"Helm, recalculate your turnaround maneuver for reversing course. Once we unload our missiles, I want you to pivot the ship through an axis inverse to the hostile bearing. I make it one-one-seven degrees relative."

"Recalculating for turnabout through one-one-seven degrees, sir," Barr-Sanchez answered.

"One more thing, Helm: we won't wait for the turnaround maneuver to be complete before thrusting. Once we reach the halfway point, punch it. You're going to have to redo our math on the new course."

"Aye, aye, sir," she answered, as if this were the most routine order she had ever received.

"Sir?" Alexander asked quietly.

Sam smiled at his tactical officer. "TAC, whoever is running the show over there is going to have a tough decision to make in about forty minutes. Once we fire our missiles and decoys, we start decelerating as hard as we can to slow our approach to his meson gun. But we know we'll be within their range well before our missiles get to their detonation distance. Right?"

"Yes, sir."

"Here's the thing. We assumed a straight-line closing problem, but our courses are oblique. Think about the firing solution from their point of view. Once we fire our missiles, the more we decelerate, the more distance between us and our attack swarm of decoys and missiles, and given *oblique* courses . . ."

"Arc of fire!" Alexander exclaimed. "We won't both be

in their arc of fire. They'll have to pick which target to engage. Acho was right."

Yes, the enemy would have to pick between protecting itself and killing the *Bay*. Those long ships weren't designed as solitary killers; they were made to act in concert, so different ships could engage targets on multiple axes. Hopefully they wouldn't patch up the other long ship soon. With two shooters, life would get a lot more complicated. So, what would he do in that case? He squinted up the duty roster and pinged Lieutenant Sylvia Norquist in the launch bay.

Yes, sir, she answered, excitement apparent in her voice.

"Ms. Norquist, I'm only going to have you launch two of those Mark Fours you have down there when we fire the main attack swarm. Move the other two to the launch cradles and keep them ready."

Two missiles with the main swarm, two on the launch cradles. Aye, aye, sir.

"Once we start our deceleration burn, keep your crew ready. After ten minutes, I'm going to cut the burn for two minutes, to give you zero gee to get those other two missiles out the door. Can you get them deployed in two minutes?"

Yes, sir. Can do.

Lieutenant Homer Alexander felt the perspiration trickle down the center of his spine inside his shipsuit. He turned up the cooling control on his life support and checked the battle clock: one hour and fifteen minutes since the two long ships had emerged from jump. His broad spectrum electromagnetic passive feed lit up and Chief Josephine Bermudez in the Tac Two seat to Homer's right called out, "Energy discharge. Bandit One just fired something."

"He's way out of range," the captain said. "What's he firing at?"

"It's not the firing signature of a meson gun, sir," she answered. "At least not like the one we recorded back on Destie Four."

Homer could see that on his own display. "Something smaller," he said. "It might be a missile launch, except our prisoner said they didn't use missiles. Maybe a sensor remote. Active radar has something . . . looks really small. *Might* be a missile, sir."

"Track it," the captain ordered, "and try to build up some imaging."

"Evasive action, sir?" Barr-Sanchez asked from the helm station.

"No, not yet. Let's find out if there's anything to evade."

Another light flashed on Homer's display, this one a reminder he had programmed himself.

"Range coming up on ninety-four thousand to target, sir," he said.

"Closing velocity?" the captain asked.

"Forty-three kilometers per second."

"Good enough. Helm, secure from acceleration. TAC, deliver your ordnance."

Homer suddenly became weightless as the thrusters fell silent, and then he felt a shudder as the coil gun delivered its first payload.

"First decoy packet launched," he said. He checked the close-in optics. "Getting a good dispersion on the decoys."

After about forty seconds the *Bay* shuddered again, this time launching the first of their Mark Five missiles. They would launch, in staggered sequence, four decoy clusters and three Mark Five missiles, all followed by a passive sensor drone. The Mark Fives and the drone left the coil gun cold and should be virtually indistinguishable from the hundreds of decoys in the swarm, and so were coded Cold Alpha, Bravo, Charlie, and Delta. At the same time, Homer knew Lieutenant Norquist's small craft subdivision was ejecting two big Mark Four missiles from the docking bay. Those had their own booster rockets but for the moment, those were simply ejected into space. Once all the other ordnance was delivered the *Bay* would begin its deceleration burn, to stay out of the range of the enemy meson guns for as long as possible. That's when they would remotely fire the big solid fuel rockets on the two Mark Fours—coded Hot Alpha and Hot Bravo. The rocket exhaust would show up as hot targets on the enemy sensors, and hopefully draw fire away from the deadlier Mark Fives.

"Bandit is firing again, sir," Chief Bermudez reported.

What the hell were they firing? Homer wondered. "Very well, Chief. Track it and see if you can pick up any sign of a small projectile cloud on the same trajectory."

"You think it's something like the buckshot ordnance the uBakai used in the last war?" the captain asked him.

"I don't know, sir, but it's got to be something."

Once the last coil gun package was fired and he received his report from Norquist, the captain ordered the *Bay* turned to begin its deceleration. In the moment of slight dizziness as the ship turned around its central axis, Homer listened to the calm voices issuing routine-sounding updates on range and closing velocity, as if the minutes they counted down might not be all the minutes any of them had left and he wondered if he was going mad, or if they were all mad.

The numbers . . . nothing but numbers and he felt as if he lost his bearings, no longer knew what any of them meant. He looked at the captain. Bitka's head was tilted slightly back, eyes half-closed, as if the numbers painted an elaborate picture in his head, as if he understood everything. What did he see?

Homer visualized the attack swarm—the mix of Mark Five "colds" and decoys. It took two hundred and eighty seconds, almost five minutes, to launch the entire array of missiles and decoys. Since they left the coil gun at four kilometers a second, by the time the last ordnance launched, the first one was over a thousand kilometers downrange. The decoys would spread out, but only a few kilometers, so their attack "swarm" actually resembled a long, thin, ghostly spear hurtling toward the enemy.

No, not toward the enemy, toward where the enemy would be in thirty minutes. But the *Bay* would be in range of their meson gun almost ten minutes before their own missiles could start engaging. What then?

Homer's tactical display lost much of its resolution as they finished their turn. Now the starlike hot torch of their fusion thruster was directly between the *Bay* and the long ship, blanking out their own onboard sensors. The only target information they had was from the passive sensor drone following the missile and decoy cloud.

"Fire the boosters on Hot Alpha and Bravo," the captain ordered. Behind them the two Mark Four missiles, floating on their own in deep space after Norquist's bosun's mates had ejected them from the launch bay, fired their solid-fuel rockets and leaped toward the enemy ships. There was no telling if the Guardians had picked up their attack swarm, but these two missiles would show up on their thermal sensors like two miniature stars. The plan was for the Guardian ship to concentrate its fire on these and assume the more deadly but cold and nearly invisible Mark Fives, sandwiched in amongst hundreds of decoys, were just part of the diversion. But that would all happen after they were within range of the enemy's meson gun. And why had the captain only discharged two of their Mark Fours, and not all four of them as planned?

Minutes later Homer watched the range tick down to sixty-eight thousand. The battle clock now read one hour twenty-seven minutes.

"Helm, secure from acceleration," the captain ordered. "Have Norquist discharge the last two Mark Fours and then resume full burn."

In those two minutes while Norquist's bosuns ejected the other bulky Mark Fours, the tactical display sharpened up again with the fusion torch no longer between them and the enemy. The range dropped to under sixty-four thousand, about twenty-thousand kilometers out of the range of the meson gun, but still closing at thirty-six kilometers a second. The thrusters kicked in again, pressing them back in their chairs and fuzzing the tactical display.

Missiles Hot Charlie and Hot Delta successfully deployed, Norquist reported to Homer and Captain Bitka on the command commlink channel.

"TAC, fire the booster on Hot Charlie," the captain ordered.

Homer sent the remote firing signal and one of the two Mark Fours they had just deployed fired, showing up as an intense signature on the thermal tactical display, heading toward the alien ship. Homer glanced at the captain, not sure what he intended with this change in plan but not sure he should ask. The captain met his eye and shook his head.

"Haven't got it yet, TAC? Think it through. Range and closing rate?"

"Range sixty-one thousand, closing now at thirty-three and a half kilometers per second. Eleven minutes until we're in range of their meson gun, sir."

"And how long until our attack swarm starts engaging them?" Captain Bitka asked.

"Nineteen minutes, sir," Homer answered.

"So, we'll be in their range for eight minutes before we can do anything about it. That should be an exciting eight minutes. And that Mark Four we just lit off, how long until it's within the meson gun's range?"

"A little over six minutes, sir. It'll take twenty minutes for it to get within its own engagement range."

"Well, I don't expect it to live that long, TAC."

Homer glanced at the captain again. He appeared completely calm and relaxed. He seemed mentally engaged, interested by the problem, but somehow emotionally detached. But when the captain looked at him, when their eyes met, the intensity of his stare startled Homer. It frightened him a little, too.

"TAC, in five minutes our missile and decoy swarm will be in the enemy's engagement range. What do you think Bandit One is going to do?"

"I ... I think they'll start shooting decoys."

The captain seemed to think that over.

"Possibly. If so, they won't be able to shoot at Hot Charlie when it gets into their outer range band, not without turning their ship and lifting fire against the main swarm."

"Yes, sir, but they've got another fifteen minutes to deal with it."

The captain's gaze moved back to his own display. "That's the way I think they'll figure it," he said, as calmly as if talking about the game plan of an opposing soccer team. "We'll see pretty soon."

Homer felt sweat run down his forehead and he wiped it from his eyes. He reached to turn down the temperature in his suit again, but realized he was already shivering from the cold. On his display the range numbers ticked down and the minutes passed, and he wasn't sure if they seemed to go faster or slower than usual. Both. Neither.

"Bingo!" Bermudez said from Homer's right. "I've got a return echo from a particle cloud. Very faint radar signature, sir. Must be much smaller particles than the pellets the Varoki used in the last war. More like sand or fine grit. The larger return echo we got must be from the launch canister that held the sand."

"Closing rate?" Homer asked.

"Forty-seven kilometers per second, closing on our

attack swarm. Actually, it's aimed at our original trajectory, so it will pass behind the attack swarm. The second discharge will intercept the attack swarm in sixteen minutes."

Homer felt the tight knot of muscles at the base of his neck ease. "Too late. It's close, but our missiles will fire before that."

"Wait, another firing signature." Bermudez studied the display for a half-dozen heartbeats before nodding. "This one's coming at us, sir, on our new course track."

"I think we can evade that, provided we live that long," the captain said. "TAC, where is our attack swarm?"

"Crossing the outer limit of their gun range right now, sir," Homer answered. He checked the battle clock: one hour thirty-four minutes since jump emergence. "No firing signature from Bandit One." He waited another thirty seconds. "Still no firing signature, sir. Why isn't he firing? You think he's counting on that dust to take out the missiles?"

"Maybe. I think he's either holding his fire for Hot Alpha and Bravo following the attack swarm, or he's repositioned his ship to fire at Hot Charlie, and then kill us when we cross the range boundary. We won't know until he actually fires. Let's give him something else to think about. Light up the last Mark Four we kicked out the door."

"Aye, aye, sir," Homer answered. "Firing boosters on Hot Delta."

"Time?"

"Four minutes to meson gun range. The attack swarm is twelve minutes from engagement range."

"Meson gun firing signature!" Chief Bermudez called out. "*Hit!* He just took out Hot Bravo trailing the attack swarm."

The captain's forehead creased in concentration. "Next, he'll take out Hot Alpha behind the attack swarm and then...then it will get interesting. Te'Anna said these beings were raised for war. We'll see how smart and tough this guy really is. Helm, prepare to secure from deceleration and commence lateral evasion. Make your axis of displacement one five degrees. TAC, get ready to fire the warhead on the Hot Charlie missile."

"Aye, aye, sir," Homer and Lieutenant Barr-Sanchez said almost simultaneously. Homer brought up the missile direct detonation control on his display, but it was still forty thousand kilometers out of its own effective engagement range.

"Bandit One has fired again," Chief Bermudez reported. "Hot Alpha is gone."

For almost a minute the bridge fell silent, waiting.

"He's gone longer than his previous firing cycle time, sir," Homer said. "Why isn't he firing at the attack swarm?"

"Ha!" the captain said and sat back in his command chair. His face showed a ferocious, predatory grin Homer had never seen before. "*T-S-T-L!*" the captain said, "Too Stupid to Live. He's turning his ship to fire at Hot Charlie and then us. He thinks there's nothing left in the attack swarm but decoys. That cocky bastard's going to get one hell of a surprise when those Mark Fives rip his guts out. Helm, secure from deceleration and prepare to evade. Reactor on standby and go to low-emission mode."

"Securing from deceleration, reactor on standby, low-emission mode, sir," Barr-Sanchez answered, and Homer felt himself float forward against his restraints, again in zero gee. Without the ship's fusion torch between them and the bogies, the tactical display sharpened again.

"TAC, detonate Hot Charlie."

Homer punched the detonate signal and the tactical display showed an intense white flare where the missile had been and again the tactical screen lost resolution. Their own sensors could not penetrate the cloud of superheated and radioactive debris, but the drone in the attack swarm, at an oblique angle, could see past it, and then Homer understood.

The enemy ship, the *Bay*, and the attack swarm were not lined up with each other. Because the courses of the two ships converged, but at an angle, the ships and the swarm formed the three corners of a triangle. But the two Mark Fours the captain had held back and fired later *were* lined up between the Bay and the enemy ship. Part of the tactics Bitka had developed in the uBakai war was use of nuclear warheads to temporarily blind enemy sensors. That was how he was going to buy the time they needed.

"Helm, lateral evasion, fifteen degrees of arc," the captain ordered.

Barr-Sanchez sounded two short blasts on the klaxon and then fired the ACT thrusters, pushing Homer up and to the left.

"Making lateral burn on one five-degree axis," Barr-Sanchez reported.

"We'll be in range of their meson gun in ninety seconds, sir," Homer added.

"Understood. TAC, prep a firing solution for the Mark Five in the tube to put it right between us and Bandit One. Code it Cold Echo. Helm, give me ten more seconds of lateral burn and then turn the boat through one-eighty and point us at that guy. Then deploy the thermal shroud."

Boat, Homer thought as he worked the numbers on the missile launch problem. The captain had said, *turn the boat*. A slip of the tongue. Transports and cruisers were ships, but a destroyer rider, the type the captain had commanded during the war, was technically a boat because it lacked a star drive. The captain must be back in a part of his mind, a part of his psyche, he had not used since those desperate hours in the uBakai War. Homer wondered if Bitka had put this part of his soul away, thinking he might never need it again.

"Captain, the firing solution for Cold Echo is to bring the target to a bearing of two three zero with an angle on the bow of two degrees," Homer said.

"Helm, make it so," the captain said, and then shook his head. "I hate to burn a Mark Five as just a sensor jammer. Don't see an alternative, though."

"Meson gun firing signature!" Bermudez in the TAC Two chair called out. "Bandit One has fired at us and missed. We've got a sensor image capture. Looks like he fired at our position based on last known course. Energy pulse passed one point six kilometers from the hull, bearing one nine five degrees."

Homer felt himself instantly covered in sweat and he was grateful to be strapped into a chair and in zero gee. He might have fallen down if there had been a "down."

At a range of forty-two thousand kilometers, a miss of one point six kilometers was *nothing!* Less than a tenth of a mil of deflection.

Beside him, the captain laughed.

"One point six kilometers?" he asked. *"Really?"*

"Affirmative, sir," Bermudez answered.

The captain laughed again. Why would he laugh at a time like this? Was he crazy? Homer tried to keep the alarm from his face as he turned to him. The captain looked back, his eyes burning with excitement and humor.

"One point six kilometers, TAC. Don't you get it? He *missed us by a mile!"*

Homer heard a few nervous laughs on the bridge, and then a few more, and then he found himself laughing. He didn't think it was funny, but for some reason he couldn't help himself.

"Ship steady on target bearing two three zero," Barr-Sanchez reported. "Angle on the bow two degrees. Thermal shroud is fully deployed."

The thermal shroud gave no direct protection against a meson gun, or any other weapon, but the enemy couldn't hit what they couldn't see.

"TAC, go ahead and launch Cold Echo and then load another," the captain ordered, "although I hope we don't need to use it."

Homer hoped so as well. They had started with thirty-six Mark Fives, which had sounded like more than they would ever need, but between the fight at Destie Four and now this one, they had fired off seven of them, and four of their twelve Mark Fours. How many more long ships would they have to face? There were at least four more out there, and more could show up.

"Missile Cold Echo on the way," Homer said as he fired the missile and felt the Bay shudder. He shuddered himself but tried to concentrate on his display. The battle clock read one hour thirty-eight minutes, range now down to forty thousand, still closing at a little over thirty kilometers a second.

"Meson gun firing signature," Bermudez said, her voice now level. Maybe they were all getting used to being fired at, Homer thought. "Energy pulse passed two nine zero kilometers from hull, still bearing one nine five degrees."

"Yeah," the captain said, "if we're not on our old course, we must have tried to deflect, and what better way to deflect than directly away from our attack swarm, to make him turn his ship more. At least that's what he figured. This guy really is Mister Obvious. Helm, give me ten seconds of lateral thrust at one hundred degrees."

Homer's tactical screen started gaining resolution.

"Sir, I'm getting a better picture here, and I think that means he must be as well. Even if he can't see us on thermals, his active sensor radiation will be getting through."

"Okay, TAC, detonate Hot Delta. Helm, better give me ten seconds of lateral thrust at one four five degrees."

With trembling hand Homer brought up the missile control display and detonated the last of the Mark Fours as Barr-Sanchez sounded two klaxon blasts. Again the tactical screen showed the blooming heat signature of a nuclear detonation and then grew fuzzy.

For four more minutes they coasted, the bridge crew

silent except for the periodic reports of the long ship's fire by Bermudez, and then the captain's order for a different evasive burn. The screen interference began to fade.

"Okay, TAC, better detonate Cold Echo," the captain ordered.

Homer did so and the screen flared again.

"Cold Echo detonated. Cold Foxtrot is in the tube, sir. Should I launch?"

"Let's wait and see," he said. "We're a little under four minutes from our attack swarm being in engagement range."

Homer's chest felt tight and each breath came hard. He swallowed hot spit, fought down the nausea and rising sense of panic. His vision had narrowed to the universe of his tactical display, where the battle clock read one hour forty-five minutes. He couldn't think clearly, couldn't see beyond the next second, wasn't sure what he was supposed to do.

"Range thirty-one thousand," he reported, trying to keep his voice from cracking.

"Thanks, TAC," the captain said quietly.

The minutes and range ticked down, but now with glacial, excruciating slowness. Homer thought his display was growing clearer but he wasn't sure. His own vision seemed to be losing color resolution and its field narrowing. Was he about to pass out?

"Range twenty-four thousand," he managed to say, and then he saw a new thermal flare on his display.

"That's Cold Alpha in the attack swarm detonating," Bermudez called out. "Thermal spike on the target! We hit the son of a bitch!"

A cheer of desperate relief went up from the bridge crew. Homer realized he hadn't been breathing, took a long, gasping breath, and felt his vision begin to gain focus again.

"Settle down!" the captain ordered, but without the edge the command had had over Destie-Four. "Work your stations. We're not done yet. He's still showing pretty hot, so he's got power. Let's see where he shoots. Bermudez?"

"Sir, on the firing cycle he's been keeping to, he would have fired ten seconds ago."

They waited and seconds ticked by. Homer felt irrelevant to the battle. Everyone else's brain was working while he had become a powerless spectator.

"He's either lost his gun or he's turning his ship to engage the attack swarm," the captain said. "Either way, he's screwed."

Fifteen thousand kilometers away from them, in the middle of the attack swarm, the missile coded Cold Bravo became a tiny sun for an instant. Thirty x-ray laser pulses connected the new star with the alien long ship for too brief a time for the human eye even to register, but long enough to transfer an avalanche of its deadly, searing energy.

The long ship's fusion reactor containment must have failed because the stern section of the enemy ship suddenly became its own miniature sun.

CHAPTER TWENTY-EIGHT

Minutes later, aboard USS *Cam Ranh Bay,*
outbound to Destie-Seven
16 June 2134 *(one hundred twenty days after
Incident Seventeen)*

Sam should have felt the tension ebb from his body but did not. This wasn't over. He looked at the battle clock: one hour fifty-three minutes. Two minutes since the Cold Charlie had fired and cut the other long ship, the one disabled by the jump mishap, in half. Two minutes since he had begun decelerating again. His own sensors couldn't see the alien ships now, and the sensor drone was still partially obscured by the detonation of the three Mark Fives in the attack swarm. Both alien ships were wrecks, but really big wrecks, with some sections fairly intact. There was no telling how much it would take to finish them, although taking out one of their reactors was certainly a good start.

"Helm, where are we going to be when we match velocity with the wrecks?" Sam asked.

"Sir, we'll decelerate to match velocity with them in forty-four minutes," Barr-Sanchez said, "but by then we'll have overshot them by over twenty thousand kilometers. We're just going too fast to stop before then, even at full thrust."

"How close will we come to them as we pass?" Sam asked.

"About five thousand kilometers, sir," she answered.

"That'll be inside point defense laser range," Alexander said, "or in their case, particle accelerator range."

Sam was pleased to see the TAC Boss seemed to have recovered his composure. It had been touch and go with him during the battle, but he'd kept it together.

Close-in combat was not what Sam had been thinking about, but it was worth considering. If those ships had any close-in weaponry still functional, they could make things ugly. Even throwing sand at them at close range, given the velocity when they passed each other, could cause a fair amount of damage if the *Bay* didn't maneuver fast enough to avoid it.

"TAC, program the Mark Five we have in the pipe to divide its energy dump between the three large remaining hull sections. Open the iris valves on the one-five gig lasers and extend the heads. We're going to be in range in a couple minutes. COMM, see if you can get a tight beam to either of those wrecks."

"No power over there, sir," Bohannon answered.

"No active power plant," Sam said. "There could still be stored energy, like our power ring. Give them a shout."

Three minutes later they were just inside their own laser engagement range. Sam had waited about as long as he thought prudent when Lieutenant Bohannon jerked forward in her chair. "Sir, I've got someone! Text message using the system we worked out with the New People. Message reads: *What more do you want from us, S'Bitka World Destroyer?*"

World destroyer. That's what they thought of him, and not without some justification.

"COMM, make the following reply: Am I speaking to the leader of the ship, or to the ship itself?"

"Incoming reply, sir," Bohannon said and read it, stumbling slightly on the names. *"The Ships are dead. I am Rhaunu by-Vrook through-Reokwikki."*

"Sounds like the pedigree of a racehorse," Alexander said.

"Too bad it's not a ship," Sam said. "That one ore carrier we ran into wasn't bad. Okay, make this reply: Surrender at once and I will do what I can to assist your survivors. If you do not surrender, I will destroy you. Sign it and send it."

"Think they know what surrender means?" Alexander said.

"The New People did," Bohannon answered as she punched in the text. "Who knows if these things do? They aren't New People, that's for sure. That vid of P'Daan's made them look like big roaches, but without antennas. But they understand the common Guardian language, and it has a number of ways of expressing the concept of surrender."

"*Roaches?*" Alexander said. "I think they just got a nickname."

Sam's commlink vibrated, and he saw Ka'Deem Brook's ID tag.

"Yes, XO."

Captain, I just read your text. I have to protest. We have no business stopping for survivors.

"Mister Brook, if they surrender, we are obliged by custom, law, and regulation to render assistance."

Exigent circumstances! Brook almost shouted.

"Not in my judgment, XO. Sorry I didn't bring you into the loop on this, but there wasn't time. If we're going to take them out with another missile, we have to get a firm answer before we get in range of their close defense weaponry. Minutes count."

How do you know you can trust them?

"How do you know you can trust anyone, XO? You don't ever know for sure."

"Son of a bitch!" Bohannon said from the COMM chair beside him. "Captain, I have an answer. They give up."

"Helm, once we're stopped, calculate a burn to get us back to proximity with the enemy wrecks, then decelerate to bring us to zero close rate at a range of ten kilometers."

"Aye, aye, sir," Barr-Sanchez answered.

"TAC, secure the Mark Five in the tube but keep the two big laser heads extended. We're going in, but not emptyhanded."

"Alea iacta est," Alexander said. Sam wasn't sure what that meant or what his TAC boss thought of all this, but right now neither one really mattered.

Captain, the last time you trusted anyone connected with the Guardians, our landing party was murdered and eaten, Ka'Deem Brook said through the commlink. *This decision is reckless and I formally protest it.*

"Noted."

★ ★ ★

Senior Chief Bosun's Mate Edward Wainwright, "Boats" to most of the officers and crew, relaxed in his self-selected battle station in the docking and small craft launch bay. He had no specific duties to perform while at general quarters and so got to pick his own station. He took a chair in the launch bay because that's what he'd done until the captain and XO Running-Deer had bumped him upstairs. That's what he told everyone, anyway. The real reason he'd picked this position was to keep an eye on Lieutenant Junior Grade Sylvia Norquist, the First Lieutenant.

First Lieutenant—that was an interesting title. Whenever Brits heard it they assumed it meant the same as First Officer, which is what they called their XOs. But all it meant was the lieutenant leading the First Division, and by tradition it was usually the most junior lieutenant on the ship. First Division was responsible for the deck, which meant general cleaning and maintenance, as well as docking, and the launch, piloting, and recovery of the ship's small craft, the *Bay's* six PSRVs.

Not much usually happened in the First Division when at general quarters, especially since the PSRVs weren't armed, but the officers had dreamed up a way to use the PSRV launch cradles to deliver Mark Four missiles. Totally nuts. The idea that their improvised shackles would hold a two-ton missile in the cradle while under one gee acceleration was a disaster waiting to happen. But it had held—after Wainwright supervised a little creative reinforcing of the shackles.

The next crazy idea had been that Norquist, the most junior lieutenant on the ship, could manage to launch four of those monsters out the docking cradles while under combat acceleration. Wainwright had wanted a front-row seat to that circus, and he wanted to be there to step in if necessary. But it hadn't been necessary. Norquist got all four of the missiles deployed within the two narrow launch windows and did it without crushing any of her bosun's mates. The captain had cut the acceleration, so that helped, but still—not too shabby. Now Wainwright had nothing to do but watch the deck crew securing the empty shackles and observe Norquist's new dose of confidence. She wore it well, with modesty, like just one more job squared away.

He felt his commlink vibrate and saw the captain's ID tag.

"Yes, sir."

Boats, there are over two hundred surviving crew in the remaining compartments of those alien ships. You've got about twenty-five minutes to put together a rescue and repair mission. Mister Ma's Engineering department will provide the EVA personnel and on-ship fabricators, Ms. Acho's logistics crew is putting together bottled oxygen and some sort of trauma response, Major Merderet loaned us a fireteam of Marines before we de-docked with the habitat ring. We'll put them in hard suits for security. Ms. Norquist's small craft subdivision will ferry personnel and material to and from the wrecks in our PSRVs.

Wainwright wondered what sort of trauma response they could offer for a totally alien species. Spray bandage and rubbing alcohol, he supposed. Maybe just bandage.

"Sounds like all the bases are covered, sir. What do you want me to do?"

Take charge and keep it from turning into a cluster fuck. We're about thirty minutes from rendezvous. After that you've got twelve hours before we have to break off and rejoin the spin habitat.

"We know what those things breathe, sir? What their body chemistry is?"

Not yet, Boats. That'll be your first job: atmosphere and tissue samples. Then see about helping them with repairs, although how you repair a living ship that's apparently dead is a good question. At least they all speak the Guardian standard language and you'll have autotrans loaded in your commlinks. That should help some. But all we can do is our best. If they die, let's make sure it wasn't from our lack of trying.

"Aye, aye, sir. Maybe we can lash something together over there that'll keep them alive for a few days. Are their friends going to stop and help them?"

That's their call, Boats. This is mine.

"Yes, sir."

Okay, I've got an incoming comm from Mister Haykuz, our Varoki diplomat. Maybe I should have brought him in on the diplomacy part. What do you think?

Wainwright could hear the suppressed humor in the captain's voice even through the commlink, and why not? They'd been jumped by two long ships, had taken them out, and had suffered no damage and no casualties. And they'd done it with an armed transport. A small ration of celebration was in order.

"Captain, if he thinks he can do better than an unconditional surrender, let's give him a shot at it next time."

Captain Bitka laughed.

Laptoon Haykuz waited with his commlink channel open, expecting a call-back message, but was surprised when the captain personally answered after less than a minute.

Yes, Mister Haykuz?

"Captain, first I wish to congratulate you on this victory which, I understand, was bloodless."

Bloodless for us, anyway. Not so much for the other guys. But thank you. Now, if that's all, I'm a little busy right now.

"I can imagine you are, directing the rescue effort, and I apologize for intruding on your work, but something occurred to me. If we are going to spend some time helping the aliens, I wonder if I might be allowed to open a dialog with one of their representatives."

For what purpose?

"To find out whatever we can about this other new alien race. They are not at all like the New People, I understand."

Haykuz felt his heart accelerate as the silence grew. Perhaps he really could accomplish something useful, but why would the captain trust him, after all? Then Captain Bitka spoke again.

Well, it can't hurt. Permission granted and good luck. But how are you going to manage it from back on the habitat wheel?

Haykuz let out a breath he had not realized he had been holding. "Oh, I intend to do everything by text and holocomm. I am no hero, Captain."

Heroism is highly overrated, Mister Haykuz. Just do what you can.

Something he had not previously considered occurred to Haykuz, and the thought made his ears twitch and his skin tingle.

"Oh, one more thing, Captain. I wonder if I might call on one or two others to help me."

As long as they aren't involved in the rescue effort or ship operations, be my guest. I imagine Dr. Däng could be of help.

Haykuz thanked the captain and broke the connection. Dr. Däng might indeed be of assistance, and he would ask her, but that was not who he had in mind. He sat for a moment, gathering his courage and resolve. Then he rose, left his quarters, and walked nearly halfway around the habitat wheel. He explained his purpose to the two Marine guards and then walked across the threshold of the stateroom he had dreaded entering for so long. Strangely, today the dread was gone.

"Ah, the little Varoki-thing returns," the Guardian Te'Anna said, and she stood up, perhaps in order to look down on him. Her shoulder feathers spread in a menacing fashion and her halo grew bright. "Have you reconsidered the possible origin of your species?"

"Yes," he answered, and held up his hands as a display. "Observe: four fingers and a thumb, but your creations seem to mimic your own three-fingered hands."

He flexed his long, slender fingers, turned his hands to show the range and complexity of their motion. "Also, I observe your work is not so fine as this. Perhaps you have little need for nimble-fingered slaves."

The Guardian sat back down and considered him with her unblinking eyes the color of stone. "Perhaps you are right. Did you come just to tell me this?"

"I came to ask if you would like to do something with me, something I think you will find very interesting."

CHAPTER TWENTY-NINE

The next day, aboard USS *Cam Ranh Bay*,
outbound to Destie-Seven
17 June 2134 (*one hundred twenty-one days
after Incident Seventeen*)

Homer Alexander sat with his hands in his lap and stared at the bowl of steaming whole-grain porridge that was his breakfast.

"Food's getting a little boring," the captain said, "but Acho says we'll have some ripe tomatoes in a few days. That'll be a treat, won't it?"

"Yes, sir," Homer answered.

It was actually Ensign Gutierrez from engineering's place in the breakfast rotation, but Homer had prevailed upon her to switch places with him. He'd told her he had tactical developments he had to discuss with the captain, and that was almost true. Over the course of the last twenty-four hours Homer had been forced to take a long, hard look at himself, and he didn't like what he saw. He remembered what a college creative writing teacher had once told him about growing up: children think about what they want to *be*, while adults think about what they

371

want to *do*. She had been talking about people who want to be writers but don't actually like to write, but it was a more universal observation, wasn't it? How many wanted to be firemen, but didn't particularly want to run into burning buildings? Or get hot?

He wanted to *be* a tactical officer, but was that what he wanted to *do*? Was he even capable of it? He'd taken such pride in it, and now that all seemed like vanity, very silly vanity, and misplaced.

"TAC, we've still got a couple decoy packs, don't we?"

"Three, sir," Homer answered.

"I've been thinking about what the Guardians will decide after seeing this fight. Those two ships following us from Destie-Four, I want you to fire a decoy cluster back down our course to intercept them. It will take a few days to get to them but I want to see what they'll do about it. Displace out of its way and so lose a day or two catching us? Or maybe try to kill every decoy. They can't know whether or not there's a live missile in there, so they pretty much have to do one or the other."

"I'll see to it as soon as we finish breakfast, sir," Homer said.

The captain studied him before speaking again.

"So, what are you chewing on, TAC? It sure isn't your oatmeal."

"I've been thinking about my performance in the battle sir. I think . . ." He wasn't sure how to finish the sentence. What *did* he think?

"Yeah, you screwed up there at the end," the captain said as he took another spoonful of oatmeal. "You let yourself get scared. But you held it together, I'll give you that much. You managed to at least read off the instruments, but your brain shut down, didn't it? Most important weapon a TAC boss has is his brain, Mister Alexander, and you disarmed yourself. You can't afford to ever let that happen again."

He said this without fire or contempt, more the way an instructor would correct a classroom problem done wrong. *You forgot to carry forward the residual velocity, Mister Alexander. Don't let it happen again.* But it wasn't that easy.

"I . . . I don't know if I can manage that, sir. I may not have what it takes."

The captain looked up at him and for the first time, a shadow of anger crossed his face.

"What are we, cavemen?" Bitka demanded. "Sitting around the fire in loincloths, praying to some stupid god of war, to give us courage? And if he doesn't it must mean we aren't *worthy*, or some bullshit like that?

"When you get scared, your heart races. When your heart rate gets above a certain speed it's beating faster than the chambers can refill and so your blood pressure drops. Then your brain gets starved for oxygen, higher brain functions shut down, and all that stuff you experienced during the battle happens. You think it happened to you because you don't have what it takes? No, Lieutenant, it happened because you were the only person on that bridge who forgot your tactical breathing routine. Jesus Christ, how hard is it? Inhale for five seconds, hold it for five, let it out for five, wait five, repeat. That's how you control your heart rate in a crisis, and damnit, you *know* that! What did you think, *real* men don't need to breathe tactically? This is the twenty-second century, Alexander. We don't need war gods anymore; we got science. Watch your biomonitor, remember your training, do your job, and . . . and eat your breakfast before it gets cold. Hungry children on Bronstein's World would kill their siblings for that breakfast."

Homer felt such a flood of relief that for a moment he became lightheaded. He took a slow, careful breath and for the first time since the battle it came easily. He picked up his spoon and took his first bite of oatmeal. It tasted extraordinary.

"Kill their siblings? That's pretty dark, sir."

"I am a very bad man, Mister Alexander."

He said it lightly, but Homer knew people often hid the truth in jest. Did the captain really believe that about himself?

Major J. C. Merderet looked away from the flux welder as it attached the big magnetic anchors to the souped-up utility pod. She regretted having ordered it. The austere, functional lines of the utility pods—the one-person vehicles the engineering crew used to make repairs on the exterior of the ship in vacuum—had a sort of beauty which the improvised magnetic anchor and weapon pack had completely destroyed.

She saw Wisnowski, her wing sergeant major, stick his head down through the overhead hatch and wave to her.

"Old Man's on the way, Ma'am."

"Sergeant Major, you watch who you're calling old, you. He's younger than me."

"You'd never know it to look at you, Ma'am," he answered with a grin.

Merderet turned back to the utility pod but only as an excuse to avoid eye contact with anyone else. She needed to collect her thoughts and put on her game face. As squid officers went, Captain Bitka was one of the better ones, but he was still a squid.

The tremor had returned to her left hand. She watched her hand tremble for a few seconds and then clenched it in a fist. That stopped it. The tremors didn't seem to be coming any more frequently, which was good. Probably not neurological, just psych, which figured. Her biomonitor would have picked up any serious physiological problem.

Just psych. Tough it out.

"Congratulations, Captain," she said as soon as Bitka rode the manual conveyor down through the hatch to the machine shop in forward engineering. "Damned fine shootin'. Two long ships dead and one helluva rescue."

"'Boats' Wainwright was the miracle-worker on the rescue, Major," Bitka said once he stepped off the conveyor and to the deck. "He came up with the idea of docking the stern section of their first ship with the surviving habitat module from the second one, then had Lieutenant Ma's A-gang help the bugs get their stand-by reactor running to give them power. I don't know how he did it in twelve hours, but those roaches ought to make *him* their new god."

"They could do worse, sir. Seems we got a bit more gravity this morning, too."

"That's what I wanted to talk to you about," he said. "I kicked our acceleration up to over a tenth of a gee, going to damn near drain the HRM tanks but it will get us there six days sooner. These guys have seen too many of our tricks. We have to speed it up, get this thing wrapped up. So, do you have a workable assault plan for hitting the Destie-Seven-Echo highstation?"

"Yes, sir. Grab 'em by the throat and choke the shit out of 'em till they say *je me rends!*"

"Grab them by the *throat?*"

"In a manner of speaking, sir. Life-support. They got thick security at all the C3I nexi on that station, but we think we can take and hold life-support at a lower cost."

"By we you mean . . . ?"

"Me, my two company commanders, my Ops boss, and my wing sergeant major. Consensus plan, sir."

"Okay. And the intel on where their defenses are thick? Where did that come from?"

J. C. knew what he was getting at and made one quick nod of agreement. "Yes, sir, it's all from the alien prisoner Te'Anna. If we've got anything better I'll be happy to redraft the plan based on that."

The captain squinted and scratched his close-cropped hair, then shook his head.

"No, we don't. Hell, I know that's all we have. I'm just not crazy about it."

"I ain't neither, sir."

"No chance of just threatening them with bombardment? After what we did to their complex on Destie-Four, that should have some credibility."

"Well, that's your department, sir, and you're doing pretty good at engineering surrenders. If it works out that way, that smacks. But when they call your bluff, we're ready to go."

"*When,* huh? You think they'll know it's a bluff."

"Well, sure. How we gonna get home if we blow up the one place can fix our jump drive? Bet they figured that out by now. Meantime, we been turning your utility pods into ugly-ass death machines, along with some help from Lieutenant Ma's A-gang. Adapt, improvise, overcome. One more thing, sir, it's important I take this ride with 'em."

"We've gone over this before. I can't afford to lose you, Major."

"I never bucked you before, but with respect, sir, this time it's different. What you *can't* afford is for this assault to go south. If we blow it, game over. If we pull it off, we probably won't need to drop again. But either way we get exactly one shot at it."

The captain frowned and then asked the question she knew was coming.

"Is that the only reason?"

"No, sir. There's a personal reason as well, but I didn't mention it because it shouldn't influence your decision."

"Or yours," the captain shot back.

"Understood sir, and I can't promise it didn't. But even if it did, that don't change the rest of it. Best place for me is controlling the assault wave."

Captain Bitka studied her. She wondered what he thought he saw. He shifted uncomfortably before he spoke, and when he did it was slowly, thoughtfully.

"You know, when we get back—assuming we do— Somerset and Thibodaux are going to be heroes."

Somerset and Thibodaux were the two Marines who had died with the landing party.

"Way I see it, sir, they're heroes whether we get back

or not, but I know what you mean. People will *know* they were heroes."

"Yes. I want to put Thibodaux in for the Medal of Honor. I watched the vid again." He paused and closed his eyes just for a moment before continuing, not much longer than if he'd just blinked, but a little longer. "He died trying to get to the XO, trying to save her."

He probably believed that, J. C. thought, maybe needed to believe it. She hesitated before replying.

"Sir, I don't think that's true. I mean, put him in for the medal, I think he deserved it, but don't do it for the wrong thing."

"Major, I *saw* him reaching for her."

She needed him to let her take this next ride, but she was damned if she'd tell a lie over the body of a dead Marine to get it. How to make him understand about Thibodaux, though, that was another thing.

"Thibodaux was in Delta Company, my old command, sir. Went down with me in the first wave on K'tok, landed a hundred meters from the downstation. I saw him come down and even in battle armor I *knew* it was him, just the way his feet touched the ground. Lord, he was one beautiful, graceful man, him. Funny, we travelled over a hundred and fifty light-years from Earth to do that assault drop on K'tok, and where do you think he come from? Pointe a la Hache, Louisiana, just two parishes over from where I grew up. What do you think of that?

"Sir, Andre Thibodaux was a coon-ass no-nonsense Marine who knew the score. We all watched that vid too, sir, quite a few times. Drank some beers and cried some tears. Near as we can tell, he killed two Desties and crippled another, barehanded, before he died. I can tell you that when Thibodaux made that lunge at Lieutenant Running-Deer, both he and she were mortally wounded, and I believe he knew it. He wasn't trying to save her, sir."

"Then...why?"

"She was the only one carrying a sidearm. Thibodaux was trying to get to her gauss pistol, take a couple more Desties with him. If he's going to get a medal, give it to him for that. I know you'd rather it be for him tryin' to save a life, but all due respect, that ain't the business we're in, sir."

She watched the captain think about that, or think about *something*, who knew what?

Then he sighed. "I know, Major. I know. When your Marines go into that highstation, I don't want to lose one of them if I can help it. I'd say go in guns blazing if it'd keep them alive, cut down anything that looks like resistance. But we have to remember—*they* have to remember—every Destie they kill might be the one who knows how to fix our drive. Taking that station isn't worth a can of navy beans if it doesn't get us home."

"Understood, sir, but there's no way to make that tactical call by remote control. All you can do is put the assault wave over there and trust the judgment of whoever's leading it."

The captain watched the petty officers work on the utility pod for a while and then gave her a sour look of surrender. "*Shit.* Okay, you win. You lead the assault wave. But you better not get shot, Major."

There were worse things than getting shot, J. C.

thought as the captain rode the conveyor up through the hatch.

Laptoon Haykuz found Captain Bitka where the watch officer—the "Officer of the Deck" the Humans called her—had told him he would be: in the fabricator compartment in forward engineering. He would have become lost were it not for the frame numbers displayed prominently at the various bulkheads. Forward engineering was at frame sixty-two in the main hull. After months of living in a wheel, where everything eventually linked up with everything else again, finding his way in a straight line was surprisingly disorienting, but he grew accustomed to it by the time he had made his way from the lifts aft through the docking bay, past the auxiliary bridge, missile room, and the long doorless passages which he knew traversed the enormous liquid hydrogen tanks.

Haykuz was becoming used to so many different things, he wondered—in the event he actually survived to return home—how he would ever adapt to his old life. That the current watch officer, the officer in charge of the ship and everyone on duty on it, was a *female*, he no longer found odd enough to comment on. The only thing odd about the moment was that he did not find it odd at all.

On Varoki warships there were no female personnel of any rank, nor were there any in government or positions of authority in business or education. A handful of Varoki nations had begun to adopt a less traditional view of gender roles, but only because they were weak and powerless among the Varoki, and so sought influence among the Humans and the other like-minded species.

Or was that really the case? Was it really weakness which drove them to break with the past? It was what he had been taught, had always believed, but now he wondered. Perhaps their weakness liberated them. Perhaps power and influence were heavy chains which kept a nation from growing. Perhaps.

The stench of the fabricator room assailed him as soon as he entered. The captain, speaking with a crewperson, nodded a greeting to him but turned back to the swarthy human male.

"It's basically a Databot Seventeen-Thirty," Captain Bitka explained to the crewman. "King Defense Industries licensed it, put a different casing around it, slapped their own name on the outside, and called it the M-Seven, because it sounded more military. They hardened about five parts against electromagnetic pulse, made sure the Navy specs were written to specify those five special modifications, and then charged about two and a half time the street value of a Seventeen-Thirty. That's how you make money doing business with the Navy, Cisneros."

"How's that, sir? First screw us blind and then saddle us with this broke-dick piece of shit?"

Haykuz felt his ears fold back defensively and was surprised to hear Captain Bitka laugh. Was that sort of casual disrespect of the service tolerated?

"Well," the captain answered, "hire a retired officer from BuOrd as a lobbyist to write the specifications the way you want them, and then persuade whoever it takes to get them adopted. That's the *legal* way you screw someone blind. But that's not our concern, Cisneros. Despite all the trouble this thing is giving you, the Seventeen-Thirty is basically a good fabricator. It's just not very operator friendly, which might sound like a bad thing, but it does tend to generate additional training and field modification revenue streams for the manufacturer. The problem's all in the rear top injectors. I'm willing to bet they are saturating your rear mold cavity and you're getting blowout and overfills. Right?"

"Yes, sir."

The captain then began a long back and forth conversation with the technician, laced with references to injector nozzles and feed temperatures which completely escaped Haykuz, but by the end clearly satisfied and impressed the crewman.

"Keep this guy running, Cisneros," the captain said by way of conclusion. "It's the best fabricator we have for turning out thermal pipe. We might not be as lucky next time as we were in this fight. Those big-ass radiators of ours stick way the hell out and will tend to get shot up. The quicker we can fabricate new pipe and get it installed, the quicker we can get the reactor back to maximum power. Maximum power is good."

"Yes, sir."

The captain took another look around—a *longing* look, Haykuz thought—and nodded.

"Okay, carry on, Cisneros." He turned and walked carefully to Loptoon in the gliding shuffle of low gravity. "Sorry to keep you waiting. Mister Haykuz. We had some trouble with this fabricator during the rescue operation and I wanted to make sure we had it under control. Besides, I like hanging around the machine shop. I like the smell of working fabricators. Nothing quite like it."

No, Haykuz thought, there was nothing like that smell of ozone and hot composite. *Dreadful.* How strange to be nostalgic for it. They walked together into the main corridor. While they were under acceleration it had become a shaft leading up through the center of the main hull, and they stood together on one of the hand conveyor platforms which carried them up along one side of the shaft.

"Your description of procurement in your navy sounds depressingly familiar, Captain Bitka. I sometimes fear the Varoki way of doing things may have corrupted the species we imagined we were helping."

"Oh, I wouldn't worry about it, Mister Haykuz. I don't think the Varoki had a thing to teach Humans about graft and corruption. If anything, I'd say it's the other way around."

Haykuz could not dispute that. Humans were known throughout the *Cottohazz* as its most daring, accomplished, and resourceful criminals. There was something of that roguishness in Captain Bitka, Haykuz thought.

"So, I got your report on the diplomacy with the bugs," the Captain said. "*Troatta*, that's what they call themselves, right? When you asked permission to round up some help, I never imagined you'd tag our prisoner Te'Anna, but it sounds like it paid off. You think the Troatta commander really thinks he's stuck in the middle of a Guardian civil war?"

"She, not he. It appears all the Troatta ship crew are female. I believe she suspects there is some sort of internecine conflict, Captain Bitka, but I was careful never to make such a claim. Any claim which can be directly disproved diminished the credibility of everything else, but clues subject to various interpretations are a different matter. Te'Anna's presence and obvious willing cooperation were sufficient to plant the seed."

"Sounds like Te'Anna had a good time," the captain said, "which is very weird, but then what about her isn't?"

"I agree," Haykuz said and felt himself color. "She . . . I believe she made a sexual advance to me afterwards."

He had removed himself from the situation as tactfully as he knew how. It was not simply the idea of interspecies sex which appalled him, it was the idea of a female of any species seeking sexual favors from a male. Were Varoki the only sane, modest beings in the universe? He cleared his throat before going on. "Once she understood the Troatta might think there was strife among the Guardians, I think she was as intrigued by that idea itself as by the actual negotiations."

"If you're thinking she might sign on for something like that, for some anti-Guardian revolution, I wouldn't be too hasty," the captain said. "She might appreciate the entertainment value, but that's not enough to stick with a real war. Not nearly enough."

Haykuz knew Captain Bitka was correct, but the captain's disagreement had not been expressed as a reprimand or as evidence of superiority. Instead it was almost an opinion shared by an equal. The thought disoriented Haykuz for a moment.

"Your actions helped as well," he said to Captain Bitka.

"Mine? How?"

"By expending so much time and effort in the rescue operation, you made it clear your quarrel is with P'Daan, not with the Troatta, and so by extension not with their Guardian lord, Y'Areez."

"Huh. Okay, but what's that get us, exactly?"

Haykuz dipped his head to the side, the Varoki equivalent of a shrug. "I doubt it will cause an open breach, but some friction now may lead to interesting developments later. One never knows exactly what. I suppose diplomacy is not a very satisfactory occupation for those impatient for immediate and unambiguous results."

The captain laughed again, an easy, comfortable laugh. "Fair enough. Okay, fill me in on everything the Troatta representative said."

CHAPTER THIRTY

Objective is secure, Sam heard Major Merderet report via tight beam commlink. *I say again, Destie-Seven-Echo-Highstation is secure. All resistance ended, all hostile personnel incapacitated or prisoners, enemy leadership target is in custody unharmed. Two friendly casualties, no fatalities.*

Sam released the breath he had been holding.

"Well done, Major," he said. The bridge crew cheered and he wanted to get up and dance himself, but that would have been neither dignified nor professional. He settled for a very broad grin. Finally, something was going right.

"Lieutenant Ma and your follow-on force are waiting in the PSRVs. Are you set up to receive them?"

Give us ten minutes, sir, and then send them over. We can use the extra bodies. Got a shitload of EPWs to watch.

"Will do, Major. And Merderet . . . well done," he said,

his voice suddenly thick. "Well done." It seemed such an inadequate response, he had to resist the temptation to say it yet again, as if repetition might somehow inflate it to the proportions required by the moment.

Twenty minutes later Sam met with his advisory group and department heads, with Lieutenant Bill Parker from engineering standing in for the absent Koichi Ma. The other novel addition was the Guardian Te'Anna, along with her two silent Marine escorts, complete with gauss pistols and neuro-wands. Sam was happy to see the wands collapsed and in their small holsters on their web belts. It would be stupid not to carry them, but he didn't want to rub Te'Anna's nose in them.

Why did he care? Well, she could be an invaluable asset in understanding and hopefully thwarting P'Daan's plans, but that wasn't all. He was starting to . . . maybe not *like* her but sympathize with her. She wasn't just a template for what all Guardians must be. She was a unique, sentient being trying to find something to make her life worth living. She could almost be one of them, aside from being immortal, oversexed, and a bird.

"It's been a hectic day," he began, "but I'm glad to say our Marines have the highstation and Lieutenant Ma has transferred there to begin interviewing the Guardian K'Irka and her senior technical staff to get a handle on fixing our jump drive. In the meantime, we are breaking Destie-Seven-Echo orbit and bending course for a Molniya-style highly elliptical orbit around Destie-Seven itself. That will take us deep into the gas giant's atmosphere on our closest approach and we will scoop hydrogen to refill our HRM—that's *hydrogen reaction mass*—tanks. We'll make three orbital passes which will get us up to about seventy percent of our full tankage. Then we'll head back to the highstation and hope Lieutenant Ma has some progress on the drive front."

"How long will that take, Captain?" Doctor Däng asked.

"Each orbital pass will take about sixteen hours, so with transit time back and forth to the Highstation, about sixty hours total."

Sam saw the flicker of a frown on the biologist's brow.

"What's wrong, Doctor?"

"Oh, I am only concerned about my friend Koichi. It seems like a long time for them to remain on the station without possibility of assistance from us."

"A very long time to be with K'Irka," Te'Anna said, her first words since joining them. Everyone in the room turned and stared at her. She looked around at them and then ran her fingers through the fine feathers on her neck and head, fluffing them out, an unmistakable preening gesture. She did love attention, Sam thought.

"I wouldn't leave if we didn't need that reaction mass," Sam said, "but he's hardly alone over there. Major Merderet's there with a heavily reinforced company of Mike Marines, over a hundred grunts, armed to the teeth. Most of them are veterans of the assault landing on K'tok. You won't find a better trained or more experienced force of close combat troops in the *Cottohazz,* and I bet you won't find their match anywhere around here, either."

Doctor Däng turned to Te'Anna. "What did you mean, about the Guardian K'Irka? Is she dangerous?"

"Oh, yes," Te'Anna answered, and she nodded for emphasis.

Nodding, Sam noticed: a Human gesture of agreement the Guardian had picked up over the course of her weeks with them. Although she spoke Guardian, and the others in the group understood her by means of commlink autotrans, none of them wore vox-boxes, nor needed to, for her to understand them. Te'Anna had developed a near-perfect understanding of English, the language spoken by everyone present. Her spoken English was almost as good as the auto-trans. Sam wondered at her ability to learn a new language so quickly, especially as she had never in her entire memory encountered any language but her own. If, as Choice claimed, she was a biological machine, she was a pretty impressive one.

"How is she dangerous?" Däng asked.

"K'Irka is the most accomplished gene sculptor I have ever encountered," Te'Anna said, "certainly the best in this realm."

"She's under guard," Sam said. "She's not doing any gene sculpting now."

"No," Te'Anna agreed, "not *now*."

The words sent a surge of unease through him that made him shiver.

"How could she know what to sculpt, or how?" he asked. "She's never even seen a Human, or heard of one before we got here."

"You are probably correct, Captain Bitka," she answered, and she leaned back in her chair, a model of idle grace. "It is unlikely any of the genetic material left from the circulatory fluids of your party—which soaked the audience ground—was recovered at P'Daan's orders, analyzed, and then the data sent by tight beam to K'Irka. After all, your enemies have only had a *hundred days* to do so, and they are probably too stupid to have even thought of it."

Damn! She had an uncomfortable way of making a point. Sam squinted up the duty Comm chair, Signaler First Lopez.

Yes, sir, he answered from the bridge.

"Lopez, get me a tight beam commlink to Major Merderet."

Around him everyone else in the conference room fell silent. After less than a minute Merderet's voice sounded in his head.

Yes, captain?

"Major, our guest Te'Anna suspects her friend K'Irka has prepared some sort of trap for your people."

I think so too, sir. Taking the station was too easy.

"Yeah, now that you mention it. She thinks the threat is biological in nature. Don't let up on your biosecurity."

Sir, we found four compartments we sealed off and we pumped them down to hard vacuum, then filled them with virgin air brought over in tanks from the Bay by our supply echelon. Nobody desuits except in that safe zone, and not until after a thorough suit scrub, including live steam and a UV burn that would give a virus melanoma.

Sam couldn't think of anything else to do. He looked at Te'Anna but her eyes told him nothing. "Okay, Major, sounds good. I'll check back after each scoop."

Te'Anna did one of her head duck and neck stretch motions, then looked at the ceiling of the conference room and rolled her head from side to side. "My *friend*, K'Irka," she said, mimicking Sam's words, and then repeated it, as if listening to it for some hidden meaning. She looked around the conference room, her eyes coming to rest briefly on each person there, and she leaned forward as she spoke.

"You, the one named Parker. I know your name but nothing else about you. Alexander? I have heard of you but we have never spoken. Strangely marked Human female named Choice, we have spoken once but shared nothing interesting. You, Buran-thing: I will never know you. But the rest of you . . . understand me when I say each of the rest of you is a better friend to me, in the sense you mean the word, than is K'Irka. Why would I think such a thing? I still look for answers, as do you. K'Irka found her answers long ago. She found them at the cellular level and her mind dwells there, not here."

"And what about P'Daan?" Sam asked. "Does he search for answers?"

She leaned back, again relaxed and made a graceful gesture with her hand, as if to reveal something, or perhaps dismiss it. "P'Daan has no need to; he simply makes them up."

Two hours later Ka'Deem Brook found Captain Bitka in the officer's gymnasium in the habitat wheel, working on the resistance machines with a studious intensity which made Ka'Deem wonder what demon the captain was trying to cast out.

"You sent for me, sir?"

The captain stood up from the lower back machine.

"XO, I'm getting a sense of what P'Daan has in mind and it's making me nervous."

Ka'Deem couldn't imagine understanding what went on in the mind of a Guardian. The captain obviously believed he could, but Ka'Deem thought there was as much vanity as insight in that belief. Ka'Deem waited as the captain wiped his face with a towel.

"Those two long ships around Destie-Four have broken orbit and are accelerating down, out of the plane of the ecliptic. They have been for over a day."

"You think they're getting ready for another in-system jump, sir? But P'Daan is with that division of their fleet. I thought you were certain a Guardian wouldn't take that sort of personal risk."

The captain paused and looked at him carefully, as if for a moment sensing Ka'Deem's true hidden feelings. The captain's face remained a blank mask, however, as blank as Ka'Deem kept his own.

"I still am," the captain answered. "He keeps peppering me with these angry rants by holocomm, but I think he's just going through the motions to keep me distracted or something. Comm records them and I look at them when I get time. You watch them?"

"Yes, sir."

"Notice anything different about the last one?"

Ka'Deem thought back. He'd only half-watched it, not paying that much attention. As the captain said, the messages had become boring and repetitive. "Not really, sir."

"I saw a crewman on that last vid, just for a second. It was a Destie—a New Person. P'Daan is transmitting from a Destie ship or orbital station. He's not on one of those Troatta battleships anymore, which means he's going to send them against us, jump in above the plane of the ecliptic and have their residual velocity carry them down toward us. Only question is when. Are they going to wait for the two ships trailing us to catch up or go sooner with just two?"

"If I were them, I'd wait, sir. They know we can beat two ships. It's safer to wait until they have all four."

The captain shook his head. "I sure hope you're right, XO. If they think that way, odds are we'll be gone by the time they get here. But if they come early with two ships, we're in trouble. They know our main trick, which is to throw off their sensors with a thermonuclear warhead. If they're smart—and these Troatta are supposed to be good at this stuff, even if P'Daan is an amateur—they'll realize our tactic worked in part because they were down to one ship but also because they were in tight formation. If they come in spread wide, we have to use twice as many warheads to block their sensors, position them just right, and that assumes they don't have a sensor drone they can send out as a flanker.

"We'll also have to send two different attack swarms. We're fabricating more decoy clusters but we don't have an endless supply of missiles. We've used four of our twelve Mark Fours and six of our thirty-six Mark Fives. I've been stingy with them so far, but next time we're going to have to fire them as fast as we can clear the coil gun. If we have to fight again, it's not going to be so bloodless."

The captain wiped his face again and Ka'Deem

realized the perspiration might not all be from the exercise, and that thought made Ka'Deem's heart rate climb.

"I want the ship at Readiness Condition Two for the entire duration of the scoop. Everyone on their toes. And I want you to have Mister Alexander work out the solution for a Mark Five shot that will take it straight up above the plane of the ecliptic. Fire that one off by the end of the watch. We'll follow it with one more every watch for the run in to the first scoop and then the next two watches afterwards. If they come from up there, we might get lucky."

"The odds of them emerging anywhere near one of the missiles . . . is that worth shooting four of our remaining Mark Fives, sir?"

"Well, long shots are about all we've got at this point, and those missiles aren't drawing interest sitting in our hold. Make it so, XO."

"Aye, aye, sir," he answered, his heart still pounding in his ears. Bitka knew the long ships were coming for them, knew where they would come from, and Ka'Deem knew, just looking at him, that the captain had no idea how to beat them.

CHAPTER THIRTY-ONE

Two days later, **aboard USS *Cam Ranh Bay*,
in scooping orbit around Destie-Seven
13 July 2134** (*one hundred forty-seven days
after Incident Seventeen*)

Eleven thousand tons of HRM—hydrogen reaction mass—scooped in two passes. *Not bad,* Sam thought. He thumbed his signature to the watch log as the tactical sensor array extended again and the bridge display began showing detail of their surroundings.

"Coming out of ionization," Lieutenant Barr-Sanchez reported from Ops One. "Comms and sensors coming back online."

"Contacts!" Alexander called out from TAC One. "Two bogies, great big ones, seven degrees relative, angle on the bow eighty-nine, range three million and change."

Sam brought up the tactical display on his workstation. They'd expected this sooner or later but his hand still trembled from the sudden jolt of adrenaline. "What's the closing velocity?"

"Sixty-nine kilometers a second, sir," Alexander answered. "That's pretty good for those big tubs."

"Yeah. Well they spent four days accelerating. What's that work out to?"

"A fiftieth of a gee continuous burn for ninety-six hours would get almost seventy klicks, sir," Barr-Sanchez answered. "That's probably as high a burn as they can manage for that long and still have reaction mass in the tank to turn around."

"Why that high a closing rate, sir?" Alexander said. "That helps us. And they'll be here in twelve hours, way before their other two ships get here."

"Excellent question, TAC. How far out is the first Mark Five we fired?"

Chief Bermudez in the TAC Two chair touched her display. "Cold Alpha is six hundred ninety-one thousand kilometers out, sir."

Sam did the quick math in his head. "About ten hours to missile detonation, unless they start decelerating. Chief, please tell me it's going to pass within range."

"Sorry, sir. Cold Alpha will pass about three hundred thousand kilometers away at closest approach. Cold Bravo is also a miss, but Cold Charlie will pass within four thousand kilometers, unless they change course."

"Sir," Bohannon in COMM One said, "I've got an emergency tight beam from Major Merderet at the highstation."

Emergency? Now what?

"Patch her through."

Captain Bitka, he heard Merderet's voice in his head, but it sounded hoarse and strained. *I don't know how, but she got to us, and it's coming on fast. Elevated temperature and heart rate, vomiting and diarrhea, dizziness, blurred*

*vision, skin lesions. We've been pulling blood samples for
the last hour and running them through the breakdown
scanner. I've got a burst data dump ready for Doc Däng.*

Sam looked at the main display, saw the closing track of
the two long ships. Had they timed their jump emergence
to coincide with symptom onset? Well, why not?

"Send the databurst now, Major, and keep taking
samples."

*Sending now. I pulled all our security people back and
we're locked down in here.*

She paused and Sam could hear her vomiting. Her
voice was weaker when she resumed talking.

*We'll keep at it as long as we can, but at this rate we
aren't going to be upright very long. Can't keep enough
fluids in to keep our body chems right. Lieutenant Ma
wants to add something, sir.*

After a pause, Ma's voice joined the feed.

*Captain, as near as I can tell nobody on this station
knows how to fix our jump drive. All they manufacture
here are in-system cargo haulers and the occasional
patrol/rescue craft. No starship technology or the
apparent ability to make it.*

Sam felt suddenly lightheaded as Ma paused to vomit.
They were right back where they'd started. Worse. He had
over a hundred Marines on an orbital shipyard with some
sort of galloping rot, and two battleships, wise to his tricks,
screaming down on them.

Here's a good one for you, Ma continued. *The New
People who used to work on jump drives were the ones
who tried to kill their Guardian overlords. They're still
alive, down on the surface of Haydoos, what we call*

Destie-Seven-Echo. I guess they're there in case the Guardians ever need to pick their brains or something. I've got all the information the station has on their habitat and I've got a databurst ready to send.

Whatever bug we have is bad and progressing rapidly, and none of our filtering and sterilization techniques can contain it. Sir, you need to get those Desties on Haydoos to fix the drive and then get the hell out of here. Don't get everyone else killed trying to save us. Major Merderet and I are on the same page about this.

Sam paused before replying, wanting to be sure his voice betrayed none of the emotion he felt. "Send the databursts, Mister Ma. Yours and the major's recommendation is noted. I cannot in all honesty promise I will get you out of this alive, but I'll do my best, and alive or dead I *will* get you home. I will be damned if I will leave you or anyone else behind."

He cut the channel, pinged Doctor Däng, and told her what he knew, asked her to go to the medbay and look over the incoming data burst. He could hear the agitation in her voice. She and Ma had been close since before Sam had come aboard. She'd already lost Boniface, her other close friend. Sam wasn't sure how well she would hold up if they lost Ma as well.

He looked back at the tactical display, forced himself to focus on the oncoming ships. He turned to Alexander.

"TAC, what would we do if we didn't have a package of silent death on the way to greet them?"

"Maybe get some started, sir."

"Yeah, I'm thinking the same thing, and I wonder if that captain is as well. Ten thousand tons of HRM is all we'll need for this. Helm, cancel the third scoop. Bend orbit for Highstation."

Barr-Sanchez triggered the lateral acceleration klaxon and then began turning the ship for deceleration.

"TAC, get a decoy cluster loaded in the coil gun and then prep a Mark Four. We'll launch straight from the dispenser in the wheel. Decoys from the coil gun followed by one hot missile, easy to see. How many sensor drones we have left?"

"Six, sir."

"Okay, we'll burn one. Punch him out at a steep slant angle away from us. When the Cold Charlie bird detonates, I want eyes far enough out to see around the detonation cloud and assess damage."

"Aye, aye, sir."

Sam felt the deceleration kick in, about a twentieth of a gee. enough to lower their velocity relative to Destie Seven from thirty kilometers per second to half that in about seven or eight hours, enough to match orbit with the Seven-Echo Highstation.

"COMM, get me all ship."

"You're live, sir."

Sam took a moment to compose his thoughts and his voice before he started.

"All hands, this is the captain. We have two situations and I'm pretty sure the timing isn't coincidental. Our people on the Highstation have come down with some sort of illness, almost certainly inflicted by the Guardian there. At the same time, two more Troatta long ships just exited jump space three million miles above the plane of the ecliptic, coming down after us.

"We're heading back to the Highstation and we'll get there about the same time the long ships get within range of their meson guns. That will be in about twelve hours. We're going to stay at Readiness Condition Two for at least the next eight hours, unless they start accelerating. Catch up on your rest and make sure you get something to eat. If there are no changes before then, we'll go to General Quarters in nine hours, when Blue Watch is due to come on duty. We'll take care of these two long ships first, then we'll sort things out on the Highstation. Carry on."

Sam hoped that sounded sufficiently confident. He turned to Alexander again.

"Let's get that ordnance launched, TAC. When you're done, deploy the big survey sensor arrays. I want as good a look at those bandits as I can get. The ship is at Readiness Condition Two, Material Condition Bravo, bending course for Highstation. Power ring is fully charged, reactor hot, shroud secured, sensors active. Mister Alexander, you have the ship."

Te'Anna studied the captain as he entered the dining hall and crossed to the table where she and her Marine escort ate their midday meal. His body warmth was normal but his heart rate was slightly elevated, as was his respiration. His blood pressure seemed higher than normal as well, although not dangerously so. It was difficult to tell in this reduced gravity, which altered the distribution of pressure throughout their body. Humans had very limited means of controlling it. You could normally tell so much about them from their blood pressure. Now she could not tell how much of his physiological state was due to anxiety and how much to excitement. There was a muscular tension as well which suggested suspicion or hostility.

He greeted her, sat, and explained the situation. She studied him, pretended to listen, but it was nothing more than what she had expected. K'Irka had prepared a trap and of course their defense mechanisms proved unable to guard against it. Why the Humans had thought their mechanical-based material culture could mount a defense against biological attack from a material culture based on bioengineering was beyond her, but she supposed if she could understand everything about them she would not find them so interesting. But the news that the station had no solution to the problem with their star drive—that was an unexpected development.

"I sent over a hundred people into that station," the captain said. "Now they may be dying, and it was all for *nothing*. Why did you tell us the Echo Highstation could repair our drive?"

Ah, that was the basis of his suspicion and hostility. He thought she had led him into a trap. Well, it was a perfectly reasonable belief, wasn't it? She had done exactly that, but not deliberately.

"Captain, I told you the truth as I understood it. It has been a very long time since any starfaring ships were built in this system, but we do retain the capacity to do so, and that capacity resides in the shipyard complex. It is H'Stus's responsibility, both the complex and the ability to craft the heart of the drive."

"There's no Guardian there named H'Stus. There's just K'Irka."

"No H'Stus? That is very odd. K'Irka and he have usually worked together. I wonder where he is. Have you asked?"

"He apparently left the complex by shuttle," the captain said, "not long after we broke away from the bulk carrier and began heading in this direction. If the complex had any flight trajectory data on his shuttle, we haven't been able to find it and now our people there are in no condition to keep looking. Lieutenant Ma said something about the New People down in the surface of Seven Echo having the information."

"Oh, how ironic! Yes, it was a cabal of engineers serving H'Stus who rebelled and who were punished with eternal life on the unpleasant surface of the moon Haydoos."

Captain Bitka talked more then, spoke brusquely about the condition of the humans on the shipyard complex, what they were trying to do to help them, and what he expected Te'Anna to do, although her mind was elsewhere. He finished talking and was waiting for a reply. She replayed his words: *illness, Däng, help.* Yes, of course she would help with the disease, but she had to do more than that, had to find a way to insure all these beings escaped P'Daan. She wasn't yet sure why she felt that need, but she could explore her motives at her leisure. For now, she had to recapture their trust, and that would have to start with helping preserve the lives of the people infected by K'Irka's plague.

"You understand," she said, "these microscopic pathogens are not my primary interest. That does not mean I am uninterested in the outcome, only that my knowledge on the subject of gene splicing is limited. But

I will do what I can. I feel strange concerning Lieutenant Ma. He irritated me and so I was most unkind to him, deliberately attempted to torment him, and I succeeded. I find I regret that success, and it has been a long time since I have felt regret."

"You want to make it up to him?" the captain asked.

"Make it up to him?" she repeated, trying to think through the complex weave of meanings that expression must have for Captain Bitka. He had such a bewildering lattice of obligation and responsibility, moderated by formal law, traditional practices, the general Human notions of morality, and his own unique versions of those notions. And the moderators differed in strength and salience depending on the situation.

She had witnessed highly ritualized cultures where actions were constrained to the point of predetermination. She expected something similar from Captain Bitka, but he surprised her. He always surprised her. His life seemed like an exercise in navigating between a black hole and the unpredictable flares of a variable star—sucking, crushing constraint on one side, lancing, terrible danger on the other. And yet he managed to find a way. He always seemed to find the ability to act, to maneuver, to follow his own path, but never by violating those constraints. How? How did he do it? It was by understanding those constraints in meticulous detail, wasn't it? He must love rules to study them so closely, and yet love finding ways around them even more.

"Make it up to him?" she said again. "I would have no idea how to go about doing such a thing. It is all so complicated. Do you know, Captain, what constitutes the sufficient penance for an injury deliberately inflicted? Have your people codified this?"

"No, Te'Anna. I don't know how you can atone for a deliberate injury."

"Oh. What a pity," she said. She tilted her head to the side to get a different view of the tension of his facial muscles and the dilation of his pupils, and she felt a little puff of breath escape her mouth, a sign of her frustration. Bitka *must* know but was unwilling to tell her. Who better knew the treacherous waters of their system of ethics and customs than Bitka? Still, he must have his reasons for withholding the answer.

"In any case," she said, "I will assist Doctor Däng, and we will do our best to save poor Lieutenant Ma and the others. These unexpected complications can add texture to a journey, but K'Irka really is quite difficult to bear sometimes."

"Difficult to *bear*?" he said, and she saw, felt the anger rise in him. "You know, Te'Anna, you Guardians just don't make sense to me. You've been around for thousands of years so I keep expecting to see a glimmer of... *enlightenment*. I know you only remember a few hundred years, but that's still a long time. Humans—most Humans—acquire at least a little wisdom after half a century or so. But you guys..." He shook his head in frustration and disgust.

"I imagine some Humans acquire wisdom, but not all," she answered. "I believe one aspect of enlightenment must be the understanding and acceptance of the concept of *enough*. If enlightenment means accepting that at some point you have had enough life, then after tens or hundreds of thousands of years, how many of our own enlightened ones do you imagine would still be alive? Almost by definition, none. Or did you imagine they would still be playing at being gods, but they would be the *good ones?* Only the P'Daans and the K'Irkas are left." She paused and fought her own wave of emotion, swallowed it down as if it were gorge rising in her throat. "And the Te'Annas."

Sam sat at the desk in his stateroom and looked at the walls, which again showed the exterior view, but no longer a field of dead stars. Instead the upper atmosphere of Destie-Seven nearly filled the wall and floor beneath him. Like many gas giants, a lot was going on down there, including two storms, each one as large as Earth. Ops had done a good job bending orbit to avoid their turbulence in the scoop maneuver.

He turned on the holovid recorder.

"Hey, Cass. Interesting day so far and likely to get more interesting, especially as I have no idea what I'm going to do next. I'm throwing some very stupid tricks at them, desperate stuff, really, just so the crew will know we're doing something. I don't really think it's going to work, though. What it will come down to is brute force: pump out as much ordnance and decoys as we can manage and hope something gets through. If we didn't have people in trouble on the Highstation, we could just run. Those Troatta battleships have a big head of steam but can't exactly turn on a dime or slam on the brakes. If we could just lay low for twelve hours, find someplace to hide, we could let them sail past and maybe be on our way before they could turn around. Nothing to hide behind in space, though."

He stopped and looked at the smartwall again, filled with the enormous bulk of the gas giant Destie-Seven. He stared at it and then shook his head and laughed.

"Nothing to hide behind? Man, am I an idiot!"

S'Bitka's ship turns away from the shipyard, Ship Ninety-Three's voice rumbled inside the brain of the Troatta Chief Helm, Kakusa by-Vrook through-Kuannawaa.

"Does S'Bitka run?" Kakusa asked, ashamed that she hoped the answer was affirmative. Let him run away! She and her sister, Helm Tamari by-Vrook through-Kuannawaa on Ship Ninety-Six, had spoken many times together, and with their two Ships. They had experienced the recordings of the disastrous battle of their other sisters, the destruction of two Ships and most of their crews, and had considered how to fight this devil. They kept a wide berth between their Ships so S'Bitka could not mask them both with one hellstar, as he had before, but how many did he have? Lord P'Daan said he cannot have many. How did the Lord know that? If he could look into S'Bitka's soul, why did he need Troatta battleships to throw at him? Oh, let S'Bitka run!

He does not run, the Ship told her. *He makes a polar orbit around the gas planet. It will place him on the far side of the planet as we pass, and his orbit will keep the gas planet between us and him while we are at closest approach.*

Her communicator tingled and then her sister's voice, the Helm of Ship Ninety-Six, chirped in her head.

You have heard?

"Yes, Sister, I have. He turns. At this course and velocity, he will hide behind the planet as we pass. The diameter of the gas planet and its atmosphere are three times the range of our beams. Even were it not there, the distance alone would keep him safe."

Kakusa's sister did not speak for twenty beats of the heart.

So. We must either decelerate or weave our course with his.

"That is what our Loan-Lord P'Daan commands."

Her sister paused again before replying.

My Ship is reluctant. S'Bitka saved the soul of Ship Eight-Seven, repaired it, brought its consciousness back from darkness. He saved our sisters as well.

"Those he did not kill!" Kakusa fired back. "Ship Eight-Seven lives, if you can call that crippled, addled existence life. Ship Eight-Eight is gone forever along with over a *hundred* of our own nestmates. Shall we congratulate him for not slaughtering them all?"

I say only he is a worthy foe, Sister . . . and a dangerous one. My Ship does not love him, but it does not hunger for revenge either. It fears him. I fear him.

By the Lord Guardians, Kakusa feared him as well! But fear was woven into her life. Fear kept her alive, so long as she did not allow it to master her.

"We are commanded to engage and destroy him if we can, and if not, to damage him, delay him until the others arrive. Deceleration now will not slow us enough. We must bend course toward the gas planet, pass close enough to engage him there, and stagger our formation so he cannot hide from us both.

"He *is* a worthy foe, and we will give him a worthy death. Our names will be remembered as the slayers of the demon S'Bitka, and if we take care, we will live to share that memory."

CHAPTER THIRTY-TWO

Seven hours later, **aboard USS *Cam Ranh Bay*,
in polar orbit around Destie-Seven
14 July 2134 (*one hundred forty-eight days
after Incident Seventeen*)**

"Sir," Sam heard Homer Alexander report, "the ship is
at Readiness Condition Two, Material Condition Bravo,
in polar orbit around Destie-Seven at an altitude of two
hundred twenty thousand kilometers. Power ring is
fully charged, reactor on standby, shroud deployed,
sensors passive and also receiving passive feed from
Drone One."

"Very well, I have the bridge, Mister Alexander," Sam
replied as he strapped himself into the command chair.
"Now tell me something I want to hear."

Alexander smiled before answering. "You were right,
sir. They've kept making that same lateral acceleration
ever since they saw our orbital shift. Looks like a thirtieth
of a gee, same as what we figure their initial burn was. It's
displaced them a little over a hundred fifty thousand
kilometers toward Destie-Seven, which means they'll pass
well inside the orbit of Seven-Echo. If they keep it up

they'll pass really close to Destie-Seven's atmo. They're definitely spoiling for a fight."

"And?"

"And that displacement has put them well out of range of our decoy attack cluster, and the Cold Charlie bird, but they're bearing right down on Cold Bravo. It's going to have a shot in about thirty minutes."

The first of his stupid long shots, Sam thought. Had they done enough to distract the Troatta admiral that they might get a lick in after all?

"And they haven't seen it yet?"

"Hard telling, sir. It's really small, black, and nonreflective. They're at about a hundred and twenty thousand kilometers, and it's almost invisible on radar at that distance unless you know exactly where it is and what you're looking for. HRVS couldn't see it unless it occludes a star or something. And it's damn near as cold as the background. But the thing is, it's got to get to within *five* thousand kilometers before it can sting him, and that's a different matter."

Yeah. Still a long shot.

"Where's the Cold Alpha missile?"

"Nowhere near firing range, sir. One hundred two thousand from target, already well downrange."

Sam looked at the battle clock: nine hours eleven minutes. In about thirty minutes the Troatta would be within meson gun range of the Cold Charlie missile and if they saw it, they would kill it. Nine or ten minutes after that, if they hadn't killed it, Cold Charlie would be able to hit them.

"We're coming up on the watch change, TAC. Let's go to general quarters."

"General quarters, aye aye, sir," he answered as he leaned forward and touched his workstation. The general quarters gong sounded throughout the ship, although Sam noticed that most of the stations on the bridge were already manned and the rest of the battle station's bridge personnel showed up very quickly, probably waiting in the corridor outside or the crew forward break room. Sam waited for five minutes to be sure most of the crew was at their stations throughout the ship.

"Comm, give me all-ship." When Bohannon gave him a thumbs up he started. "This is the captain speaking. Since I spoke to you last, things have changed. We've bent course into a polar orbit around the gas giant Destie-Seven to use it as cover against the two Troatta long ships. They're going fast enough they can't actually stop any time soon, so if we could keep Destie-Seven between us and them as they shot past, it would have been a pretty low-risk battle. I can't speak for all of you, but that's the kind I prefer. But they've decided to come after us and mix it up around Destie-Seven, which should make for a confused knife fight of a battle. We'll have the edge, though: bigger variety of weapons, time to plant some surprises in Destie-Seven's ring system, and the fact that all we have to do is stay alive for about ten or twenty minutes and then they'll be down the road, and they won't be able to return for a week. They spent over three days accelerating at their maximum thrust to get going this fast. It will take them the same time to decelerate to a stop and then at least as long to get back here.

"But first, we've laid a trap for them and now we'll see if it can take a bite out of them before they get here. Look to your stations. Things are going to be interesting for the next half hour. Then we'll have some work to do to get ready for the next round. Carry on."

Sam turned to Alexander.

"TAC, Detonate the Cold Alpha missile and go active with Drone One. I want tight beam radar on those two Troatta ships."

Alexander touched his workstation.

"Cold Alpha detonated," he said, and Chief Bermudez in TAC Two added, "Drone One active, painting targets with radar."

They waited. Six seconds later the main tactical screen showed the flare of a thermonuclear warhead over eight hundred thousand kilometers away: three light-seconds. It took three seconds for Alexander's command to reach the missile and then three more seconds for the light of the detonation to get back to them. Ten or twenty seconds later Bermudez spoke.

"Sir, targets have ceased acceleration. Target aspect ratio changing, I think they're rotating their ships, sir."

Sam said nothing, not wanting to jinx what was happening out there with premature self-congratulations, but he knew what he wanted that Troatta admiral to think. He wanted her to remember Humans used nukes to prevent detection of threats. Sam had detonated the Five-One missile, which had already passed them by, to make the Troatta think the threat was coming from behind them. Sam wanted that admiral to turn her ships so their meson guns were ready to engage any missiles emerging from the hot debris cloud that a moment before had been Five One. He wanted those ships pointed the wrong direction—and looking the wrong direction—until it was too late.

"TAC, how much power does Drone One have left?"

"Seventeen minutes at maximum output, sir. Six hours on high-res passive, seventy-two on low power standby."

"Okay, drop it back to passive mode for now. We're going to need it later."

Now nothing to do for half an hour but watch the battle clock, stare at the tactical displays, and wait. Might as well do something to fill the time.

"Say, is that damned bridge drink dispenser still on the blink?" he asked.

"Still broke-dick-no-workee, sir," Chief Bermudez answered as she sent the command to Drone One to power down.

Sam squinted up the commlink to the ready wardroom. *Yes, Captain?*

"Steward, I got a bridge full of thirsty people. Think you can manage to send some delicious beverages up here? Make mine coffee black and take everyone else's order."

Doctor Däng Thi Hue had been the first person on the ship to speak to Te'Anna, had defended her against the imagined murderous intentions of the captain—incorrectly imagined, as it turned out—but she and the Guardian had hardly spoken since then. Whatever Hue needed to do her work had involved tissue samples, not conversation. Now Te'Anna stood here in the medbay where Hue had spent so many hours studying the Guardian's chemical, cellular, and genetic makeup. She had come to help Hue save the lives of Koichi Ma and one hundred twenty-seven more. Hue had not been sure what to say at first but, once they began examining the structure of the biological agent in the blood of Koichi and the infected Marines, their shared curiosity took over and within an hour they had formed a desperate partnership— desperate because of the aggressive, virulent agent they observed in the samples.

"My God, it is actually re-engineering their DNA," Hue said, sitting back from the display screen. "Have you ever heard of anything like this?"

"Oh, yes," Te'Anna replied calmly. "This is a favorite technique of K'Irka's. It requires more work in the original invasive construct, but once that construct is introduced it works very quickly. Notice how she has sped up metabolism. Also, the viral agent stimulates cells to replicate more often than normally. Both changes speed the transformation. The subjects are already shedding their outer epidermis. The extreme body and joint pain is symptomatic of accelerated bone replacement."

"But why? She could have just killed them."

Te'Anna did one of her peculiar neck stretches and then looked at Hue with her head turned nearly on its side. "There is no art in simply killing, Doctor Däng."

"Did you say *art?*"

"Yes. K'Irka thinks of herself as an artist, and one whose work runs to the ironic and grotesque. *I* think she is simply pretentious, but then I cannot recall ever appreciating art of the more challenging sort."

Art, Hue thought. K'Irka was turning Koichi and the others into twisted caricatures as an expression of art. What was wrong with these so-called Guardians, these . . . these *things*?

"What can we do to counteract this virus?"

"We can do nothing," Te'Anna said.

Hue felt unsteady for a moment, and then experienced a surge of rage, murderous rage. "I want to kill K'Irka," she admitted. "I know it's wrong, and yet I want to very much. I want to do it with my own hands."

"That seems a very sensible reaction," Te'Anna said, "and yet you think it is wrong. Humans have so many rules. It makes me dizzy just thinking about them."

"We can do nothing to save Koichi," Hue said, "so all I am left with is vengeance."

"Why do you say we cannot save Lieutenant Ma? There is nothing *we* can do to reverse the virus, but I am certain K'Irka can. It is only a case of finding what will motivate her to do so."

Twenty minutes later Sam looked at the battle clock: nine hours and forty-one minutes. The lead Troatta battleship crossed the forty-three-thousand-kilometer line—meson gun range—from the small, cold, silent cylinder of the Cold Charlie missile. The battleship did not fire. The next nine minutes seemed to Sam to last an hour. One minute before their missile was within detonation range of the enemy, Alexander spoke.

"Captain, we've got something interesting here. If we wait eight more minutes after we're within detonation range of the lead long ship, we'll have both of them in range of Cold Charlie. We can split fire and maybe cripple both of them."

Both? Two with one blow? The odds of killing them both were vanishingly small, but still . . . damage on both ships, even a little, would put them back on their heels. But the missile would have to live eight extra minutes. At what point would the Troatta close-in collision avoidance sensors pick it up?

"No. Take the shot we've got as soon as we've got it. All laser rods aimed at the proximate target."

"Aye, aye, sir," Alexander said, and Sam sensed no disagreement, no resentment in the voice. He'd had an idea, made his recommendation, but was happy with someone else making the call. Either that or he was a good actor.

"Firing range in twenty seconds, sir. Ten seconds. Firing range . . . *mark*."

"Fire," Sam ordered.

The Ship was in pain. Chief Helm Kakusa by-Vrook through-Kuannawaa felt the ship's pain in her own arms, immersed in the living orifices of the control interface. She felt the pain rippling up and down her limbs.

"Is it bad, Ship?" she asked.

It hurts, but not so much as that time we fought in the last great battle against the Keen-Kee Armada. My long eyes and long legs are broken. My short legs are as well, but I think I can repair them with the help of our crew. Some of our crew are broken, also. I am sorry.

"I know, Ship," she answered. "I am sorry too."

How did he attack us from behind? it asked.

"It was my fault, Ship. My fault. I let him deceive me, turned to face a threat which was not there. Repair your short legs if you can. The long legs are unimportant for now."

They did not need the Ship's *long eyes*—active sensors—so long as her sister's Ship still had its own and the datalink between them remained active, and the *long legs*—star drive—could indeed wait. But the *short legs*—the Ship's thrusters—were needed to slow the Ship and eventually bring it back to the shipyard for repairs. Without them, they would probably all die. The Ship itself certainly would. She felt the tingle of her sister, Helm Tamari, trying to open contact.

Sister Kakusa, are you alive?

"Yes, Sister Tamari, most of us still live. There is damage, however, and it is serious. Our active sensors are inoperable as well as both our star drive and reaction drive. The reaction drive may be repairable."

We will dock with you and help make repairs.

"No! Our mission remains unchanged. S'Bitka has won the first contest, but there may still be a path to our own victory. You must listen and follow my instructions exactly."

"TAC, what am I looking at?" Sam said.

"I think it's a crippled Troatta long ship, sir," Alexander said. "It's cooling, so its powerplant is either inoperable or she's playing possum. The ship is still on its original course and will pass between Destie-Seven and Seven-Echo, but it's not radiating energy and it's tumbling slowly, about one rotation every seventeen minutes. The other ship has resumed lateral thrust, so it's not going back to render assistance. That can mean a lot of things."

Yes, it could, Sam thought. He was glad to hear Alexander wasn't jumping to any conclusions. They knew they'd hit that one ship, knew they'd done something to it, but what? Either it was so lightly damaged it didn't require assistance, or so badly damaged it was a lifeless shell, or the Troatta admiral wanted Sam to think it was one of those two things, or maybe it meant something else entirely. One thing was clear: the remaining ship was still bending orbit to get as close to them and Destie-Seven as they could when they made their fly-by.

"What sort of firing solution can you put together on the undamaged bandit?" Sam asked.

"Nothing simple, sir. The gas giant's gravity well is so deep it's got an escape velocity of about sixty kilometers per second. We've got an orbital velocity of twenty-six klicks, and we can only put about four more klicks per second on a Mark Five with the coil gun, so all we can do it throw it into a higher orbit. We can lob stuff at them, but they're likely to see it coming."

Sam brought up the course projections on his display. At the current closing rate, they'd be in range of the Troatta's meson gun in under three hours. If the Troatta kept up the lateral acceleration, they would just about graze the upper atmosphere of Destie-Seven. He still had twenty-five Mark Fives and eight Mark Fours.

"Helm, time to disengage from the spin habitat. As soon as we're clear we'll burn some of that reaction mass we just scooped. Give me a full gee for twenty minutes, kick us into higher orbit and leave the spin habitat down close."

"One gee for twenty minutes, aye, aye, sir," Barr-Sanchez answered. "Do you want a second correction to even out the orbit, sir?"

"No, let's leave it eccentric, give them something to do with those fancy computers they're supposed to have.

TAC, give me some firing solutions on the active long ship: decoys and Mark Fives in sequence. Keep the Mark Fours in their canisters and hold back a couple Mark Fives, but throw at least twenty missiles at her. Give me one decoy cluster and one Mark Five on the cripple, too. Let's see how crippled they really are."

The next ten minutes were consumed with preparing the ship to undock with the habitat ring, and then actually undocking. Alexander was silent the entire time, absorbed with the firing solution calculations and course projections. As the Bay's main hull cleared the habitat ring, Alexander's head snapped up.

"Captain, don't accelerate!"

"Helm, belay acceleration," Sam ordered and then he turned to the TAC boss. "Time is limited, TAC. This better be good."

"I hope so, sir. I may be crazy, but look at these orbit tracks. I'm not used to fighting this deep inside a gravity well, but orbital eccentricity . . . I think we can really mess them up. We don't have to just lob missiles at them. We can do all sorts of screwy things, like shoot a missile down into the atmosphere and get a slingshot effect. I mean, we'll have to retard the decoy release until after the missile clears atmo, but—"

"Settle down, TAC. Take a breath. Why does that matter?"

"There are so many different ways of putting a missile on target, I think we should do *all* of them, sir. Some missiles will get there quicker, some slower, but if we stagger the launches, we can time them all to get there at about the same time. And here's the kicker: some of them are going to come from weird angles. Arc of fire, sir. I think we can flood the zone, overwhelm their point-defense ability, hit them from more directions than they can bring fire to bear against. Look, sir." He pointed to his display. Sam saw a tangle of missile tracks, but all converging on a common point. "The thing is, we've got a very narrow launch window. For this to work we've got to start launching *now*, not twenty minutes from now."

Sam felt an almost overpowering urge to begin crunching the numbers, to see how the solution worked—or didn't work—but he resisted it. Alexander already had crunched the numbers. That was his job.

"Is this fire plan ready to execute?"

Alexander's eyes opened wider and for a moment Sam thought he would falter, but he swallowed and then nodded. "Yes sir, it is."

"Okay. It's your boat, TAC. Execute."

The next twenty minutes were physically as well as psychologically disorienting. The *Bay* spent much of the time rotating, coming to new firing bearings at Alexander's commands. The sound of the acceleration klaxon became as familiar as the shudder of the ship when it fired a missile or decoy cluster from its coil gun. Sam did not give a single command the entire time; Alexander executed the fire mission without bravado or self-consciousness. His personality seemed to disappear into the job. Sam spent the time crunching the numbers, making sure the solution would work. If it wouldn't it would at least keep the Troatta busy for a while and he would have to come up with something else, but the numbers worked. By the time the last missile was fired, he was convinced the

Troatta were dead. Now the only thing left to do was convince them of that.

"COMM, get me a text link to both Troatta ships. Mister Alexander, that is one brilliant attack plan. Well done, TAC. Well done. Now get me a copy of our fire-plan course trajectories, but code all the decoys as live missiles as well."

Pride and confusion fought for mastery of Alexander's face. "Sir?"

"We're warriors, Mister Alexander, not murderers. If they want to fight and die, we'll oblige them, but they should at least have the chance to surrender. Because I'll tell you the truth, TAC, that's the only way they'll survive the next two hours."

Sam hoped they would surrender. He'd killed enough. Whatever score there was to settle was settled many times over, and these beings had no part in the murder of his landing party. He'd like to take a piece out of P'Daan, but how many of his own crew was he willing to expend on that item of personal satisfaction? Not a single one. He squinted up his contact list and pinged Haykuz.

Captain?

"Mister Haykuz, I have a diplomatic task for you, one which if carried out can save a lot of lives. No one has dealt with Troatta senior officers more directly than you. I need you to persuade these two Troatta ships facing us to surrender. You've got some leverage: we have them in a hopeless tactical situation. Negotiate any terms you like, so long as they're out of the fight long enough for us to finish our business on Seven-Echo and get away."

I will do what I can, Captain Bitka.

CHAPTER THIRTY-THREE

The next day, aboard USS *Cam Ranh Bay,*
approaching Destie-Seven-Echo Highstation
15 July 2134 (*one hundred forty-nine days
after Incident Seventeen*)

The light in the medbay was so bright it hurt Sam's eyes
at first, but this was where Doctor Däng and Te'Anna
wanted to give their report. He could taste the coffee
coating his teeth and tongue. That was one thing the
galley still had. They'd been carrying a big shipment of
concentrate in the cargo hold, which was a good thing.
He'd been running on coffee for the twenty hours since
the two long ships had emerged from J-space—all
through the strangely one-sided battle, the temporary
truce negotiations with the two alien ships, the tense
moments until the one undamaged ship had begun
accelerating away from Destie-Seven and toward a
rendezvous with the cripple, the inevitable recriminations
from Ka'Deem Brook, and the agony of listening to and
seeing the last conscious moments of their people on the
shipyard highstation. Running on coffee and protein bars
made by Acho's logistics crew: pressed soy protein with

dried seaweed for texture and flavored with hydroponically grown beet sugar.

Yum.

"So what do we know?" he asked.

Doctor Däng glanced over at Te'Anna, but if she believed she would get any comfort there, Sam thought she was mistaken. Whatever sense of fear or loss Däng felt for her friend on Highstation was foreign to their Guardian . . . their Guardian *what?* Not really prisoner so much these days. Guest? Traveling companion? The continued presence of the two armed Marine guards suggested otherwise, but the relationship had definitely altered since the battle with the pair of long ships. The *first* pair of long ships.

"We know the agent which infected Koichi and the Marines," Doctor Däng said, "and probably the means by which they were infected. The delivery system is a retrovirus, human-specific, clearly engineered for this one very specific purpose."

"How did it get past Merderet's security precautions?"

"It did not, Captain Bitka. We believe it was always present in the space they selected as a safe environment. It does not require oxygen and so reducing the space to vacuum did not destroy it."

"That's crazy. How did they know to put it in those specific spaces?" Sam asked.

Doctor Däng shook her head. "They did not, nor did they need to. Since it is human-specific, it is harmless to both Guardians and New People, so we believe they simply spread it everywhere in the station, assuming our landing party would have to choose some place as a refuge."

Däng again glanced at the Guardian and this time Te'Anna spoke.

"There may be a way to rescue Lieutenant Ma and the others. But you must first promise to release me to K'Irka. This is actually an essential part of the plan, but I cannot explain it to you until you agree. And your agreement must be without condition. I believe the term is 'a separate peace.' In your capacity as senior military official of the United States of North America, or at least senior of all officials present in the theater of war, you agree to a cessation of hostilities between your realm and the Guardian Te'Anna, effective immediately."

"I don't know if I have the authority to do that," he said.

"Of course you do," the Guardian replied. "Your authority in this star system is absolute. It is possible your superiors will disallow such an arrangement when you return to their authority, but that is not important to us for now, is it?"

No, it wasn't. If they could actually get to a place where his superiors could overrule him, they'd have won. What would she do with her freedom, though? Well, he could still have her escorted, still keep her out of sensitive areas, still physically prevent her from taking action harmful to the ship and its passengers and crew. If she tried something, he could clap her in the brig again. He wasn't giving her immunity from their rules, after all, just changing her status. He looked at Däng.

"Doctor, what can you do for our people over there?"

"Nothing, Captain. Believe me, I wish the answer were different, but I have no option to offer you. The only way we can save them is to force or persuade the Guardian K'Irka to reverse the process she started. The best we have is a possible vaccine against the agent, but that will not help those already infected."

A vaccine. Sam could vaccinate his two remaining platoons of Marines and put them over there if it came to that, but then what? Sam turned back to Te'Anna. "I don't understand why I need to agree to this as a precondition."

"It is not necessary to understand," Te'Anna said, "only to do. In this I ask you to trust me."

"That's asking a hell of a lot."

"I am aware. If it is of help, Doctor Däng has come to trust me and you should consider her opinion on the matter. She is certainly very intelligent and has won some sort of prize, I forget its name. Although honestly it seems you have as many prizes as you have rules. My Marine friend Showalter said that his daughter had won a gold star for reading, and someone else told me you won a silver star in your last war. Which colored star is better?"

Sam glanced at Private Showalter, whose face was turning red, and he suppressed a smile of his own.

"Gold, definitely."

Sam looked at Doctor Däng who shrugged, a gesture he had never seen her use before and which struck him as disingenuous. Te'Anna could not have put this proposal together on her own. She didn't know enough about their laws and customs. Still, he had two choices, and while neither of them was particularly attractive, he knew which one offered the most opportunity for success.

"Very well, you have a deal," he said.

"Not a deal, Captain Bitka. You give me my freedom

without condition, or requirement of any specific act in recompense."

"Okay, I understand. Te'Anna, you are no longer considered a prisoner and hostile combatant. Your status is now a neutral noncombatant. Furthermore, I undertake to repatriate you as soon as it's practical. We'll draw up an official document, but for now Doctor Däng and your two Marine . . . *friends* will serve as formal witnesses to my decision."

"Oh, good!" she said. "I feel better already. It happens I *do* have an idea how we might save your people on the shipyard. Would you like to hear it now?"

As the orbital shipyard grew larger on the PSRV's control display, Sam considered his parting from Ka'Deem Brook. The XO had not questioned Sam's decision to change Te'Anna's status or to go along with her plan, and it occurred to him those were the first decisions of Sam's in quite a while the XO hadn't taken issue with. He'd actually seemed fairly cheerful saying goodbye and wishing him luck. Sam had a funny feeling Ka'Deem Brook didn't think he was coming back from this adventure, and that the thought didn't bother him a bit. Wait for the crazy captain to get himself killed or infected, send a landing party down to Seven-Echo and find someone who could fix a jump drive, then get the hell home. Of course, that probably meant abandoning all their people on the Highstation, but their memories would be honored, probably with a plaque somewhere. Sam unbuckled the restraints that held him in the copilot's chair.

"Boats, as soon as we're in the station airlock, get the PSRV clear and head back to the *Bay*."

Chief Wainwright glanced at him without moving his head, keeping most of his attention on the instruments. "You might need a ride in a hurry if things go south, sir. Why don't I take up a parking orbit about a kilometer away?"

"I appreciate the offer, but do as I say. If this does go south, I doubt I'll be at liberty to leave."

"Hell, why don't you take a gauss pistol, sir? Shoot your way out if you have to."

Sam laughed. "I don't even remember how to take the safety off one of those things. Wainwright, if something does happen, you've been a hell of a senior chief bosun, and God knows I needed one. It's been a privilege serving with you. But once the Guardian and I are on the station, you get your ass away, understood?"

"Aye, aye, sir. And for what it's worth, I don't think anyone in uniform could have done a better job with this mess than you have, and that goes no matter how this last trip comes out."

Sam finished unstrapping from the copilot station but before he pushed off he held out his hand and Wainwright shook it. Sam kicked lightly up and back and floated to the rear of the main cabin to join Te'Anna, the only other passenger.

"How's that vacuum suit fit?" he asked.

"Not as well as I would like. It is tight across my shoulders and under the arms. I hope that will not limit my mobility too much."

"Engineers only had a few hours to fabricate it. I just hope it holds atmosphere if you need it."

She turned that unblinking gaze on him for a moment

before replying. "I am less likely to need it than will you. Try to keep your helmet closed as long as possible."

"You having second thoughts about the vaccine you and Doctor Däng cooked up?"

She tilted her head to the side before answering. "We also only had a few hours to fabricate it. I just hope it does not kill you."

Just what he needed, Sam thought, a Guardian with a dark sense of humor.

"There is something I would like to say, Captain Bitka, while we have a moment," she said in a different tone and without looking at him. "I have wanted to say it for some time but my circumstances were such you would have interpreted it as an effort to curry favor and so would have discounted it. I hope you will not do so now, since at this point I have nothing to gain from it. When your delegation came to the Eye of P'Daan, I was visiting his compound but was not party to any of the negotiations leading up to the meeting. I was invited to participate in the offering, and it is expected that all Guardians present will do so under those circumstances, but I did not know this was other than a voluntary offering of appeasement. I regret my participation. Regret is a very foreign emotion to me and although I value novel sensations, I do not like this one."

Sam wasn't sure what to say, wasn't sure how he felt about that. Just being reminded of the "offering ceremony" sent a shudder of revulsion through him. He believed her regret was sincere; he just wasn't sure what to do with that regret.

"I'll have to think about that," he said.

★ ★ ★

A half-dozen Desties relieved both Sam and Te'Anna of their helmets as soon as they were in the station. Other Desties stared at them as they first floated through the zero-gee docking area and then made their way into the station's rotating habitat wheel. It felt to Sam as if it was spun up to about nine-tenths of a gee. That was light for the Desties, but then he remembered that comfort of the Guardian would trump everything else. Ten minutes later they were brought into in a large machine shop, judging from what looked like robot machinery lining the walls. Sam took it to be robotics, but some of it looked more alive than mechanical and he again wondered where to draw the lines between machine and creature; the Guardians had certainly managed to blur the line in his mind.

Speaking of which, a Guardian, who Sam assumed must be K'Irka, waited for them in the center of the large open work area. She was shorter than Te'Anna but still taller than he was. Unlike Te'Anna, her feathers were mostly yellow and pale red, and her glowing aura also had a reddish tint. The difference in the heights of the two Guardians made him wonder about Choice's theory these were the biological machines left behind by a vanished race: why make functionally identical versions of your machines different sizes?

"Te'Anna," the Guardian said without any other greeting to either of them, the words translated in his head by his commlink, "so it is true you have gone over to the invaders?"

"Did those Troatta-things say so? They must not be very intelligent. I was a prisoner. The invaders had me go with one of them while he spoke with the Troatta. I did so. But I am no longer a prisoner; this one has decided to release me to you."

K'Irka looked at Sam and tilted her head to the side. "So. This is the one called S'Bitka, the Destroyer of Worlds."

"Well, that's an exaggeration," Sam said. "I've only destroyed one world . . . so far."

K'Irka turned to Te'Anna. "What bargain did you make with him for your freedom?"

"None. He released me without condition, as a gift to you to establish his good faith."

K'Irka studied Te'Anna's face carefully for several long seconds, then let out a sharp explosive puff of breath. "Pha! He must be a fool."

"They are sentimental and hopeful, like most mortals," Te'Anna said, walking slowly across the floor to join K'Irka. "I am not positive this is invariably a weakness, but in some circumstances, it can certainly be a disadvantage. He has come here to get you to heal his followers and let them go so they can return to their home, which is certainly an act both of hope and of sentiment. Could the On-Living Engineers really have repaired their star drive?"

"Of course they could, if they would agree. I cannot imagine they would. I doubt the invaders could even get their attention, the On-Living ones have become so fixed in their behavior."

Te'Anna stopped next to K'Irka and lightly touched the other Guardian's shoulder feathers. K'Irka twitched in impatience and turned away.

"Don't turn away, my friend," Te'Anna said. "It has been so long since I have been with and touched one of my own."

"Why the others value your wisdom escapes me," K'Irka answered, turning her back to her. "You are a silly creature."

"Oh, let me feel you in my arms," Te'Anna said and enveloped her from behind, one arm around K'Irka's throat, the other behind her neck in the classic choke restraint Marine Private Showalter had shown her and practiced with her for over an hour. K'Irka's eyes bulged and her mouth opened but no sound came out. The Destie guards moved forward in alarm, energy weapons raised.

"*I am your Guardian!*" Te'Anna's voice rang out in a tone of command Sam had never heard. "This business is above you. Attempt to raise a hand against me and you will join the On-Living on the surface of Haydoos, and your pain will never end."

The guards exchanged uncertain looks and then stepped back, lowering their weapons. Then Te'Anna put her lips close to K'Irka's ear and spoke in a tone too low for Sam or the guards to hear. She spoke for what seemed a long time as K'Irka's struggles weakened and then became simply twitches. Te'Anna had told Sam she would persuade K'Irka to help them, but he remembered her distaste for this other Guardian and wondered if she had changed her mind, and the plan now was to simply kill her. He nearly spoke, nearly stepped forward to remind her they needed K'Irka alive, but he didn't. With guns in nervous hands all around him, the balance in this tableau was too delicate to upset. He had to trust her, and trust that her sense of obligation to Lieutenant Ma would not let her kill the one being who could heal him.

Te'Anna relaxed the pressure of her arm and K'Irka slumped but did not collapse. Sam let out a breath he hadn't realized he was holding.

Te'Anna supported K'Irka and helped her to a seat on a low vertical casing, and then she turned to the Destie guards.

"It is over. All is well between us. Return to your other duties. We will send you instructions soon."

The Desties hesitated, but then K'Irka raised her face and gestured to them, and despite their clear uncertainty the Desties filed out. Sam waited until they were gone to approach the two Guardians, still not entirely sure what had transpired between them and where he stood. Time to find out.

"So, what can K'Irka do to cure my people?"

The seated Guardian rubbed her throat and Te'Anna answered for her. "I think the restoration will take some time, but it can be accomplished. The important thing is that her expertise is at our disposal." She turned to the other Guardian. "You will get to work on that right away, won't you?"

K'Irka wagged her head from side to side.

"That is an affirmative response," Te'Anna explained.

Sam had his doubts. Agreement forced under the threat of imminent death was only good as long as the threat could be maintained, and right now he didn't see much way to do so beyond Te'Anna following K'Irka around with a gun at her head. What was to keep her from going back on the deal once she was back with her guards? Honor? From what Sam had seen, Guardian honor was too frail a reed to support the weight of their future.

"Your fears are groundless, S'Bitka," he heard K'Irka say, her voice raspy. "Yes, I see your suspicion. Te'Anna has persuaded me to assist you and accompany you back to your realm."

She stood up and walked to him and then examined him, shifting her position to see him from different angles. "I believe what she says is true. You were not raised up by Guardians. You evolved independently. And there are five other species in your realm who also have evolved into intelligent life without manipulation. We have no recollection of ever encountering such a thing, although if it has happened with six species in such a concentrated area of space it must have happened elsewhere. Your stars, they are all high metallicity late-blooms?"

"I don't know what that means. I'm not an astrophysicist."

"I cannot imagine any other explanation," Te'Anna said.

K'Irka looked at her with an expression Sam took as something approaching scorn. "Te'Anna, when will you learn that the universe is not limited to what you can imagine?"

Sam felt a jolt of adrenaline as he remembered having said almost the same thing to Homer Alexander. When was that?

"S'Bitka, I must know more," K'Irka continued, turning back to him. "I must understand the steps of the process. All of our creations resemble us, because we made them. But structurally you resemble us as well. If that was not the result of deliberate manipulation, what was the operant principle at work?"

"I can't tell you, but I have a biologist onboard who might. She's a widely renowned scientist, honored for her work, although I don't really understand it."

"Structural ubiquity," Te'Anna said.

K'Irka turned to her. "What?"

"That was the work for which Doctor Däng was honored, and it is the operant principle you seek. Regardless of the chemistry of organisms, the engineering path nature uses to build large structures from smaller ones is essentially the same, hence the external similarities in form and function."

"I must speak with this doctor-thing," K'Irka said, her voice firmer now.

"She is very concerned for the recovery of our people over here," Sam said, trying to steer the conversation back to something practical. "She will want to discuss that with you first. If you restore them to health, I'm sure she will be grateful to work with you."

"Oh, yes," Te'Anna added. "She was deeply impressed with your work on the transformational retrovirus. You know much more about the genetic and cellular aspects of life, but I think she can open an entirely new world of inquiry to you, the various naturally branching trees of life leading to intelligence."

K'Irka closed her eyes and leaned her head back, taking in a long, slow breath. She seemed to fill up, come more alive, and Sam knew they had her. She opened her eyes.

"Oh, but the star drive is unlike your machines. It lives,

an enormously complex colony of microscopic organism. Reprogramming it without degrading its function is extremely difficult. Only the On-Living Engineers and H'Stus know how to do so, and H'Stus is far beyond our reach."

"You don't have the information in some sort of memory storage?" Sam asked.

"Of course, but it will take a year or more to train new technicians in its use. You have only days before the arrival of the rest of the Troatta ships."

"The engineers live below, on Haydoos, don't they?" Sam asked. "Can't you order them to help us."

"It is not that simple," K'Irka replied.

CHAPTER THIRTY-FOUR

Four days later, **Destie-Seven-Echo**
19 July 2134 (*one hundred fifty-three days after*
Incident Seventeen)

Hell must look like this, Sam thought as he rode the needle down to Destie-Seven-Echo's poisonous yellow surface, yellow from its omnipresent coating of sulfuric volcanic ash. No shortage of that on this world. Once the passenger compartment slid down through the last cloud layer, he saw a bleak vista of bare rocks and dead or dormant volcanic cones lit by the glow of active volcanoes scattered in every direction to the horizon.

It's like Io with a dense atmosphere, he thought. As a newly minted ensign a decade ago he'd orbited Io, Jupiter's fifth moon, on his first duty rotation to the outer Solar System. Now here he was, about to get out and walk around on this apocalyptic landscape and hope the coating on his hazard suit was as good as advertised against sulfuric acid. There probably hadn't been much problem with that until the Guardians decided to give the place an oxygen-rich atmosphere. What were they thinking? He remembered a rhyme from middle school chemistry:

439

Johnny was a chemist, but Johnny is no more
For what he thought was H_2O, was H_2SO_4

He rode in the passenger compartment only with Te'Anna, who looked very odd in her own hazard suit. It was comforting to know the Guardians weren't impervious to acid. They were immune to just about everything else. He now had an opportunity to ask what had been bothering him for several days.

"Why did you make me release you without telling me your plan? Was it a test of my trust?"

"No. At least I did not intend it to be. I told you it was necessary for my plan to work, and it was. It enabled me to tell K'Irka nothing but the truth, including that you had given my freedom without condition. I seldom if ever lie; it damages one's credibility and usually to little purpose as a lie is so easy to detect. She certainly would have detected a direct lie from me."

"Well, you didn't lie, but you certainly deceived her."

"Oh, I think sentient beings mostly deceive themselves."

Some of his skepticism must have shown in his face. She wagged her head from side to side.

"Sometimes I help them a little," she admitted.

He looked back out at the lifeless yellow landscape rising up to meet them. *No, not entirely lifeless,* he thought. There were thirty-seven New People down there who had lived on the surface of Haydoos for over five hundred years and were likely to continue doing so for a very, very long time. Usually they were dispersed across this hemisphere of the moon in work parties, recovering rare transition metals in volcanic rock, vomited up from the molten core of the moon.

Hard telling how those transition metals got there to begin with, but they were there, mostly lanthanides but a fair chunk of actinides as well. The Guardians needed those elements for advanced electronics as much as the *Cottohazz* did, but it was hard to find them in concentrations high enough to make extraction practical, unless you had a smallish moon with a molten metallic core rich in them and a lot of active volcanism going on. Then you just had to locate the surface deposits, mine the ore containing the good stuff, process and smelt it, and send it up the needle to the shipyard.

But the New People working down here, the ones the Guardians called the On-Living Engineers, spent much of their time so dispersed it would have been nearly impossible to find the ones they needed and enlist their help, partly because they were so singlemindedly dedicated to the job, or at least so K'Irka claimed. Sam and Te'Anna had waited four days in order to time their arrival with one of the periodic gatherings of the ore miners at the needle downstation to begin the smelting process, the only time most of the ground personnel gathered in one place. The wait made Sam nervous. They had negotiated a three-day truce with the Troatta warships, a truce which had expired yesterday. Newtonian mechanics gave them three more days; the Troatta had only managed to decelerate to a dead stop relative to Seven-Echo today and would take those three extra days to get back here, but if all went well the *Bay* should be gone by then.

If.

"You sure this is going to work?" he asked Te'Anna.

"Of course it will *work*," she answered. "The only questions is *how* it will work: usefully or disastrously."

Sam looked at her and shook his head.

"I think you do that on purpose," he said.

"I have no notion what you mean," she answered. She tried to ruffle her neck feathers but her gloved fingers encountered the hazard suit fabric instead. She shifted her balance from one foot to another and Sam realized she was nervous about the outcome. She had no real skin in this game, was likely to come out fine no matter who won. Guardians apparently didn't kill other Guardians, despite her assault of K'Irka. But she was still nervous, which meant her anxiety was for Sam and the others. She really had been surprised the station had not held the answer to the problem, and now she was genuinely frightened for them. She actually *cared*.

"Thank you, Te'Anna," Sam said, "for all the help you have given us. Whether this works out usefully or disastrously, we will never forget what you have done."

And then he did something he had never imagined doing. He put his arm around her shoulder and hugged her. She stood still for a moment, then turned to him and enfolded him in her arms, head lowered and resting on the top of his helmet.

"Oh," she said, a plaintive note in her voice, "yet another unaccustomed feeling."

Te'Anna stood with Bitka near the wall of the enormous enclosed receiving bay, and she marveled at the noisy swirl of vehicular activity, eight-wheeled ore carriers with huge solid-looking tires backing up and dumping their loads into broad bins set into the floor, where mechanical conveyors moved the rocks away for processing. The floor and walls were yellow with sulfur dust, the air thick with it.

New People shuffled through the vehicle traffic, waving and directing the massive vehicles, but they were unlike any New People Te'Anna had ever seen. They were hairless, weathered, tough-looking workers who moved with assurance, barked orders, and wiped perspiration from their damaged faces. And they *were* damaged, much of their skin showing the glossy texture of scar tissue. Acid burns, undoubtedly. They all wore protective clothing, but accidents happen—after five hundred years, *many* accidents. She knew all of this, had heard of it, but actually seeing it was different, and deeply unsettling.

The New People worked in the receiving dock with their respirators pulled off their faces and Bitka made to take his off as well, but she stopped him.

"No, Captain Bitka, their lungs are more robust than yours or mine. P'Daan's object was not to kill them slowly, but punish them forever. He meant them to serve as an object lesson, but they have not turned out as he anticipated. He may still kill them someday."

"These guys are about the hardest-working and most organized crew I've ever seen," Bitka said. "Are they on a tight deadline?"

How to explain the On-Living Engineers?

"No, there is no required schedule. There was one originally, but they exceeded it, and kept exceeding every schedule given them. Now they are simply allowed to work at their own pace, which is what you see." She realized there was something very impressive about it, but also perverse.

"See how the ones on foot weave in and out of the traffic?" Bitka said. "It's like they know in advance where every vehicle is going to be ten seconds from now. And they do, don't they? They've been doing exactly this job, and only this job, for *hundreds* of years. No wonder they're so fucking good at it! But why are they ignoring you?"

"You and I have nothing to do with their task," Te'Anna said, and moved him gently back to make way for a small maintenance vehicle. "It is very hard to get them to stop concentrating on their task, but K'Irka gave me something which is supposed to help. I have never interacted with the On-Living Engineers before. They act almost as if they are in a trance."

"No," Bitka said, "they act as if they're real and we aren't. They act as if we're ghosts, or me anyway. Everybody they ever knew is dead, aren't they? Everyone alive now will die and they will go on. Just them, along with you Guardians. For them, I'm just a ghost waiting to happen."

She looked at him, surprised as she so often was at the insights which seemed to just come to him, and this one brought her a moment of pain. "Yes, you are, Captain Bitka. Part of me misses you already."

Bitka looked away, seemed to take a deep breath. "Okay, let's get this show on the road."

What an odd expression, she thought. "I assume you mean let us begin. We will in a moment. We must wait for their break period."

Bitka looked back at her, his face a portrait of skepticism. "They actually *stop*?"

Twenty minutes later, Sam's commlink vibrated. He was about to shift it to message mode when he saw Brook's ID tag and the *Urgent* flag on the command channel. Sam stepped away from Te'Anna and into a corner of the work area.

"Captain here. What's wrong, XO?"

We just got hit with some kind of inert attack weapon, small pellets at high velocity.

"From the station?"

No sir. The station got hit as well, but it didn't do any serious damage to them. We back-calculated the trajectory and it looks like it was fired from the other inhabited moon, Destie-Seven-Golf.

"Damage?"

Pretty bad, sir, most of it to the primary hull. Three of the four radiators are off-line, two cells of the power ring are torn up pretty badly, one of the one-point-five gig lasers is a total write-off, and we took a cluster of hits in forward engineering that wrecked all of our fabricators. The coil gun is inoperable, but Parker from engineering thinks we can get that back online, but that's about the only good news, sir.

"Casualties?"

One rating dead, sir: Machinist Third Camorra from the auxiliary division. One chief, seven ratings, and four civilians injured but expected to recover, assuming we get out of here.

Sam tried to remember Camorra but couldn't put a

face with the name. Killed by inert pellets at high velocity, about as simple a weapon as there was. In the previous war the uBakai had hit Sam's ship with a weapon like that at the very start of hostilities, killing half a dozen shipmates. Fleet Intel had dubbed it *buckshot*.

"We need to shut down whatever hit us from Seven-Golf."

Yes, sir. Alexander is on that. That Guardian K'Irka on the station sent us the ground layout of the Seven-Golf facilities. They've got a big mass driver they use to launch ore into orbit for transfer over here. Looks like they shot us with it. Our coil gun's still down but we have our Mark Fours. Alexander's working on a firing solution now, sir, and we have active sensors saturating the area, looking for additional incoming clusters.

"Very well, XO. Fire when you have a solution. Keep me informed but act on your own initiative."

Aye, aye, sir.

Te'Anna looked at him inquiringly.

"Bad news. The other inhabited moon threw some rocks at the *Bay* and messed it up pretty bad. Not so bad we can't still get out of here, but we need to get moving on a solution."

"This cannot be rushed, Captain," she answered. "It should not be long now, however."

Half an hour later the On-Living Engineers, without any signal, all parked their vehicles, dismounted, and trooped through a hatch into the quarters section of the downstation. Te'Anna gestured for Sam to follow her and in short order they found themselves in a room with food and drink dispensers and a number of tables and chairs.

The On-Living Engineers did not wait in line before the dispensers; each one seemed to know when it was their turn and rose to draw their meal. Sam and Te'Anna stood all but unnoticed by a blank wall until she spoke in that voice of command he had heard earlier.

"I am the Guardian Te'Anna and I have a message for the coordinator from K'Irka and H'Stus. Who is the coordinator?"

One of the New People raised his hand briefly without looking up from his meal. Te'Anna walked over to the table where he sat, took a metal vial from the pocket of her protective suit, took the cap off, and gave a quick spray of aerosol in front of the coordinator. He inhaled, paused, and then inhaled more deeply. He put down his fork and looked up from his food, an expression of surprise on his face. Sam came up beside her.

"Jesus, you drugged him? I guess that's one way of getting cooperation."

"Not a drug," she answered. The air current carried the gas or whatever it as down the table and the other four New People seated there showed various signs of reaction, and in moments had stopped eating. Te'Anna had their undivided attention.

"It is not a drug, Captain Bitka. It is simply the aroma of their homeworld. There is no more powerful sensory experience, persistent memory, or emotional catalyst, than scent." She turned to the coordinator. "You understand who you are and who I am?"

"Yes," he said. "I remember. How is the Lifeground?"

"Not as well as you remember it. P'Daan has brought strangers, ignorant of our ways. There was violence, death, and much destruction. It will take generations for the wounds to heal."

The coordinator lowered his face into his hands.

"P'Daan still seeks the strangers. Their leader stands here with me. They came here against their will, meant no one any harm, and wish only to go on their way. Their star drive is locked, however, by P'Daan. You must unlock it for them so they can depart and the killing end."

"What damage to the Lifeground?" one of the others asked.

"How many were killed?"

"How did it happen?"

Te'Anna held up her hand to quiet them. "It happened when the Eye of P'Daan attacked the strangers and they defended themselves. That much I saw myself. The strangers defended themselves, and killed the Eye of P'Daan, along with G'Baxus and De'Na."

"The killed three Guardians?" the coordinator asked and looked at Sam with an expression he couldn't read. Wonder? Possibly. Maybe some envy. After all, these Desties were here being punished for trying to kill one Guardian, right? But they hadn't succeeded. Sam had actually killed three of them.

"P'Daan wishes you to stay?" he asked.

That's right, Sam thought. The guy who made you immortal so he could stick you in this hellhole of a mining moon and torture you forever would be really unhappy if the *Bay* got away. How would that be for payback?

"We will never help you," the coordinator said.

It took over an hour to sort everything out, for Sam to

start understanding what was going on. Te'Anna used her spray capsule to arouse the others, get them involved, part of the decision. It didn't make any difference.

At first Sam thought it was a sort of Stockholm Syndrome, where the abused prisoners begin identifying with their captor, and maybe it was, but not like any case he'd ever heard about. They didn't identify with P'Daan at all; they despised him and lived to frustrate his plan for them. But how do you do that when he's holding all of the cards? When a guy makes you immortal just so he can punish you by making you do the shittiest job in the universe, *forever*, what can you do about it?

A few of them killed themselves, but P'Daan apparently had some kind of automated mobile auto-docs that were really good at recovering and resuscitating the recently dead. The recovery process was pretty excruciating. Some Engineers managed a good enough job of the suicide they couldn't be brought back, but the ones who were left had decided allowing P'Daan to force them to kill themselves was a form of surrender, and they didn't feel like surrendering. So what option did that leave them with?

Own the job. Don't just do it, don't just do it well, take joy and pride in doing it better than anyone ever could. Because if you really love it, *it's not punishment.* That was the only way they could cheat P'Daan out of his vengeance. That's what Te'Anna had meant when she said things had not turned out as he planned, and that he might end up just killing them after all. But if he did, that would be *their* victory, which was probably all that kept P'Daan from doing it. They were one tough, stubborn bunch of bastards, and that meant they were not going to do anything that P'Daan could interpret as a sign of discontent. It was too bad for the people on the *Bay*, but as far as the Engineers were concerned, their struggle of wills with P'Daan would go on long after everyone on the *Bay* was dead, no matter what they did or did not do to help.

Sam's commlink vibrated.

"Yes, XO."

Captain Bitka, we've got a Mark Four on the way to take out the mass driver, but radar says those two Troatta ships you and that Varoki so-called diplomat let get away have managed to reverse course and are accelerating back toward us, looking for a fight. They'll be here in three days and the two ships from the inner system will be here the day after that.

The ships he and Haykuz *let get away?* Sam was surprised to feel himself nearly overwhelmed by a wave of animosity toward Ka'Deem Brook. He wanted to ride back up the needle to the highstation, get a PSRV over to *Cam Ranh Bay*, and punch Brook, physically hurt him. Sam closed his eyes and breathed deeply, slowly, letting the anger flow through him and, to some extent, away. *Why was he so angry?* Why was he ever angry? His anger was always at himself, but then redirected to someone else.

He was angry because he'd let the Troatta go to avoid the uncertainties of battle, uncertainties which could have left the *Bay* a crippled wreck after one lucky shot, and now that's exactly what it was anyway. His truce with the Troatta had been temporary, had to be, because they would never surrender while they had power and weapons. Those crippled wrecks earlier had been one thing, but their code of honor wouldn't allow ships still capable of killing the enemy to just throw in the towel. That's not who they were. Haykuz had learned that about them and Sam understood it. The truce was the best they could manage, a respite to let Sam find the solution to everything else, because where there was a chance, he'd find a way. He always did, didn't he? But now that solution was crumbling before his eyes, and he was angry because Ka'Deem Brook's insinuation of failure was right on the money.

Captain, are you still there?

"Of course I'm still here, Mister Brook. Where else would I be? Keep me informed of any additional developments."

Sam cut the circuit and turned back to the Engineers, those scarred, magnificent, immortal sons of bitches whose stubbornness was the stuff of legends and which was going to get his passengers and crew killed, or worse. He walked back to the table and used his vox-box for the first time.

"I have a proposal for you. Will you repair my ship and help my people escape if in turn I can help you do a service to P'Daan which he will value above everything else? It is something he burns for, but he and all the warships he has brought into the system have been unable to attain it. After his failures, for you to be the ones to give him the prize will be his ultimate humiliation."

"What is the prize?" the coordinator said.

Te'Anna looked at him and then reached out, touched his arm. "Oh! Oh, no."

PART IV:
Home Is the Sailor,
Home From the Sea

Sam
Somewhere . . .

Pain. Searing, rippling, incandescent pain. Pain that bubbled up from inside him and came out as watery yellow vomit flecked with blood. Water sprayers hosing his naked body down, flushing the shit and vomit and urine down the drain in the low part of the floor. Sounds—strange sounds—inside his head or outside fighting to get in? Skin on fire, voice long since gone from screaming, muscle spasms that snapped him backwards, arching his back, bending him double.

The room never changed. Same light, same temperature. How long? Days? Weeks? Years? Naked and bruised, exposed except his left arm locked into the support machine. That must be what kept him alive. Nutrients. Fluids.

Drugs.

Sleep impossible. Instead, periods of partial lucidity alternated with wild hallucinations.

"S'Bitka," a voice said from all around him. "S'Bitka."

Was the voice real or another hallucination? He knew the voice.

What? he mouthed without making a sound from his ruined throat.

"S'Bitka."

What?

"S'Bitka, I am going now to destroy everything you have ever known and loved. Before I destroy them, I will tell them I do this thing because of you, and they will die cursing you."

No.

"S'Bitka, before I go, I want you to understand. You believe fulfillment lies in the others of your species, that you are strong when you work together, sacrifice for each other, take joy in each other's company, comfort each other, caress each other. You think this is the highest attainment of sentient life.

"S'Bitka, that is nothing more than arrested development on a species-wide scale. You are young animals, litter mates, rolling around and playing with each other. Your civilization is built on the logic of the litter and on the desperation of the prey. You huddle together and pretend that makes you safe, but the hunter circles, strikes, and then there is one fewer in the litter.

"S'Bitka, you are a child from a race of children. Only the solitary hunter is adult. I go now to do an adult's task."

No!

But the voice was gone. The pain returned, more violent than ever.

Time passed, or stood still, or came uncoupled. Then

hands lifted his body, wiped him dry and clean, laid him on a soft pallet. Different drugs flowed through him, warm drugs. Finally, he slept.

CHAPTER THIRTY-FIVE

Two months later, **Outworld Coalition Headquarters, the planet K'tok 15 September 2134**

Commander Cassandra Atwater-Jones, Royal Navy, listened to the droning questions and glib answers and she wondered if anyone on the Board of Inquiry other than her wanted to scream. This Ka'Deem Brook, this pompous puffed-up little nothing of a man, had left Bitka behind, had left him to a fate literally worse than death, because it would go on forever. Now he was second-guessing Bitka on one of the most difficult decisions she could imagine a commander having to make, the decision how to respond to a brutal and unprovoked attack by an alien civilization. He was analyzing and dissecting and deconstructing arguments and possibilities in the sort of detail a commander on the spot never had the luxury to do.

And half the board was nodding as if this all made perfect sense.

The Board of Inquiry had started out routinely, had looked as if Ka'Deem Brook's patent disloyalty to Bitka, and his timidity bordering on cowardice once in command, would end his career. Then after a single day of testimony, the Guardian P'Daan had arrived in the K'tok system with four Troatta battleships. While the Coalition presence in the K'tok system had been drawn down with the ceasefire, there was still a substantial force. But P'Daan had not come to fight; he had come to negotiate, possibly integrate the *Cottohazz* into the Guardian Realms, or perhaps P'Daan's realm. He wanted something, but no one quite knew what yet. He was still in the blustering phase.

There were a lot of things to talk about, but the big one was the "unprovoked attack on a peaceful planet" by the *Cottohazz*. Yes, the "unprovoked" business was patent claptrap, but the "peaceful planet" was true enough. But the main card P'Daan held, and it trumped everything else, was the secret to immortality. Not for everyone, of course, that would never work out. But for the best minds, to preserve them . . .

That was when, without anyone ever saying it in so many words, the insidious, despicable drift toward the easy solution to everything had begun, that solution being: *blame Bitka*. If everyone could just agree on that, then everyone could get along and maybe the lucky ones would get to live forever.

The lucky ones. Somebody sure needed some luck; there wasn't much good news in the *Cottohazz* since the *Bay* had returned. The news spread by jump courier and most Varoki nations had already denounced the whole incident as a Human fraud, cooked up to discredit the large trading houses and the intellectual property covenants. Varoki news feeds declared that even the Varoki passengers were either brainwashed or in on the scheme: zombies or blood traitors. Everywhere else, though, the reaction had begun to unleash what Cassandra thought was a century or more of pent-up resentment. All this time the Varoki had lorded it over the other species, and now it turned out it was a lie! There was going to be blood and there was going to be fire, and Cassandra saw little chance of avoiding it. Oddly, she couldn't seem to care very much about it all. Almost all that mattered to her now—all except her daughter—was going on in this room, even though it was beginning to look a bit like rearranging the deck chairs on the RMS *Titanic*.

"If I may clarify a point, Leftenant Brook," Cassandra said, keeping her voice calm and level, trying to sound as bland and detached as had Captain Lucinda Karlov, the U.S. officer who had been all but guiding Brook through his testimony. "I see here you have presented your formal objection to Captain Bitka's decision to launch the Marine rescue insertion, arguing that precipitated hostilities."

"I wouldn't call it a rescue mission, Commander," Brook said, and Cassandra looked up from the virtual folder cataloguing the little weasel's carping disagreements with his commander.

"What would you call it?" she asked mildly.

"It was clearly a revenge mission. He wanted to hit back and the Marines were handy."

"He later destroyed the complex with a bombardment strike. Why send the Marines first, then extract them, and then launch the strike?"

"Well . . . he had to go through the motions."

"The motions?"

"Of a rescue. But that wasn't his intent."

Cassandra sat back in her chair and folded her hands. "You seem to have a unique and special understanding of the psychological makeup of your captain. Please, tell us more."

He shifted in his chair before speaking. "I see what you're implying. You think you understood him better than I do, because of your . . . relationship. But I actually knew him longer than you did, worked with him more closely. He wasn't the man you thought he was."

"And what sort of man was that, Mister Brook?" she asked. She tried to look uncertain of herself, afraid of the answer. She didn't want to frighten the fool away from the edge of the cliff he was about to step off.

"I don't see how this is relevant to anything," Karlov said, the beginning of anger in her voice. Of course she was angry; she was smart enough to see where this could go, but she'd stepped in and saved her callow pawn from disaster.

Cassandra turned to Karlov and looked at her for a moment before replying. "He is testifying not as to what Captain Bitka did or said, but what he *thought*. As I think it safe to assume this board does not countenance the notion of mind reading, we might profitably explore what other foundation the witness can provide for this claim." She turned back to Brook but she knew already that line of attack was futile now. Dull as this rabbit was, he had seen the snare. But before she could try another approach, Rear Admiral Goldjune spoke.

"That's a fair point," he said, "but I'm danged if I understand what all this talk about Captain Bitka's intentions means. We aren't here to inquire into *Bitka's* actions, and I don't see why you keep pushing this witness that way, Lucinda. We may not agree with every decision Captain Bitka made, but that's one smart, brave officer out there in a terrible situation, and some of this is coming pretty close to pissing on his grave. Yeoman Williams, let's change that to 'spitting' in the official record. If this were an inquiry into Captain Bitka's actions, Commander Atwater-Jones wouldn't be sitting on the board, and that is not a negative reflection on her integrity or judgment. It's just not a position anyone would put her in, or any other officer similarly situated. For what it's worth, Commander, I commend you for the restraint and composure you've displayed."

He really was an old dear of a southern gentleman, and she still couldn't understand what had gone so wrong with his son.

"I appreciate that very much, sir," she said. "But with your permission I would like to follow this line of questioning just a bit further as I believe it does bear on our main issue."

The admiral's eyebrows ticked up no more than a few millimeters, but he nodded. She leaned forward and rearranged the contents of the virtual folder displayed on the smart surface of the conference table.

"As I was saying, Mister Brook, I have here a considerable document trail demonstrating the extent to which you disagreed with the judgment of your commanding officer. For decision after decision, I see formal letters of protest. The decision to drop the Marines. The decision to use a bombardment munition. The decision to use nuclear warheads to take down the Destie-Four satnet." She looked up from the folder with what she hoped was a look of honest curiosity. "These formal protests are dated some time after the actual events."

"There wasn't opportunity to draft a formal letter of protest at the time," he said. "We were in the middle of a battle—an unnecessary one."

"Of course," she agreed. "It is perfectly acceptable to file a formal record of a protest once things have calmed down. You did actually issue a verbal protest at the time?"

He hesitated, thought for a moment. "Something like that, to the best of my recollection."

"You were at general quarters on the auxiliary bridge, and he was on the main bridge. Your only means of communication would be by commlink, and all communications would be recorded and part of the battle log. I'm sure we can find the protest."

Brook shifted in his chair uncomfortably, but his complexion was so dark it was impossible to see if he was blushing. "I'm not certain there was a verbal recorded protest at the time, but the captain knew how I felt about that decision."

She sat back in her chair. "Ah, so Bitka could read your mind as well as you could read his?"

"Cass," the admiral warned.

"I apologize, sir, and I withdraw the question. I'm done for now." She folded her arms over her chest and smiled at Lieutenant Brook. She was going take this little wanker apart the way she would break open a lobster, and she would enjoy it every bit as much. He left Bitka in that Dante-esque nightmare.

He left Bitka.

They'd already heard testimony from the communications officer Bohannon, the tactical officer Alexander, Doctor Däng Thi Hue, and the Varoki diplomat Haykuz, all via holoconference from *Cam Ranh Bay*, unlike Brook's physical presence at the board proceedings. The picture was clear enough: Bitka had run out of options. He only had one thing important enough to trade to the On-Living Engineers in return for fixing his ship, and that was himself. There had been some objection from P'Daan, a desire to capture all of the passengers and crew, but the Troatta had ended up deciding the matter. They were tired of fighting Bitka, and they had no way of knowing how badly crippled *Cam Ranh Bay* really was, so the two battleships returning to Seven Echo laid down the law: take Bitka as a prisoner for P'Daan, fix the ship, let the other aliens go.

Brook had been reluctant to take Lieutenant Ma and the infected Marines back on board, for fear of contamination, despite the assurances of the two Guardians, but Bitka had ordered him to do so, his last official act as captain. Once all his people were aboard the *Bay*, Bitka turned over command to Brook, turned himself over to the On-Living Engineers, and then they fixed the drive. They had walked right into the drive compartment, opened it up, and adjusted it. Whatever the Guardians did to them to make them on-living, the microbial colony that made up the drive core recognized them as Guardians and did not attack them. Then Brook and *Cam Ranh Bay* had left.

The two Guardians had stayed behind: K'Irka because P'Daan had made her participation a condition of his acceptance, and Te'Anna for reasons which were unclear to the people on the *Bay*. Maybe she had never really intended to accompany them, or maybe she had had a change of heart. It would be hard to go without contact with anyone of your own species, even if everyone treated you with kindness and consideration.

What must it be like for Bitka? The On-Living Engineers at least had a small group of acquaintances they shared the experience with, but Bitka was so completely alone, three thousand light-years away.

Now Brook's testimony was coming to the very heart of the matter: leaving Bitka behind. Karlov was again walking him through it, making sure she posed the questions everyone wanted answered, but leading him to the right answers.

"Isn't it true that some of the crew wanted you to break the agreement and just go in and rescue the captain?" Karlov asked.

"Yes, ma'am," Brook answered calmly, "but I couldn't do that without breaking the second truce Mister Haykuz had negotiated with the Troatta, or without violating Captain Bitka's direct order to me."

"Thank you, Lieutenant Brook," Karlov said. "I think that answers every question I have."

She turned to Cassandra with a smile. *Gawd*, Cass thought, the fool believed she had won.

"I have just a few more, I'm afraid," Cassandra said, "with your permission, Admiral Goldjune." The admiral nodded. Cassandra took a moment to be sure her feelings were absolutely under control. The slightest show of anger or contempt would distract from the truth of what she was about to make clear. She must submerge her inclinations, lest they compete for attention with what was more important.

"You have already told us that you objected strenuously to the first truce with the Troatta, the one negotiated while in Destie-Seven orbit."

"Yes, we had them on their backs. The captain should have finished them when he had the chance."

"You counseled this even after the truce was agreed to."

"It still wasn't too late," he said. "The ordnance was still out there. All we had to do was push that detonation button."

He said this with the sort of relish which someone who has never actually taken a life often exhibits, undoubtedly because they believe it makes them appear a ferocious warrior—as opposed to the depraved adolescent they actually resemble. She knew she tread on dangerous ground with her next question, but she could not resist.

"Have you ever actually killed someone, Mister Brook?"

"No, Ma'am, I have not. Have you?" he added with a slight smile.

Cassandra looked up and studied the ceiling of the conference room and thought for ten seconds, possibly longer, and she was aware every eye in the room had fastened on her. Then she looked at him. "I am afraid I am not at liberty to say."

She saw his eyes grow slightly wider, saw the veneer of cocksure self-confidence calve away like the face of an ice shelf sliding into the ocean, and she spent a moment enjoying this absurdly easy victory. She was military intelligence, had been deployed under cover, and of course she was not at liberty to say whether she had or had not ever killed someone in those circumstances. *Of course* she was not! But it was the time she spent thinking about the answer that was the artistry in the scene, and she had known he would give her that opportunity as surely as if she had been allowed to see the future.

"Why did you decide to leave Captain Bitka in the hands of the Guardians?"

"It...it wasn't my decision," he said, still obviously shaken and off balance.

"You had recommendations from your officers to launch your remaining combat-ready Marines and bring him back, with a high likelihood of success."

"I couldn't do that. The truce—"

"But truces are things to be broken, aren't they? If there is a clear advantage to be gained? That's what you just told us."

"It's not that simple," he protested.

"No, being the actual *captain* is never that simple, is it? And you were the captain, finally sitting in the command chair—"

"This has gone on long enough," Captain Karlov broke in.

"You had your turn, Lucinda," the admiral said with quiet patience. "Carry on, Commander."

"Mister Brook, you were then officially in command of USS *Cam Ranh Bay*. Captain Bitka had turned command over to you. It was your decision what to do, and you decided to *not* intervene, to *not* save Captain Bitka, even though it was apparently well within your ability to do so. Why?"

"He gave me an *order*," he said, his voice now almost pleading. Cassandra sat back in her chair and shook her head.

"Mister Brook, he gave you *command*. After that, the orders were entirely your responsibility." She turned to Admiral Goldjune. "Sir, I have no further questions for this . . . this officer."

Nine million kilometers away, on USS *Puebla*, between the orbits of K'tok and Mogo, Larry Goldjune could feel everything slipping out of his control. He didn't know what to do about it, but he knew the cause: Sam Bitka. That career-killing fitness report was bad enough, but Larry could have gotten past that. The disappearance of *Cam Ranh Bay* made things more complicated, made it harder to undercut Bitka's credibility. No one wanted to hear anything bad about someone who couldn't defend himself, especially if it might turn out that he was a hero. And damned if he wasn't! Got his ship and crew back and sacrificed himself to do it. Not just a hero, a *fucking martyr!* Politicians would be getting into fistfights to give his eulogy. And what was the last official correspondence of the late, great Samuel M. Bitka before he disappeared into legend? That fitness report—like a last will and testament. The damned thing was, Larry couldn't figure out why he did it. He and Bitka never really got along, but he'd never done anything to undercut him, not really. A few cross words—no reason to ruin a man's life. And it looked more and more like Bitka had ruined it, *meant* to ruin it, was willing to damage his own career just to be *sure* he ruined it. That kind of hatred was just plain evil—or crazy, like an obsession. Maybe that's why he sacrificed himself—just to make damned good and sure that fitness report stuck, just to be certain he ruined Larry Goldjune's life. Jesus! If people only knew that, they wouldn't think he was such a hero, would they? Just a bitter, spiteful mediocrity who got a little lucky once and used it to destroy someone with more promise. That was it, wasn't it? Jealousy. Bitka had his fifteen minutes of fame but he was going nowhere. He was just a nobody and he couldn't stand that Larry was *somebody*. Somebody who would wear stars on his collar someday. Bitka would never have that, so what did he do instead? Ruin Larry's chance. Like . . . like not being able to paint, so slashing pictures instead. Bitka was lucky he hadn't come back. If he had, Larry would have killed him. He'd never killed anyone, but as he sat there, feeling everything he'd ever wanted slip away, he knew if he had the chance he would kill Sam Bitka. But now he couldn't even do that, and it made him want to weep. He was losing everything else, and now he'd even lost his chance for revenge. Nobody had ever had as raw a deal as this. Nobody. It wasn't fair.

And then he did weep.

CHAPTER THIRTY-SIX

One hour later, Outworld Coalition Headquarters,
the planet K'tok
15 September 2134

Takaar Nuvaash, formerly Speaker for The Enemy of the
uBakai Star Navy's First Striking Fleet, now between
assignments and technically still a prisoner of war, relaxed
on the couch in Commander Atwater-Jones's office, awaiting
her return. He had seen the video proceedings of the Board
of Inquiry, seen the session adjourned, and knew how far it
was from the conference room back to the office: no more
than a hundred steps and a one-floor lift ride. Unless she
had been intercepted and detained, she should be back—

The door burst opened and she strode in, tossed her
hat on her desk, and turned to him with a sour look.

"Well, what did you think?"

"I think you made your opinion of Lieutenant Brook
abundantly clear," Nuvaash said.

She walked behind her desk and sat down, shaking her
head. "I hardly think so. I did not physically assault him. I
did not spit in his face. I thought I was remarkably
restrained."

"I did too," Nuvaash heard through the partially open door, from the voice he now recognized as belonging to Rear Admiral Goldjune. The admiral entered the room and Atwater-Jones jumped to attention. Nuvaash stood up as well, although not quite as quickly. He was, after all, something of a guest.

The admiral looked at him and frowned. "You hang around here a lot. What are you doing?"

"Until a moment ago I was sitting on this couch, and a few minutes before that I was watching the vid feed of the proceedings, and before that reviewing the news concerning the imminent collapse of civilization. Before that—"

"Yeah, okay. So how do *you* feel about this revelation that the Varoki didn't invent the jump drive?"

"Speaking as a Varoki, you mean," Nuvaash said, and he spread his ears wide to make the point.

"Speaking as a military intelligence specialist who is *also* a Varoki," the admiral answered.

"How do I feel? I feel a great many things. Fear. Relief, oddly enough. And a certain intellectual satisfaction. Honestly, the story of how we supposedly invented the drive was never very satisfying from a logical point of view. This explanation makes much better sense."

"How many of your people are going to agree with that?"

"*My* people, by which you mean Varoki? Very, very few at first, but much will depend on what accompanies the news."

"Hard to deny it, now that there's a Guardian spacecraft making the glide into K'tok orbit. Probably get here in a week."

"You are aware that several Varoki news feeds have already claimed Captain Bitka was never onboard *Cam Ranh Bay*, and has been sighted at five different locations throughout the *Cottohazz*?" Nuvaash said. "It is not hard to deny anything if you want to badly enough, Admiral Goldjune. Not unless the sceptics are allowed to witness the vivisection of this new Guardian, and as all the sceptics cannot be fit in the room, the rest will claim even that was a hoax. Some of those in the room will doubt as well."

"I doubt that Guardian P'Daan would volunteer for the process," the admiral observed. "Why won't they believe? Near as I can tell, the average Varoki gains no more material benefit from the jump drive patents than the average Human or Katami or Zaschaan."

"Very true, sir. But the trading houses all but control government and public discourse, and they have made the jump drive monopoly a point of pride."

"Pride," the admiral said, turning away from Nuvaash, "the universal vice of fools." He sank into the chair in front of the desk and waved for Atwater-Jones to sit as well. Nuvaash did at the same time, hoping to revert to being an observer rather than participant in the conversation. You never learned much of interest by talking.

"Never-failing, sir," Commander Atwater-Jones said as she sat.

"How's that?"

"Alexander Pope called pride the 'never-failing vice of fools.'"

"So, you trust him?" the admiral asked Atwater-Jones, nodding toward Nuvaash, which Nuvaash found interesting but somewhat strange.

"That is a simple question with a complicated answer," she said. "I trust his discretion and I trust his word. I also trust his sense of loyalty to his nation and duty to his service to take precedence over whatever friendship he feels for me."

"You've run agents before. Can we turn him? He'd be a hell of an asset."

She glanced over at Nuvaash and then back at the admiral. "You know he can hear you, sir."

"So what? If we can turn him, we can. If we can't, we can't."

"We cannot, sir."

Admiral Goldjune turned slowly to Nuvaash. "Is that so?"

"Absolutely," he answered. "Not that the thought of being a double agent lacks romance and excitement, but in truth I would be a triple agent, and I am certain Commander Atwater-Jones would discover that almost at once and be forced to kill me. I like her far too much to ever consider putting her through an experience that traumatic."

"It would undoubtedly scar me for life," she agreed with a nod and a crooked smile.

"You two should take this act on the road," the admiral said. "In fact, I'm going to give you the chance. Right answer, by the way, Nuvaash. Will you please open your commlink, Vice-Captain?"

Nuvaash hesitated for a moment—he was not in the habit of lowering his e-guard for just everyone, and he was still technically a prisoner, which gave him some legal recourse in the matter, but he had come to trust Rear

Admiral Goldjune and he did as requested. He felt the tingle at the base of his skull which meant a data transfer. No, two.

"Two documents," the admiral explained. "First one is your complete parole. We'll haggle with your government over details for a while, but one way or another, there's going to be peace between the uBakai and the Outworld Coalition. With this Guardian business going on, everyone has bigger fish to fry. Until the peace is official, you're a free agent, at least from our point of view. Second document you better read yourself. Got a pair of viewer glasses?"

Nuvaash shook his head but Atwater-Jones, a look of both surprise and curiosity on her face, handed him the pair lying on her desk.

The first document was indeed his official parole. The second message was an order from the uBakai Star Navy Fleet Operations Directorate attaching him to Rear Admiral Goldjune's staff for "extraordinary duty as directed by your acting superior, subject to the mandates and strictures of the uBakai Star Navy Code of Behavior." Nuvaash took the glasses off and looked at the admiral, trying to fathom what this meant. The admiral was smiling, and why not? As the Humans would say, he was certainly having the last laugh.

"Those orders came to me through your armistice negotiating team," the admiral said. "You'll want to verify them, of course."

"Of course," Nuvaash said, "but I have to say I have never heard of such a thing in my entire career."

"You've been assigned to Human naval staffs before. I

know that from our own intel people. You even did time as a liaison officer with the US Navy."

"But not while in a technical state of *war* with them. How is this supposed to work?"

The admiral's smile broadened and he leaned back in his chair. "Lots of good will, I suppose. You probably wonder why your superiors ever agreed to such a cock-and-bull setup. Until the formal peace is signed, we're still working under the terms of the provisional ceasefire agreement. Article Nine includes a proviso which requires your government to render all reasonable assistance in the event of unforeseen and/or extraordinary circumstances which may threaten the stability of the K'tok system or the welfare of its inhabitants."

"Ah," Nuvaash said. "Well, I would say the appearance of the Guardian P'Daan counts as both extraordinary and unforeseen. Very well, admiral. I am honored to serve on your staff. What are my duties?"

"Deputy to Commander Atwater-Jones."

"Cryptanalysis Department, sir?" she said. "But that's all highly classified. You can't mean—"

"Heck, that job was just an excuse to keep you on staff after they closed down the Incident Seventeen Working Group. You don't actually *do* any of that stuff, do you?"

"Well . . . Lieutenant Commander Nightingale does keep the department ticking along rather well on his own," she answered.

"'Course he does. He can take over and it'll look good on his record. I've got a new job for you: head of our Guardian intel collection and analysis desk."

"We have such a thing?"

"We do now." The admiral thumped her desk with his hand twice. "Right here. Far as I know it's the first Guardian desk anywhere. Hell of a responsibility for you, Cass. Hell of an opportunity, too. You're right at ground zero of this with a shipload of intel assets just coming out of quarantine. Play this right and it can make your career. That's got to mean something."

"Survival of Humanity as a free species ranks rather higher, sir, but repairing my career would not be an unwelcome bonus."

She said this lightly, but Nuvaash saw the light in her eyes, heard the excitement in her voice, and knew it was not simply about survival or ambition. It was a hunger to know, and to know before anyone else did. He understood because he felt it as well.

"And Leftenant Brook?" she asked, her expression darkening.

"I know this board of inquiry is important to you," the admiral said, "but it's time we looked beyond it. After what you did today, Brook's finished. I've got a fairly junior commander sitting on the beach who's anxious for a command, and the *Bay* needs someone with more rank than a lieutenant anyway, so I just signed the papers for Commander Beauchamp to take over *Cam Ranh Bay* effective tomorrow. There won't be a finding from the Board for another few days, so I'm calling this a routine relief.

"You know how this works as well as I do, Cass. What he did was contemptible, but within regulations. I imagine the board findings will hint at the first and officially find the second. We can all wish he'd broken that truce and grabbed Bitka, but as an official organ of the Combined Fleet of the Outworld Coalition we can't very well reprimand him for *not* violating the Articles of War. He'll revert to his job as XO until I can find a loose lieutenant commander to fill that slot, and then he'll revert to his original job as Ops Boss. They'll take the *Bay* back to Earth for repairs but, with both orbital shipyards still wrecked, that's not going to happen any time soon. They'll put her in a parking orbit with nothing but an anchor watch, and reassign the crew to other duties.

"Navy's a small society with a long memory. I doubt Lieutenant Brook will find his next assignment very interesting, or his next promotion board very pleasant. He'll carry a yellow stain on his name as long as he's in the Navy, which probably won't be that much longer. Two promotion boards pass on him and he'll be out. Navy don't cotton to old lieutenants. Satisfied?"

She leaned back in her chair and studied the ceiling before answering. "No," she whispered after a moment, and sighed. "I suppose if I had his gutted carcass here on my desk and his bloody heart in my hand—like one of my Celtic ancestors—I would still feel unsatisfied. Nothing will satisfy me except Bitka's return, alive and intact if possible, but his return in any case. Tell me that is at least part of the negotiations with that *thing*, P'Daan."

"It's on the agenda," the admiral said, but without much force. "It has to be. Can't *not* say we're concerned about bringing a hero home. But he's become a damned inconvenient hero."

"He always has been," Cassandra said, "but I never expected to hear you say that, sir."

"Not my thinking," the admiral answered, "but my thinking doesn't carry as much weight as it used to. Now it's all about my brother and his circle. You saw how the tone changed in our proceedings just in the last few days."

"Your mean your friend, Captain Karlov," she said.

The admiral nodded sadly. "Lucinda and I used to be friends, as a matter of fact. Times change." He looked down at his feet for a moment. "They wanted to turn this board their way. That didn't work, thanks to you, so now there's going to be a separate Court of Inquiry. Going to examine Bitka's actions at the start of this new war, if war's what it is. Damned if I know what to call it."

Atwater-Jones sat forward in her chair, eyes flashing. "A *court*? Who's to be on it? Certainly not me, but who?"

The admiral looked up at her. "I have no idea. I'm not the convening authority; the CNO, my brother Cedric, is, same as with this board we're finishing up. He meant to blindside me with this new court, but I've still got some friends on his staff he doesn't know about. But knowing it's coming and doing something about it are two different things. Like as not he'll load that court up with folks like Lucinda Karlov, folks he can count on to make the *right* decision."

"Blame Bitka," she said.

"What's one man when the stakes are war, peace, and immortality?" the admiral asked.

"You mean aside from standing for something, as opposed to just grasping for everything you can and devil take the hindmost? Aside from *that*?"

"You know where I stand in this, Cass," the admiral said and then turned to look at Nuvaash. "Does that surprise you, that two Human brothers could be on opposite sides in a fight this big and important? Does that strike you as a peculiar example of Human behavior?"

"Peculiar?" Nuvaash repeated and then pretended to think. "Compared to what?"

The admiral stared at him and then shook his head. "So that's why you two get along like thieves: you have the same sense of humor."

"You know, sir," Atwater-Jones said, "it's not just the temptation of immortality at stake in these negotiations. There's also the matter of the jump drive, and the return of a prisoner."

"Oh, God preserve me from that damned jump drive!" Admiral Goldjune said. "I got three rooms full of JAG lawyers trying to sort out the legalities of that mess. Who owns what? Who owes what to whom? 'Course, law's one thing and what we decide to actually do is another. But unless we show some backbone, we may just be trading Varoki control for Guardian."

"If so, sir," she said, "I imagine the day will come when we look back on Varoki stewardship of the secret with genuine nostalgia. I've read the report prepared by Doctor Johnstone and Ms. Choice. If they are correct, I cannot see the Guardians voluntarily surrendering control of the secret to us. Their exclusive control of it is too important to maintaining their position in their realms."

"P'Daan's already hinting at releasing control under some circumstances."

"Hinting is cheap, sir. I cannot imagine he has the power to do so, and even if he does I see no reason why he would choose to. Why give up anything to us unless we have something to offer in return? All we have is ourselves."

Rear Admiral Goldjune nodded, and Nuvaash took from his expression that he believed that was exactly what was being discussed: trading some control over the citizens of the *Cottohazz* for . . . for what? Although he maintained rigid control of his exterior affect, inside, Nuvaash shuddered.

"So, in all of this, how are we to get P'Daan to agree to return Bitka?" Cassandra asked.

The admiral shook his head. "Damned if I know. If you got any spook tricks you've been holding back, now would be a good time to try them out."

But Nuvaash could see from the expression on his friend's face that she did not have any "spook tricks" at her disposal, at least not any applicable to this situation. As it happened, he did, but as much as he liked Commander Atwater-Jones, and admired Captain Bitka, delivering his former adversary from Guardian captivity was not his task.

CHAPTER THIRTY-SEVEN

Eight days later, on board CCS-7 USS *Olympus Mons*, in orbit above K'tok
23 September 2134

Admiral Cedric Goldjune, the Outworld Coalition's chief of naval operations, looked up as Captain Deepa Chakrabarti, his Indian Navy chief of intelligence, entered and waited for the door to slide shut behind her. Her round, dark face bore an expression which matched his own mood.

"*Goddamnit*, what in the hell is that feathered freak trying to pull?"

"Good morning, Admiral," she answered, crossing to his desk. "I take it you have been watching the early flat vid feeds of P'Daan's nocturnal broadcast concerning the state of negotiations."

Cedric waved her into the chair across from him. "Of course I've been watching. Who hasn't? Does he really want the whole *Cottohazz* Executive Council to come here to talk to him?"

"Who can say what goes on in his mind?" she said. "I have been reading the summaries Commander Atwater-

Jones put together of the reports of Doctors Johnstone and Däng. I will want to interview Johnstone before he leaves, and we may wish to retain him here for at least a few weeks. He could be useful. The main point of consideration is that the Guardians have never contacted a separate civilization. Ever. All the cultures of their elevated subject races are of their own creation. Those cultures are hierarchical and authoritarian, and are structured not only to serve, but also exalt, the Guardians. Although they may have to negotiate among themselves, they are used to doing so with other beings similarly endowed with absolute decision-making authority."

"Good luck finding that here," Cedric said.

"Yes, sir, that is precisely the point. P'Daan clearly grows impatient with our inability to commit to anything on behalf of the *Cottohazz*. It is the very diffuse nature of authority that frustrates him. We received word that the Council has sent a special envoy plenipotentiary to begin formal negotiations. His ship arrived in-system yesterday but he is still days from K'tok, and even when Envoy e-Lotonaa arrives his authority will be limited. Were the entire Executive Council to come here, they would still not be able to satisfy P'Daan. He demands we accept his authority over all the worlds of the *Cottohazz*, that in effect we become a protectorate under his authority. Even the entire Legislative Assembly does not have the authority to accede to that, no matter what sort of limitations he might be willing to accept. It would require plebiscites throughout every political jurisdiction, and the outcome would be by no means certain."

That's for sure, Cedric thought. *What would the*

average voter gain? Nothing. And what would they lose? Some freedom, for sure, and maybe more than just some. Whatever deal they came up with, he didn't think anyone could sell it.

"Captain Chakrabarti, I need to know where you stand."

"Sir?" she asked, clearly surprised by the question.

"The things we've devoted our professional lives to, the traditions and values we cherish, are all wonderful things, but their time may be coming to an end. The world—our world—is changing very quickly. The old systems may be slipping away forever, and the time between when they cease operating and a new order takes their place is likely to be very brief. People who understand that must be ready to act and act with decision. When that moment comes, I have to know where your loyalty will rest."

She looked somewhat frightened by his words and he saw her swallow and think before nodding. "I trust you, Admiral. Who else can guide us through this?"

"Good. P'Daan has been negotiating with the armistice commission, because that's the highest civilian authority in the K'tok system, at least until the *Cottohazz* special envoy gets here and that won't be for a week. We already know they aren't going to get anywhere, so we need to open talks with him ourselves."

"Ourselves? But . . . we don't have the authority—"

"Yes, we do. They have armed ships in the system and we are responsible for seeing that no unfortunate incidents occur. To that end, we need to open a regular liaison channel with them to coordinate ship traffic and avoid misunderstandings. Isn't that so?"

She smiled. "Of course, sir. I assume that at some point the subject matter of those talks may broaden."

"I don't see how we can avoid it. P'Daan wants firm answers and someone who can back them up. He's not going to get either of those from any delegation the *Cottohazz* sends. If it comes to a question of survival of our species or loyalty to the *Cottohazz*, it's not even a contest for me."

"And what is our negotiating position? What do we want and what can we offer in return?"

"I'm still working on the details, and I need to learn more about how he thinks, but what he has to offer is simple: peace, the stars, and immortality. It's what we're willing to give up for those—that's where the negotiations will get complicated. But let's start assembling a small working group of people who we can trust and who can help with this."

Chakrabarti shifted uncomfortably in her chair. "I know there are personal issues between you and her, but I'd like to have Atwater-Jones working with us. Right now, she's really the top person on Guardian culture, technology, and psychology."

Cedric shook his head. "We get copies of all her work and we have access to her database. We don't need her here and she'll never go along with me on this. I'll tell you something, Captain, she is really not very intelligent. She's one of those people who acts more intelligent than everyone else and so foolish people believe her. Bitka's another one. They were made for each other. Neither one of them's smart enough to see what it takes to solve a big problem; they're just clever enough to cause trouble. It's a good thing that uBakai admiral in the last war was such a fool. Anyone could have beaten him, even Bitka."

About forty thousand kilometers below USS *Olympus Mons,* in the fleet headquarters complex on K'tok, Doctor Däng Thi Hue followed the young man in the strange naval uniform. After half a year on board *Cam Ranh Bay,* she had grown used to seeing service people in a shipsuit and nothing else. Shirt and slacks seemed both casual and old-fashioned by comparison.

They reached a door and the young mariner pressed the entry panel. "The commander's waiting for you," he said as the door slid into the wall. Hue saw the tall British woman rise from her desk and walk briskly around it to meet her, her hand extended. She was not beautiful, Hue thought, so much as striking, with her sharply pointed features and shock of curly red hair. Hue realized it was largely the woman's self-possession which rendered her particularly attractive.

"Doctor Hue, I am very glad you were able to make time for me," Atwater-Jones said. She gestured to a sofa against the wall and they sat. "I hope the period of quarantine was not too unpleasant. I know you must be very anxious to return home."

"Home," Hue repeated, and she wondered where that was. The concept had become somewhat diffused in the last six months. USS *Cam Ranh Bay* was now part of it, in a way. She had been offered priority transport back to Earth, and she would take it, but she felt disloyal doing so, as if she were abandoning a friend who had given much to bring her home.

"I had planned to come see you as soon as I was able," Hue said, "and then received your request for an interview. May I ask why?"

"Certainly," Atwater-Jones answered. "I am a military intelligence specialist currently attached to the staff of Rear Admiral Goldjune. He has tasked me with assembling a complete assessment of the nature and capabilities of this new civilization you encountered, especially given the unfortunate circumstances of that encounter. I have already had a very enlightening holoconference with Lieutenant Alexander, the ship's senior tactical officer. I have appointments with Doctor Johnstone and Ms. Choice this afternoon, and I hope to speak with Lieutenant Ma as soon as he has recovered. But I wanted to speak with you in particular and face to face. No one understands their biology better than do you. I have read your very extensive report, of course, those parts which I was able to understand, but I was wondering what personal insights you could add."

"Personal insights," Hue repeated, and thought about that. "I had personal interaction with two Guardians, the ones called Te'Anna and K'Irka, and I viewed a number of holocons and messages from the one called P'Daan. Of course, I also witnessed the video of the slaughter of our landing party as it was taking place, and I think that may render my personal insights . . . biased. But based upon the behavior of those three examples, I would characterize the Guardians as highly idiosyncratic with distinctly different personalities and worldviews. What they share is a lack of empathy—to varying degrees—and a tendency toward self-absorption."

"Don't you think that is a natural product of their extended lifespans?" Atwater-Jones asked.

"Possibly, although I am reluctant to accept a conclusion based more on prejudice than facts—even a prejudice I fully share with you. I will be happy to explain my thoughts to you later, but for now I have a task of my own to complete. I mentioned I had intended to meet with you before leaving and it was for personal rather than professional reasons. I disliked Captain Bitka very much when I first met him but came to respect and value him greatly, although we were never intimate friends. Before we parted, I told him a poem. He took no possessions of any kind with him other than the shipsuit he wore, so he made me repeat the poem several times so he would remember it."

"I didn't know Bitka fancied poetry," Atwater-Jones said, and Hue saw surprise and regret in her eyes. There must be much about the captain she did not know, and now never would.

"I don't know that he did, as a general rule," Hue said, "but this one touched him. I shared it because the captain reminded me of the author of the poem in many ways."

"You know the author?"

Hue smiled. "That would be difficult. He has been dead for nine hundred years. He was a warrior, a rebel, an adventurer, a leader of guerrillas in a time of great trouble, later a general, a man of unbending principle—which was in some way his undoing—a lover, and eventually a poet. He was Chinese, his name was Xin Qiji, and this is the poem I gave to Captain Bitka. It is called, 'To the Tune of the Ugly Slave.' I should explain that this style of poem was not actually named, but was meant to be recited with a song played in the background, and it followed the rhythm of that song. Unfortunately, we have no record of what that song originally sounded like, but here is the poem."

When I was young
and hadn't known sorrow,
I loved to climb high places,

loved to climb high places
and write poems
that strained for sorrow.

Now that I have tasted
all there is to know of sorrow
I hesitate to speak of it,

hesitate to speak of it.
Instead I say, "This cool
autumn weather is so fine."

Hue sat quietly for a time after finishing the poem, allowing Atwater-Jones to regain her composure, or rather struggle to maintain it, a struggle which at length she won. Hue then understood something of Atwater-Jones.

"You hesitate to speak of it as well."

Atwater-Jones's mouth trembled again for a moment and she nodded, a single firm, quick gesture.

"I have two other things for you which the captain entrusted to me for delivery. I believe the first of them is a sort of diary directed to you." She drew the data tab from her pocket and handed it to the British officer, who sat for several long seconds looking at the tab resting in her palm. Then her eyes closed as the fingers of her hand curled over it, and she held it against her chest for a moment before slipping it into the pocket of her uniform blouse.

"Thank you," she whispered.

"And one last thing. I know this will upset you and for that I am sorry, but it is necessary. This is the last possession Captain Bitka gave up as he left." She handed her the hologram of herself. Atwater Jones looked at it as it played through its recorded sequence and then again closed her eyes. Tears ran down her cheeks but her shoulders did not shake and her mouth remained firm— a woman of extraordinary self-control. Hue gave her a minute or more to shore up the composure which clearly was so important to her.

"Commander Atwater-Jones, whatever influence you have in the strategic counsels of your military, use it well. P'Daan, and whatever Guardians share his worldview, will enslave us if they can. I think they will attempt to seduce us first, with the lure of immortality."

"Would that be so terrible?" the British woman asked.

"Captain Bitka believed it would be and I now do as well. I have thought a great deal about what moves us, Commander. About what molds us. The universe is built of facts, but facts do not move us. They have no meaning by themselves. Stories change us, because stories have meaning. Do you understand?"

"Perhaps. But why can't an endless life have meaning?"

"Because a story has a beginning, a middle, and an end.

The end is what gives the story meaning. Without an end it is not a story, it is only a tiresome, rambling, and pointless anecdote."

"I don't know that I believe that," the British woman said. "I don't think it has to be that way."

Hue examined the woman's face and saw something Captain Bitka's love and admiration must have blinded him to: her fear. Fear was the great enemy, always. Every contemptible act she had seen Ka'Deem Brook commit, he had committed from fear. Every moment of anger Hue had felt, every shameful desire for retribution, had been her own fear speaking.

This woman had weaknesses Captain Bitka had never understood, but that did not mean she could not find her strength when the time came. Hue had no option but to trust she would.

"Whether we accept their offer or not, Commander, the Guardians' self-image will not allow them to live with us as equals. On the moon Destie-Seven-Echo, which they call Haydoos, Captain Bitka saw what could be our future. He sacrificed himself in part so you—*specifically you*—could know the enormous evil and terrible danger facing us. He did not simply love you; he trusted you to find a way to stop P'Daan."

Six hours later, Vice-Captain Takaar Nuvaash again realized that he never quite got used to Rear Admiral Jacob Goldjune's habit of simply striding into Atwater-Jones's office unannounced and flopping into a chair.

"Alright. Now look, Commander, I have about twenty minutes before I have to be at a reception for the U. S.

congressional fact-finding delegation headed by the senior senator from the great state of Jalisco, so tell me what you've got and then I'll go. In fact, you should grab your hat and come along."

"Senator Ramirez y Sesma is here?" Nuvaash asked, unable to remain silent at this news.

Rear Admiral Goldjune, brother of the Coalition CNO, frowned at him. "How is it you know who the senior senator from Jalisco is?"

Nuvaash tilted his head to the side. "It was my responsibility, as Speaker for The Enemy, to study the political as well as military command structures of all the nations of your coalition. Ramirez y Sesma is the vice chair of your Senate Armed Services Committee, and if Senator Perkins does not run for reelection, as is rumored, and assuming the Federalists continue to hold a majority in the Senate, Ramirez y Sesma will become the chair in another year. He is rather strident in his anti-Varoki beliefs."

The admiral stared at him in disbelief.

"Really, my knowledge is not that extraordinary," Nuvaash said. "Commander Atwater-Jones, who is the uBakai deputy minister of naval armaments?"

"Sodanl e-Tso'ja," she replied immediately, and when the admiral's astonishment was directed at her, she shrugged. "Everyone knows *that*, sir."

The admiral shook his head. "Damned birds of a feather. Now, where was I? Oh, yeah, you had something for me."

"Just this, sir. For the last several days the Troatta ships have been launching small probes. We believe they are sensor probes, passive collection devices. They are not emitting in any frequency or wavelength except for what appear to be routine telemetry and diagnostics."

The admiral frowned. "How many?"

"Fourteen to date."

"*Fourteen?* What's orbital control doing about it?"

"Nothing, sir. They have received orders from Admiral Stevens, First Combined Fleet commander, not to interfere with them. I made a discreet inquiry and it seems the order came to him from your brother, the CNO himself, but only in response to a request from the armistice commission to do nothing which might provoke a breakdown of the negotiations with P'Daan."

"Why on Earth . . . ?"

"As I understand it, the armistice commission is most concerned with your brother's possible response, and I have to say, sir, with some reason. During the recent war, he justly earned a reputation as an officer quick to take provocative action and consider the possible consequences at his leisure."

"Well, that's Cedric all right," Admiral Goldjune said. He frowned, his eyes on the floor. "Those probes—not weaponry?"

"That is impossible to say positively, sir. Given the Guardian aversion to nuclear warheads, it is difficult to see how something this size could be any sort of conventional weapon. It could have an offensive electronic warfare function. It is of course *possible* they are what the Troatta claim. On the other hand, I have been reading the summaries of the negotiations with P'Daan. They are going over old ground. It is as if P'Daan had a script but has exhausted it and is starting over."

"That makes no sense," the admiral said.

"I am sure it makes sense to him, sir. We just cannot fathom his intentions. But it seems to me he is waiting for something."

The admiral snorted his skepticism and then stood up. "Okay, I'll make some discreet inquiries of my own, maybe even comm Cedric. Brothers need to stay in touch. Grab your hat, Commander, and I'll introduce you to the VIPs. They will find your accent charming." He turned to Nuvaash. "But not you, Vice-Captain. I'm looking to charm Ramirez y Sesma, not infuriate him."

Nuvaash heard this, but his attention was now on his commlink, which vibrated insistently. He realized from their expressions that both the admiral and the commander were experiencing the same phenomenon. He saw his call was from an acquaintance, an uHoko Speaker for The Enemy, on the staff of the armistice commission. He opened the link.

Takaar, I don't know where you are, but you should get to a viewer. Our picket craft tell us that a ship exited jump space above the plane approximately five minutes ago. The signal has just reached our sensor platforms as it exited over fifty million miles out. It matches no known ship profiles of any Cottohazz member state and it is not a Troatta battleship. It has been sending a tight beam flat vid signal since emerging, but it is an empty carrier signal. We expect they may begin transmitting once they know they have found a receiver.

"Thank you, my friend. I will remember this favor."

He cut the connection but saw Commander Atwater-Jones already turning one smartwall of her office to viewer mode. She switched it to the US Navy Channel Four—Restricted Live Feed. "This is where they'll show whatever they have. If it isn't too dreadful, they will rebroadcast it later on the public feeds."

They watched the blank screen for what must have been three or four minutes before it flickered and an image appeared, the image of a being Nuvaash felt as if he almost knew, having heard so many stories and watched so many vid feeds and holocon records. In the subdued light of the ship from which the image was transmitted, the Guardian's halo shimmered and sparkled.

"I am the Guardian called Te'Anna, and I have come a very long way to give you a message of great importance."

CHAPTER THIRTY-EIGHT

Moments later, on board CCS-7 USS *Olympus Mons*, in high orbit above K'tok
23 September 2134

Admiral Cedric Goldjune, the Outworld Coalition's chief of naval operations, watched the flat vid speech with a growing sense of unreality. This wasn't how the game was played. This made no sense. It had to be some sort of trick. Almost everything P'Daan was bargaining for, everything he offered in exchange for some portion of their freedom, this Te'Anna was offering as a gift, without conditions: the secret of large organism immortality and the means to implement it, for those who so chose—and who in their right mind wouldn't? And the secret of the jump drive. She was even throwing in their advanced data-processing technology, which was the key to both of the other advances, something P'Daan had not mentioned.

The only thing P'Daan could offer which Te'Anna couldn't was *peace*, and Cedric had to admit peace was the thing he valued least. Her offer was like a dream come true, and he did not believe in dreams coming true this easily. People didn't just give you the things you longed for, you had to take them. That was the way it should be: you appreciated them more that way.

P'Daan would probably make them fight, and the rumor was P'Daan could find a thousand ships to throw against them. Cedric had been going over the fleet intel archives, and the various navies of the *Cottohazz* could easily double that, more like triple it, in terms of deep space armed combatants of one sort or another. They weren't all as capable as the latest Human or Varoki cruisers, but enough of them were. Let P'Daan bring his thousand ships. The *Cottohazz* could meet it with a hell of a combined fleet.

And someone would have to command that fleet.

Forty thousand kilometers below, Cassandra and Rear Admiral Goldjune walked in step toward the reception in the headquarters complex. As they approached the guards at the entrance, both in the uniforms of Nigerian Naval Infantry, she remembered something she had wondered earlier but had gotten lost in the rest of their conversation.

"You say there's a new special envoy from the Cottohazz executive council *en route*?"

"Yes," the admiral answered, "entered system yesterday but won't get here for nearly a week. He's Varoki, named Labonna, Latonna, something like that."

"Arigapaa e-Lotonaa?" she said and momentarily broke stride.

"Yes, that's the one," the admiral said and turned to her. "How'd you know? Oh, yeah, enemy command structure and all. But the *Cottohazz* Executive Council isn't exactly the enemy."

"Not as of yet, sir, but the evening is still young. In one way, it makes perfect sense they would send e-Lotonaa. He's had more direct experience with K'tok than anyone else in the *Khap'uKhaana*—that's their diplomatic corps, sir. He was even interim governor while they were transitioning to independence. Of course, with all this business about the jump drive, I'd say he has a devil of a conflict of interest."

"How's that?"

"His adopted daughter is heiress to the largest share of the e-Traak holdings, probably the largest private fortune in the *Cottohazz*. Traak was one of the supposed inventors of the jump drive. He and another of the inventors, a chap named Simkitic, formed a partnership which has become quite successful."

"Good Lord, you're talking about Simki-Traak Transtellar?"

"Yes, sir, now one of the two largest manufacturers of jump drives in the *Cottohazz*." She remembered, but did not mention, that they had manufactured the jump drive the admiral had earlier sent her to inspect.

"So, is this gentleman a bad *hombre*?"

"I'm afraid much worse than that, sir: he is an unknown quantity. As much as we know about him, we have been unable to clearly identify him with any internal faction within the government, which means either he is remarkably good at disguising his positions or he is a loose cannon, neither of which is comforting."

"I don't suppose just being an honest and conscientious government official is very likely, huh?" the admiral said.

Cassandra did not answer what was clearly a rhetorical question.

Cassandra liked diplomatic receptions, as a general rule. If she had more rank and prominence it would have been different. Important people would have watched her, taken note of what she did. As a comparatively junior officer she could mingle with the other junior staff, who were generally more interesting and certainly more informative to talk to. Unfortunately, she found herself under tow by the admiral, at least for the moment.

The reception was hosted in a large meeting room from which the tables and chairs had been removed. White-jacketed naval steward's mates crisscrossed the open area with platters of sparkling wine, cocktails, and *hors d'oeuvres*, those for Human consumption made with indigenously grown ingredients, and so mostly variations on what they called Crab K'tok.

"Come on, Commander, I'll introduce you around."

"Oh, thank you so much, sir, but really, that's all right."

"No, I don't mind. Now where . . . ? Well I'll be dipped! Look at that, the senator talking to two Varoki diplomats as if they were old pals. Looks like we could have brought Nuvaash after all. I never thought I'd see Ramirez y Sesma so chummy with Varoki. Think it's because the folks back home won't know about it and it's all been an act?"

"Anything is possible, sir, but I think it more likely because the world's turned upside down. The Varoki are no longer the greatest threat, and so they become potentially the most valuable ally."

The admiral looked at her. "That is a strangely unsettling thought."

They made their way through the crowd and in moments were beside the senator and the two diplomats. Ramirez y Sesma was in his mid-fifties, tall and handsome in a distinguished sort of way, complete with graying temples in his wavy black hair. Admiral Goldjune introduced Cassandra. The senator took her hand and gave her a look she was certain had melted hearts— probably a great many hearts. He had that intangible but essential ingredient of attractiveness—self-confidence— and his was accompanied by a warm, generous smile which enfolded everyone around him in the embrace of his confidence, let you know his confidence extended to you as much as to himself. He wordlessly complimented her with his undivided attention, as if she and he were suddenly the only people in the room, and when he had to turn back to Admiral Goldjune, a look of regret flashed across his face so intense it bordered on the tragic.

An aide appeared at his elbow, speaking softly but insistently and gesturing to another clump of civilians. The senator made his formal farewell to the diplomats and Admiral Goldjune, then kissed her hand and shot her a sad, helpless smile of apology as he allowed himself to be led away. *Ah,* his eyes seemed to say, *what might have been were it not for the call of duty.* He actually kissed her hand! *Lord,* he was good at this! It was all theater, of course, but so was Shakespeare, Cassandra thought, and no one looked down their nose at that.

The admiral was soon involved in conversation with the Varoki diplomats from the armistice commission and

Cassandra made her escape, acquiring a flute of sparkling white wine in the process and an *hors d'oeuvre* which resembled crab meat wrapped with seaweed, but somehow tasted remarkably like *rumaki*. She took both of them from trays prominently marked "Human Consumption Only," a precaution necessary in such a mixed crowd. She saw all six of the intelligent species represented in the reception, an extraordinarily cosmopolitan gathering on a sparsely populated colony planet such as K'tok. The world was indeed turned upside down.

She saw Choice at the reception but the musician was surrounded by a half-dozen admirers, listening with serious concentration to her discourse. Cassandra couldn't make out what it was over the babble of voices in the hall but imagined it concerned music. People do not hang on every word like that if it has to do with cybernetic systems analysis, at least not at a reception like this. Within five minutes Cassandra had struck up a conversation with a massive, shambling Zaschaan diplomat. She was always somewhat astonished there were any among the notoriously ill-tempered Zaschaan capable of such an occupation, but he was surprisingly good-natured and she was again astonished to realize he had a very dry, ironic sense of humor. Within a few minutes he had her laughing. When she felt her commlink vibrate and saw the ID tag for Nuvaash, she felt genuine regret as she excused herself.

"Yes," she said after opening the link.

There is a development you and the admiral should be aware of, Commander. Minutes ago, the Troatta remote probes began broadcasting a powerful coded signal. At the same time, we detected seventeen jump departure signatures from what seem to be the equivalent of jump courier missiles, all launched by the Troatta battleships.

Cassandra felt the blood drain from her face and for a moment she fought dizziness. She thought they would have more time than this. She looked at Rear Admiral Goldjune, standing near a Katami military officer, but could tell both of them were listening to their own commlinks, and as she scanned the room she realized the babble of conversation was fading as more and more guests began receiving commlink messages. She made her way toward the admiral, but he saw her and moved to meet her. As they approached each other she saw he was talking to someone, undoubtedly by commlink.

"... got a clear recording of the broadcast? Good. Tight beam it up to one of our jump courier missiles on standby and send it off to Eleventh Fleet on Bronstein's World. Make sure it's not set to broadcast, though, understand? Just tight beam data transfer. As soon as it's loaded, dispatch it."

He looked up at her and shook his head. "I should have commed Cedric as soon as you told me. *Son of a bitch!*" he added in an uncharacteristic display of profanity. Around them the babble of voices began growing, taking on an increasingly insistent tone. "Come on, let's get to the communication center. At least it has a Marine guard on duty who'll keep this mob out of our hair."

They walked quickly and purposefully out into the corridor, waving away the questions of the civilian guests. The people in uniform were either still talking on their commlinks or hurrying out as well. No more than halfway to the communications room the Admiral received another comm. Cassandra heard only half of the conversation.

"What do you mean it's down?...Well then load it to another courier missile and send that." He stopped walking and his eyes widened for a moment. "What do you mean they're *all* down?...Well, get it to a ship that...How can every ship's jump drive be *down*?...Very well, I'll be there in five minutes."

He looked at Cassandra and shook his head, clearly unsettled by this new development. "Well, I think we know what that broadcast was. New fleet policy is to routinely decouple jump drive cores from their actuators so no malicious signal can trigger a jump. This signal just made every jump core in the system go to sleep, maybe permanently."

"Oh, God!" Cassandra said. "Those jump couriers the Troatta sent. What if those are carrying similar broadcasts to the other *Cottohazz* worlds?"

The admiral shook his head. "No. P'Daan probably backtracked the course of the probe that took *Cam Ranh Bay* to him, but how could he know where the other *Cottohazz* star systems are?"

Cassandra had no answer to that, but it did not make the dull sense of dread recede. *Where were those probes going?* Admiral Goldjune's head rose slightly and turned to one side, which she took as another incoming comm.

"Yes...Say again?...*How* many?...Very well. I'm almost there. Better set up a holoconference with Vice Admiral Stevens and the CNO." He looked back at

Cassandra, his face visibly paler. "More jump emergence signatures: *thirty-one* of them, very large, and they don't look like they're ours."

Admiral Cedric Goldjune, Outworld Coalition Chief of Naval Operations, tapped his Annapolis class ring nervously on the arm of the chair in the holosuite on USS *Olympus Mons*, waiting for the others to materialize. His younger brother, Jacob, appeared first and they exchanged nods. Then Vice Admiral Gordon Stevens—"Gordo" to most other flag officers—commander of First Combined Fleet, physically walked into the holosuite and sat down at the station next to Cedric. He looked harried.

"Gordo, what the hell's going on?" Cedric asked.

"Sir, near as we can tell every *Cottohazz* jump drive in the star system is offline, apparently as a result of that broadcast from their so-called sensor probes. A couple civilian ships are still running diagnostics, but that's what it looks like."

"Goddamned civilian diplomats!" Cedric said. "I told those fucking idiots we needed to deal with those probes, but they wouldn't listen. Now look at us!"

Well, he knew that was a bit of an exaggeration, but he'd mentioned something about it and wanted it in the record as soon as possible. His brother Jacob looked preoccupied, and was used to his explosions in any case.

Stevens looked surprised, and then skeptical. "Yes, sir," Stevens said. "We're stuck here. Hopefully when no word shows up back home or on Akaampta, someone will think to send reinforcements."

Cedric wasn't sure Stevens was the right man for this

job. He'd mishandled the whole fitness report issue between Bitka and young Larry, six months ago, and now he looked like he might be trying to second-guess his superior. But if Cedric fired Stevens, who could he put in charge? Not his brother. Maybe he could take command himself, but as disaster-prone as the situation was, that was more exposure than he really wanted.

"Hope you're right, Gordo, but I'm not sure you are," Jacob put in.

"Why's that?" Stevens said.

"I got a pretty sharp intel officer down here wondering where all those jump missiles went to that left about the same time. If somehow P'Daan figured out a way to locate the other major worlds of the *Cottohazz*, and seeded them with more of these ECM probes, this isn't going to just be our problem."

Hell! If it really was *Cottohazz*-wide, Cedric realized, they might be in deeper trouble than he'd thought.

"Gordo, what's the word on those new ships that showed up?" Cedric asked.

"They're Troatta battlewagons, all right, what Bitka's people call long ships, thirty-one of them. They emerged from J-space nineteen million kilometers above the plane and they're closing at fifteen clicks a second, so we've got fifteen days, little more if they decelerate to enter orbit. P'Daan's squadron is standing away from K'tok, presumably to rendezvous with the new ships, or maybe try for an intercept on that other Guardian ship, Te'Anna's, before it makes orbit. Their mean orbital radius right now is about seventy thousand klicks and they're nearly at escape velocity."

"They join up," Cedric said, "and they'll have thirty-five of those long ships. What have we got?"

Stevens gestured with his data pad but didn't consult it, probably knew the roster by heart. "Not counting auxiliaries and transports, First Combined Fleet has twelve cruisers, one destroyer carrier, eight mint-condition destroyers, and three beat-up ones. The *Cottohazz* Peacekeeping Squadron has three more cruisers: two Zaschaan, and one Katami. The uBakai armistice delegation's escort squadron has three more Varoki cruisers: two uBakai and one uKaMaat."

"So, eighteen cruisers and eleven destroyers?" the CNO replied, nodding. "That's better than I thought. We've almost got numeric parity. Hell, Bitka beat them outnumbered two-to-one and with only an armed transport—*twice!*"

Stevens looked like he wanted to argue with that but Jacob beat him to it. "Bitka fooled them, with a different trick each time. They aren't going to fall for anything like that again. And those Troatta ships weren't designed to be used in pairs, they're designed to fight as part of a phalanx, a solid wall of firing ships, which is how they'll come at us. You throw our ships against that wall of meson gun fire, they'll shoot us to pieces."

"He's right, sir," Stevens said. "It's like boxing with someone whose arms are longer than yours. They hit us before we can get close enough to land a punch."

"Our missiles have more reach than those meson guns," Cedric reminded them both.

"Not really, sir," Stevens said. "We can launch them from farther out, but they've still got to get to within five thousand kilometers before they can hurt them. Our destroyers and some of the cruisers can actually start punching at ten thousand kilometers with their lasers, but when the Troatta can hit us from over forty thousand klicks, well ..."

"Defeatist crap!" Cedric shouted. "You're saying there's no way to beat them? That they can just come in here and crush us any time they want because they have longer-range directed-energy weapons?"

"No, sir," Stevens answered. "They have some vulnerabilities, chief among them being how slow they are. Our ships are a lot more maneuverable. And I'll tell you, they seem pretty shy about making in-system jumps. If it was our only option left to us, I'd say send some ships to jump in behind them, especially while they're still above the ecliptic plane and there's very little risk of annihilation events. Turn their flank. But they took that option away when they shut down our jump drives."

"Okay, so what about a decapitation strike? Their big fleet is two weeks away. Let's go after P'Daan and his squadron now. Four warships and his command vessel—we should be able to take them out." But Stevens was shaking his head again.

"We've got six cruisers here at K'tok, two beat-up destroyers, and three armed transports. Most of the rest of the combatant fleet is at the gas giant Mogo, except *Puebla*. She's about halfway between here and Mogo, not sure why. One of your black ops projects, Jake?"

"It was," Jacob answered and turned to look at Cedric. "The CNO has authority for it now."

Stevens looked from one to the other and when neither

of them said anything more he shrugged and went on. "Well, in addition to our ships at K'tok, the uBakai contingent is here as well, but I'm not sure we can persuade them to undertake offensive action. Even if we do, it's moot. P'Daan still has working jump drives, unless he's a total idiot and didn't customize the broadcast command to our drive systems only. As soon as we start after his personal ships he can just jump away, jump out-system, wait a week or so, jump back and join his main fleet. There's no risk jumping away and he's about far enough out of the gravity well to do it already.

"So, without our own jump drives there's not much we can do, sir. I've already sent a warning order to the ships at Mogo to prepare to bend orbit for K'tok. As it is, it'll take most of the two weeks for them to get back here. Might want to pull *Puebla* back in as well. Looks as if its trajectory is going to take it close to P'Daan's personal squadron."

Cedric pretended to think about their tactical options, but his mind was on Stevens himself. He definitely wasn't the man for this job. All he saw were problems, their own problems. The enemy had problems too, must have. They always did. It was just a matter of figuring them out, but Stevens couldn't see past any of the clutter.

In a way, this whole mess was Stevens' fault. If he'd handled the fitness report issue better to start with, Bitka never would have been in command of the *Bay*. That young exec would have been, and even though Cedric didn't have much use for Bitka, he doubted the exec could have gotten the ship out of that mess. Probably got it blown up or something and that would have been the end of that. One missing ship, no explanation, pin it on the uBakai and then take care of business. Instead they had this.

"So, what do we do instead?" Cedric demanded. "It's your fleet, Gordo. What are your plans?"

Stevens looked at him and then at Jacob and shook his head. "It's not like I like the guy, but right now I wish Bitka was here. He'd probably come up with something."

"Bitka!" the CNO spat out. "The hell with Bitka. He wasn't all that smart, just lucky."

"Well," Stevens said, "smart *or* lucky, I'd take some of either one right now."

Cedric saw Jacob nodding in agreement. Jacob had always been a worrier, too. Cedric needed someone with some goddamned confidence, someone who would actually *commit* to getting the job done. That's how problems got solved: find someone willing to do it, *whatever* it took, and then back them all the way. If they failed, well, that was their fault, wasn't it? Fire them, find someone else, give the job to them. But this time there might not be a second chance, and if they lost . . .

He'd have to wait to see if contact with Earth and the rest of the *Cottohazz* really had been cut. They'd know for sure long before the battle came, but if P'Daan could turn off every jump drive in the *Cottohazz*, the war was over, and the first people to recognize that were going to be the only ones who had very good long-term prospects. If they really didn't have any good military options, they might still have a diplomatic one, but not through those idiots on the armistice commission. This wasn't a task he could job out. He would have to handle this himself.

CHAPTER THIRTY-NINE

Four days later, **on board LAS-17 USS *Cam Ranh
Bay*, in high orbit above K'tok
27 September 2134**

Lieutenant Homer Alexander strapped himself into the
command chair after relieving Ensign Bob DaSilva as
OOD. There wasn't much to do at anchor watch, but they
still had to stand it. Too much crap going on to act like it
was business as usual. Jesus! They'd come all this way
back, got to K'tok, and instead of the brass letting them
go home, they'd been slapped in quarantine. No sooner
were they out than P'Daan breaks their jump drives. So
now they were as good as his prisoners, but no crazy
Destie mechanics around to fix their drive. No Captain
Bitka, either.

"Anything interesting, Joe?" he asked Signaler First
Lakhanpal in the Comm chair beside him. Homer had
relieved DaSilva an hour early so Lakhanpal was still on
but had been here for the last five hours as well.

"Te'Anna shook that Troatta long ship off her tail like
it was standing still, sir. Bandit gave up about four hours
ago. We got so used to how slow these battleships are, it's

kinda weird thinking of a Guardian ship that's fast. But that little bird of hers has some goddamn *legs* on it, that's for sure. I didn't even know she had a ship of her own, sir. Did you?"

Homer shook his head. "No idea, and now I wonder what she's thinking, coming here."

"Can't ask her, sir. Orders."

"Yeah, I know, Joe. Comm blackout to and from except authorized stations, which we ain't. Just wondering, that's all."

"You think it's a trick, sir? Like maybe she's in with P'Daan now?"

Homer stretched as he thought about that and started to link his hands behind his head, but then remembered how many times he'd seen the captain do exactly that in this chair and he just scratched his scalp instead. He'd never spent enough time with Te'Anna to know what to make of her. He knew the captain trusted her, but what good had that done him?

"I really don't know, Joe. I'd love to, and that's a fact."

"You think maybe she busted him out and is bringing him home?"

Homer turned and snapped, "Don't say that. Don't *ever* say that again!" It came out louder than he meant it to and the other two petty officers on duty turned to look, then quickly turned back when they saw the scowl on his face.

"Sorry, sir," Lakhanpal said quietly.

"Ah, shit, I'm sorry for blowing up. It's just that . . . don't *say* it, okay? You might jinx it."

Lakhanpal's face cleared and he nodded. "I get it. Aye, aye, sir. Mum's the word."

Homer smiled. "That's right, Joe. Mum's the word. So, any signal traffic between Te'Anna's racer and K'tok?"

"Lots of it, sir, but all tight-beam and restricted. About all I know I get from the vidfeed, comes up the needle to highstation and then on to us. Once in a while they release a clip of her talking about what she's offering, no strings attached. What do you think, Mister Alexander? You want to live forever?"

"I've always wanted to, Joe. In a way, I guess I never believed I was going to die, not really. Now that maybe it's a possibility . . . I don't know. I'll have to think about that."

"Well, her ship's getting real close, sir, retro-burning hard to get into orbit. Lieutenant Barr-Sanchez says looks like she's going to dock with Highstation later today. Maybe you ought to make up your mind. Might have your chance sooner than you thought," he said with a grin.

"I guess," Homer said. "I'll tell you what, I sure would like to look inside her ship, see if anyone's with her. I sure would."

The bridge hatch opened, Ka'Deem Brook entered, and all conversation stopped. He looked around and met Homer's eyes.

"*XO*," Homer said with deliberate emphasis, a title he enjoyed using since Commander Beauchamp had come up the needle to relieve Brook a week earlier and Homer no longer had to call him *Captain*.

Brook nodded, looked around again, his eyes empty, and he left.

The conversations resumed.

★ ★ ★

"Senator," Admiral Cedric Goldjune said, rising from his chair and extending his hand. "I am honored you chose to accept my invitation. Please, shall we sit in my lounge? You must be exhausted from the ride up the needle."

"Actually, I feel quite good, Admiral," Ramirez y Sesma said as he sank into a large armchair. "I caught up on my sleep coming up. The last few days have been very busy and the respite was much needed." He looked around the office, his gaze lingering on the smartwalls which showed the exterior view: the near orbital space around Highstation, the two dozen other ships, most of them commercial vessels, seemingly motionless there, the two or three tiny shuttles moving among them, and he nodded. "Your flagship is an impressive vessel."

Cedric sat down in another armchair. "Thank you, sir, but technically USS *Olympus Mons* is not my flagship. It is assigned to Vice Admiral Stevens, but we're sharing it for the duration of my visit."

"Ah, and how long will that be now? None of us knows. Tell me, do you believe there will be a battle?"

Cedric pretended to think about that for a few seconds, but of course he knew what he had planned to say. "I believe P'Daan will wait until his combined fleet is closer and then deliver an ultimatum of some sort. If we fail to accept, there will be a battle."

"And how will that battle turn out, do you think?"

"We are outnumbered and outgunned. We will certainly lose."

They sat in silence for some time and Cedric watched a utility shuttle move away from *Olympus Mons* toward Highstation.

"We have no options?" the senator asked eventually. Aside from his eye movement having sped up and his voice now being pitched a bit lower, probably to compensate for the tendency to rise, he gave no evidence of his fear, but that was enough.

"Well, sir, I think our only options are *policy* options, not military ones. But I don't make policy; I only follow orders. If we really are cut off from the rest of the *Cottohazz*—and every additional day without contact makes that more certain—there will be no orders for me from anywhere, no policy direction. We cannot even be sure there is anyone left to make such a decision. Who is to say this is the only Guardian fleet which has come? Our best intelligence suggests the Guardians in the near stellar neighborhood of Destination might be able to muster a thousand ships, and we have only seen thirty here.

"I think someone has to make a decision, and quite frankly sir, the members of the armistice commission are not intellectually or temperamentally equipped to do so." Cedric left unsaid who he hoped might have that equipment, although he could see his mention of a thousand Guardian ships had started the senator sweating.

"I have no such authority, unfortunately," Ramirez y Sesma answered, his eyes darting nervously about the room.

"Senator, if I may speak frankly, allow me to point out that no one anywhere within the former extent of the *Cottohazz* currently has legal authority to do anything. I say former extent advisedly, because the harsh truth is that once all interstellar travel and communication was interdicted, the *Cottohazz* as a practical, functioning political entity ceased to exist. You can't speak for the *Cottohazz*, but you are the senior elected civilian official present from the governments of the four nations of the Outworld Coalition. Senator, as CNO of the Outworld Coalition, I will follow your orders, as will every coalition ship in this system. I think it is a safe bet the various *Cottohazz* ships will join us out of necessity, although it may take some hard convincing once the time comes."

Ramirez y Sesma took a handkerchief from his breast pocket and wiped his face before answering. "But to what end, Admiral? You said yourself our military options are nonexistent."

Cedric keyed open a virtual folder on his desk and then tapped it with his finger. "This is Johnstone's report on the sociology of the Guardians. Those Troatta battleships are on loan to P'Daan. Someday they'll have to go back home to their own gods, or whatever they call them. How is P'Daan going to manage the one hundred and seventy-one sovereign nation-states, comprising six different intelligent species, of the *Cottohazz*? These people have never had to manage anything as complex as this. All they know is a planet or two where everyone already agrees on everything, particularly who's in charge. Who's going to manage that? Who's going to serve as liaison between P'Daan and the *Cottohazz*? Don't you think, sir, that our people's welfare will be better served if the liaisons are of their own species?"

"Quislings, you mean," the senator said, his face unreadable.

"To be thought of that way is probably a burden such

people would have to carry. Not everyone would have the strength to pick that burden up."

The senator's gaze returned to the smartwall as he thought that through.

"This Te'Anna's ship arrives in a few hours," the senator said, still looking at the spacescape through the wall, "and e-Lotonaa, the day after. Special envoy plenipotentiary for the Executive Council." He turned back to Cedric. "Plenipotentiary. *Tasyvaalt'aynoon* in aGavoosh. God, the Varoki love that word! Lord knows why, because it keeps getting them into trouble. But it means he actually has authority to speak for the *Cottohazz*, particularly in an emergency such as this. The Guardian Te'Anna and Special Envoy e-Lotonaa—how do their arrivals affect your calculations?"

Cedric sat back in his chair. "How many battleships are they bringing with them, sir?"

Cassandra Atwater-Jones longed to know whom, if anyone, Te'Anna had brought with her, much as Homer Alexander onboard *Cam Ranh Bay* longed to know. Unlike him, she was able to satisfy that longing nine hours later—watching the live vid-feed on the restricted access Naval senior staff channel, as Te'Anna debarked from her ship's shuttle at Highstation. Te'Anna was not alone. There were two other Guardians with her, whom Te'Anna quickly identified to the waiting staff as K'Irka and H'Stus. Cassandra brought up several intelligence folders and then watched as hazmat-suited station crew searched and decontaminated the small shuttle, and she received the reports of the other crew who had done the same to the

Guardian's main ship in orbit near the station. There was no one else.

She sat back and closed her eyes. She had not dared to hope he was there, but admitted the possibility. She tried to identify how she felt about this new reality, but she simply felt empty. Her commlink vibrated and she saw the ID tag for Rear Admiral Jacob Goldjune.

You watching this, Cass? she heard in her head when she opened the link.

"Yes, sir. I'm also looking at some still visuals from *Cam Ranh Bay's* records. The second one does appear to be K'Irka, based on its markings. We have no visual imagery on the Guardian named H'Stus. The crew of the *Bay* never had any sort of contact with him."

I was about to ask you if we could verify any of this. Glad you're on top of it. He paused before speaking again. *Sorry he wasn't with them.*

Cassandra closed her eyes and took a steadying breath before replying. "As am I, Admiral, but I am not surprised. I doubt you were either, but I appreciate the sentiment. Has the CNO developed a plan for dealing with P'Daan's fleet?"

If either he or Gordo Stevens has, no one's told me, and that makes me nervous. Your new friend Ramirez y Sesma was gone most of the day—up-needle, but he's back now. Something's going on and we're out of the loop. Only one thing to do when that happens.

"Make our own loop," Cassandra said, and she heard the admiral laugh softly.

God, I do love the way you think. The Guardian new arrivals are coming down-needle and they'll meet with you first and alone. I'll run interference, but you size them up, get a handle on what they really want.

"With an eye toward what end, sir?"

Will they help us beat P'Daan, and if so, how?

"And if your brother has other plans?"

Well, I hope that's not the case. I really do. But if it is, I have your sidekick Nuvaash working on another option.

Cassandra heard the regret in his voice, and was reminded that whatever their differences now, Jacob and Cedric were still brothers. "What other option, sir, if I may ask?"

The Executive Council's new special envoy has said he wants to talk to that Varoki diplomat who negotiated with the Troatta back at Destination. Haykuz, right? Isn't that his name? The special envoy wants to meet him tomorrow when his ship docks. Nuvaash is talking to Haykuz tonight.

She wasn't sure what Haykuz could do other than vouch for them to the special envoy, but that was something. Perhaps it was the means to open an informal line of communication.

"Excellent idea, sir. We have to have e-Lotonaa behind us, and ideally the senator as well. If we do, the military will likely fall in line."

Yes, Cass, but that doesn't mean beans if we don't have a military plan to go with it. So work on those Guardians. See if they can help. Judging by the fancy maneuvering they had to do to get by P'Daan's ships, I'd say they're willing to help. Able is another story. You know, if we beat P'Daan here, really beat him, we still have a chance of getting Bitka back.

Cassandra said nothing at first. He meant well, but one reached a point where prolonging those sorts of vague hopes was simply an exercise in cruelty.

"On a different subject, sir, what is our cover story for my exclusive first interview with the Guardians?"

Te'Anna requested it.

"Will your brother accept that?"

He'll have to. It's the truth. She asked for you by name. They're on the needle now. Expect them in your office in two hours.

He signed off and Cassandra thought through what she would need. They knew Te'Anna spoke good English, and Cassandra had the best version of Destie autotrans loaded in her commlink, so even if the others spoke she would be able to understand them. But would Te'Anna have to translate everything Cassandra said to the other two?

She pinged her yeoman administrative assistant on her commlink.

Ma'am?

"Jones, I need a vox-box, something like what they used on *Cam Ranh Bay*. And I need it programed for English to Destie. And I need it in under two hours."

Aye, aye, ma'am, he said, as calmly as if all she had asked for was a watercress sandwich and a cup of Earl Grey. He really was extraordinary, a member of that informal network she had heard one of her US Navy colleagues call *the E-4 mafia*. Chief petty officers knew everything about how to get things done, but had certain constraints on their behavior due to the positions of responsibility they held. The petty officers first and second class had ambitions to become chiefs. But petty officers third class—whom Americans loved to call by their pay grade, E-4—had no such lofty goals and a select number of them were, so far as she could tell, both fearless and contemptuous of Navy regulations. Some day they might develop ambitions, those who were not summarily discharged along the way, but in the meantime, they navigated the tortuous passageways of Navy bureaucracy like ninjas with a death wish, and Yeoman Third-Class Jones, Thomas K., was *her* ninja.

Less than an hour later, Jones delivered her vox-box. She also received a brief commlink call from Nuvaash, who reported a very successful meeting with the diplomat Haykuz, details to follow. She spent the remaining time refreshing her familiarity with what was known of the three Guardians and going over a short list of key needs, the first and most important of which was a means of repairing their jump drives, as soon as possible. From what she understood, the Guardian called H'Stus would be critical for that task, as he was the one who headed up the ship construction operation back in the Destination system.

She received a commlink notification the three Guardians had arrived safely at Downstation and that Rear Admiral Goldjune had provided a platoon of Mike Marines, half of them in powered armor, as a security detail. That seemed rather much, Cassandra thought, but better too careful than not enough. The admiral mentioned the Marines, one of the two uninfected platoons from *Cam Ranh Bay*, had volunteered for the duty. The Guardian Te'Anna had been instrumental in recovering their stricken comrades from the Destie-Seven-Echo Highstation. US Marines were every bit as serious about repaying their debts of honor, at least in her experience, as were Royal Marines. Gambling debts were a different matter, of course.

She received notification when they left the underground shuttle tube at the platform under the headquarters building, again when they left the lift on her floor, and then her commlink vibrated again with the ID tag of Yeoman Third Jones.

"Yes," she said.

Ma'am, your 1630 appointments are here, he said in that infuriatingly calm voice.

"Thank you, Jones. Please show them in," she said, in as blasé a tone as she could muster, and then she added with a smile, "Oh, and I don't think we'll be needing tea."

The door slid open and Jones stood to the side, gesturing politely in, rather like a doorman. Te'Anna was first, much more imposing in person than in vid-feed. Cassandra rose from her chair in welcome. The Guardian was a good two meters twenty in height and ducked her head a bit passing under the door frame, even though it had originally been constructed for Varoki use. Her aura glowed yellow around her head, her plumage colors were soft, mostly white and pale gray, and Cassandra particularly noticed her strikingly large gray eyes, with no sign of white in them. Her expression changed as soon as she entered the room, eyes growing even wider, and her mouth curved in what was unmistakably a smile.

"Oh, you look just like the hologram!"

K'Irka was second, somewhat shorter, not much over

two meters tall, aura pinkish, plumage more yellow and pink, incongruously feminine-looking to Cassandra. Given the reports that K'Irka seemed less emotional and empathic than Te'Anna, a more monochromatic palette might have been a better fit. K'Irka looked around the office, her large gray eyes taking in its objects, recording the information without apparent reaction. Cassandra was just one more of those objects.

H'Stus was the third through the door, H'Stus whom they had never seen before. He wore a Guardian SA frame, the sort she had seen in the video record of the landing party massacre. His aura glowed blue, plumage deep black except for his head, which was mostly white, and a splash of deep red on his throat and upper chest. His large, ornamental shoulder feathers filled out more to the sides, emphasizing his breadth of shoulder, and his neck was shorter. *My God*, Cassandra thought, *he looks like a vulture!* Unlike K'Irka, he looked directly at her, only at her, and it made her uneasy.

Before Cassandra could speak, Te'Anna apparently heard a noise in the anteroom for she turned and reacted. "Oh, look! It is Doctor Däng! Come, K'Irka, you will like her best of all the Humans," she said and dragged her Guardian companion with her, leaving the other one, the vulture in leg braces, standing alone in Cassandra's office staring mutely at her. The door slid closed. What was going on here? Te'Anna had asked for a conference with her by name and then wandered off. Was she always a scatterbrain? As the seconds stretched out and the creature's gaze did not waver, Cassandra became even more uncomfortable and began fumbling with the vox-box. She doubted any of them but Te'Anna could speak English.

"You don't need that," it said. She swallowed and looked at it, and for the first time in recent memory Cassandra was certain she was going to faint. The towering Guardian clumped across the floor and sat heavily in the chair, which creaked under its weight. "I didn't mean to stare," it said in Sam Bitka's voice, but lower, rougher. "It's just so good to see you again. I didn't think I ever would."

She sat down herself, her knees no longer supporting her. She looked at it, unable to speak, unable at first even to breathe. Finally, she managed two or three gasping breaths, and felt the hot tears run down her cheeks.

"Oh my God!" she whispered. "What have they *done* to you?"

CHAPTER FORTY

At the same time, on board Troatta Ship Ninety-Six, *en route* to join the Troatta main fleet
27 September 2134

Chief Helm Kakusa by-Vrook through-Kuannawaa sat in the detention cell on Ship Ninety-Six and awaited her fate. It would not be long now. When the other four operational Troatta ships from P'Daan's Realm had gone with P'Daan as escorts, Ship Ninety-Six had joined the Troatta Main Striking Armada, waiting in deep space to join P'Daan when it received the signal. She had felt the space-bending when they moved into the enemy system and were moving on the enemy principal world. That much her sister Tamari, commanding helm of Ship Ninety-Six, had told her. She had also told her that Lord Y'Areez, their Guardian creator and master, their living God, accompanied the armada. He would deal with her disobedience directly, and she knew he would do so without mercy.

Why had she defied P'Daan and made the truce with S'Bitka, the one which allowed his ship to escape, even if S'Bitka himself remained behind as P'Daan's eternal plaything? More importantly, what would she tell Y'Areez when he demanded an accounting?

The truth. She would tell him the truth. No lie she could construct would gain her any measure of mercy, so she would speak the truth to God, so that God would know the truth. But what was the truth?

Guardians could die. *Gods could die!* That was a truth she had learned. S'Bitka had destroyed a world, but he had killed three Guardians as well. The New People had whispered this by tight beam to them, safe from the ears of the surviving Guardians in P'Daan's realm. Should she tell Y'Areez this truth? No. He might decide the heresy must be rooted out, destroy all of her sisters who had been sent to P'Daan's realm, and they were guilty of nothing but heroic service at considerable cost. Almost one part in five of the Troatta who had gone to P'Daan's realm had perished, fighting a battle which was none of their concern.

Guardians could make errors. That was another truth she had learned. P'Daan had underestimated S'Bitka, a mortal like Kakusa, and P'Daan had been bested by S'Bitka repeatedly, despite having overwhelming force. *Guardians could be bested by mortals.* Another truth she would not share with Y'Areez.

The message panel above the doorway pulsed a rainbow of colors and made a soft tone. She inserted one arm in the communication sleeve beside the room's single chair.

"I am here."

Sister, she heard Tamari say, her voice thick with emotion, *the time has come. Prepare for a holocommune with Lord Y'Areez.*

"I am ready. Goodbye, Tamari my sister."

Goodbye, sister of my soul.

The holorecorders in the corners of the room glowed, capturing her image, and then two figures seemed to materialize in the room with her, side by side and standing no more than two spans distance. One was Troatta, like her but a male, his carapace painted the sacred reddish-black nightshade color of a holy interlocutor. The other, the Lord Y'Areez, towered over both Kakusa and the interlocutor, nearly twice their height. His feathers were a uniform blood red and his features ferocious. Kakusa by-Vrook through-Kuannawaa faced God with the courage which comes from having abandoned all hope.

Despite herself, Cassandra leaned back away from the Guardian before her who spoke with something that sounded like Bitka's voice.

"I'm sorry to scare you like that," it said. "but we had no choice. We monitored enough of the comm chatter to know how things stood. P'Daan has made me the bad guy and Admiral Goldjune is looking for a bus to throw me under. If they know I'm here, I'll spend all my time answering charges, and we don't have time to waste with that."

"But what did they *do* to you? They've turned you into a Guardian!"

"God, no! This is a disguise, like our skin masks, only a little more elaborate and . . . alive. I'd take it off and show you but we can't repair it down here, so you'll have to take my word for it. It's still me—*physically* me—under this."

"A disguise? But . . . your height."

"It's this SA frame. We had to modify it so the knee

joints are higher up and the shins longer, see? Basically, a set of stilts, but you have to look hard to notice. K'Irka did do some alterations to me, but not what you think. I'm still human, still *mortal*, still got all the standard equipment. She double-crossed P'Daan on that deal."

"Some . . . *alterations*? But why change you at all?" The unreality of the moment, sitting and talking to a giant bird which had Bitka's voice and vocal mannerisms, left Cassandra feeling detached from herself, as if watching the scene play out to someone else.

"Had to," it said. "They changed my digestive system, but that's all they fiddled with, and most of that was changing my gut bacteria rather than me. There was only so much Human food left behind and once it was gone, I'd have starved. They had to do it to save my life."

"Your voice sounds different," she said. "Is that because of their . . . alterations?"

"Indirectly. They had to make it look real. I didn't know myself till later. P'Daan was watching me by video feed at first and some things you can't fake, so . . . I had to go through the process without anesthesia." It paused and looked away. "I found out why people scream under torture. It makes it hurt less. It really does. The louder and harder you scream, the less pain. So, I screamed and screamed, as loud and as long as I could, until I blew out my vocal cords. When they healed, my voice was lower and rougher." It looked back at her. "Don't look like that. It's okay, really. It feels like it happened to someone else."

She wondered if it *did* happen to someone else. She wondered to what extent this thing really was Bitka.

"How did you escape?"

"I didn't. I was rescued, but even that sounds more melodramatic than it was. P'Daan had already left the system, once he was sure I was being altered and wasn't enjoying the process. Te'Anna came back to the station for me, persuaded K'Irka to release me and come with us. It wasn't that hard since K'Irka had already agreed to not go through with the full slate of modifications to me. The hard part was convincing the New People on the station this was on the up and up."

"Why did she?"

"Why did K'Irka agree? I'm not sure. She's an odd one. I almost said 'an odd duck,' but with all the feathers that sounds too much like a joke. No joke here, she is *seriously* strange."

"No," Cassandra said, "I meant why did Te'Anna come for you? That is a remarkable step, to turn on her own species like that, and suborn treason by another member of it."

It looked down and to the side in thought, a gesture which seemed so familiar to Cassandra it sent chills down her spine to see this alien do it.

"I'm not sure she thinks of it as treason. Turning on her species, I mean. I don't think she feels much, if any, loyalty to her species as a group. Maybe she did once but now her loyalty has become . . . personal."

"But you captured her, wrecked a planet she helped govern, killed those other Guardians. What would make her give that sort of loyalty to *you*?"

The thing's mouth twisted in Bitka's ironic, self-effacing smile and Cassandra felt a sudden tightness in her chest and throat.

"Me of all people," it said.

"Oh, I didn't mean that!"

"Yeah, I know you didn't. As to Te'Anna, I just accepted it for the gift it was. It seemed sort of rude and ungrateful for me to demand an explanation. You'll have to ask her yourself."

"I believe I shall."

For a while they sat in silence, the thing calling itself Bitka looking at her.

"What?" she said.

"Nothing," it answered and shook his head with another Bitka smile. "It's just really good to see you. For a long time, I had to rely on memory."

"How do I compare to your memory."

"You look older," it said.

"*Gawd,* just what every girl longs to hear!" Why should it bother her that this thing said that? Why should it bother her that Bitka would?

"Older's not so bad," it said. "It means you're mortal and, scary as that sounds, I have a whole new appreciation for mortality, having nearly lost mine."

She looked away and shook her head. "This is so . . . surreal. You talk about losing your mortality the way young girls talk about their virginity." She took a long, slow breath, then let it out and looked back at the alien. "Very well. I cannot completely accept this on an emotional level but I must accept it intellectually. What is your plan?"

"Stop P'Daan."

"That is not a plan," she said. "It is merely a goal."

"Yeah, I know, but I was hoping you wouldn't notice," it said, one eyebrow raised.

She felt a momentary flash of irritation, a so, *so* familiar irritation which, once she recognized its source, sent a pain lancing through her chest and momentarily took her breath away.

"Oh God! You really *are* Bitka!" And then she turned her swivel chair around so he would not see her as she finally gave way and sobbed uncontrollably. He didn't rise and come around the desk to comfort her. He didn't make little solicitous sounds. He just waited, as she knew he would. He was good at waiting for her. Better than she had ever been at waiting for him.

An hour later, Cassandra kept the first meeting small: herself, Nuvaash, Rear Admiral Goldjune, Te'Anna, and Bitka, although neither the admiral nor Nuvaash knew his identity yet. Admiral Goldjune was the last to arrive, and when he entered the conference room, she and Nuvaash stood up, as did the Guardian known as H'Stus. The admiral's eyebrows went up a bit at that. He gestured to the vox-box on the conference table.

"Please tell him I appreciate the courtesy but it is not necessary for him to stand."

Cassandra looked at the vox-box for a moment and then back to the admiral. "As it happens, sir, he *is* obliged to stand in your presence. You may want to sit down for this."

The Lord Y'Areez never spoke directly with his flock, always through an interlocutor. Kakusa listened to the questions from the nightshade-painted Voice of the Lord but then gave her replies directly to Y'Areez himself, being careful to never look into his eyes. She did not know whether Y'Areez and the interlocutor shared a communication link or if God could somehow place his thoughts in the mind of his servant. But if so, why not put them in her mind instead? That, she realized, was yet another blasphemous question.

"Why did you agree to the first truce with S'Bitka?"

"He showed us the approach tracks of his missile patterns, and our sensors confirmed them. They would certainly have destroyed both Ships before we could close to engagement range. I was willing to sacrifice the ships entrusted to me, but only if it could achieve the end Lord Y'Areez desired. To throw them away for nothing would be to injure my Lord's interests, not safeguard them."

"Was that your decision to make?"

"Yes, it was."

She thought this answer surprised at least the interlocutor. She could not, or rather would not, see the expression of Y'Areez. After several heartbeats' worth of silence another question came.

"And the second truce? Did P'Daan not order you to attack the Human ship?"

"He did."

"And you refused?"

"Yes."

"Explain."

Kakusa drew two long breaths through the respiration membranes on her flanks and gathered her thoughts. This was the essence of her sin and she wanted it understood for what it was.

"P'Daan had told us our task was to capture the criminal S'Bitka, and S'Bitka agreed to surrender himself.

We had already lost two of Lord Y'Areez's Ships and another, my own, was crippled. Over two hundred servants of Y'Areez had gone into the Darkness already. There was no certainty my two Ships would have prevailed in another battle. I had been ordered to obey P'Daan, but I also had been given responsibility for the useful application of the force Y'Areez had loaned to his brother god. These two charges had become incompatible. I chose to preserve the children of Y'Areez while insuring P'Daan's goal was achieved. In doing so I knew I was violating the order given by P'Daan and that I would be punished for this unforgivable sin. I now willingly accept God's punishment."

She rested her arms on the arms of the chair and closed her eyes, waiting for the end. She breathed in and out, and the air in her compartment bore the scent of burnt wood, her favorite room scent. She wondered why. What memory in youth before leaving her hive had triggered this pleasant association? She couldn't remember, and in a way, that made it all the more pleasant. She was not ashamed of what she had done, and she would die with the scent of burnt wood in her flank tongues.

She sensed a restlessness and opened her eyes to see the legs of the interlocutor shifting, his weight going from one to the other, as if in distress at what he heard from God. She closed her eyes again.

"Lord Y'Areez has decided the punishment for disobedience will be the death of Chief Helm Kakusa by-Vrook through-Kuannawaa. But Lord Y'Areez also desires the skills of the one called Kakusa should not be lost to his host, and so they will be transferred to another servant."

She looked up at the interlocutor. "Such a thing can be done?"

"Great is the power of Lord Y'Areez. Your consciousness will go into the body known as Tatak Seven by-Noom through-Katchawaa. All of the deeds and honors of Kakusa die with that name and Tatak begins as a common helm. When this Ship joins the main fleet, she will transfer to Ship One-Two-One and take command from the current helm of that vessel, who has proven unsatisfactory."

"When is this transformation to take place?"

"It already has."

She sat back and looked at her hands. They looked like the same hands. The compartment still smelled of burnt wood, and she still savored the aroma. "I did not feel any change."

"Great is the power of Lord Y'Areez," the interlocutor said, and then the two holograms winked out.

CHAPTER FORTY-ONE

An hour later, Outworld Coalition Naval
Headquarters Complex, the planet K'tok
27 September 2134

Sam looked out through the disguise which was becoming
more comfortable over time rather than less, which
worried him a little. Hopefully he wouldn't need it much
longer. Rear Admiral Goldjune had a hard time accepting
the reality of his identity, but both Te'Anna and Cassandra
had answered every question he had, and Sam had done
some answering as well. The Varoki intel officer had also
been shocked, but had taken it calmly after the initial
surprise wore off. He said very little, listened a lot, and
Sam could tell his mind was working constantly. Sam
remembered he'd met Nuvaash twice before, back when
Sam and Cassandra were still together. There had been
something about him Sam hadn't quite trusted then, and
there still was now, but he at least trusted him to be on
their side against P'Daan.

"All right," Admiral Goldjune said, "I guess I accept
that you are Lieutenant Commander Bitka. I suppose I
see the necessity of the disguise up until now. The longer

P'Daan is in the dark about you being here, the better. But we can't keep this secret from the chain of command. I've got a duty to report your presence and you'll have to answer for your actions at Destination."

"All in good time, sir," Sam said. "But why don't we deal with P'Daan first?"

"I agree, Bitka, but it's not up to me."

"That is correct, Admiral," Te'Anna said. "It is actually up to me. My rescue of Captain Bitka was conditional upon his acceptance of service to me, I believe you call it parole. For the term of that service, he is my thrall. I am, of course, willing to loan his service to you toward achieving our common end."

Goldjune looked from Sam to Te'Anna for a moment and his expression darkened. "A coerced agreement won't hold water, and I'd call the conditions Lieutenant Commander Bitka found himself in coercive, beyond which his agreement cannot bind me."

Sam smiled and nodded. "Yes, sir. Why don't you get some JAG lawyers working on that? But in the meantime, if you want Te'Anna's assistance, you're going to have to agree to her terms."

"Damned blackmail is what it is," the admiral said.

"I assure you it is not aimed at you, sir," Sam said. "I think you know what I mean."

The admiral straightened up and turned to Cassandra. "Commander, is this meeting being recorded?"

"Oh! I knew there was something I forgot to do. You know how I am sometimes, sir."

"I sure as hell do." He frowned, but turned back to Sam. "Okay, so we're off the record. First, I have one very important question. Those jump probes P'Daan sent out. Were they aimed at other *Cottohazz* systems?"

Sam looked at Te'Anna, as did everyone else.

"Oh, certainly," she answered, and Sam saw Cassandra nod as if in grim confirmation of her suspicions. If anyone would have been mentally out ahead of this move, it would have been her.

"How did he know the location of the other worlds?" Goldjune asked.

"The same way he knew to come here," Sam said. "The same way Te'Anna did. It turns out all previous points of origin of interstellar transit are encoded in the memory of each drive. The On-Living Engineers copied all the locations from *Cam Ranh Bay*. Fortunately, it's a new ship, and so had only four origin points, other than the chain of deep-space origins on our trip out to Destination. The four important points were K'tok, Rakanka, Bronstein's World, and Earth. You only picked up the high-power broadcast P'Daan's probes made at the end, but before then they were probably using low-energy tight beam to interrogate the jump drives of other vessels in the system. He must know the location of every world in the *Cottohazz* by now."

Admiral Goldjune nodded, his expression grim. He turned to Cassandra. "Looks like you were right, Cass."

"I take no pleasure in it, sir," she answered.

Goldjune turned back to Sam. "Okay. Tell us your plan, and it better be good."

Captain Beauchamp was particular about his afternoon staff meeting with the department heads on *Cam Ranh*

Bay, including the OOD on that watch attending by hologram from the bridge. Today that was Homer Alexander's turn. He lowered his helmet's visor and found himself seated at the familiar conference table with the captain, Brook, Acho, Bohannon, and Parker.

"Good morning," Beauchamp began. "I've read all your morning summaries and everything looks shipshape. Only two items on my agenda. Lieutenant Acho, what's the follow-up on that one-point-five gig laser head?"

"K'tok Base has it coming up the needle, sir. There's a maintenance shuttle standing by docked at Highstation. We should have it onboard in seven hours."

"Parker, make sure your EVA crew is ready to install it as soon as it's here. I feel naked with only one heavy laser mount. Well done, LOG.

"Next item: Captain Rodriguez on *Spratley Islands* has called a tactical holoconference of the captains and TACs from the ships in the transport division for tomorrow at 0830. She expects hostilities with the Guardians and believes every armed vessel may be pressed into service, even beat-up transports. She wants to familiarize the command staffs with enemy tactics and capabilities, and begin forming contingency plans to deal with them. Lieutenant Alexander, I recommended that you make the main presentation to the group and lead the discussion."

"Me, sir?"

"Of course, you. No one in any *Cottohazz* navy outside of this ship has fought the Guardians or the Troatta, and of our officers no one knows more about their tactics than you do. We need your expertise, Homer. Just tell us what you know, and then what you think all that means. You've got a day to put together the presentation, but don't overthink it. Just keep it simple. The rest of us are beginners at this."

Homer wasn't sure what to say, other than . . .

"Aye, aye, sir."

"Would you like me to helmet up for the conference as well, sir?" Ka'Deem Brook asked.

Beauchamp looked at him and hesitated only a moment, his face expressionless, before answering.

"I appreciate the offer, XO, but that won't be necessary."

Sam sat back in his chair and let out a huff of breath. Okay, what *was* his plan?

"Admiral, I've spent months, literally months, thinking of ways to beat those Troatta long ships, but they all involve using a jump drive. As outnumbered as we are, and without the use of our jump drives, I don't think we have many other options. I would like Vice-Captain Nuvaash to get whatever readiness information on the other *Cottohazz* warships in-system. We'll all need to pull together on this."

"Of course," the Varoki intelligence officer answered. "I believe I can provide that information immediately from my own files."

"Even the non-uBakai ships?" Sam asked.

Nuvaash smiled slightly and dipped his head to the side in a Varoki shrug. "Call it my hobby."

Cassandra laughed softly.

"Okay, good hobby," Sam said. "I especially want to know if those uBakai cruisers, or any others, have that coilgun-launched ordnance you used on us in the last war, what we called buckshot."

"Both uBakai cruisers do as well as the lone Katami cruiser. The others do not."

"Well, that's a start. But our number one priority has to be to fix our jump drives, and I don't see why we can't do it. Are Councilor Abanna Zaquaan and Choice still here?"

"All the civilian passengers from *Cam Ranh Bay* are," the admiral answered.

"Good. We need to crack the broadcast code they used, dig out the command codes, and construct a counter-command which will turn the drives back on again. The Buran councilor was the first to see the similarities in control language between the first probe and the ship control codes in the Destination system. Choice is good with cybernetic data systems and has a very powerful, logical mind. She can connect dots, make connections between different disciplines. Te'Anna can answer a lot of general questions about the drive and system interfaces."

"And if I may suggest," Cassandra added, "Lieutenant Commander Nightingale, the admiral's acting chief of cryptology, is something of a savant when it comes to cracking ciphers."

Goldjune nodded. "If that's acceptable to you, Te'Anna, it sounds as if we have a pretty good working group there. Cass, get staff on it and set them up a workspace and living quarters here in the compound. Put cots in their workspace if you want. They work around the clock until they come up with an answer. Anyone else?"

Sam nodded, and sighed. "Yes, I'd like Lieutenant

Koichi Ma in the group as well, but I understand he's still in recovery from that bug K'Irka gave him and the others."

"He's got some psychological issues they're working on as well," Cassandra said. "What is he needed for?"

"Physics. How the damned thing works. Te'Anna explained it to him, and I think understanding it upset him, but I'm convinced he understood."

"You said she can explain everything to the working group," Admiral Goldjune said.

"Yes, sir, that's true, but I'm not sure they will be able to understand its significance. Ma, as a physicist, could understand what Te'Anna meant and probably make it understandable to someone who didn't know all the math. Maybe we can find another engineering officer with a strong background in physics."

"Walter Wu," Cassandra said, and the admiral immediately nodded.

"Who's Walter Wu?" Sam asked.

"Not an engineer, but a physicist, and quite a good one," Cassandra answered, and threw a furtive glance toward Nuvaash before continuing, "at least so I've heard. He is stranded here with everyone else. Just our luck."

"I think I know where Wu is," Admiral Goldjune said, "and I'm sure he'll be eager to help. And what will you be working on, Commander Bitka?"

"An engineering project, sir, a way to give our missiles more range, a way to get through their kill zone. I'll need some help there. Specifically, I need a cruiser with a good engineering department."

"Why a cruiser? Why not a fleet auxiliary?" Goldjune asked.

"We're short of time. We won't be going far, but we need to get there quick. I need a ship with some good legs on it. Te'Anna's would do for speed but it doesn't have a fabricator division, a machine shop, or a bunch of EVA snipes."

The admiral nodded. "The *Fitz* might do for that, but it's not under my command. Well, we'll see about that next." He looked around the table for a moment. "It's a good start at the tactical end, but if we don't have a unified and reliable military striking force, it won't do us much good. Vice-Captain Nuvaash, I understand you've laid the groundwork for contacting the *Cottohazz* special envoy when he arrives. I'll want to pursue that contact as soon as practical. Cass, since you've already got Senator Ramirez y Sesma's attention, maybe you can approach him about working with the special envoy."

Sam looked at Cassandra and she studiously avoided his eyes, looking instead at the admiral and nodding seriously. A *senator*? Huh. He might need to get out of this bird suit sooner than he'd planned.

"In the meantime," the admiral continued, "we need to get Vice Admiral Stevens in on this, and I'll need to borrow you for that, Bitka, assuming Te'Anna concurs. Gordo Stevens can free up the *Fitz*. If we can get the special envoy and Admiral Stevens working with us, I'm pretty sure my good brother will see the light as well."

"I'll do whatever you need, sir," Sam said, "but I better warn you that Vice Admiral Stevens doesn't have much use for me."

"You'd be surprised, Bitka. Lot of surprises today, and before we get totally carried away with the mission, let me just say it's a privilege to meet you at long last. I admired your conduct in the last war, and your handling of the *Bay* has only added to that admiration. And by the way, damned fine set of design recommendations you sent me at BuShips on the DDR modifications. Welcome home, son, even if you do look like a big vulture—and I'll take your word for the fact that's temporary. Welcome home."

Home. He was home, wasn't he? This had become his home: these people, this navy. He nodded to the admiral but found he couldn't speak.

CHAPTER FORTY-TWO

The next afternoon, Outworld Coalition Naval
Headquarters Complex, the planet K'tok
28 September 2134

Vice-Captain Takaar Nuvaash and deputy envoy Laptoon
Haykuz waited in a VIP lounge for the arrival of the next
passenger capsule at the needle downstation, the capsule
which would carry the Honorable Arigapaa e-Lotonaa,
special envoy plenipotentiary of the *Cottohazz* Executive
Council. Nuvaash could tell from his flushed face and
twitching ears that Haykuz was nervous. Understandable,
considering both what was at stake and how far the special
envoy's station was above that of Haykuz. Nuvaash had it
easier: military rank established a comfortable and
unambiguous social positioning for those who held it.
Knowing exactly where you stood was strangely liberating,
provided you accepted it—or pretended to.

When the arrival warning tone sounded, Nuvaash and
Haykuz walked to the restricted VIP arrival area and soon
the special envoy and his surprisingly small entourage
passed through the broad exit from the customs and
security area. Nuvaash recognized the special envoy from

the numerous dossiers he had studied. He was accompanied by two armed security guards and only three staff assistants. One of the security guards was Human and female, shorter and less bulky than most Humans and nearly dwarfed by the Varoki around her. Dark hair and fine features, but otherwise undistinguished from most Humans. She shared the cold, blank eyes of the Varoki security specialist.

Human security guards were not uncommon. Humans shared a reputation for a willingness to undertake violence, and a certain animal cunning, which made them useful, and in some circles even prestigious, security guards. What was much more surprising was that one of the three Varoki staffers was also female. It was not unheard of, but extremely rare to see a Varoki female in a position of responsibility such as this, but e-Lotonaa had a reputation for eccentricity.

The special envoy exchanged a word with his staffers and then the three of them hurried off, possibly to locate and take charge of the group's baggage. E-Lotonaa and his bodyguards then approached Nuvaash and Haykuz.

"Good evening," the special envoy said. "It is evening here, is it not?"

"Yes, it is . . . well, late afternoon, Honorable Special Envoy. Nearly evening," Haykuz stammered. They exchanged shallow bows.

"And this must be Vice-Captain Takaar Nuvaash, the uBakai Speaker for The Enemy."

"Honorable Special Envoy," Nuvaash answered with his own bow.

"I see an empty private lounge," the special envoy said.

"Let us take a moment and get acquainted here, where there is less chance of our conversation being overheard and recorded." The special envoy's two guards took position outside the room, to either side of the doorway. The special envoy and the others entered the room and Nuvaash closed and locked the door behind them.

The special envoy looked at them. "This is my third trip to K'tok, and I have enjoyed none of them. It may be I will die here, but if Providence allows me to leave, I do not intend to come back again. That requires that what we do here be done *completely*, with no loose threads which someone may pull on and so unravel our tapestry. Do you understand?

"Good."

He turned to Haykuz. "I bring personal greetings from your sire. He wishes you to know you have brought pride to the family and he looks forward with pleasure to being able to welcome and congratulate you personally."

Haykuz flushed with embarrassment and pleasure, but shook his head. "That will never be possible unless we can prevail here. I was forced to speak with circumspection over even a closed diplomatic holocon channel, but the danger is enormous. We need your leadership to—"

The special envoy put his hand on Haykuz's shoulder and nodded. "Yes, yes, I know. Believe me, I could read your meaning quite clearly and I have been studying the situation to the best of my ability during the long coast in. We will see about dealing with it shortly, and you will have a role to play. Prepare to carry even more responsibility than you have so far."

He turned to Nuvaash. "I suspected you would be

present as well, Vice-Captain. I counted on it, in fact, and so did not voice such a request. No need to advertise my interest. I bring a message for you as well, Vice-Captain, from your superior."

"Admiral e-T'maa, the chief of Naval Security?"

"No, Nuvaash, your *real* superior. This is the message: *We are the arrows of destiny.*"

Nuvaash swayed unsteadily for a moment. As practiced as he was at never showing his reactions and at being prepared for every foreseeable eventuality, he had never anticipated this. The special envoy knew his personal activation code. *The special envoy!*

"Our fiery trajectories extinguish the darkness," he answered, and the special envoy nodded. Nuvaash saw Haykuz staring from one to the other in confusion and the special envoy turned his gaze to him again.

"Here is the first of the responsibilities you must carry from now forward, Haykuz. You must never reveal what you have heard in this room, or what you will hear shortly. Vice-Captain Nuvaash is an undercover agent of CSJ."

Haykuz turned to Nuvaash, his eyes wide. "The secret police? A Co-*Gozhak* provost? You?" Then he turned back to the special envoy. "Then you must be one as well?"

The special envoy smiled broadly and shook his head. "Oh, no. I am exactly what I appear to be: an official of the *Khap'uKhaana*, a diplomat and bureaucrat. More often than not, the policies we recommend to the Executive Council run counter to those of the CSJ, sometimes diametrically so, but our principal goal is the same: survival of the *Cottohazz*. We usually differ as to how that is to be accomplished, but occasionally we agree even on that. When the commandant of CSJ, Field Marshal Lieutenant e-Loyolaan, learned of my mission here to K'tok, he made available the services of the one agent he knew to be well-placed."

The special envoy turned to Nuvaash again. "Very well-placed, although it appears largely by chance, as this was not your assignment."

"Entirely by chance, Honorable Special Envoy. Chance dictated I was rescued from the wreck of the uBakai flagship and thus captured, chance dictated I would share a needle capsule with the Human intelligence officer Atwater-Jones, and chance helped those two coincidences move me to my current position."

The special envoy nodded. "Your commandant is curious how it was that you survived the destruction of the flagship and yet the object of your surveillance, Admiral e-Lapeela, did not."

He seemed to be waiting for an answer, and Nuvaash remembered what his friend Cassandra had said during the Board of Inquiry. "I am not at liberty to discuss that," he said.

"Of course, I understand," the special envoy said. "The less I know about your former mission the better, at least for now."

Nuvaash relaxed a bit. He did not wish to lie, but he also did not think telling the special envoy the truth—that he, Nuvaash, had *executed* his former commander— would help them build a relationship of trust.

"Now, Nuvaash," the special envoy said, "begin by telling me what you know about the Guardian Te'Anna, and then your assessment of these three Human admirals."

"Perhaps I should tell you about Bitka as well, Honorable Special Envoy."

"The missing Human ship captain? Is he important?"

Haykuz laughed, and then gulped his laughter down when Nuvaash and the special envoy looked at him, nearly choking on it and turning a shade of purplish red. To Nuvaash's surprise, the special envoy smiled.

"Perhaps you *had* better tell me."

Gordo Stevens knew something was rotten when Jake Goldjune offered to come up-needle for a face-to-face but wanted it on Highstation, not *Olympus Mons*. Highstation was part of Jake's command—K'tok Base Area—not Gordo's First Combined Fleet, so maybe it was a turf thing, or wanting the home field advantage in whatever negotiations were going to take place. That made sense, but he didn't buy it. He thought it was because Jake didn't want to be anywhere near his brother Cedric, the CNO. But why? Gordo knew not to ask, though. As long as he could pretend it was just a turf thing, taking the meeting was not a deliberate act of insubordination. Once he knew what Jake wanted, then he'd decide what to do.

It was funny—a month ago he'd never have agreed to this. Too politically dangerous. He'd have gone to the CNO right away. That had changed, though. It wasn't just careers and pensions at stake anymore. Gordo understood that. It was hard getting used to, and he wished things could get back to business as usual, but he didn't see how. It was like navigating without a chart. He hated it.

The Marine lance corporal led him to the meeting room Jake had reserved and showed him in: a small room, and Jake was the only other one there. He rose from his chair and extended his hand, but his expression remained serious. Never any false *bonhomie* from Jacob Goldjune, and Gordo liked that.

"Gordo, thanks for taking this meeting. I know you must be busy as hell."

"I am, Jake, but I figured this must be important for you to come up here and want it face to face. Are we on the record or off?"

"On, but the record is going to stay sealed for a while. You'll see why and I won't keep you in suspense. I am going to fulfill a wish you expressed a few days ago." Jake squinted and turned aside, then said, "Yeoman Saud, have the lieutenant commander join us."

The door opened and the officer entered.

"Jesus Christ, Jake! He looks just like Bitka. Where'd you find him? Hey, what have you got going here?"

"Not what you think," Jake answered. "He doesn't *look* like Bitka. This *is* Lieutenant Commander Samuel Bitka, in the flesh."

Gordo looked at him and shook his head. "Bullshit! Not fucking possible. How did he get here? Magic?"

"The Guardian Te'Anna brought him."

"*Bullshit.* My people scoured every inch of her ship."

"He was disguised as the third Guardian. Even fooled me, but I watched him take the disguise off myself. Damnedest thing I ever did see."

"The hell you say." Gordo stared at Bitka again. He didn't just look like him, he had that . . . *attitude*. Maybe more so. *Shit*, it really was him, wasn't it?

"Well, Bitka, you fucked me over again. My financial

advisor said not to sell my Simki-Traak stock, said only suckers sell when the price is low, said it was sure to bounce back. Now this news your crew brought back—hell. Simki-Traak and all the other old houses are stone cold dead, aren't they?"

"Possibly so, sir."

"Yeah, and there goes my retirement. Guess I'll have to keep wearing this uniform until they kick my ass out, which might not be that long once the CNO gets wind of this meeting. So, you're probably going to fuck me one last time. Is there a reason for this meeting, other than to torpedo what's left of my career?"

"Bitka's got some ideas, but he needs some things I can't give him," Goldjune said. "You can."

"Uh-huh. God, I'm afraid to ask. Okay, what do you need, Bitka?"

"Sir, I need twenty-four Mark Five fire lance missiles, and a light cruiser with working fabricators and a good EVA team. I understand USS *John Fitzgerald Kennedy* might be available."

Gordo looked at Bitka for a while. He'd known young lieutenants and lieutenant commanders who could stand there and talk to a vice admiral without fear or bluster. Some were academy-educated whiz kids who knew they were destined for stars themselves. Others were just dumb fucks who didn't know any better. Bitka sure wasn't the first type and Gordo didn't think he was the second, either.

"Is that all?" he asked with sarcasm.

Bitka shifted his weight and looked down before replying. "Well, sir, there's also a CPO named Joyce Menzies, recovering from reconstructive surgery on USS

Mercy Island but due for release. She was my CPO-Weaps on *Puebla*. Hell of a missile monkey. I could use her, too, if you could arrange it."

"Missile monkey, huh? I assume you two are aware the *Fitz* doesn't have a coil gun so it can't shoot those Mark Fives."

"'Course we are," Goldjune said with a smile.

Legally, this was entirely his call. He was the fleet commander and he didn't have to ask permission to move one ship in his command or shift around a few missiles. It was Bitka's presence that made the situation potentially explosive—Bitka's along with the CNO's. This wasn't something the CNO *had* to be told, but it was something he would *want* to be, since he was right next door in *Olympus Mons*. Why was his brother Jake reluctant to let him know? For that matter, Gordo wondered why *he* was himself reluctant to bring the CNO in on this. Probably because of all those private meetings between the CNO and Senator Ramirez y Sesma, and a sudden silence from him about how Gordo was to prepare for the coming fight. He didn't like what that added up to.

Gordo looked at the other two officers and knew he was standing on the edge of a cliff. The thought scared him, but he was also getting really, really tired of being scared of all this political bullshit.

"Well, my ass is really hanging out here, but you got it, every bit of it, provided the plan makes any sense."

"Happy to hear that, Gordo," Jake said. "May as well let you know, I've got some class-A composite-armored ass coverage for you. Open your commlink and I'll transfer it."

Gordo felt a tingle and squinted up the incoming document. Then he laughed.

"All military forces in the system are officially called into *Cottohazz* service? What the hell, Jake, you could have saved me some sweat by just telling me up front. You just want to see me squirm in the hot seat?"

"The truth is, Gordo, I wanted you to have the chance to do the right thing on your own. You did."

"So, who is this leatherhead e-Lotonaa?" Gordo asked, ignoring Goldjune's compliment.

"Never met him before today but he's got some starch in him, and he knows his mind. I think we could have done a lot worse."

Gordo nodded. Maybe so. They sure weren't getting what he would call decisive direction from the CNO. "Okay, Bitka, tell me what that devious mind of yours has come up with."

"Oh, actually sir, there is something else I need."

Goldjune started laughing then. "Yes, and it's only a couple *billion* dollars worth of Navy hardware he's going to blow up in the process. You'll love it, Gordo."

CHAPTER FORTY-THREE

Two days later, **Outworld Coalition Naval Headquarters Complex, the planet K'tok 30 September 2134**

"A senator, huh?" Sam asked as Cassandra sank into the armchair across from him in the field-grade officers' lounge. They were the only two there. Sam hoped it stayed that way.

"Are you jealous?"

He thought about her question for a while, really thought about it, examined what he felt and why, and then shook his head. "I would have been before, but not now. So why did I ask? I guess it surprised me is all. A senator doesn't sound like that much fun."

"How do you know how much fun a senator can be behind closed doors?" she demanded, but it sounded false to him, sounded defensive.

"You willing to live your life behind closed doors? You're a private person, Cass, but not out of shame, and not to cater to someone else's shame, either."

She looked away before replying. "You are going with the fleet."

"Sort of. Vice Admiral Stevens appointed me his Tac boss. I'm taking your pal Nuvaash along, found him a berth in the N-2 shop."

"I thought you didn't trust Nuvaash."

"Well, I trust him enough for this. We need a good liaison with the Varoki fleet elements, and he knows their ships' capabilities better than anyone else around. We're heading up-needle this afternoon, but I'm bound for a light cruiser, the *Fitz*. I'll shove off this evening. The rest of the fleet—what there is of it here—starts accelerating tomorrow. We want the point of contact to be as far from K'tok as we can get, and with as high a closing velocity as we can manage."

She looked at her hands folded in her lap and the silence grew.

"Bow-on Bitka," she whispered.

"Bullshit. That's not who I—"

"Don't lie to me!" she snapped, suddenly turning on him, eyes intense. "For God's sake don't lie to me about that. Not now. That's exactly who you are. You think I don't know how your mind works? All these different schemes you're working on, all these different forces you and Stevens are trying to assemble … It's not to put P'Daan off balance, not to bluff him, not to confuse him or trick him into some elaborate mistake. You aren't fencing with him. Your plan is simply to smash him, any way and *every way* you can. You see, I've been studying the logs and archives on the Fourth Battle of K'tok, the climax of the last war. I know what your attack plan was."

"Commodore Bonaventure commanded," Sam said quietly.

"Yes, but it was your plan. His log says as much. And what was that plan? Drive into the heart of the uBakai fleet, fight your way right through it, and come out the far side, doing as much mayhem along the way as you could. You probably don't know much British naval history, but in 1666 one of the largest naval battles in history took place, in the English Channel between the Royal Navy and the Dutch. Part of the outnumbered British fleet was all but engulfed by the Dutch fleet at one point, seemed to be swallowed up by it, but then emerged from the far side, *erupted* out having fought their way through in fire and thunder. They won a victory so remarkable the poet John Dryden wrote about it in one of his masterworks, *Annus Mirabilis*, the *Year of Miracles*. One verse has always stayed with me. I understand you've developed an appreciation for poetry."

"One poem, anyway," Sam answered.

"Well, here is another for you:

Our little fleet was now engaged so far,
That, like the sword-fish in the whale, they fought:
The combat only seem'd a civil war,
Till through their bowels, we our passage wrought.

"He could have been writing about Fourth K'tok. That's you, Bitka: *through their bowels*. You won't nibble at the edges of the Troatta fleet, will you? You aim to gut it."

Sam felt a coolness wash over him, a calmness and clarity which once would have been alien to him but, since deciding to turn himself over to K'Irka on Seven Echo Highstation, had come with greater frequency. "There's no other way."

She looked up into his face, her own forehead creased in distress. "There's no other way *for you*. That's who you are, Bitka. Don't pretend it's not, and for God's sake, don't be ashamed of it."

Don't be ashamed of it. That was an interesting way to put it. Was he ashamed? No, not really, but he wasn't entirely comfortable with the notion, either. But that didn't change the truth of what she said.

"Yeah, I know you're right. I guess I've known a long time, ever since the *Third* battle of K'tok, not the Fourth."

"Where you destroyed the uKaMaat salvo cruiser," she said.

"You *have* been doing your homework. Well, you always were thorough and methodical." Sam stood up. "Time for me to exhibit the same qualities. I have three staff meetings before I catch the needle. I'd hoped we'd have a chance to talk more, get some things said. I guess that's going to have to wait. Maybe I can put your mind at ease on one score. I won't be with the main fleet. I have another job, and it doesn't involve even getting into the line of fire."

Cassandra shook her head and stood. "No plan survives contact with the enemy. In my experience, most don't even survive contact with reality. I don't count on you coming back this time, Bitka. Hope sometimes makes things harder, not easier. I did listen to your holovid diary."

"What did you think?"

She closed her eyes. "Heartbreaking, to be perfectly honest."

Sam shook his head. "Didn't mean it to be. Well, I was a long way from home, frightened and lonely, and there were some things I hadn't worked out yet. By the time I had, there wasn't as much time to do those entries."

"Or as much need," she said quietly.

"Or as much need," he agreed.

"So, let me at least say this much to you, Bitka. Of course, I love you. *Of course,* I do. But I am not certain I am in love *with* you, and I am even less certain we could manage to build a satisfactory life together."

"*Satisfactory?*"

Her brow creased in anger. "Oh, don't be an ass, Bitka! That's the way I talk, as you very well know, and you also know exactly what I mean: a joint household in which we would both feel happy and satisfied and fulfilled."

Sam couldn't keep from smiling. He hadn't said it to set her off, but he really did love to see her angry— preferably not at him. Anyone who thought the warrior spirit was incompatible with femininity had never seen Cass under a full head of steam. Boudicca must have looked like this, exhorting her Celtic warriors to charge the hated Roman legions, or Joan of Arc getting ready to take back another French city from the Limies.

"Happy, satisfied, and fulfilled," she repeated. "Is there something you would care to add to that list?"

"You didn't mention sex."

"Yes I did, three times. It's simply not all I mentioned. Now go, and don't tell me we'll talk when you get back. I am ... superstitious about pronouncements of that sort. God bless you, Sam Bitka." She gave him a quick kiss on the cheek, hugged him harder than he thought she was capable of, and then she was gone.

★ ★ ★

Ten million kilometers above the plane of the ecliptic, and closing on K'tok at fifteen kilometers per second, Helm Tatak Seven by-Noom through-Katchawaa—who had once been called Kakusa by-Vrook through-Kuannawaa, but through the magic of Lord Y'Areez had been transformed into another body, one which looked and felt exactly like the old one, but certainly was different because Lord Y'Areez assured her it was so—*that* increasingly skeptical Troatta of uncertain name sat in her command chair, and she brooded.

Guardians lied! Their powers were great, including the power to make life and bend space. But really, their *devices* did those things, didn't they? Claiming credit for the work of devices was one thing, but lying about a miraculous transformation which never took place was something else. The idea of the transformation was absurd. There were still three small nicks missing from the carapace of her strong-side forearm, chips broken off when an atmosphere circulator had dropped on her. When they transferred her mind to a different body, did they transfer the nicks as well? And how did they get that body into her compartment? And where had her old body gone? No, it was all clearly a lie, and it was a lie *aimed at another Guardian*. She was just incidental. P'Daan demands punishment for her disobedience. Y'Areez kills the miscreant—her. But he doesn't want to lose the services of a trained helm, and so makes up this lie to satisfy P'Daan.

Guardians quarrel. And they didn't just lie to each other. There were now Guardians on both sides of this war, which made her wonder about the two other great

wars the Troatta had fought, led by Y'Areez, always against
rebellious races, or races led by demons. The enemy they
fought had always thought *they* were led by a Guardian
as well. They were mistaken, weren't they? It had always
been an impostor, a false god who had deceived their
enemies and seduced them into wickedness, for which
they paid a terrible price. Wasn't that what the
interlocutors told them? But *Guardians lied*.

Guardians erred. P'Daan's handling of their eight ships
had been embarrassing until it became deadly and tragic.
Tatak-who-had-been-Kakusa could have done much
better. Most of the helms in the fleet could have, and
P'Daan was a Guardian! Y'Areez had never made mistakes
such as those, and she had assumed that was because he
was a Guardian. But no. His skill was independent of his
identity as a Guardian, wasn't it? Otherwise, P'Daan
would have shared it.

And Y'Areez had also made an error. He had left Tatak-
who-had-been-Kakusa alive. The thought chilled her. She
shuddered with fear thinking that at some point Y'Areez
might recognize his error and correct it, but so far not.
She had been willing to die before, willing to give her life
for her disobedience because she believed doing so was a
way to better serve Y'Areez, her God. Now she had
doubts.

New helm-thing, Ship One-Two-One murmured
through the arm contacts of the control station.

"Yes, Ship."

*Lord Y'Areez desires audience by holocommune. Are
you ready to confront God?*

"I am, Ship," she answered, although suddenly she was

far from ready. Had God repented his error? The hologram of God and his interlocutor materialized in the bridge space. Y'Areez again towered over her, but the effect was slightly marred by the fact his lower legs seemed embedded in the machinery console on the left side of the bridge. Only a hologram—not his actual physical presence, but she had always known that.

"Helm Tatak Seven by-Noom through-Katchawaa. Great is the power of Lord Y'Areez, and great is his mercy," the interlocutor said.

"Great indeed," Tatak/Kakusa replied.

"Your essence was kept alive for a purpose. You have fought the *Cottohazz*-things, commanded the eight Ships of Lord Y'Areez at Lord P'Daan's Realm. How will they attack us?"

Tatak/Kakusa withdrew her arms from the control sleeves, folded them across her torso, and held her shoulders. She wanted her breathing flanks open as she took a moment to pant and fight off the effect of her first flush of panic. She also needed to gather her thoughts, give as good advice as she could, but not pretend it was worth more than in truth it was.

"Noble servant of Lord Y'Areez, I will gladly answer your question, but I must make three things clear. First, we fought a single ship, and so how that ship fought will not tell us how a fleet fights. Second, they fought against pairs of ships, not a combined fleet, and so their tactics will not necessarily be the same. Third, the ship we fought was commanded by S'Bitka, who was clearly an ungoverned being of erratic behavior, and may not reflect the practices of others. In any case, S'Bitka is P'Daan's prisoner and so will not play a role in our fight."

There was a pause in which an exchange between Y'Areez and the interlocutor might have taken place. The nightshade-painted male then turned back to Tatak/Kakusa. "What you say is true and Y'Areez knew these truths when we came here, so speak."

Tatak/Kakusa took several deep breaths to calm herself and then began. "The *Cottohazz*-things use their hellstars to blind our sensors and cover their approach, and the approach of their missiles. They launch swarms of them, but we believe many of those objects are not hellstars, but decoys, making it harder to know which contact to engage. They are clever at striking simultaneously from different directions. Fighting well away from a planetary body is wise, as they use the world's gravity to sculpt the course of their hellstars. I believe they will split their force of ships in order to strike from different directions. I also believe the lower our closing rate, the longer our main guns will have to destroy the approaching hellstars and their decoys. The fleet's current speed is adequate."

After a short consultation, the interlocutor spoke again. "You mention only their hellstars. Are these their only weapons?"

"S'Bitka threatened that they had weapons he had not used on us, but we could not verify the truth of that claim. Hellstars are the only weapons S'Bitka used the two times we fought him. The record of the fight at P'Daan's World shows him using coherent light weapons against satellites, but they would have much less range than our own beam weapons."

When she finished, Y'Areez remained motionless for

long seconds. God was inscrutable, but she wondered if he was thinking more of what she had just told him, or about what he should do about her. The nightshade-painted interlocutor shifted his weight after perhaps a minute and looked at Y'Areez, who bent his head slightly in a show of assent. The interlocutor turned to her.

"Lord Y'Areez is pleased. Continue to serve him well. Great is the power of Lord Y'Areez."

And then they were gone. Just as well. She did not know how long she could maintain her façade of worship in the face of mounting lies and errors from her omniscient and infallible god.

CHAPTER FORTY-FOUR

Twelve hours later, on board USS *John Fitzgerald Kennedy* (the *Fitz*), CLS-222
1 October 2134

Captain Rockaway met Sam in the receiving bay of the *Fitz* with a salute and a handshake as the chief bosun's mate piped him aboard.

"Welcome back," she said. "You're looking good, Bitka, for someone we all figured as dead or worse."

Sadie Rockaway looked almost the same as when he'd last seen her, almost but not quite. The lower left side of her face had a slightly shiny look to it, which of course "Rocky" would never have considered toning down with makeup. That was the only evidence Sam could see of the reconstructive surgery she'd gone through to repair the injuries she'd suffered in the final battle of the uBakai War. Her expression, which had always been serious, looked strained.

She'd briefly been his commanding officer in that battle, only for a couple hours, from the time Commodore Bonaventure was killed until her own ship was knocked out. After that, no one was in charge. They'd worked together well then, but he did not notice any sign of pleasure in seeing him again.

"Thank you, Ma'am. Good to be aboard. Congratulations on the command," he said, looking around the docking bay, which was similar to that on the *Bay*, but smaller. "They got you back on your legs pretty quickly."

"Yeah," she said, and then nodded to the chief bosun's mate, who waved her side party to take Sam's luggage and follow her toward the hatch aft. Rockaway watched them go and as soon as the hatch clicked shut behind them, she turned back to Sam.

"So, enough chit-chat. When I said welcome back, I meant back to the *Cottohazz*, back to Human space, back home in general. I have to tell you, I'm not all that excited to see you on my ship. I still have nightmares about the fight here at K'tok. That was *your* plan."

Sam almost took a step back, surprised by the display of animosity. Sadie Rockaway had a reputation as one of the toughest, most professional captains in Destroyer Squadron Two, their former unit, and she hadn't blinked once in the long, confused fighting around K'tok. Had her wounds and close brush with death taken something out of her? Or had she just been a really good actor? Or what?

"Um . . . I didn't realize you objected. You didn't say anything before."

"It all happened so fast I didn't have much time to think, just do. Later, in the hospital, I had a lot of time to think about it. To remember the crazy thing we did."

What was that line from the poem Cass had quoted?

"Till through their bowels, we our passage wrought," he said.

"What?"

"A poem a friend of mine quoted to me, said it reminded her of what we did at Fourth K'tok. Shot our way right through their guts and came out the other side. She didn't exactly mean it as praise, either, but she did say not to be ashamed of it. It's what I know, Rockaway. If you've got some better ideas, I'm all ears."

She looked away and shook her head. "No. Maybe there wasn't any better way to approach the problem, but . . . you didn't have to *enjoy* it so goddamned much. I just hate the nightmares, that's all." She turned back to him. "Do you have nightmares?"

"Not about that."

After his reception from Rockaway, Sam wasn't sure what to expect from Chief Menzies, but when she saw him her face lit up with a grin.

"Captain Bitka!" She turned from the workbench in forward engineering, moved toward him half a step, almost as if to hug him, then remembered herself and came to attention, magnetic boots holding her to the deck.

"At ease, Chief," Sam said and held out his hand to shake hers. He saw the same evidence of scar tissue on her hands as he'd seen on Rockaway's face, more noticeable here. A liquid hydrogen leak had seriously injured her hands in the last battle of the uBakai war. In a sense, her hands were her life. Music was her real passion, and her civilian career.

"Good to see you," he said. "How are the hands doing?"

She held them up and flexed them.

"Good enough to bolt missiles together," she answered.

"How about for keyboard?" he asked.

"Oh, yes, sir. You been gone, so you didn't know, but I formed a local band—mostly swabbies like us. We been playing holoconcerts beamed down planetside. Been drawing real good, over ten thousand last show."

"That many?" Sam said. "Who's your audience? Service personnel?"

"No, sir. Mostly civilians—Varoki civilians from the colony. *Great* fans, sir! Really into *Terrakultur*, you know? Only thing is, they can only clap on the one and three. Tried to show 'em how to hit the two and four, but they just *can't* get it."

Sam laughed. "Well, keep at it, Menzies. Maybe you can show them the light. So, tell me what you think of my crazy idea for long-range shooting."

She nodded, but her expression became guarded.

"Very interesting idea, sir," she said. "Revolutionary even. Should really surprise them."

Sam waited for more and then shook his head. "Come on, Chief. I didn't get you assigned here to kiss my ass and tell me how smart I am. What's wrong with it?"

"Well . . . too many *ostie de crisse* moving parts, sir. All these things gotta happen in just the right order, and then they gotta fire simultaneously, it's like . . . A-B-C-D-Z and then a *de saint-sacrament* miracle occurs. Like the nose cones. They all have to eject and clear away before the tracker heads can make any target locks. But the missiles aren't going anywhere in real space, so why even have the nose cones on? And the missiles are mounted facing forward so they release and then turn laterally to find targets. Why not mount them *facing out*? And these securing brackets look like they'd take a couple gees of acceleration, but they don't have to take *any*, so why have them, and then have to have these explosive bolts to separate the warheads from the ordnance carrier—all of which have to fire simultaneously? Why not replace the brackets with a *de crisse* piece of dental floss? Well, little more than that, but you know what I mean, sir."

Sam grinned. "Yeah, I know what you mean. Make it so, Chief."

A tingle at the base of Sam's neck alerted him to an incoming comm. He squinted his menu open and saw Captain Rockaway's ID. Sam held up his hand to Menzies and turned to the side.

"Yes, Captain?" he said.

Commander Bitka, we're getting an incoming comm you need to see. Would you join me on the auxiliary bridge?

"Yes Ma'am, right away." He cut the connection and turned back to Menzies.

"I have to go. We've got about nine hours to high orbit. Get the design modifications locked down. Once we make stable orbit and cut the acceleration, I want to start cranking the fabricators right away. Make this thing work, Chief. Oh, and . . . where the hell is the auxiliary bridge?"

Sam found the auxiliary bridge empty except for Rockaway in the command chair. Sam slipped into the TAC One chair to her right and buckled himself in.

"I was a little harsh when you came aboard," Rockaway said without looking at him.

"It's nothing," Sam said.

"I'm trying to apologize," she said, turning to look at him. The anger in her voice suggested otherwise.

"Okay," Sam said, "go ahead."

"God, you're an asshole," she said, and she punched the button on her console that lit up the main tactical display in the front of the room.

That must have been the wrong thing for him to say, but suddenly he didn't care. "You're not exactly the first person to notice that about me," he said.

The holodisplay darkened for a moment and then Sam was face-to-face with P'Daan, whose head filled the air only meters in front of him and loomed over him, easily ten times life size. Sam's muscles tightened and he felt as if the acceleration chair was pressing him toward the image.

I know that S'Bitka has escaped and is among you.

The commlink translated the strangely melodic speech of the Guardian, the words seeming to echo in Sam's head.

As retribution for the bombardment of the world you call Destie-Four, this fleet will bombard the surface of the planet you call K'tok, and will destroy every large structure on its surface. Then we will travel to the Human homeworld and bombard it. Then we will accept the surrender of the underspecies of this Cottohazz of yours, and destroy all those who resist. All of this is S'Bitka's doing. As long as he lives, this will never end.

Then the image clicked off and the room fell absolutely silent except for the faint hum of machinery from somewhere. Sam realized he was wet with perspiration and his hands trembled.

"You let yourself be *his* prisoner to get your crew

home?" Rockaway said and then shook her head. "Okay, Bitka, you and I got off on the wrong foot. Let's try this again. Are you going to be able to kill that son of a bitch? Because he needs killing."

"Believe me, we're working on it," Sam said. "But here's the thing that's bothering me right now. P'Daan's big fleet that showed up right after he shut off the jump drives and sent out all those jump couriers—that fleet must have been waiting out in deep space, no more than a single jump away. One of the jump courier missiles he sent out in that big wave of departures had to have been to it to call it here, because it showed up immediately, right?"

"Right," she said.

"Aside from that fleet, we haven't picked up a single jump emergence signature in the K'tok system since I got here in Te'Anna's ship."

"Not as far as I know," she said. "So what?"

"So . . . how does P'Daan know I escaped?"

Four hours later, Te'Anna waited for the holocon circuit to become active and struggled with a sea of unfamiliar and contradictory emotions. She must have known feelings like this once. Otherwise she would not have the capacity to feel them now. Had she forgotten? Can someone forget to *feel*? They can forget to feel for others, she supposed. But they can remember, too.

The circuit came alive and Bitka appeared.

"Captain Bitka. You look well as a Human, although I have to say you look better as H'Stus than H'Stus does. I am very happy to hear you will not be directly involved in the upcoming battle. I would not like for you to expire sooner than necessary, although really it is not an absolute necessity for you to do so at all. But I am trying to respect the latticework of rules you seem intent to impose on yourself, even if they make little sense to me. Aren't we to speak with Lieutenant Ma?"

"In a moment," he said. "I wanted a word with you alone first. There's something I've been wondering. Why didn't P'Daan ever come to gloat once I was his prisoner? I mean, he did that one time, sent that one message, but that was it."

Oh, *that* question, she thought. She sometimes forgot how clever he was for someone his age. She thought about trying to dissemble, but what was the point? He would work his way through it eventually.

"What was there for him to gloat about? You beat him. Your ship and crew escaped and you were the instrument of delivering yourself into captivity. He had not yet won."

"Not yet," Bitka repeated, and he nodded as if he expected the answer. "He let me go. Did you know he was using you?"

Te'Anna rocked her head from side to side in barely contained mirth. "Did I know? *It was my idea!* How else could we have engineered an escape except with his acquiescence? We had already sided with you once; he was hardly likely to trust us. Of course, I had to make him believe he thought of it. But he believes he is more intelligent than everyone, so that part was not difficult."

"Son of a bitch," he said. "Cass thought P'Daan was waiting for something before making his move, and he was: *us*. They knew we were coming all along."

"P'Daan knew, but I doubt he has shared the

information with anyone else. After the ships and Troatta lives it cost Y'Areez to capture you, I doubt the news P'Daan had let you go to assist the defense would be well received.

"Oh, Captain Bitka, if you could see your face. The irony! P'Daan found your capture unsatisfying because it was your doing, not his. Now you find your escape unsatisfying because it was his doing, not ours. I would say you are suited to each other, except I know you both and you have very little else in common."

"So, this is just going to go on and on until one of us is dead?" he asked.

Te'Anna regarded Bitka. "It distresses you to be at the center of this. Many of your species would be flattered, but not you. P'Daan may eventually lose interest, but not during your lifespan. I suspect that, for your purposes, you are correct: it will go on until one of you is dead."

She saw the news sat heavily on him, as she suspected it would. That was why she had not told him sooner, but she had always suspected he would puzzle it out. He looked up.

"You still have my gratitude, Te'Anna. P'Daan's dissatisfaction might have been expressed in a number of different ways, most of which would have left me dead or altered beyond recognition. Thank you for giving me back my life and my freedom. Now, I see Lieutenant Ma is waiting to join us."

How odd, Te'Anna thought, *that he considered himself free.*

Another figure appeared to their side, a figure she at first did not recognize.

"Oh! Lieutenant Ma," she said in anguish. "What we have done to you!"

He looked only vaguely Human. His proportions had changed, making him squatter, broader, rounder. His features were altered, coarsened, and had partially disappeared in facial fat. His hair was gone but he now had short, stiff, but widely spaced bristles over much of his body, at lease the parts Te'Anna could see. He had been a handsome creature before, and now was hideous.

He held up his hand and looked at it, turning it so he could see the back covered by bristles and the smooth palm in sequence. When he spoke, his words were somewhat slurred from the altered shape of his mouth and tongue.

"It's not so bad. You get used to it and it isn't permanent. The antidote stopped the retrovirus, but the physiological changes were so traumatic it would have killed us to change back right away. We're building up our strength, though, and when we're strong enough . . . well, this time we'll have pain blockers. That will make it easier."

She saw Bitka nod in understanding, and she remembered the heartrending sounds of his agony. *What we did to them!*

"Te'Anna," Captain Bitka said, "the reason I called this meeting was the working group tells me you have held back some information about the jump drive. They aren't sure it is critical to solving the problem, but—"

"*It is not!*" she said, cutting him off. "There is no need for them to know everything."

Bitka watched her for a few moments, and he looked sad.

"Te'Anna, I owe you almost everything my life will be from here forward. There is no limit to my debt to you, and I think I know you as well or better than any of us do. I asked Lieutenant Ma to be here because I think he is the reason you won't share this information with the working group."

Te'Anna wanted to just turn the cameras off, get up and walk away. She wanted to be anywhere but in the presence of Lieutenant Ma, that horrific reminder of what *Guardian* must mean to these people, what it was beginning to mean to her. But her debt to Ma was too great to walk away from.

"Te'Anna, you don't have to be guilty about what K'Irka did to me and the Marines," Ma said. "You didn't do it. You *saved* us, made K'Irka cure us."

"That is not my greatest burden, Lieutenant Ma. As terrible as this transformation of you has been, my words hurt you more deeply, damaged you more thoroughly. I am so truly sorry for that."

Bitka looked to Lieutenant Ma, who rubbed his eyes with the palms of his hands and then nodded. "You mean what you told me about how the jump drive works. Well, I figure you didn't *mean* to destroy my faith in reality, drive me half insane. At least half. You had no way of knowing how I would react. It was just a mistake."

"No, Lieutenant Ma, it was not a mistake at all. What you suffered is precisely what I intended, and that is what I regret: my *intent*. My fault was not a deficiency of judgment, but rather one of character. I will never again be the instrument of another sentient being losing their way. Never again. Never."

"But, Te'Anna," Bitka said, "we are going to need that information. The working group may need it now. Later, if we're going to resist P'Daan and the others like him, we're going to have to understand this technology. You know that."

She did know that, she knew all of it, but she also knew she would never again risk telling a human what she had told Lieutenant Ma.

"No," she said.

The three of them sat in silence, Bitka and Ma staring at her, Te'Anna not knowing how the others felt, but feeling her misery as if it were a heavy, wet cloak wrapped around her, chilling her, smothering her, weighing her down. After a long silence, Lieutenant Ma nodded.

"I understand. Some burdens are too heavy to carry. But I owe you my life, Te'Anna, so I'll carry this burden for you. Captain, if you'll set up the holocon, I'll brief the working group on everything I know. This is my gift to you, Te'Anna. Oh, and Captain? We need your head clear and firing on all cylinders, not full of worms. Sit this one out, sir. I'm serious."

Choice actually felt dizzy when she saw what Lieutenant Ma had become. She had disliked him intensely, hated his arrogance and casual dismissal of anything which did not line up with his narrow and judgmental world view, but she would never have wished this on him. She looked away, her eyes falling on the others, and she saw Lieutenant Commander Nightingale's face twist in revulsion, the physicist Walter Wu simply stared, his unlit cigar forgotten for the moment. She could not tell what the Buran linguist felt, or if it had any reaction at all.

Ma stared past them, his eyes too wide open to be actually focused on anything. After a while he winced, as if a tooth had gone bad in his mouth, or he remembered a lie he'd told years ago which still shamed him.

"I guess it starts with Einstein—"

"Well, that figures," Nightingale, their "commander" said.

"—and Podolsky and Rosen," Ma continued.

"Who were they?"

Ma shrugged. "Couple more physicists. The three of them came up with this thing, the EPR Paradox it's called."

"EPR?" Nightingale said. "What does EPR stand for?"

Walter Wu shook his head. "It stands for Einstein, Podolsky, and Rosen, okay?"

"Oh, sure. Okay, I'm with you. Go on."

"This is very approximate," Ma said, "but try to follow. Particles alternate between existing as probability waves and then sometime as actual particles. When they are actual particles, not waves, they have certain characteristics, one of which is spin. When a particle is in its wave state, you can't tell its spin, but if you measure it, it drops from its wave state to its particle state. One principle of quantum physics is that its spin is random. Not only can we not tell its actual spin while it's in its wave state, the universe itself doesn't know until the instant the particle drops into its particle state."

"That's kind of weird," Nightingale said, and beside him Walter Wu laughed.

"Oh, we're just getting started with weird," Ma said. "It's possible for two particles to be *entangled*, which means we know their spin characteristics are balanced: one particle will spin up and one down, but while they are in their wave state the universe doesn't know which is which. It just knows that if one spins up, the other spins down.

"So, Einstein, Podolsky and Rosen set up this thought experiment: what if you could separate two quantum entangled particles while in their wave state and just measure one of them. Logically, the other particle has to collapse to its particle state and exhibit the opposite spin characteristic. The thing is, it has to do so instantly, and since the universe doesn't know what its spin was before, how does it communicate that spin to it? You've separated them, moved them away from each other, You see the problem? The speed of light is an absolute speed limit, but somehow that information is transmitted from one entangled particle to another *instantaneously*, which is faster than light speed. By what mechanism does the universe transmit that information? Einstein called it, 'Spooky action at a distance.'"

"But you said it was just a thought experiment," Nightingale said.

"Sure, it was for those guys, two centuries ago. They didn't have atom smashers to play with. We do. We've been running the experiment in particle accelerators since before the Varoki showed up. It works just as predicted: measure one particle and the other collapses from its wave state as well. We can actually watch it happen in the lab."

"How does it work?" Nightingale asked.

"Well, that's a hell of a question, sir. Einstein said the paradox shown by the experiment meant one of two things. It might mean quantum physics was all wrong, and the experiment wouldn't actually come out that way. But since the experiment works, we know that's not it."

"What was his second thing?"

"That there's something wrong with our understanding of the concept of *location*." Ma paused and his eyes again got that far-away look. In a few moments, he came back to them and looked around at all of their faces in turn.

"If a tree falls in the forest," he said, "and there is somebody there to hear it, does it make a sound?"

"You mean if *nobody* is there, don't you?" Choice asked.

"I mean what I said."

"No, it does not," the Buran said in its dead, hollow voice. "Sound is made by the being hearing it. There is no sound in the universe outside the brains of living beings. There are only vibrations in a solid or fluid medium. Auditory sensors convert those vibrations to a sensation in the brain we equate with sound."

Ma nodded. "Very good. There is no sound in the universe, except in our heads. Sound is an illusion. So is sight. There are electromagnetic waves of different intensities and wavelengths. Our eyes interpret radiation in what we call the visible spectrum as shapes and colors, but those exist only in our head. The universe doesn't actually *look* like anything. Scent is an illusion. Taste, an illusion. Touch, an illusion. We already knew that. But what is far more difficult to grasp is that *location* is an illusion as well, although we should have known it two centuries ago, when Niels Bohr was unravelling the secret of the atom.

"Electrons are locked into orbits, and if one of them gains energy, it moves to a higher orbit. But it doesn't do it like a spacecraft moving from one orbit to another, gradually passing through the space between the orbits. It is in one orbit, and then it simply is in another. It *jumps*. And the reason it does not move through the intervening space is that . . . *there is no such thing*.

"From here on, it gets disturbingly strange, but in a way, it is also obvious. Painfully obvious."

CHAPTER FORTY-FIVE

Five days later, **on board USS** *John Fitzgerald* *Kennedy*, **CLS-222, in high orbit around K'tok** **6 October 2134**

Sam waited for the holocon circuit to come alive and fought the urge to fidget. He breathed deeply and regularly. He didn't want to appear out of breath or nervous.

The camera lights came on and the compartment in front of him disappeared, replaced by a sea of seated ship captains, mostly men and women, but a few Varoki and Zaschaan as well, and one Katami, its elaborate cranial crest rising above the crowd. It must be hard to face this sort of struggle all alone, the only Katami ship in a fleet of twenty-nine warships of one sort or another. As motley a fleet as had probably ever been assembled, its elements scattered through a span of space a couple hundred thousand kilometers across. USS *Puebla* far prograde, or spinward, depending on how you wanted to look at it, in the direction the planets moved around K'tok's star. Rear Admiral Crutchley's Task Force Twelve far to retrograde, or trailing, coming in fast from Mogo. Task Force Eleven with Stevens, Sam, and the other ships from K'tok in the middle, closing with P'Daan and his Troatta phalanx of ships head-on at almost sixty kilometers per second. The Troatta had not decelerated and they were not taking any evasive action.

The officers in the conference were arranged within the virtual array the same as for a large live briefing: junior officers in back and the senior to the front, with the four other flag officers of the fleet in the first row. Sam understood this was done to make the junior officers feel less self-conscious, not being under the eyes of their superiors. Sam and Stevens sat on the virtual stage facing the others. Larry Goldjune sat in the very back row, among the most junior of ship captains, and Goldjune's face lost its color as he recognized Sam.

"Good day," Admiral Stevens said. "I'm going to turn this briefing over to the fleet's new acting Tac boss. Some of you know him and most of you have heard of him— well, *all* of you since P'Daan's broadcast five days ago. There's a hell of a story behind how he managed to get back here to join us, but that's for another time. For now, our focus is on the fight ahead of us. Lieutenant Commander Bitka, over to you."

"Good morning," Sam said but he paused when he saw a ripple of movement at the front of the virtual space. Three Human officers stood up. He knew two of them: Rear Admiral Victoria Crutchley, Royal Navy, and Brigadier General Robert Irekanmi, Federal Nigerian Navy. The third he did not recognize but he wore the uniform of an Indian Navy rear admiral. For a moment Sam thought this might be some sort of protest, but he had been on good terms with both Crutchley and Irekanmi. Then they began clapping.

Then the Zaschaan Squadron-Guiding admiral beside them stood and joined them, and then the others rose and applauded as well. Even the Varoki.

Even Larry Goldjune rose and clapped, although his heart was clearly not in it. Sam had difficulty speaking. The tribute, the welcome, was clearly heartfelt—well, *mostly* heartfelt. After perhaps a minute the applause subsided and gradually the officers took their seats.

"Thank you," Sam said and nodded to them, particularly the flag officers in the front of the space who had begun it. "It's good to be home. You can't know how good it is, and I sincerely hope none of you ever finds out. It's our job to make sure no one else ever has to.

"Vice Admiral Stevens has asked me to give you a final summary of the situation and a review of our plan of action. Task Force Eleven, under Admiral Stevens, is currently at four hundred and thirty thousand kilometers from the Troatta. Admiral Crutchley's Task Force Twelve is at about three hundred thousand, but is closing at a lower velocity. We anticipate going to general quarters in one hour and will begin firing ordnance thirty minutes later. At Task Force Eleven's closing rate of sixty kilometers per second, this will be a very short, sharp fight. The task force will have passed through the Troatta fleet in less than two hours from now.

"The Troatta battle fleet is divided into six squadrons of six ships each, although the reserve squadron has only five. Each squadron has five ships deployed in a cross formation and one more ship to the rear, either the commander or a reserve ship to fill in a loss. The fleet is deployed in the same way: five squadrons in a cross formation with one more squadron behind in reserve. We have watched them practice a number of maneuvers over the last three days and know the squadrons on the periphery are prepared to wheel to face attack from several directions.

"Our plan is to force them to do exactly that.

"Their tactics are based on massed meson gunfire, and their formation reflects it. We gain no advantage from physical proximity, so our formations are dispersed and we are going to threaten them with attack from as many directions as possible: Task Force Twelve incoming from Mogo, Task Force Eleven outbound from K'tok, and USS *Puebla* from out in the boonies. At the same time, USS *Kennedy* in high K'tok orbit will join in with some very long-range shots, once we get the jump drives working.

"One hour ago, the uBakai squadron and our sole Katami cruiser from Task Force Eleven began firing inert munitions into the path of the Troatta—what we Humans called buckshot. We don't know what their defenses against inert munitions are, but we at least hope they will have to maneuver to some extent and perhaps disrupt their formation.

"Now, some news. Thirty minutes ago, I received word that a special working group we assembled has isolated the command code which turned off our jump drives."

Sam had to pause for a few seconds to let the sudden exclamations and then cheers run their course.

"Yes, great news, but we're not all the way home yet. They still have to construct a coded message which will overwrite that instruction and turn our drives back on. We're committed to the attack and we don't know when, or even if, they will get that work done. The good news is we're all less than a light-minute from K'tok, so when they have the code, we'll have it right away. USS *Kittyhawk* in Task Force Twelve should keep its destroyers in-cradle until the admiral gives the word to release. If we can get the drives working, *Kittyhawk* with its eight destroyers is our ace in the hole. One of them, anyway. *Kennedy's* long-range shooting will be the other."

Sam stopped and looked at the faces of twenty-nine ship captains, four of whom he knew: Larry Goldjune of *Puebla*, his face an expressionless mask, Kropotkin of USS *Arleux*, Ranjha of HMS *Exeter*, and of course Rockaway of the *Fitz*. He saw captains and flag officers from four Human, two Varoki, one Zaschaan, and one Katami navies, and he had to swallow the lump in his throat. This mix of species and nationalities had never before gone into battle together. It took a common enemy, a terrible enemy, to force it, but it was here, it was happening, and he wondered where it would lead.

"I just took a moment to look over all of your faces, and you should do the same. Some of us won't be alive in two hours, perhaps a lot of us, but what we're about to do together makes us brothers and sisters. I hope that whoever of us survives, and whatever comes after today, we all remember these two hours. Now Admiral Stevens has a few words for you."

But as Stevens rose, the hologram flickered and then became heavily pixilated. The background noise took on the sound of loud, uneven static.

"Bitka, where'd you go?" Stevens asked, looking directly at Sam.

"I'm still here sir," Sam answered, but the confused look on the admiral's face suggested Sam's hologram was no longer visible.

"Captain Rockaway," Sam transmitted on his commlink. "Is something wrong with our tight beam transmitter?"

Negative, Bitka. We're picking up some electromagnetic radiation from the Troatta fleet. It looks like directional ECM jamming. We're not in their jamming arc, and probably too far away to have much effect on us anyway, but it's flooding the receivers on the fleet. We can pick up their transmissions, but they can't receive from us.

Admiral Cedric Goldjune felt the vibration of his commlink and opened the channel. "Yes?"

"Sir, I have a holocon request from Senator Ramirez y Sesma. Are you in?"

"Patch him through." Cedric sat back and waited for the connection. What did the senator want now? They couldn't make any sort of move until they knew what the outcome of the fleet action was. Cedric didn't have a lot of faith in Stevens' ability to win this fight, especially considering what a mishmash of ships he had to work with. Still, they didn't lose anything by waiting. Maybe Ramirez y Sesma had found out something useful about the Varoki special envoy. The senator's image materialized in Cedric's office. He looked upset.

"Good morning, Senator. What can I do for you?"

"Explain to me why you didn't see fit to tell me that

your Captain Bitka had returned."

Cedric stared at him for a moment but tried to hide his surprise. *Bitka back?* What sort of crazy rumors had the senator been listening to?

"That's impossible, Senator. Captain Bitka is still a prisoner of the Guardians back in the Destination system."

"Are you lying to me?" the senator said. "Or can it be you don't know yourself? I have it from a reliable source that, as we speak, Captain Bitka is with your battle fleet and is serving as the planning officer for Admiral Stevens."

"*Bullshit!* That's crazy talk. That's . . . wait, let me pull up First Fleet's staff roster. We'll see who the N-5 is." Cedric touched the smart surface of his desk, searched for the latest update of the staff roster, and opened it. *N-5 Planning Officer: Lieutenant Commander Bitka, Samuel M.*

Cedric felt the room sway around him. How could this be? Was it a mistake? A joke? How could it happen and Stevens not tell him? He felt his face grow warm with a mixture of shame and anger. *Stevens had fucked him!* He didn't know how or why yet, but he'd done it. *Gordo Stevens!*

The senator's hologram disappeared.

Ninety minutes later, Sam felt unsettled, nervous, and at first he wasn't sure why. This was more than pre-battle jitters. He felt a growing anxiety and sense of helplessness he had never before felt on the eve of battle. Part of it was they still did not have workable jump drives. That was part of it, but not all. Then he realized what it was: this was the first time he had prepared to enter battle when he was not in command of a ship. He was just a staff wonk, a passenger. He hadn't realized the extent the responsibility of command had distracted his thoughts from his own personal danger—not that there was much of that, sitting in K'tok orbit.

Maybe he should have asked for a command, but which one? They sure weren't going to give a cruiser to a brevetted lieutenant commander. Maybe the *Bay*. Why not? It was there in the task force, along with its sister ship USS *Spratley Islands*. Everything with a coil gun or a missile rack was. Too late to ask now and besides, he'd heard good things about Beauchamp, its new skipper. Instead he sat in the TAC One chair on the *Fitz's* bridge.

"Captain," Chief Turnbull, the senior sensor tech, reported, "USS *Puebla* is accelerating harder than the tactical plan calls for."

Sam shifted the view on his workstation display and saw the heat signature of *Puebla's* fusion drive, and the shifting length and angle of its course vector. Was Goldjune bugging out?

"What the hell?" Rockaway said. "What's he up to, Bitka?"

"No idea, Ma'am."

Sam watched *Puebla* continue to accelerate. It wasn't running away.

"Crazy son of a bitch," Rockaway said. "Stevens will have Goldjune's ass, if he lives through this."

"Don't kid yourself," Sam said. "*If* he lives, Larry will use the ECM jamming for cover. No direction from the admiral due to the comm blackout so Larry acted on his own initiative. Trust me, nobody who survives this fight is going to get in trouble for running *toward* the Troatta."

She turned and looked at him, her expression cautious. "*If* he survives."

Yeah, Sam thought. And if he didn't survive this stupid stunt, he'll have taken Sam's old crew with him—Moe Rice, Marina Filipenko, Rosemary Hennessey, all the others. Elise Delacroix, Chief Menzies' fiancé, was out there on *Puebla*, too. The next hour was going to be tough for her to sit through.

"Range from the Troatta to Task Force Eleven has closed to one hundred nine thousand kilometers," Chief Turnbull reported. "One minute to their firing point. Um . . . energy spike from enemy battle line," he added. "May be accelerators firing."

Rockaway turned and looked at Sam. "Too far out for meson guns. You think they're firing sand?"

"That's my guess."

"Task Force is firing its coil-launched missiles," Turnbull reported.

In Task Force Eleven all the coil gun ships were US Navy: two General-class heavy cruisers, two assault transports, and one beat-up destroyer, USS *Arleux*. The other five cruisers in the task force would join in with their missile racks once the decoy cloud was on its way, as would the three Varoki cruisers, now several thousand kilometers off their port quarter.

Rockaway turned and began talking on her commlink. At the same time Sam's own commlink vibrated. He squinted and saw the ID tag for Lieutenant Commander Nightingale, head of the jump drive working group.

"Bob, I hope this is good news."

We've got the code. We're ready to transmit.

"Do it!"

Sam bumped Rockaway's shoulder, who turned from her conversation with a scowl. Sam gave her the thumbs up sign and her face broke into a broad grin.

"Now we'll show those bastards what we can do," she said. "COM, as soon as you have a complete signal package from K'tok, pass it to TAC and engineering. TAC, feed that package to our missile carriers as soon as you have it."

"Troatta fleet is changing formation," Turnbull reported. "One squadron turning to face *Puebla*, two turning to face Task Force Eleven. The Task Force Eleven ships with missile racks have opened fire. Thirty-two hot missiles outbound."

Sam checked the battle clock: *forty minutes.* Jesus, where had the time gone?

"All Troatta ships maneuvering," Chief Turnbull said, "have turned to one seven zero degrees relative, angle on their bows forty-two degrees."

"They must have picked up the incoming buckshot from the Varoki task group and are turning to face," Sam said.

"Warhead detonations," Turnbull said, and Sam could see them on the situation model on his workstation, blotting out the Troatta battle fleet but also blotting out the task force's own missiles from the Troatta view. These first missiles had detonated before they were in range, to mask the ones coming behind them.

Rockaway stared at the large tactical monitor and shook her head.

"Look at Task Force Twelve. *Kittyhawk* has released her destroyers. Why? She's supposed to jump with them in-cradle, come out behind the Troatta, and then release the boats."

Sam looked and then understood.

"*Oh shit!* The ECM jamming. They can't receive the jump descrambler code. The Troatta are jamming the hell out of them, so none of them have their jump drives up. They're back to a head-on attack and just try to plow through that wall of sand and meson gun fire."

"Oh my god," she whispered.

"Yeah," Sam said. "But we're still in business."

CHAPTER FORTY-SIX

Moments later, **on board Troatta Ship One-Two-One 6 October 2134**

Tatak-who-had-been-Kakusa grew increasingly uneasy. Using the stardust weapon as a shield against their hellstars was a brilliant innovation by Y'Areez, and it also seemed to disrupt the formation ahead of them as it scattered in three directions to escape the dust-which-kills. But then they had detected approaching enemy stardust and the entire fleet had turned toward it to deploy their anti-dust armor. But that had meant that the golden squadron, in which Tatak/Kakusa's Ship One-Two-One was the down-weakside vessel, had had to turn away from their own targets, the enemy squadron approaching from the system's large gas world. There would be time to turn back after the dust-that-kills had passed, but still, she felt the situation was becoming confused.

Helm, have we been reinforced from home? the Ship asked.

"No, Ship. Why do you wonder this?"

There is a jump emergence signature within our formation.

Tatak/Kakusa brought up the close tactical display and saw the red hostile signature between the lead squadron and the reserve, and then saw the reserve sweep by it, too soon to react to it. The red signature then became five red signatures.

Kakusa nearly took control of the ship and turned it to face the new contacts, but she did not. The dust still came. It was a known threat. These were unknown, and how could they be hostile? P'Daan and Y'Areez had taken the life from the enemy's star drives.

And then the threat became known, as four red dots turned into rapidly blooming white globes of star-hot plasma. *Hellstars!*

Sam checked the clock: forty-five minutes.

"Second jump emergence inside the Troatta formation," Turnbull said.

"What sort of damage are we seeing?" Captain Rockaway asked.

Sam had been checking the sensor reports, which were faint at this range anyway, and badly garbled by some of their own warhead detonations and the jamming, but he knew the warheads were hurting them. "Ma'am, our first package of four warheads definitely left a mark. Two of their ships are completely off-line, cooling and not firing their meson guns. I think we have probably a dozen more hits, but no way to assess damage."

"There goes the second cluster," Turnbull said and Sam saw four more hot radioactive debris clouds mushroom seemingly in the middle of the Troatta fleet, and then saw one of the Troatta ships break in half.

"That is damned good shooting, Bitka," Rockaway said. "What are those courier missiles running these days? About a half-billion dollars each?"

"A lot less than one of our ships, Ma'am. Sure as hell less than what it takes to build one of those Troatta battleships."

"Well, I have to hand it to you, Bitka, you earned your pay the day you thought to strap four Mark Fives to a jump courier missile and throw it at them through J-space. I just hope it's going to be enough."

"The task force's own missiles are entering their meson gun range, sir," Turnbull said. "They're taking scattered fire, but some of the Troatta ships are reversing direction, to fire to the stern, and two squadrons are turning back toward Task Force Twelve. Their missiles are getting close as well. Whoa! What the hell?"

What the normally unflappable chief reacted to was a very large ball of white-hot energy in the middle of the Troatta formation, which momentarily obscured the entire central squadron. Sam immediately knew what happened.

"Annihilation event," Sam said. "Our third jump missile must have come out right inside a Troatta ship."

"All right!" Rockaway said.

Sam felt a surge of excitement as well, but he knew they weren't home free, far from it.

"Incoming tightbeam from Task Force Eleven Actual," the communication officer to Rockaway's right called out. "Text reads: To USS *Kennedy* from COMKTOKFLEET. We cannot receive but assume you can as you have operational jump missiles. We are approaching heavy wall of high velocity sand, expect high damage rate from transit same. Pour on the missile fire. Good hunting. Signed, Stevens."

"You heard the man," Rockaway said, and as she did the tactical screen lit up with a ripple of exploding fusion warheads.

"Fourth cluster detonating," Turnbull reported.

There were still a lot of Troatta ships out there and from what Stevens had said, the taskforce was taking a beating. This wasn't going to work. Sam pinged Menzies on the commlink.

Sir? she answered.

"Check firing," he ordered.

Aye, aye, sir. Check firing.

Rockaway turned to him, eyebrows coming together in part question, part challenge.

"I know," Sam said, "But this isn't working. We're hurting them but not enough to stop them. They are going to just keep on going and then fry K'tok."

"Well . . . what the hell do you suggest?"

"You said it yourself earlier: *kill that son of a bitch.* Retarget our last two clusters. We can't see much anymore, but we need to hit the trailing ships, not the leading ones. That's where P'Daan is. Chop the head off the snake . . . or in this case the tail."

"Okay, we'll try it. TAC, feed the targeting information for the trailing Troatta squadron to Chief Menzies."

"Aye, aye, Ma'am," Turnbull answered as Sam triggered his commlink again.

"Chief Menzies, new targeting information coming. Load it and fire our last two clusters in succession."

★ ★ ★

Tatak-who-had-been-Kakusa had seen the disaster of the annihilation event on her tactical display, had seen the core Ship of the Silver Squadron become a miniature sun, saw the damage to the other five Ships in the squadron, one of them broken in half, one dark and without power, and the other three damaged to some degree. The reserve would normally have moved forward to fill the gap, but the reserve did not accelerate. The reserve of four Ships consisted of the command vessels of P'Daan and Y'Areez and their two escorts, and Tatak/Kakusa did not expect them to accelerate. Guardians do not become directly involved in the killing.

Then the hellstars had come again, but this time slashing at the reserve squadron. When the screens cleared, one Ship was dark and the other three showed signs of damage.

Helm, the Fleet Guide is sending a holomessage.

"Very well, Ship."

The Fleet Guide, painted nightshade the same as interlocutors because he was privileged to speak for Y'Areez, appeared in her bridge, as he did on other bridges at the same time.

"Iron Squadron, engage the enemy force to trailing. All other squadrons close formation and engage the enemy force coming from the target world. Defeat them and our path is clear. Concentrate all fire on the enemy hellstar missiles, even after the enemy ships are within range. The hellstars are the greater hazard. Leave the enemy ships to the stardust."

He disappeared from her bridge, and then two of the four Ships of the reserve task force did so as well, bending space to wink out of existence here, and materialize presumably at the fleet rally position. One remained, other than the dark wreck. This must be the second escort vessel, left behind by the two departing god-Ships.

Helm, the Fleet Vice-Guide is sending a holomessage.

The Vice-Guide? He served P'Daan. Had Y'Areez left and P'Daan stayed?

The Nightshade-painted Vice-Guide appeared on her bridge and spoke.

"Continue as ordered. The God P'Daan accompanies us and shares our fate. Never before has a Troatta fleet been so honored. Fight, and know he watches."

Fight? What was left? All six Ships of the Iron Squadron responded to the Guide's order. Of the twenty-four Ships in the remaining line squadrons, only seventeen still showed on her tactical screen as under power and capable of maneuver. Still, seventeen Ships made a formidable force. The battle was not lost unless the enemy had more of the space-bending hellstars which had nearly torn their formation apart, but she had not seen any more for several minutes. Perhaps they had survived the worst the enemy had to offer. Perhaps Y'Areez had been too hasty in fleeing. She would like to see how he reacted to a battle lost under his command and then won back in his absence, commanded by the inept P'Daan. Oh yes, that would be a thing to see.

She felt the slight acceleration from side to side as the Ship swung its nose to engage target after target with the meson gun. Tatak/Kakusa could not really tell how much damage they were doing to the swarm of hellstars. It was hard to know how many of their targets were genuine missiles and how many were decoys, harder still to tell which were anything but twisted metal after passing through the stardust, and the occasional detonations of hellstars clouded her sensor picture. The enemy ships had crossed the outer boundary of their engagement range but the Fleet Guide was correct: kill the hellstars first. There would be time to deal with their ships soon enough.

Now the passage of time seemed to accelerate. The first hellstar detonated within killing range of the fleet and she saw two Ships lose power. Then another hellstar detonated and one Ship went dark. Then two hellstars, then three more, and her tactical screen no longer showed a coherent picture. It was time to shift fire to the enemy ships, but she no longer had a good target solution on them. Another hellstar detonated somewhere ahead of them, and another, further clouding her screen. How many had gotten through?

And then she saw the large signatures of enemy ships, but they were so close!

"Ship! Engage the enemy, close action!"

"We missed him," Rockaway said, surprise in her voice.

Sam studied the tactical display, but it was clear she was right. The Troatta fleet, much battered and reduced in numbers but still a cohesive force, had passed through the remnants of Task Force Eleven and were on course for K'tok. A small rearguard was almost within engagement range of Task Force Twelve, but a stern chase was going to be a tough fight to win. The closing times on the missiles would be longer, the numbers nowhere near as good. And P'Daan was definitely alive down there; he'd already broadcast one boasting, self-congratulatory message.

"Chief, have you got a fix on that broadcast by P'Daan?" Sam asked.

"Yes, sir. It came from the contact flagged Bandit two-six."

Rockaway looked at him. "What are you thinking, Bitka?"

"Just wondering . . . I know these light cruisers have no coil guns, but don't you have missile packs on the spin habitat?"

"Yes," she said cautiously, "we have two launcher modules installed, with six Mark Four missiles total. But we don't have a jump drive to get them to P'Daan."

Sam raised his eyebrows.

"Oh, no," she said as she realized what he meant.

"Hey, I'm open to suggestions if you have a better idea," he said.

She looked down and thought for a long moment but then shook her head and sighed. "Okay, I guess *Through Their Bowels* it is. And I was so looking forward to retirement."

"You're my age," Sam said. "Way too young to be thinking about retirement."

Her expression became almost haunted, and she answered quietly, meant only for his ears.

"Since Fourth K'tok, it's about all I think about."

Tatak-who-had-been-Kakusa leaned her forehead against the slick metal of the control console between the two command sockets. Ship Ninety-Six had disintegrated in the brief but incredibly violent melee when the two fleets passed through each other. *Ship Ninety-Six.* Her sister Tamari, *gone!* If the stardust had not damaged the enemy ships so heavily, she doubted any of the Troatta vessels would have survived. S'Bitka had never used such powerful lasers on them in P'Daan's Realm, but then they had never fought his ship at such close range.

Incoming communication from the Fleet Vice-Guide, Ship said.

"Very well," she said, sitting up straight.

The message this time was simply voice, not hologram. Perhaps the holotransmission equipment on P'Daan's Ship was damaged. She imagined every surviving Ship had suffered some damage.

Reform the firing wall and Ships rotate to engage to rear. The enemy pursuit force is being damaged and disorganized by the Iron Squadron. We will destroy the enemy remnants. The command Ship will pass through the fleet and command from the far side until the pursuing fleet is dealt with.

"Ship, open the command channel to the surviving Ships in Golden Squadron." Since the destruction of the Ships carrying the two senior helms of the squadron, Tatak/Kakusa had assumed command. Once she had a connection, she passed the orders on to the two other surviving squadron Ships and in triangle formation they rotated their vessels to bring their meson guns to bear on the pursuing fleet.

She saw the passage of the command Ship through the line on her tactical display. Curiosity drove her to summon a high-resolution visual graphic of the Ship and she saw the latticework of its jump drive generator twisted and dark. Interesting. Would P'Daan have stayed with them had his jump drive been functional? She didn't know. There was something manic and driven about this Guardian, and in those cases, it was impossible to tell what triggered their decisions.

All the sterns of the Ships were now facing in the direction of their course, toward the world the *Cottohazz*-things called K'tok. They would have to turn back in order to engage the enemy orbital defenses, but that would not be for at least another day or two. For now, their concern was behind them, the pursuing fleet. She remembered her fight against S'Bitka in P'Daan's Realm, remembered turning her Ships to face a threat she thought was behind them, and then being attacked from the unexpected direction. Her respiration membranes shivered in anxiety. No, surely not.

Jump emergence, the Ship announced in its flat, calm voice.

Tatak/Kakusa saw it at once on the tactical display, *to their Ships' sterns!* They hurtled toward the new contact but with all of their weapons pointing the opposite direction.

Again!

"Ship, power up our close-range particle accelerators and engage any missiles it fires. Transmit this to Golden Squadron: *Rotate Ships and engage new enemy.*"

One Ship was facing the new contact, however: P'Daan's command Ship. It did not fire at first, must be turning to bring the enemy target into its arc of fire. Like the other enemy jump missiles, this one had very little velocity of its own and so the fleet raced toward it. But unlike the others, this one fired two hot missiles. *A warship, not a jump missile!* She saw the energy signature from P'Daan's Ship as it fired, saw the heat spike from the enemy ship showing it was hit.

Sam's workstation rebooted and then died again as the bridge emergency lighting came on. Beside him he could see Captain Rockaway talking on her commlink but couldn't hear her, as both had their helmets closed and were on suit life support. They still had some atmosphere in the bridge, but not much. The battle had been very brief and they were taking a beating, but they had managed to fire at least one fire lance and hit P'Daan's ship before they lost power. Now Sam wasn't sure what was happening, and without a functioning workstation he felt deaf and blind. He looked around and didn't see any workstations running. He hoped auxiliary bridge was in better shape, and then he felt a tingle from his commlink. Captain Rockaway.

Bitka, P'Daan's ship is crippled and we have two more fire lances in detonation range, target-locked on the forward command module. You want to say anything to him before I blow his shit away?

For a brief moment he considered transmitting something, maybe, *Who's the hunter now?* But that was stupid.

"Nah, just kill him. *Quick.*"

The voice of the Fleet Vice-Guide was cut off as the command Ship went dark on her tactical screen and then was replaced with an intense star-like spike of energy as its reactor exploded.

And then the new enemy was past them as the fleet raced on toward K'tok, leaderless but alive. *They still lived!* She lifted her arms and panted, sucking air in through her breathing slits. The tactical screen slowly cleared as superheated debris and gas cooled. Then a thermal bloom—another hellstar! The missiles from the pursuing enemy fleet, the one approaching from the outer system, were reaching them, and the ships themselves were within minutes of overtaking them and passing through their formation, the formation now badly disordered by the last attack.

Then is this the end? her Ship asked.

"Perhaps, Ship, but perhaps not. Give me the common channel to all surviving Ship helms."

It is so, the Ship answered.

"I am senior surviving helm and I take command of this fleet. By my order, all Ships cease firing immediately." She knew many of her helm sisters would wonder at this order, question its propriety, but she also knew they did not wish to die today for nothing. She had assumed command, and so the responsibility was on her.

"Ship, now give me a broadcast channel to the enemy."

It is so.

She took two breaths and then discarded forever her false identity. Whatever time she had left, she would live as herself.

"I am Kakusa by-Vrook through-Kuannawaa, she who defeated S'Bitka, Destroyer of Worlds. I am now senior surviving helm of the Troatta Armada, and I surrender these Ships and their crews in the name of Y'Areez the Eternal."

Can such a thing be done? the Ship asked.

She did not answer, because she did not yet know whether in fact it could be done. Then a voice came back over the communicator.

Kakusa by-Vrook through-Kuannawaa, I remember you. I accept the surrender of all of your ships. Have them turn their guns away from the approaching fleet and we will cease fire. You know you can trust my promise.

"S'Bitka?"

CHAPTER FORTY-SEVEN

Four days later, on board USS *Andrew Jackson,*
CGS-223, approaching K'tok orbit
10 October 2134

Vice Admiral Gordo Stevens felt good, very good, as he looked again at the final inventory. He beamed at the hologram of his tactical officer, who was already at K'tok Highstation, having been picked up, along with the rest of USS *Kennedy's* crew, by FGS *Thuringer,* the flagship of Task Force Twelve. USS *Kennedy* was an abandoned, twisted piece of junk, but the crew casualties had been surprisingly light.

"Damn, Bitka, what a haul! Thirty-three long ships bagged. Eight of them are just radioactive slag and drifting junk, thirteen are dead hulks, ten more pretty heavily damaged, but two of them are pristine. BuOrd is going to have a field day pulling them apart and looking at those meson guns."

"They can pick through the wreckage and the hulks," Bitka said, "and look as long and as close as they want to at the live ships, but BuOrd isn't pulling any of those functional ships apart."

"*Oh, no?* And just exactly why not, Lieutenant Commander?"

"They're enemy prisoners of war, sir."

Gordo laughed and then he looked at Bitka again. "Jesus, you're serious!"

"Yes, sir. I'm about as serious as I can get. Those ships are self-aware sentient beings, mostly organic. What you're talking about is no different than live vivisection of human prisoners."

"Well...what if they promise to put them back together when they're done?" Gordo said.

"Chop up some humans, glue their corpses back together, and see who thinks that's okay. Those ships are alive, they think, they *feel*."

Gordo shook his head, half in frustration but half in amusement. "Damnit, Bitka, do you stay up nights trying to figure out ways to make everything harder?"

Bitka shrugged. "I feel like I got to know them, sir, a little bit anyway. And there are over a thousand Troatta prisoners. I know we recovered some rations, but we need to fabricate some big hydroponics chambers and start growing Troatta protein or they're all going to starve. We've got some seed stock from the hydroponics in the captured ships. K'Irka may be able to help, too."

This Bitka was a funny guy, and Gordo still didn't really have him figured out, but he was interesting, that was for sure. Gordo thought he might be more concerned about those damned prisoners than what this victory meant for the two of them. Still, Gordo sort of admired that in him. And if all these prisoners died in captivity, how anxious would the next bunch be to throw in the towel?

"Lot of folks wouldn't mind them starving, might even drag their feet on fixing the problem until it became moot, so tell you what. That's *your* job, Bitka, okay? And you've got my authority backing you up, anything you need. Just keep those prisoners alive."

"Aye, aye, sir." Bitka said. "I want Haykuz, if you can get him. He knows the Troatta better than any of us so far. I think he's still *Cottohazz* staff, so you should be able to request a transfer. Ask the special envoy."

"Consider it done," Gordo said. A thought came to him and he smiled. "Say, what do you think they'll call this battle?"

"Probably the Fifth Battle of K'tok."

"No, it was nowhere near K'tok," Gordo said. "They'll call it the Defeat of P'Daan or something, but I'll tell you what they should call it: The Miracle Battle. We had one hundred ninety-seven dead or missing throughout the fleet, about three hundred injured, and lost seven ships, four of which we'll probably be able to salvage. Damn, Bitka—just seven ships out of twenty-nine lost, and we nailed *thirty-three* of those big Troatta monsters! Hell, even young Goldjune distinguished himself, drew the fire of a whole Troatta squadron on his missile cluster and got through it with hardly a scratch."

Bitka said nothing, his expression darkening.

Gordo remembered what had started this whole thing six months ago and he shook his head. "Bitka, you know how the game works. When the admiral's boy pulls a gutsy move like that and *doesn't* get his boat blown up, you give him a medal and make sure his picture's in all the vid feeds."

Bitka looked down with a sour expression, as if he were looking for a place to spit. "I know, sir. But he did it out of desperation, trying to save his career. He figured he had nothing to lose, but what about the other ninety people on *Puebla*? They had something to lose. A lot of those people went through hell in the uBakai War, and for what? So Larry Goldjune could throw them away grandstanding?"

"But they didn't die," Gordo said. "Wise up, Sam. The *Cottohazz* needed a win, needed it bad, and we gave them one hell of a victory, maybe enough to pull everyone together and put some sand in their bellies. But nobody wants to hear anything about this battle unless it has to do with heroes, you understand? When you have a victory this glorious, you have lots of heroes, and no goats."

"Glorious?" Bitka said. "We got really lucky, sir. Next time it won't be this easy."

"You call that *easy*?" Gordo said, and then thought about how lopsided the victory had been. "Well, maybe you're right. But it won't be as easy for them, either, if we have all our jump drives operational next fight."

Bitka nodded. "Well, that's true. And besides, P'Daan's dead. If we're lucky, there won't be a next time. By the way, sir, thank you for letting me take the surrender. I'm getting a little history with the Troatta."

Gordo waved the thanks away, and he felt unexpectedly affectionate toward this odd young maverick officer. And why not, considering what he'd done? Gordo thought about that for a moment, wondered if he could have done all that Bitka had in the last half year, and he knew he couldn't have. The unaccustomed lump in his throat surprised him.

"This was your victory, Bitka. But you understand, only the tactical geeks will figure that out, right? For the real world, it will be mine. So, for a change, I owe you. Isn't that weird? I'll tell you one thing I can do, I bet we can get that temporary bump to lieutenant commander confirmed, make it permanent. You've even got enough years and time in service, I'm going to go for full commander, but no promises on that. I'll tell you one thing, I'll get you something more than a Silver Star this time, especially for what you did getting the *Bay* home. Jesus Christ!"

"I appreciate it, sir," Bitka said, "but you might want to save some of your political capital for yourself. You're going to have some explaining to do to the CNO. You know, about not telling him I was back."

Not for the first time, Gordo remembered the conversation he and Bitka had had six months ago. He shrugged and grinned. "Tell you the truth, that never worried me one bit. I figured with you in charge of the plan, we'd both end up either heroes or dead, and either way Cedric Goldjune being pissed wasn't going to be a problem. I told you a long time ago, if we were both heroes we could tell Goldjune to go fuck himself. Well, son of a bitch if we ain't! Now get your ass down that needle. Join the celebration down there. You earned it."

"Thank you for seeing me, Senator," Admiral Cedric Goldjune said to the hologram in his office. "It has been hard to reach you the last few days."

"There have been many demands on my time, Admiral,

as I am sure you understand. But it is always a pleasure to speak with you. What can I do for you?"

As if he didn't know! The son of a bitch looked like a potentate receiving a supplicant. The damned thing was, that was pretty much the situation.

"You can help guide the President, the SecDef, and the SecNav in their choice of the next Chief of Naval Operations."

"But Admiral, are you not already so employed?"

"Damnit, Carlos, you know this new threat means the Outworld Coalition is a dead letter. There will be a combined fleet, but it will probably be an all-*Cottohazz* operation. I'm going to be out of a job."

Ramirez y Sesma waved dismissively. "Given your experience and years of service, I am sure Secretary Padang will find employment for you."

"I'm not so sure. A lot of what's gone on could be looked at two different ways. Some of our conversations, for example."

The senator's smile disappeared and his gaze became cold and hard. "Whatever was said would damage your reputation as much as mine, Admiral."

"That's true, Senator, absolutely true. But that only matters as long as I have a career worth protecting, if you take my meaning."

Ramirez y Sesma looked at him, his eyes calculating. Cedric felt his heart rate accelerate, heard the blood pounding in his ears. Finally, the senator spoke.

"Not CNO. Not now. Perhaps someday."

Cedric thought that over. Ramirez y Sesma had a lot at stake here as well. He probably wasn't bullshitting him.

He was laying out what was real, what was attainable, and what was not. Cedric was not going to be the next US Navy CNO. He wasn't that old, though. There was still time. And there was the Guardian K'Irka, and her promise of immortality. Probably not for everyone, though. He'd have to get in touch with her, figure out what she really wanted. But first . . .

"A fighting command," he said.

The senator frowned. "Have you ever actually *fought*?"

"Hell, who has? Aside from a handful of people, I mean, and most of them don't have the rank."

"Admiral Stevens does."

Goddamnit! Gordo Stevens again. The senator was right, though. Stevens would be the hero of the hour. There were only going to be so many commands, and damned few of them would go to Humans unless the *Cottohazz* changed a lot more than he thought it would. Cedric wouldn't get anywhere trying to tack into that wind.

"Stevens may be a good front-line admiral, but he needs someone to back him up, a superior who knows how to run political interference for him, and knows how to get the resources a major campaign needs. Hell, let him fight the battles, We're a proven team."

Ramirez y Sesma contemplated him as he thought that over. Finally, he nodded.

"*Bueno.* Perhaps something can be done."

And today that was as close to victory as Cedric could expect, but it still left a sour taste. He would survive, perhaps to triumph another day, but until then simple survival fell far short of what he knew he deserved.

★ ★ ★

Te'Anna stood with the other two in the docking bay of the K'tok highstation. She already knew the Varoki named Nuvaash, but Bitka made the introduction anyway. She thought Bitka seemed uncomfortable or distressed, and so they stood together wordlessly for a while before he spoke again.

"So, you're going?" he asked her, and Te'Anna saw both affection and regret in his eyes.

"What you call an executive council has asked to meet with me in person. I think that is a logical first step. After that, I want to see your *Cattohazz*, meet its people. Doctor Däng and K'Irka will stay here and assist you with the survival of the Troatta. I will not be gone forever. Not for so very long."

"You won't be welcome everywhere, you know," he said.

"I would have asked you to guide me, but I am sure you will be very busy for quite some time, with very little time to answer my annoying questions." She saw sadness flash across his face, loss.

"Not really annoying," he said. "Not once I got used to them. To you." His voice sounded different, strained.

"Vice Captain Nuvaash, would you leave us alone for a short while?" she said.

"Of course," the Varoki said, and walked into the station interior.

"You are the first Human I ever embraced, but because of you, you will not be the last. It is important to me that you do not allow yourself to die while I am gone."

Captain Bitka smiled. "Well, you know, that's actually important to me, too."

"Yes, but there are things *more* important to you, Bitka, and that is dangerous. All your emotions and your ridiculous rules. I have been thinking a great deal about death since the passing of P'Daan."

"You don't mourn him, do you?"

"Yes, I do. He was alive, and now he is gone forever. Someone should mourn that."

Captain Bitka's expression darkened and he shook his head in disagreement, or perhaps frustration. "He was a killer. He wanted to destroy *Earth* just to settle a grudge with me. He was a mad dog that needed to be put down."

"Oh, yes," Te'Anna agreed. "But I have been reading many of your stories, and one I found was about a mad dog which needed to be put down. It was owned by a young male of your species and they had bonded. When it contracted a disease, it became dangerous and so was put down, but the story presents this as a tragedy, not a triumph. A *necessity,* but a tragedy nonetheless. P'Daan could not be allowed to live, but had he lived, he might eventually have become well. Now he never will."

"The animal in the story was a good dog before it got sick," he said.

"Do you imagine P'Daan was *not* a good dog before he got sick?"

Something flickered in Captain Bitka's eyes, his respiration changed slightly, and she knew this thought surprised him. But he shook his head again.

"I don't know about that. But I can't and I won't mourn him."

"I would not expect you to. But do not expect me *not* to. And please, Captain Bitka, do try to stay alive until I return. Think of all we will have to talk about. Think of all the *questions* I will have!"

Four hours later, Nuvaash was surprised to see the special envoy waiting for him as he disembarked from the needle's passenger capsule. He nodded to him but first turned to Bitka, with whom he had ridden down from Highstation, and shook his hand, a Human gesture he had learned many years ago.

"Goodbye, Captain Bitka. It has been a very interesting and exciting trip."

"Not captain anymore," Bitka said. "Lieutenant commander, or just commander works if you're in a hurry."

Nuvaash shook his head. "Your bewildering inter-changeable uses of ranks and positions with the same name is . . . well, bewildering. I will plead unfamiliarity and continue to address you as captain. You know, before I even knew your name, I knew you. I spent hours, days actually, going over the ground recordings of your duel with the uKaMaat salvo cruiser, the battle you call Third K'tok, trying to see how you not only survived, but de-stroyed that ship which should have beaten you easily. I never understood until it was too late, until your ships were among us at that final battle. You will always be Captain Bitka to me."

Bitka appeared surprised by that and looked at him with genuine, if guarded, interest. "Even if we're not on the same side?"

Nuvaash smiled. "Oh, *especially* then."

And Bitka actually laughed. After they took their leave,

Nuvaash made his way quickly to Special Envoy e-Lotonaa, who stood flanked by his two thugs . . . that is to say *security specialists*.

"My apologies, Honorable Special Envoy, for the delay, but I felt an obligation to—"

"Of course, Nuvaash. I would never expect you to show disrespect to a colleague. Let us walk together. The battle must have been very exciting."

"It was, although I had no real part to play once the action began. The Varoki ships performed very well, had a critical role to play both in forcing the Troatta to turn away from the main attack force, and also in their volume of fire."

e-Lotonaa nodded but Nuvaash had the feeling this was simply a conversational preamble to what interested him.

"I met you because I have a proposition to make," the envoy said after a few more steps. "It seems I will remain employed by the Executive Council in . . . in a variety of roles in the coming months, and I think the times ahead of us may end up being even more exciting than your battle. There is some question whether there will even *be* a *Cottohazz* a year hence, but it will take much bungling to bring that dire a result about. Given the continuing threat from the Guardians, which we cannot yet accurately gauge, but know to be truly daunting, the six sentient species of the *Cottohazz* must remain united. So, the question is not so much *if* as *in what form?* It will be demanding work bringing that new infant forth. I would like you to join my staff. In fact, for the most part you would *be* my staff."

Nuvaash broke stride for a moment and when e-Lotonaa stopped and turned to him he caught up and they continued walking, but in silence. Nuvaash felt his color change and he fought to keep his ears from folding back in surprise. He had never expected an offer like this, in part because of the obvious impossibility of it working.

"I am deeply flattered, Honorable Special Envoy, and yet confused. You are aware I am not simply an officer of the uBakai Star Navy. You know my other service would render this arrangement unworkable."

"Oh? Why? Field Marshal Lieutenant e-Loyolaan, your superior at CSJ, has expressed an interest in working closer with the *Khap'uKhaana*. I am confident that if I requested your services as my official assistant, but also as an unofficial liaison between our organizations, he would agree at once. I am sure he would delight in having a spy so close to my inner council, and for my part I would benefit from having a better insight into his thinking and decision-making. Both of us will expect you to spy on us for the other, as an unspoken condition of the arrangement, and each of us will expect your *true* loyalty to lie with us. I need hardly add that it will be delicious for you to know both I and e-Loyolaan will undoubtedly spend many hours privately grappling with the question of who you are *really* spying on, and for."

Well, that last part was undeniably true, but Nuvaash still hesitated.

"Why would you imagine, if I may ask, my primary loyalty might be to you?"

"Two reasons. One will simply be physical proximity, both to me and to the important work I will be doing. I think the task may seduce you. The second reason is I sense you are troubled, have unanswered questions, and I think those questions may be about your current service. I would not normally tell an agent such things, so that should be an additional data point for you."

How did he know that? Nuvaash prided himself on how little he disclosed through his demeanor. Was this a lucky guess? Was the envoy really this good at looking into another being's soul? Or did he simply know something about the dark and twisted origins of the K'tok war? That was more likely, and that is what Nuvaash hungered to understand—that and the role his superior at CSJ, Field Marshall Lieutenant Yignatu e-Loyolaan, had played in it. But there was one more obstacle in the way of agreement.

"Before I decide, Honorable Special Envoy, I must ask you an intrusive and impertinent question. I fully understand if you are unwilling to answer and beg your forgiveness for the affront. But your adoptive daughter is the principle heir of the e-Traak fortune, a fortune which it seems these revelations about the origin of the jump drive will destroy."

e-Lotonaa nodded. "You wonder about my true interests and how that will affect my actions on behalf of a united *Cottohazz*."

"Yes, Honorable Special Envoy, I do."

"One thing before all others. If you are to work for me, you must never hesitate to question me. I may or may not answer, but questions must be raised without fear. Do you understand?"

"Yes, Honorable Special Envoy."

"And simply *Envoy* will do. Now as to your question, four facts should put your mind at ease. First, I am not the financial guardian of my daughter Tweezaa's fortune. That responsibility lies elsewhere, so that is no direct concern of mine. Second, Tweezaa's financial guardian has been quietly diversifying her holdings for the past two years, so her financial future is no longer inextricably linked with that of Simki-Traak. Third, even without patent rights, someone will have to actually manufacture jump drives, quite a lot of them I think, and Simki-Traak does have an excellent industrial infrastructure in place for so doing. Damaging as these revelations will be, Simki-Traak may still survive as a viable industrial concern. Fourth, even the near-total ruination of her vast fortune would leave Tweezaa with a residue which most of the rest of us would consider enormous, and unlikely as it may sound, my daughter's life is quite austere. I suspect she will eventually give most of her wealth away. In that aim, I believe she has been greatly influenced by the example of her late father."

Her late father, Nuvaash knew, was Sarro e-Traak, who four years earlier had tried to turn the e-Traak family fortune into a trust for the Humans on the planet Peezgtaan, and who had only been stopped by an assassin's bullet. Sarro was a person widely reviled as an insane race-traitor to the Varoki species. Nuvaash had always wondered about him. Well, here was an opportunity to find out more—about Sarro and about other things.

"I accept your offer, Envoy. I should tell you immediately that I suspect the Humans have been engaged in a research project here in the K'tok system which may be in contravention of the *Cottohazz* charter."

"You mean the jump drive module from the derelict uBakai cruiser?" e-Lotonaa asked casually.

CHAPTER FORTY-EIGHT

One hour later, Outworld Coalition Naval
Headquarters Complex, the planet K'tok
10 October 2134

There was a plaza outside the Fleet Headquarters
building, with green groundcover and benches. It faced
west, and Cassandra led Bitka here so they could have
some privacy. The sun was low on the horizon and
Cassandra remembered her first hour on K'tok, walking
out of Downstation into the sunset, beside Sam Bitka.

"I doubt they'll give me a command any time soon," he
said. "Probably watch me for a while to see if I grow
another head or something. Pretty sure they'll keep me in
uniform, though. If they cut me loose, I won't have
anything to do but write my tell-all memoir, and I don't
think anybody wants that. So it's pretty much down to
keep me in uniform or kill me. I don't think they'll kill me.
What do you think?"

Yes, what did she think?

"I think you are a very strange man."

"Yeah, but *good* strange, right?" he said with a grin.

"Oh, Gawd." She shook her head. There was

something so *irrepressible* about this Bitka, she was having a difficult time coping. After a moment, she recovered the thread of their conversation.

"Of course, they will keep you in uniform. You're as sharp an officer as any I've ever known, and don't pretend you don't know it. You think those other blockheads like Admiral Stevens aren't out of their depths? Good lord, Bitka, we all are. They're just too bloody thick to realize it."

He smiled at her, his eyes sparkling with happiness. "You know, you sound pretty upset over the treatment of an *ex*-boyfriend."

"Yes, I still care about you, as you know very well! But it is also a matter of principle, and a pragmatic consideration of how we can all best survive whatever is coming."

"Principle," Bitka said, and nodded with a solemn seriousness which mocked her. "Pragmatic. Of course."

"Oh, sod off, Bitka! I know what you're on about: *love*. Everyone goes on and on about love, but what is it? No one knows, no one can tell you."

"I can," he said quietly, and his confidence shook hers, although why that would be so she couldn't say.

"Oh really? In prose or poetry—or will you sing it to me?"

He smiled again, this time with a gentle, affectionate warmth. "If you don't want to hear, that's okay. If you want to make fun, that's alright too. I just like being here with you."

Cassandra looked at him, looked hard at him. There was no sign of mockery in his face, no condescension, no guile.

"What really happened to you out there?"

Sam laughed. "Oh, so many things. I'll tell you all about it, everything I saw and felt, every mystery, everything I finally understood. It's a big story, though. Telling it could take the rest of our lives."

Cassandra shivered despite the warmth of the afternoon.

"The rest of our lives! What if I have other plans? What if I've fallen in love with someone else? You know, I believed you were dead."

"No you didn't," Sam said with a shake of his head. "Believe I was dead, I mean. I'd have seen that in your eyes. You were just afraid to hope I was alive. That's different. Have you fallen in love? Are you happy?"

Cassandra looked at him again, even more confused.

"No, I haven't. What *happened* to you out there?"

He sighed and looked around, taking in the trees the sunset was turning pink, looked at the clouds low on the horizon, as if the answer was written out there somewhere. "I found a new civilization, watched a lot of good people die, started a war I'm not sure how we're going to finish, made a couple new friends, and then came home." He turned back to face her. "To you."

"But what if I'm not in love with you?"

"That's okay."

And she thought he really meant it! But how? She stared at him, trying to see past his smile. Did she even know this man? So much of him seemed familiar, but also alien, as if something of the Guardians or whatever else he'd met out there had rubbed off on him. As if time flowed differently for them, faster for her, slower for him. He had a patience she hadn't seen before. He'd shown urgency, though, when making the case for fighting the Guardians.

"Stop staring at me," she ordered.

He shrugged, his smile still in place.

"Sorry. It's just so good to *see* you. Do you know how we're not like animals?"

The question caught her by surprise.

"Um . . . not like animals? How?" she asked.

"Any species that's survived this long only made it because it had a burning, passionate hunger for life. You can't make it for a couple million years if you're just so-so about it. But we just won't give up, so here we are."

"The animals are too," she pointed out.

"Sure. They have that same relentless drive for survival we do. Here's how we're different: we've figured out that no matter what we do, we're going to die anyway. Animals know they *could* die if they're not careful, but they don't understand their own deaths are inevitable. That's why they don't have churches."

Despite herself she laughed. "Oh, is that why? I always wondered."

He smiled back at her. "Well, now you know. It's also why we're so nuts. Nothing means more to us than life, and no matter what we do, we know we can't keep it for very long."

"You're saying our survival instinct kept us alive long enough to recognize our own mortality, and that made us insane?"

"Well, not actually insane. Just really neurotic, you know? Our grasp of reality is okay. We know just enough to torture ourselves."

She didn't know why they were talking about death and survival drive, what it had to do with their earlier argument.

"Very well," she said, "we want to live and have to die, and that paradox makes us crazy, or neurotic, or at least unsettled. I suppose people have wondered what to do about it for ages. Do you imagine you discovered the answer out in Guardian space?"

"It's not that complicated. We can't have eternal life so we have to wring the most out of every second we have here, and we all know that. Since we can't have more *length*, we'll settle for more *intensity*."

He pointed at the sunset.

"Thirty-six years I've been around. That's over ten thousand sunsets, but I missed a lot of them, so say I've paid attention to one thousand. That's still a lot. You'd think I've seen everything there is to see in a sunset. But if I share it with someone whose presence makes me see those colors in ways I never have before, makes me see them with an intensity and immediacy that makes my throat tighten up, makes me feel more *alive* than I can ever remember feeling—that's love. I love you, Cass, and that's enough for me. I don't need you to love me back. It's okay. I'm on the winning side of this."

She stared at him and shook her head. "What do you mean?"

"If the stars line up right and two people love each other—love and are loved in return—that's as good as it gets. But the stars don't always line up that way. So, if I have to choose between loving or being loved, I'll take loving every time."

"Ah," she said.

"How should we like it were stars to burn
With a passion for us we could not return?
If equal affection cannot be,
Let the more loving one be me."

"Pretty good," Bitka said. "More poetry?"

"W. H. Auden. You should read him."

Bitka smiled and shook his head. "That's okay, I'm good. I like that last line, though. *If equal affection cannot be, let the more loving one be me.*"

"Most people would consider that a tragic outcome," she said.

"Yeah, but most people aren't as smart as me . . . or that guy Auden."

Cassandra found herself laughing again.

"It's true," he said. "Being in love? *Best* feeling in the world. Wouldn't trade it for anything. Tragic outcome?" He shook his head. "Cass, I don't need to tell you what real tragedy is. We've seen enough of it together. It's people dying before their time, before they've had a chance to live out the only life they ever get. And sometimes it's people afraid to live their lives, so they just let them slip away until it's too late. But not getting every single thing you want—even if you really, *really* want it— that's not a tragedy. It's just life."

They sat quietly and Cassandra watched the shadows of the trees grow less distinct in the growing darkness.

"What's going to happen?" she said, and as soon as she said it she realized she didn't know if she meant to them or to the *Cottohazz* or to both or to something else entirely.

He looked at her and smiled a different smile, a knowing one, as if he understood her confusion.

"Lots of things. But this fight with the Guardians . . . well, who knows if there's even going to be a fight now that P'Daan's dead?"

"Do not rejoice in his defeat, you men," she quoted. *"For though the world has stood up and stopped the bastard, the bitch that bore him is in heat again."* Bitka looked at her, a question in his eyes. "Bertold Brecht," she explained. "His point being, problems are seldom ended simply by killing one bastard. Our troubles with the Guardians are, I suspect, simply beginning."

"Well, I guess that figures," he said. "But I think we're going to win, eventually. Or people like us will, people whose lives are short but bright. Those who opt for K'Irka's promise of immortality won't understand what they're giving up. I realized something during the uBakai war: the fact that we know we're going to die sooner or later sets us free. We're free, while the Guardians are prisoners to their uncertain future. They think they've escaped death, but I think they've walked away from life. They've lost its urgency, its immediacy."

And then, as if to punctuate his words, fireworks erupted in the western sky and they jumped in surprise, then laughed.

"It must be in honor of your victory," she said, but Bitka scratched his head and then laughed again.

"No! Some US Navy officer I am. It's October 10th, *Federation Day,* our national holiday. The United States of North America: seventy-one years old today. Look at those fireworks and that sunset! *Beautiful.* Damnit, we're alive, Cass. *Alive!* So give me a kiss."

★ ★ ★

Te'Anna moved through the Ship, *her* Ship, sensing it come slowly out of hibernation. She sat in the helm station and gently pushed her arms down into the control cavities, felt the moist membranes of Ship close around them, and sensed its shudder of pleasure as it came awake to her physical presence.

Is it you?

"Yes, Ship, it is me."

Has it been long?

"No, hardly any time at all."

I dreamed of you. Is this another dream?

"I told you, Ship, it is all dreams. Dreams within dreams."

Which dream is this?

"Oh, this is the best one! This is the one we dream together."

AUTHOR'S NOTE AND ACKNOWLEDGMENTS

Although it is not essential to enjoying the story, many readers will notice *Ship of Destiny* follows, in broad outline, the story of Homer's *Odyssey*. In that, the novel owes much to Adam Nicolson's *The Mighty Dead: Why Homer Matters* (William Collins, 2014), which made me understand the *Odyssey* not as a story of one man's journey across the ancient Mediterranean Sea, but rather of all our individual journeys through the challenges and heartbreaks and triumphs of life.

There are hints throughout of characters and incidents inspired by the *Odyssey*, but I made no attempt to follow its plot slavishly. Instead, this is simply the story of a perilous journey that tests a captain's wit, courage, and leadership, but also tests his soul and—in the face both of so much death and the prospect of life unending—forces him to confront the implications of mortality.

I remain indebted to my two writing groups—Writer's Café at the Osher Lifelong Learning Institute at Illinois, and the Red Herring Fiction Writers—as well as individual readers who provided both encouragement and suggestions: Nancy Blake, Rich Bliss, Craig Cutbirth, Tom Harris, Bev Herzog, and Jim Nevling. Three readers stand out as having given the manuscript very close reads and provided extensive, thoughtful comments and suggestions: Linda Coleman, John Palen, and Elaine Palencia. To Casey Sutherland, for help with Cajun dialect, *Thanks, you*. I am also fortunate to count two outstanding microbiologists among my friends: Claudia

Reich and Bob Switzer, and I appreciate their help in navigating some complicated issues and communicating them in an intelligible form.

Thanks also to Li C. Tien and John Palen for permission to include their moving translation of Xin Qiji's poem "To The Tune 'The Ugly Slave,'" from *Drizzle and Plum Blossoms* (March Street Press, 2009), their collection of Song Dynasty poetry.

Finally, my enduring gratitude to, and appreciation for, Toni Weisskopf, my publisher at Baen Books, and Tony Daniel, my editor there, who believed in this book, championed it, and contributed greatly to a much-improved final manuscript. If writing were always this much of a joy, there would be many more books in the world. But then where would we put them all?

USS *Cam Ranh Bay* Described

USS *Cam Ranh Bay* (LAS-17) (aka *The Bay*, aka *Building 17*), third ship of the *Peleliu*-class of assault transports, was constructed at the IOS (International Orbital Space-dock) facility from August 2131– March 2133. It was commissioned on May 1, 2133 but after trials was returned to the IOS for further modifications to its energy storage systems and additions to the weapons and sensor suites. Returned to service November 16, 2133. Deployed to K'tok system January 13, 2134 assigned to the Outworld Coalition Combined Fleet as part of the Orbital Assault Division *(Provisional)*.

Physical Description

    Length: 135m
    Beam: 22m (circular cross section)
    Spin habitat: 20m wide, 10m deep, 100 meters
        in diameter
    Mass (empty): 24,250 tons
    Mass (loaded, excluding reaction mass): 33,550
    Mass (loaded, including reaction mass): 54,400
    Interior Volume: approximately 108,000 cubic
        meters (51,500 main hull, 56,550 spin habitat)

Crew: 171 all ranks
    25 Officers
    22 Chief Petty Officers
    90 Petty Officers
    34 Mariner Strikers

Plus quarters for 750 Marines (480 following 2133 refit and weaponry upgrade)

Machinery
1 x Lockheed Martin SW-3000 magnetized target fusion (MTF) reactor and direct thruster, 2.25-GW output
- Drive exhaust velocity at maximum thrust: 500,000 m/s
- Energy input per ton/second of thrust: 83 Kj
- Reaction mass expended per ton/second of thrust: 0.02kg
- Maximum thrust: 27,000 tons
- Reaction mass expended per second at max thrust: 540kg (32.4 tons/min)
- Reaction mass endurance at maximum thrust: 643.5 minutes (10.7 hours)
- Reaction mass endurance at maximum thrust, main hull fuel: 489 minutes (8.15 hours)
- Acceleration at maximum mass: 0.5G
- Acceleration at maximum mass (main hull only): 1G
- "Average" acceleration of 0.6G at average mass, (i.e. with half of total reaction mass remaining)
- "Average" acceleration of 1.4G (main hull only) at average mass

1 x 375-MW thermoelectric multi-cycle Seebeck generator
- (Converts thermal output of fusion reactor, stellar radiation, and internal waste heat, to electricity for ship power and recharging SMESS. 9-min recharge time at full power.)

4 x thermal radiator panels (12m x 30m) mounted aft, for discharging unrecoverable waste heat.

3 x low-signature magneto-plasmadynamic (MPD) maneuver drives with a combined thrust of
- 4,250 tons
- Drive exhaust velocity at maximum thrust: 100,000 m/s (100 km/s)
- Reaction mass expended per ton/second of thrust: 0.1 kg
- Energy input per ton/second of thrust: 200 Kj
- Maximum thrust: 4,250 tons
- Full thrust endurance on fully charged SMESS: 468 seconds
- Reaction mass expended per second at max thrust: 0.425 tons
- Acceleration at full load: 0.08G
- Acceleration at full load (main hull only): 0.16G
- Acceleration at average mass: 0.1G
- Acceleration at average mass (main hull only): 0.22G

4 x superconducting magnetic energy storage systems (SMESS)
- Combined rated capacity of 400 Gj (sufficient to power the MPD thrusters at full power for 470 seconds, or to generate 800 pulses from original point defense lasers (PDLs), 266 from added high-power PDLs, or 214 discharges from the spinal coil gun).

Performance

Provides up to 480 Mt/sec of thrust, or approximately 386 G/minutes, or 6.4 G/hours on direct fusion thrusters.

MPD thrust using fully charged SMESS: 4,250 tons for 470 seconds (103 G/seconds).

Combined sprint thrust at average mass: 0.7G

Small Craft
6 x PSRV-7C (Planetary Surface Recovery Vehicle, Mark 7, variant C)

> **Mass:** 25 tons empty, 50 tons loaded (6 tons passengers/cargo, 19 tons reaction mass)

> **Machinery:** 30 Mj MPD thruster, generating 150 tons of thrust, (powered by 32 Gj SMESS energy storage system)

Armament (as designed)
1 x 40cm Mark 17 coil gun, spinally mounted, 1.85-Gj peak muzzle energy, for launching inert munitions.

2 x 0.5 Gj point defense pulse lasers (retrofitted)
> (Virtual) Focal array: 12 meters (6 meters actual focal diameter)
> Wavelength: 1000 Å (ultraviolet)
> Effective range: 6,000–8,000 km

28 x 40cm PBM-9KS (Planetary Bombardment Missile, Mark 9, Kinetic Energy Sub-munition) (aka "Thud")

4 x 40cm PBM-9DP (Planetary Bombardment Missile, Mark 9, Deep Penetrator) (aka "Crust Buster")

Armament (following 2133 refit)
Above weaponry plus following added:

2 x 1.5 Gj point defense pulse lasers (retrofitted)
> (Virtual) Focal array: 20 meters (10 meters actual focal diameter)

Wavelength: 1000 Å (ultraviolet)
Effective range: 7,000–10,000 km

12 x 28cm DSIM-4C, block two missiles (Deep Space Intercept Missile Mark 4, aka "Fire Lance") with integral solid fuel rocket boosters. Loaded in two 6-tube launchers and substituted for passenger modules in the spin habitat. Each missile with twelve composite laser rods pumped by the 100-kt warhead. Each laser rod generates a single pulse for 2–4 nanoseconds with a total energy of approximately one gigajoule.

Warhead: 100-kt thermonuclear

12 composite laser rods, locked on pre-set pattern for maximum hit chance

Each laser rod generates a single 1 Gj pulse for 2–4 nanoseconds

(Virtual) focal array: 0.2 meters

Wavelength: 15 Å (X-ray)

Effective range upon detonation: 4,000 km

Note: Additional missile launchers reduced troop-carrying capacity from 750 to 480.

Supplemental (Improvised) Armament

36 x 32cm DSIM-5B, block five missiles (Deep Space Intercept Missile Mark 5B "Fire Lance"), each with thirty composite laser rods pumped by the 180-kt warhead. Each laser rod generates a single pulse for 2–4 nanoseconds with a total energy of approximately one gigajoule.

Warhead: 180kt thermonuclear

30 composite laser rods, independently targetable

Each laser rod generates a single 1 Gj pulse
  for 2–4 nanoseconds
(Virtual) focal array: 0.26 meters
Wavelength: 15 Å (X-ray)
Effective range upon detonation: 4,000–6,000 km

USS Cam Ranh Bay (LAS-17)

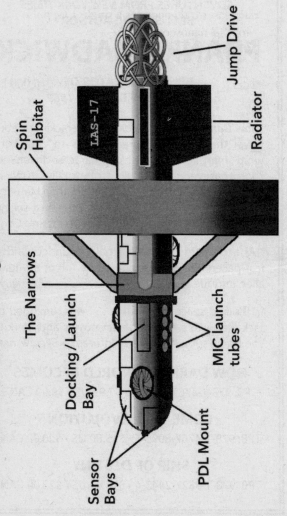

Spin Habitat

Jump Drive

Radiator

LAS-17

The Narrows

Docking / Launch Bay

MIC launch tubes

Sensor Bays

PDL Mount

THE WARRIOR'S APPRENTICE
TPB: 978-1-4767-8130-3 • $16.00

CETAGANDA
PB: 978-0-6718-7744-6 • $7.99

ETHAN OF ATHOS
PB: 978-0-6716-5604-1 • $7.99

BROTHERS IN ARMS
TPB: 978-1-4814-8331-5 • $16.00
PB: 978-1-4165-5544-5 • $7.99

MIRROR DANCE
PB: 978-0-6718-7646-3 • $7.99

MEMORY
TPB: 978-1-4767-3673-0 • $16.00
PB: 978-0-6718-7845-0 • $7.99

KOMARR
HC: 978-0-6718-7877-1 • $22.00
PB: 978-0-6715-7808-4 • $7.99

A CIVIL CAMPAIGN
HC: 978-0-6715-7827-5 • $24.00
PB: 978-0-6715-7885-5 • $7.99

DIPLOMATIC IMMUNITY
PB: 978-0-7434-3612-1 • $7.99

CRYOBURN
HC: 978-1-4391-3394-1 • $25.00
PB: 978-1-4516-3750-2 • $7.99

ADVENTURES OF SCIENCE AND MAGIC IN THE FANTASTIC WORLDS OF
JAMES L. CAMBIAS

Arkad, a young boy struggling to survive on an inhospitable planet, was the only human in his world. Then three more humans arrived from space, seeking a treasure that might free Earth from alien domination. With both his life and the human race at risk, Arkad guides the visitors across the planet, braving a slew of dangers—and betrayals—while searching for the mysterious artifact.

ARKAD'S WORLD
HC: 978-1-4814-8370-4 • $24.00 US / $33.00 CAN

"Fast-paced, pure quill hard science fiction. . . . Cambias delivers adroit plot pivots that keep the suspense coming."
—Gregory Benford,
Nebula Award-winning author of *Timescape*

". . . a classic quest story, a well-paced series of encounters with different folk along the way, building momentum toward a final confrontation with Arkad's past . . . [with] a delicious twist to the end."
—*Booklist*

"James Cambias will be one of the century's major names in hard science fiction."
—Robert J. Sawyer, Hugo Award-winning author of *Red Planet Blues*